The Ticket

Hugh Vickery

In Remembrance of Amne Vickery

We Will See You Again

Acknowledgements

I would like to thank Pastor Gary Durham and the
Red Inklings at New Hope Fellowship for reading and
commenting on this novel.

Thanks also to Glen Davis, Cecelia Marszal Iannelli,
Charlotte Stucki, and Stanley Reahard for their suggestions.

Preface

I wrote this book in memory of my wonderful late wife, Amne Vickery, who died in 2010 after a long battle with breast cancer. The story seeks to explore the intersection of grief, joy, tragedy, love, forgiveness, and grace in our lives through the eyes of a man who lost his wife to this terrible disease and was angry at God – a God he questioned even exists. It is unabashedly a Christian novel, but I hope that those who are not Christians will still find it entertaining and informative of the Christian perspective on the spiritual realm as well as the often-difficult path of coming to know and follow Jesus.

Hugh Vickery
Palm City, Florida

Forward

Unexpected. *The Ticket* is a story of the unexpected that becomes life changing. This is a captivating journey through the pain and healing of Joe Mathers where you find yourself discovering your own story and its deepest challenges.

The Ticket is an adventure worth taking. It could make some important alterations in the real story of your life.

Through the skill and creativity of my friend, author Hugh Vickery, nearly every page you turn will silhouette challenges, risks, pains, and yes, joys and beauties so they seem to be seen in a new light or even for the first time.

Trust me this book will be hard to put down.

As you follow Joe Mathers through his unexpected journey, through his unexpected encounters toward the unexpected peace and joy he wins, you will sense something authentic overarching every detail. This is because author Hugh Vickery, as good men often do, is drawing on his own real-life tragedies and triumphs and molding them into a story which can touch us all.

This is your *Ticket* to an unexpected journey capable of forever enriching your life.

Dr. Gary L. Durham
September 2025

Table of Contents

The Ticket

Chapter 1

Janice

People began to laugh at my jokes.

I am not particularly witty, although once in a while I might say something amusing. Other people mostly tolerated my humor and perhaps at times found it worth a smile or a chuckle. After the ticket, however, they found me hilarious. Even a childish pun or a bit of sarcasm conjured up peals of laughter.

I asked my sister why there had been such a change. "It's obvious. You have become famous," Cecilia replied. "Famous people can't tell a bad joke. People laugh because they are famous."

"But I haven't done anything," I retorted. "And I certainly haven't become a comedian."

"Whether a joke is funny or not is irrelevant. People laugh at their bosses' jokes even if they aren't funny. It's not the joke that matters, but the person telling it."

"So I am not particularly funny?"

"No, you are not."

Cecilia was blunt. A truth teller. That's why I valued her more than anyone else except Janice, who was gone. I bought her a car, not a fancy car but a base model Toyota, because I knew she would never accept a Lexus. She was not the kind of woman who valued luxury. As it turned out, she returned the car to the dealer and gave the money back to me.

"My Ford works fine," she said. "I don't need a new car."

"But you know it's not a burden to give you a gift," I replied.

"Everyone knows that," she said. "But I don't need a car."

We grew up together just outside Blacksburg, Virginia, at the edge of the Appalachians. Cecelia was the wise sister, two years older than me. I was the much-longed-for son of a former high school football star who ended up working in a foundry. He was a good enough athlete to excel in a small town, becoming a kind of local celebrity until graduation ended his run as a tailback and people looked for the next star. He wasn't good enough to attract attention from college coaches, much less the ones at Virginia Tech, where the memories of Michael Vick still swirled through Lane Stadium. The irony is that eventually I was the one who would hear the roar of the crowd on those Saturday afternoons, albeit from the sidelines and not on the field.

I suspect the adulation that faded away so quickly was one of the reasons my father fell into a bottle, drinking himself to an early death at 50. When the highlight of one's life occurs at 18, everything afterwards is a dreary day-to-day existence: punching time clocks and repairing the leaky roof or the flimsy plumbing of a double-wide, the only home he could afford for his young family. It is easy to see why he fell onto the slippery slope to despair. In high school, the teachers made us read Thoreau, and I came across his observation that "most men live lives of quiet desperation." Thoreau wrote the epitaph for my father.

Billy Mathers was a functional alcoholic, however. He showed up for work hungover most days, but he showed up. People covered for him. His high school teammates, who also worked at the foundry, picked up the slack when he was still drunk at 8 a.m. when his shift began. My mother made excuses for him and tried, unsuccessfully, to hide his problem from the neighbors and from us. Eventually, she broke down, and my sister became her confidante. No 10-year-old should be put in the position of counselor to a parent – and too many are – but my sister was born for the job.

I was not. I remember begging my father in tears to stop drinking after school one Friday afternoon when I was eight. If it penetrated his heart at all, I could not tell. He took two cases of Budweiser to the shed in the back of the double-wide that he had turned into a man cave decorated with memorabilia from his gridiron days and didn't reappear until it was time for his Monday shift. I suspect I added another layer of shame to his desperation, aggravating his addiction rather than helping him find the will to overcome it.

I might have grown up fatherless had it not been for football. As soon as I could walk, he made sure there was a football in my hands, showing me how to hold it high and tight so I wouldn't fumble and throwing it to me on screens and circle routes in the park at the end of the street.

I was not a gifted athlete, however. In fact, I was below average, the kid who sits on the bench until the score is lopsided in one direction or the other and finally gets a minute or two of playing time at the end of the game. Like many men, my father never fully grasped that his will couldn't change my DNA and make me what I wasn't. I was a disappointment, another reason to retreat to his shed. By my freshman year of high school, he gave up on me. That was the effective end of me having a father.

In the end, I came to understand that my mother was a survivor, far tougher on the inside than she appeared on the outside. She had won the high school lottery and snagged the star running back, basking in the reflected glory of being the girlfriend in the stands while he barreled over undersized linebackers from neighboring towns. She married him three months after graduation, five months pregnant with my sister. I often considered that year to be the highlight of her life before the twilight of grim reality fell upon her: a teenage mother in a trailer park in a depressed town.

Despite her frequent tears, Dottie Mathers held the family together. She desperately wanted something better for her two children. As my father pushed me to do something I could not do, she pushed my sister and me to do things we could do: distill every ounce of education we could out of a mediocre high school where parents and administrators cared far more about the score of the football games than SAT scores. We both were valedictorians and received scholarships from Virginia Tech. Cecilia studied nursing while I majored in physical therapy.

Both my mother and sister attended the Hokies' football games, not because they liked football – they didn't – but because I was on the sidelines learning to take care of the kind of athletes Billy Mathers never was but hoped I would become – or maybe expected me to become in the fog of delusion that comes over fathers at Pop Warner games. This same delusion existed even at Virginia Tech where every starter dreamed of playing in the National Football League. In the end, one or two might make it and any objective observer knew in advance who they were. But hamstrings are hamstrings, and I learned to take care of them along with all the other body parts damaged in horrific collisions between bulked-up young men who spent far more time in the weight room than in class.

When we were old enough to be left alone after school, my mother got a job as a cashier at the Walmart Supercenter in Christiansburg. She opened her own bank account and wouldn't let my father near the money no matter how much he howled about it and slammed doors so hard that the double-wide shook. In his heart, I suspect, he knew what she was doing, preparing for the day when his liver or heart failed. I sensed his rage was merely for show. No doubt her bank account only added to his shame.

By then the tender, nurturing young mother she had been when Cecilia was born had evolved into the hardened, older-than-her-age midlife woman one can find working at just about any Walmart in the country. She loved us fiercely while she looked forward to grandchildren that never arrived. Perhaps having lived with my father, Cecilia wasn't going to hitch her wagon to any man. As for me, Janice and I were on the verge of having children when her diagnosis ended our hopes.

I did buy my mother a fine house in the mountains, but she refused to give up her job no matter how many times I offered to give her a life of leisure. Perhaps the other Walmart employees were her second family, but I suspect the real reason was she wasn't going to trust a man again, even her own son. The ticket, and her fellow employees' reaction to it, upended her little world, and eventually she had to leave that job. She simply moved to a different town and began to work for Krogers, using her maiden name. She would work until the day she died.

As for me, I went on to get a master's degree in physical therapy, focusing on sports medicine. I applied for and was given the head trainer job for Virginia Tech, first for the football team and then for all the sports teams as a supervisor of all the trainers. My sister became a nurse practitioner. She also didn't leave the university, eventually becoming the senior nurse practitioner at its health center. When Janice died, she sold her condo and moved into my house in Merrimac.

"What are you going to do now?" She asked me one afternoon, a month after Janice's death.

"I don't have an answer yet," I replied.

"You can't go on like this," she said. "It's insane."

"I know. It's beginning to feel like a curse."

"I set before you blessings or curses, life and death, now choose life.".

"What is that?"

"Deuteronomy 30."

"Don't I get a choice?"

"You always have a choice."

"There are lots of things I didn't choose."

Cecilia had a scripture verse for just about anything that happened in life. For a strong, independent, rational woman who would not suffer fools, she had a softer, spiritual side – actually a mystical side. She could see things I couldn't see, or at least she believed she could see them. She attended a small non-denominational church just outside Radford, passing by a dozen bigger, more prosperous congregations on the 20-minute drive out of Blacksburg. My mother often went with her, and I often saw the two of them huddled in prayer in the living room of the house I bought for my mother.

It was a sore subject. My mother made sure we were raised in the church, a large Methodist congregation in the center of the city that had an energetic youth pastor who continually thought of new ways to draw children in and entertain them. We memorized scripture and had sleepovers in the church hall. I suppose out of all of this, I had an acceptable level of faith, although truth be told I hadn't given it much thought in my teenage years. But when Janice got sick, I gave the God of the Bible a chance. Even though Janice fought for far longer than the doctors thought she could, the God of the Bible, if he exists, took her from me. I saw no need to darken the threshold of any church after her funeral.

My sister was nothing if not persistent, however.

"You should talk to Pastor Brian," she said for not the first time. "He has a lot of wisdom."

"Will he tell me why Dad never stopped drinking?" I retorted, also for not the first time. "Can he tell me why Janice died?"

"Why don't you ask Him?"

"He won't have an answer."

"He may have some thoughts about the ticket."

"I am sure he might have some ideas about what I might do about it," I replied. "Everyone does."

"You may be surprised." She said with that expression she had when she was seeing things that no one else could see. Or again, thought she did.

Cecilia was right. I did have a choice. A couple of days later, for reasons I still can't fathom except that my sister is a force of nature, I made an appointment to see the Reverend Dr. Brian Cooper, DD at Radford Christian Fellowship. Not about God. Not about my father. Not about Janice.

About the ticket.

———-

The congregation of Radford Christian Fellowship met in a small steepled church sitting on a knoll bordered by farmland just outside the college town of Radford, Virginia. As I drove into the gravel parking lot, it struck me that the church was so old and worn and so much a part of the rural landscape that it seemed there had never been a time when it wasn't there. I climbed the church steps, anticipating dark wooden pews, leaded glass stained-glass windows and musty air. I wondered how Cecelia had ever found, much less been drawn, to such a church so opposite of the Methodist church of our youth and so far from her home.

I was surprised when I opened the front door to find the interior bright and welcoming, decorated with white wooden pews and soft blue walls. A rectangular oak table served as the altar, engraved with the words "Come to me all you who are weary and burdened and I will give you rest." Behind the altar, ten feet above the ground, hung a rough-hewn cross that clashed with the church's decor. It was shocking in its realism. Few would have missed the contrast between the scripture verse on the altar and the first-century instrument of torture.

"You must be Mr. Mathers," a voice said behind me.

The Reverend Dr. Brian Cooper came out of a door that must at one point have led to a sacristy but now was a small office. He was a younger man, perhaps 35, with sandy blond hair, broad shoulders and an athletic appearance.

"Call me Joe," I said as we shook hands.

"Call me Brian," he replied. "I was never much for the title of reverend."

"And doctor?"

"Scratch that too," he said. "The church board insists on advertising it, but it is pretentious."

"But you earned it."

"Dallas Theological Seminary. But until I make you say "aaah" and check your heart with a stethoscope, you can simply call me Brain."

"Brian, it is," I said.

He led me into his office, where I sat across from him on a small couch. I noticed a photograph of a woman, presumably his wife, with two small children on the desk next to a well-worn Bible, a Chromebook, and a writing pad. On a bookshelf behind the desk were the requisite theological books as well as ones by C.S. Lewis, Corrie ten Boom, John Bunyan, R.C. Sproul, D.L Moody and other authors I had heard about in sermons during my teenage years but never read.

We quickly dispensed with the small talk about the weather and the Virginia Tech Hokies' recent one-point victory over Old Dominion.

'Cecelia told me you recently lost your wife. I am so sorry for your loss. It must have been a terrible blow," he said. "Can you tell me about that?"

"Janice died two months ago. After a long illness. But I actually came to talk about something else."

"The ticket?"

"Yes, we call it that."

He paused and stroked his chin thoughtfully. "We can get to that," he said. "But I would like to hear about your wife's illness and her passing."

"What is there to say?" I asked. "She had cancer for eight years, and then she died."

He nodded, and there was silence between us for a few moments. I realized he wasn't looking at me the way other people looked at me. I could have been anybody. He didn't give the impression he would laugh at my bad jokes.

"Tell me how you met her?" He asked.

"Do we have to go there?" I glanced at the door. I wondered what would happen if I simply left. This was not the reason I had come. Janice was gone, and I had a problem that needed solving, not that many people would view it as a problem.

"I met her in college, at Virginia Tech," I finally relented. "I couldn't decide on a major, but there was a young woman I was interested in who was majoring in physical therapy. I took a class so I could spend time with her. Jancie was in that class as part of her major in nursing. I sat next to her the first day and never looked back. She was not only beautiful, she was full of life. She made me feel alive. On the same day, I found a wife and a career."

"Isn't that the way it works?" he replied. "We go looking for one thing, and then we find something completely different and better than we ever imagined. Do you have a photo of her?"

I pulled out my wallet and showed him a small photo of Janice from ten years before, prior to her diagnosis. She was standing next to Cascades Falls near Pembroke with the sun bathing her long Irish red hair.

"She was a beautiful woman," Brian said.

We both stared at the photo for a few moments, and then the dam broke. The pain I had sealed off in a dark place somewhere deep in my soul poured out. I told him about the day we found a lump in her breast, about the mastectomy, the chemotherapy, and the radiation. About the day when I hugged her as we lay in bed, and clumps of her stunning red hair fell onto my face. That very morning, I shaved her head, the hair falling onto our kitchen floor, and how we held each other as she wept afterwards. The chemotherapy drove her body into early menopause, so our hope for children of our own was lost.

"She went into remission after the first round of treatments, and her hair grew back. We thought maybe she was over it. But then two years later it came back in her bones. The doctor didn't want to tell us that breast cancer in younger women is usually more aggressive. We attacked it again with chemotherapy, and for a while the PET scans showed no cancer. We were hopeful once more. We talked about adopting children..."

Suddenly, a fresh wave of grief rose within me. At once, I was crying, in fact bawling. I have never been a person who cries, and I wouldn't have thought it possible, especially in front of another man, but I couldn't control myself. Brian waited patiently while I struggled to compose myself.

"In those last days, she was semi-comatose, crying out in pain," I continued. "She was in the living room of our home in a hospital bed. I changed her diapers, tried my best to comfort her and give her morphine but it wasn't enough. Her cries echoed through the house, and I was powerless to help her. I talked to her, but I don't know if she heard me. I prayed to God to help her but he was not listening."

I stopped to see if I had offended Brian. I had not. He simply nodded, a look of compassion on his face. He reached out and touched my hand.

"Go on," he said softly.

"I planned her funeral and the reception before she was gone – the flowers, the caterer, everything. I bought two gravesites in a cemetery outside the city, one for each of us. I even ordered her coffin online and had it delivered to the funeral home to save money. Does that sound morbid?"

"No, it doesn't," he said. "I understand."

"I kept praying for a miracle," I said. "The chemo and radiation had transformed her into a frail old woman, and I prayed that God would touch her so she could rise up cancer-free and fully restored to the woman she was before she was diagnosed. He didn't." Once again, I lost control of my emotions, and tears flowed. "Why didn't God heal her?"

Perhaps I expected a theological answer or a Bible verse from a pastor, but I was surprised when he simply said, "I don't know."

"During the last days, I started to want her to die. She was in so much agony. It was a relief when she finally did."

"Were you there when she died?"

"No, I was asleep. A volunteer from the local hospice organization came by to sit with her and give me a break. A few minutes later, I heard a knock on my bedroom door, waking me up. She said Janice had passed away."

"And what did you do then?"

"I got busy. There was so much to do. I went on autopilot. There was only one moment when I cried, when the men from the funeral home came to take her away. They put her in a body bag and wheeled her out of the house for the last time. I would never see her again."

I paused to wipe away the tears that were again flowing ."The rest is a blur. All the friends calling and visiting. The meals that showed up on my doorstep. The funeral. The eulogy I gave about her. The burial. Buying her grave marker. The whole ritual of death."

"And then the ticket?"

"Yes, then the ticket," I said. "I came here to talk about it, not about Janice, but now I don't want to."

"I understand," he said. "Perhaps we can meet again."

I brushed the last tear from my eyes and gazed at him. He projected a calmness that seemed real, as though he were absorbing all my emotions – my grief and my anger – and transforming them into a mysterious and infectious peace. I had expected religious platitudes about God's will or heaven. He offered none.

"Do you have any thoughts?" I asked.

"Perhaps one," he answered. "A scripture."

I expected he would hit me over the head with the Bible. But when he spoke, it was something I had not expected.

"From the prophet Isaiah," he said. "As the heavens are higher than the earth, so are my thoughts higher than your thoughts and my ways higher than your ways."

"What does that mean?

"It means that we can't see what is actually going on in life," he said. "There is another reality hidden from us and too great for us to even comprehend at the moment."

"And?"

"And when the journey is over, we will finally know what it was all about."

I took a deep breath. He was so sincere, so full of faith in the God who allowed Janice to die. But I was not.

"I don't believe that," I replied.

He looked me straight in the eye and spoke softly but firmly.

"God knows that," he said.

Chapter 2

Brian

"So did you make another appointment with him?" Cecilia asked as she cracked eggs to make spinach quiche for our dinner. She was a superb self-taught chef, and one of the benefits of her moving into my house was I didn't have to eat my own cooking or, more commonly, the frozen dinners sold at the local grocery store. If someone hadn't invented the microwave, I might have starved.

"I did," I conceded. "We got sidetracked talking about Janice, and we never talked about the ticket."

Celicia stopped cracking eggs for a moment and looked up at me. I wasn't going to mention the tears, but I didn't have to. She had radar and could read me. "So you finally allowed yourself to grieve?"

"I don't want to grieve," I said. "I would rather just be angry."

"It doesn't work that way," she replied and switched her attention back to the eggs.

"It doesn't work, period," I said. "I can weep all I want, and Janice will still be dead. I will still wake up in the middle of the night and find myself all alone, an empty place next to me."

Cecelia turned away to get cream out of the refrigerator. She was such an attractive woman, even as she neared middle age. I wondered why some doctor at the health center hadn't been able to decipher the combination of the lock that guarded her heart. I am sure that many had tried. I vaguely remembered she had a boyfriend briefly in high school. He broke her heart, and she spent the night alone in her bedroom crying. From that moment on, she focused on her career and her faith and had little use for dating.

Years before, she had told me one time, "Only one man has ever entered my heart. And I can't marry Him. I can only follow Him." It had taken me a few moments to figure out that she meant Jesus. I hadn't wanted to start that conversation again. We had covered that ground too many times.

"So when is your appointment?" she asked, beating the eggs with a fury.

"Tomorrow."

"At the church?"

"No," I replied. "He wants to meet at Cascade Falls."

Cecelia abruptly stopped stirring and looked at me. "He doesn't play fair, does he?"

"No," I said. "And yet I agreed. Quite frankly, I thought you had something to do with that."

"I didn't," she said and went back to stirring.

The four-mile trail in the George Washington National Forest was Janice's favorite hike, culminating in a 70-foot waterfall bordered by 200-foot cliffs. In many ways, it is where we fell in love, beguiled by the colors of the Appalachian mountains, with a hundred shades of green in the spring and countless hues of yellow, orange, and brown in the fall when the red oaks appear to be on fire. Eventually, it was the place where, on one knee, I asked her to be my wife.

"Maybe I shouldn't go," I said. "I don't want to be crying in public."

"Maybe that is the reason you should go," she replied.

"So that all the people who recognize me from the papers will wonder what such a lucky man could be doing crying by a waterfall?"

"Maybe it would be good for them too," she replied. "It will help them get over the fantasy. Maybe they will spend their money on better things."

"I never spent a dime."

"I know," she replied. "And now it's a problem everyone else would like to have."

"It's a problem," I said. "I can hardly go out in public anymore, and you wouldn't believe the new friends and relatives I have."

"So you've told me a hundred times, you poor boy," she teased.

"A lot of help you are."

"Talk to Brian about it," she said.

"Yes, the Reverend Doctor will have the answer," I replied. "It's all in the Good Book."

Cecelia poured the contents of the bowl into a crusted pie plate and put it in the oven. Then she turned toward me and used her Big Sister voice.

"You might just be surprised," she said.

——-

"How did you end up here?" I asked Brian as we headed down the trail in the chill of a March morning, snaking through trees just beginning to bud. It was still early in the morning and there were few other hikers. I wanted to be the one asking questions when we met up at the head of the Cascades Trail outside Pembroke. I was sure my sister had told him about the significance of the falls to my marriage, even though she denied it.

"What do you mean?" he asked.

"What I mean is you have a doctorate from a well-known seminary and you are pastoring a small church in the mountains of western Virginia."

"You mean I should be pastoring a much bigger church, maybe even a megachurch?"

"I was just wondering."

Brian smiled broadly. "You aren't the first person to ask that question," he replied. "There are lots of professors, senior pastors, and others who are wondering what I am up to."

"Well, what are you up to?" The thought crossed my mind that it was a double question: what was he up to in his career, and what were he and my sister up to in regards to me?

Brian didn't say anything for a few moments as we hiked further into the woods. A man walking a Labrador retriever passed by from the direction of the falls, and we stopped to greet the owner and pet the dog. When we started walking again, he returned to the conversation.

"Many people, even people in churches, view what I do as a career, like any other job, where the goal is to get promoted and work your way to the top. I thought that way when I earned my doctorate. I had worked as a youth pastor while I was studying, but then, after I published my first book, I was hired as an associate pastor at a megachurch in St. Louis."

"You published a book?"

"Yes," he said. "It's not light reading. It's a theological book exploring alternative translations from the Greek of Romans 5 to Romans 8 and their influence on systematic theology."

"A scholarly book?"

"Yes. It was well received by those who are interested in such things," he replied. "A lot of other people would find it a cure for insomnia."

"So you were an assistant pastor at a megachurch?"

"Yes, Crosswalk Church in Brentwood," he said. "Ten thousand members when I was there. It's probably bigger now."

I considered this for a moment. "One of those churches with a big stage, a rock band for worship, and thousands of seats like an arena?"

Brian nodded. "That's about it. Kind of a smaller version of Joel Osteen."

"So what happened?"

"I was there for three years," he said. "They were grooming me to open up another campus in Clayton and then, I suspect, to ultimately take over for the senior pastor when he retired."

We continued to hike in silence, climbing higher toward the falls. The thought struck me that there was only one thing that might derail someone on a successful career path: scandal. Did he sleep with a parishioner? Become addicted to alcohol or drugs? I wasn't sure I should press the line of questioning any further. Then again, he didn't seem hesitant to talk about it.

"So what happened?" I finally repeated my question.

"It's simple," he said. "I met Charlotte. Then, because of her, I met Jesus."

I groaned inside. I couldn't count the number of Cecelia's friends – not to mention Cecelia herself – who talked endlessly about meeting Jesus. Or what Jesus said to them. Or how they saw Jesus. Or the blood of Jesus. How many times had they huddled around Janice, pleading the blood of Jesus over her?

Brian detected my weariness. "You have heard a lot of Jesus talk, have you?"

I nodded. "You know my sister," I replied.

Brian laughed. "I do know your sister."

"So tell me about your road to Damascus experience?" I asked.

Brian laughed at my reference. "You know the Bible, then?"

"Taken to church for years by my mother. Sunday school, youth group, vacation Bible school. Sword drills. You name it."

Brian smiled. "So was I."

"But obviously with you it stuck. You went to seminary and became a pastor. I went to college and became a party animal. A good student, but a party animal. And when you are around the football team, you can be quite a party animal."

We stopped to admire a red oak, impressive even without its leaves. In the fall, it would transform into a fiery torch of red. We heard the faint sound of falling water. The sun had risen, and we no longer could see our breath.

"You have to understand something," he finally said. "I was an earnest, determined young man. I resolved to be a good person and, truth be told, to be seen as a good person by others. I put all my efforts into becoming that person. When I was a pastor at Crosswalk, I encouraged the young people to be like me. Instead of 'Go win one for the Gipper,' it was 'Go win one for Jesus.'"

"Isn't that good?"

Brian stopped to pick up a red leaf and examine it. "The good is the enemy of the best," he said cryptically.

I had no idea what he meant. We were distracted by the appearance of a black bear crossing the trail ahead. There are more black bears per square mile in the Appalachians than in any place in the country, so it wasn't that unusual a sight.

The conversations switched to stories about our past bear encounters. I recounted the time Janice and I were camping near Old Rag on the Hughes River, and a bear was trying to get to our food that we had hung over a branch outside of our campsite. I chased him off while Janice doubled over in laughter at my macho bravado.

I was still curious about Brian, so when there was a break in the conversation, I risked more Jesus talk and went back to my questions. He seemed to welcome it.

"How did you meet your wife?" I asked. "Was she a member of your church?"

"Online, believe it or not. A dating site."

"There's a dating site for pastors?"

Brian laughed. "No," he said. "But there are sites for Christians. I couldn't date anyone from my church for obvious reasons."

"Yes, that could get messy."

"I had no idea what I was getting into when I clicked on the link."

"What did you get into?"

"I fell into Charlotte's Web," he smiled. "And once you are in Charlotte's web, there's no escape."

I laughed, remembering the children's book by that name. "And that changed your life?"

"She saw me for what I was, a religious fraud with a doctorate," he said. "A man with Reverend before his name who had no genuine reverence for God. A man who led Christians but had no real knowledge of Christ. A religious professional, so to speak."

"That must have been hard to hear."

"It was, but she doesn't have a mean-spirited bone in her body. She spoke the truth in love. She told me the devil is not in the beer and brothel business but in the religion business, and I needed to get out of that business."

"And what did you do?

"I quit my job and spent three months living alone in a cabin in the Appalachians in eastern Kentucky, a place on a mountaintop so remote it didn't have indoor plumbing. At first, I fasted and prayed. Then I began to visit my neighbors, simple mountain folk with very little in the world. Some were in need, and I tried to help them. Others were uneducated hillbillies who knew God far better than the Dallas Theological Seminary graduate with a doctorate. I sat on their porches as they played their banjos, fiddles, and guitars and sang bluegrass songs about Jesus and the cross and heaven. Those songs and the simple passion with which they sang them penetrated my heart. It was during that time that I had a dream in which Jesus appeared to me and said two words, 'Follow me.' When I woke up, for the first time in my life, I followed Him."

"And that's how you ended up in a small church outside Radford, Virginia?"

"You don't know where he will lead you," he said. "You simply go."

"And you married Charlotte?

"As fast as she would let me."

"I would like to meet her," I said.

He looked at me with a strange look on his face as though he were seeing something unexpected in my appearance.

"I think you will," he said softly. "I think you will."

———-

"I half expected him to ask for money to build a bigger church," I told Cecelia over dinner that evening.

She had made her own version of shepherd's pie, a dish I hadn't eaten or even thought about in years. She didn't follow recipes exactly, but used them as suggestions and then raided her herb and spice rack to produce her own creation. It was the way she lived her life: dedicated to excellence but always with an unexpected twist. Once again, I appreciated the radical improvement in my cuisine.

She raised her eyebrows. "Why would he do that?"

"I don't know," I shrugged my shoulders. "I have the money I didn't ask for and not a clue what to do with it."

"So you finally talked to him about the ticket?" she inquired.

I nodded.

"But he didn't ask you for money?" It was more a statement than a question.

"No, he did not."

"So what happened? Are you going to tell me?"

I took another bite of shepherd's pie and leaned back in my chair, searching Cecelia's face for any clue that she already knew the answer to the question. As usual, I couldn't read her.

"We got to the rock that you swore you did not tell him about," I said. "The place where I asked Janice to marry me."

"And?"

"And, of course, I broke down and cried. Why would you have him take me there?"

"I didn't," she said. "But why would you agree to go?"

It was a fair question. Why had I agreed? Why hadn't I just refused to even meet with him a second time or insisted on meeting in his office or somewhere else?

"Maybe I wanted to go there," I finally answered.

"Or needed to go there," Cecelia said.

I looked up from my food and peered into my sister's eyes. This was certainly something she and Brian had cooked up to get me to properly grieve the loss of Janice.

"So you did tell him," I stated.

"No, I didn't."

"How else would he know?"

"Perhaps you showed him the photo of Janice in your wallet with the falls in the background?"

"I thought of that," I said. "But how would he know about the rock? You had to have told him?"

"I didn't," she insisted again.

We fell silent for a few moments, tucking into our dinner. It was a mystery. My sister was not a liar. However, I sensed she knew more than she was saying. The large flat rock where I had fallen to one knee to ask Janice's hand was at the far side of the pool, and it took some effort to get there. I chose it because it was relatively private, yet still within view of the waterfall. I didn't want a public spectacle even though I was proposing in public. Brian had led me there, knowing exactly where he was going.

'So did people bother you?" Cecelia finally asked.

"No, it was early in the morning and cool," I said. "There were only a couple of people there, a man and a woman. I think the woman might have recognized me by the way she stared at me, but she didn't approach us. And once we got to the rock, we weren't that visible."

Cecilia took another bite of her dinner, put down her fork, and tackled the elephant in the room. "So what did he say about the ticket?"

———-

The ticket.

I could see the headline in my mind. "Virginia Man Loses Wife, Becomes Billionaire in One Week." Every newspaper in the country had a version of the headline. Every news broadcast ran a story. And then there was the national television broadcast of the Hokies' game with Florida State on ESPN in prime time. The story was irresistible, and the camera found me repeatedly. Viewers all over the nation wondered why I was there: why I was taping the ankles of running backs and stretching the hamstrings of linebackers. His wife just died. Why is he working? He just joined the Bill Gates and Elon Musk club. Why isn't he on his own private island?

I knew I was hiding from grief: occupying my mind with knee strains and tears in bicep muscles to keep the pain at bay – at least in part – so I wouldn't think of Janice's still, breathless body lying in the hospital bed in my living room or the eerie silence that filled the house. Or that I was alone, no longer having the one person who truly understood a flawed man and loved and cherished him as though he had no flaws.

Then there was the great mystery that no one knew about except Cecilia and me. I never bought the ticket. I had never bought a ticket in my life. Across the country, millions of people stood in long lines to buy a ticket for the largest Powerball payout in history, $2.4 billion. I was not one of them.

The morning Janice died, the volunteer from the hospice organization in Blacksburg arrived at 7:30. She was a petite, middle-aged woman with graying blond hair. That's all I can remember. I had been up all night with Janice, giving her morphine every two hours, and I was exhausted. I thanked her for coming and guided her to the chair next to Janice's bed. She sat down and took Janice's hand. I excused myself to get some sleep. I sensed this was the final day of the battle, and I would need to be rested for what would come.

When the knock came at the door, the petite woman told me Janice had died. Then all was a blur. I didn't call anyone. I sat by her bed for two hours holding her hand. There were no tears, just a zombie-like state. I knew she was going to die. It was not a surprise. Yet I still was in shock.

It was a day later, after the funeral home had taken her body, after all the friends and neighbors had called, after the casseroles began to pile up on the kitchen counter, that I found the ticket as I folded up the hospital bed and cleaned the room. It was sitting on the nightstand next to the chair where the volunteer had been holding Janice's hand.

I left it where it was and paid no attention to it. I didn't notice the next day when the local newspaper reported that the winning ticket for the highest Powerball jackpot in history had been purchased at a 7-Eleven in Blacksburg. I didn't notice when the next day they reported that no one had stepped forward to claim the prize. Nor the next day or the day after. In fact, I didn't think about it until one of the basketball players I was stretching before a pre-season workout mentioned the lottery.

"Why do you think no one has claimed that Powerball money?" he asked to make conversation.

"How much is it?" I asked.

"More than $2 billion."

"What would anyone ever do with that much money?"

"I don't know," the player said. "But I wouldn't mind finding out for myself."

We both chuckled, and it reminded me of the ticket on the nightstand. That night, I retrieved it and checked it against the winning numbers on the Powerball website.

The odds of getting all five numbers and the Powerball number are 292 million to one. That means that on average, a person would have to buy a ticket for every drawing for nearly 2 million years to win once. To win a single drawing would be like being a spectator in one of 5,000 side-by-side football stadiums and having an airplane flying overhead drop a ping pong ball into your lap. Yet somehow, a volunteer from a hospice organization had absent-mindedly left a winning ticket on the nightstand of a dying woman.

Except she hadn't. Because she apparently didn't exist. Or more likely, she did exist, but no one knew who she was or how she had come to be by Janice's bed at the very moment she died.

I called the hospice organization.

"We didn't send anyone over to your house that morning," the lady in charge told me after expressing condolences for the loss of Janice. I didn't mention the ticket to her, just that the volunteer had left something behind.

"Do you have a volunteer who is a small, middle-aged woman with graying blond hair?" I asked.

"I don't know of anyone who fits that description," she replied. "Are you sure it was a volunteer from our organization?"

"You are the only ones who sent volunteers," I said.

"I don't know what to say," the lady said. "All I can say is she wasn't one of ours."

I am not one to keep something that is not mine, but I couldn't think of any other way of identifying the woman. So I waited a week, hoping she would reappear. She didn't. The newspapers moved on to the next big story.

In a bank somewhere was a theoretical stack of dollar bills 130 miles high waiting for someone to show up with the ticket I held in my hand. I knew the moment I cashed it that nothing would ever be the same. But I also knew that the moment Janice died, nothing would ever be the same.

———

"It looks like you are a billionaire," Cecelia said as she moved her possessions into my house the following week.

"I have no interest in being a billionaire," I said.

"No luck in solving the mystery of whose ticket it is?"

"No," I replied. "I'm beginning to think it's like the tooth fairy, except this is the cancer fairy. Instead of taking a tooth from under a pillow and leaving 50 cents, she took Janice and left $2 billion."

"That's quite an analogy."

"My mind is full of analogies these days," I replied. "But it was a bad deal. Janice was worth far more than $2 billion. She was priceless."

Cecelia went with me when I drove to the lottery headquarters office, a three-hour trip across the state to Richmond. My goal, of course, was to remain anonymous, which was allowed under the lottery regulations. Keeping the winner secret turned out to be impossible, however. It was in no one's interest except mine to have a faceless winner of the largest jackpot in history. Someone at the lottery office tipped off the Richmond Times-Dispatch, and a photographer snapped a picture as we exited the building. Before we got home, my photograph was splashed across the internet.

The lottery office wanted to know how I had come to obtain the ticket, of course. I told them it was purchased at the 7-Eleven. This was not a lie. I didn't claim to purchase the ticket. I only said where it was purchased, which had already been reported in the newspapers. When they checked the video footage from the store, there was no recording of anyone buying the ticket. The screen simply went blank for five minutes at the moment the ticket was bought.

In the end, they had no choice but to honor it. I chose the option of a lump sum payment of $1.6 billion rather than annual payments over 30 years that would add up to $2.8 billion. I immediately transferred the money to a brokerage account with Goldman Sachs set up by Cecelia and used it to purchase short-term Treasury bills, the safest investment known to mankind, until I figured out what I wanted to do with the money.

The irony of all of this was that while I was indifferent to state-run lotteries, not giving them much thought, Cecelia was dead set against them.

"It is a deal with the devil," she told me more than once. "Instead of taxing people to pay for better schools, the government pretends we get the money free from lotteries. But it is not free at all. The government ends up spending more on social services to take care of families that are wasting money on lotteries that should be spent on food, clothing, and rent. You don't see long lines waiting to buy lottery tickets in rich neighborhoods. It's in the poor neighborhoods that the government sells the fantasy that you can become instantly rich.

"And what happens to the winners? First, the government snatches back half the money in taxes. Then, the winners implode. Everyone thinks money is going to solve their problems, but what is really happening is nothing more than throwing gasoline on a fire. It breaks up families because everyone fights over the money. Anyone addicted to something just becomes a worse addict. Scammers con people into giving them the money. You get people with problems suddenly having money that makes those problems worse. Many of them end up broke and with no family to support them anymore."

I couldn't argue with her reasoning. I was facing a tax bill in the hundreds of millions of dollars as the government clawed back its share, and the moment the news broke that I had the winning ticket, I started to hear from relatives and friends I hadn't seen in years. Strangers introduced themselves to me in the street. My phone lit up with telephone calls from people claiming to be investment advisors pitching opportunities to put my newfound wealth to work, as though somehow I needed to make even more money because a billion dollars isn't enough.

Most of all, people didn't just start laughing at my bad jokes, they looked at me differently and treated me differently.

"Why are you here?" I heard from the grinning receptionist at the university fitness center where I had my office. It was a question repeated many times in many ways in the days after we returned from Richmond.

"I work here," I replied.

Of course, everyone expected me to quit my job and buy a 100-foot yacht or a Lear jet and never set foot in Blacksburg again. What they couldn't fathom is that I enjoyed my job and I was content with my life, with the obvious exception of being widowed. I liked working with young people, hearing their stories and their dreams as I tended to their bodies. Even though I could have retreated to a strictly supervisory role, I continued to show up on the sidelines at football games and other contests for the hands-on work of being an athletic trainer and physical therapist. I also relished being part of a campus community. I had friends on the faculty and in the administration, people Janice and I enjoyed having dinner with or bowling with on Saturday evenings.

It took me less than a week to fully understand that all was lost. The news media quickly found out about Janice, and the story was too hard to resist. "Virginia Man Loses Wife, Becomes Billionaire in One Week" was just one of the headlines. "From the Sidelines to the Penthouse," read another, featuring interviews with football players and coaches.

Reporters and cameras camped out on the sidewalk outside my house and invaded the campus, trying to find anyone who even remotely knew me. They quoted people I had never met who gave them all kinds of facts and opinions about me, few of which had any connection to reality. I found out that I jogged five miles before the sun came up, that I liked Latin music, and that I had once attempted but failed to swim the English Channel. I was shocked to find out people made things up to get their names in the paper, and reporters didn't bother to find out whether they were true before publishing them.

I hid from it all in my office and in the gym, but there was no escape. The university president, whom I had met only once, dropped by my office to see me. He had not attended Janice's funeral. He laughed at my jokes and mentioned the need to update the weight room for the football team to be competitive in recruiting battles with other teams in the Atlantic Coast Conference. Perhaps I might consider a donation and have my name on it.

"I don't know what I am going to do with the money," I told him. "I am still working that out."

He gazed at me, perplexed. "I suppose we are going to have to find a new person to supervise our physical therapists and trainers," he said.

"I don't intend to resign," I said. "This is my life. I like it."

"Well, of course," he said quickly. "You are a great asset to the university. Coach Adams has always spoken highly of you."

I barely suppressed a laugh. The odds that Coach Adams spoke to the president of the university about an athletic trainer were about the same as winning the Powerball lottery. Maybe less. At least that was true before the ticket. I am sure they had talked about me afterwards.

After all, the coach needed a new weight room to help recruit better players.

—--

Cousin Jack showed up on my doorstep two days after the Richmond Times-Dispatch and the internet made me a nationwide celebrity. I hadn't seen him in five years, and I had never called him "Cousin Jack." Apparently, he expected me to call him that.

"Cousin Joe," he bellowed loud enough for the neighbors to hear when I answered the door. He stepped forward and gave me a bear hug before I could resist. "It is so good to see you!"

Jack Hayford, 6-foot-3 inches tall and not an ounce under 300 pounds, was my father's cousin's son, which I guess made him my second cousin, although I'm not sure about that. Looking over his shoulder as he hugged me, I saw the requisite jacked-up Ford 150 parked in the driveway behind my Toyota with the requisite gun rack behind the passenger cab.

"Well, hello, Jack," I said, stepping back. "What a surprise to see you."

"I was just passing through Blacksburg on a way to a gun show – you know that's how I make my living these days – and I thought I would stop by and see you."

"That's very thoughtful of you," I replied dryly.

"Well, we haven't seen each other since the last family reunion in Harper's Ferry," he said, still loud enough for everyone on the street to hear him. "That was what, three years ago?"

"Five," I replied softly, looking around to see if anyone had stepped outside to see what was going on.

The reunion of the Mathers/Hayford/Jones clan had taken place at the Shenandoah River Resort five miles upstream from Harper's Ferry. The "Resort" was actually a line of small A-frames lining a dirt road off of Route 27 backing up to the river in West Virginia. The main office was a two-story house at the end of the road, its first floor converted into a combination front desk, tackle shop, and convenience mart selling everything from bait fish to fried pork rinds. A small pool surrounded by a waist-high fence bordered a horseshoe pit and a variety of cornhole boards, some painted with the Stars and Stripes. Nearby, a flagpole flew the American flag with the Confederate battle flag just below it.

"Wasn't West Virginia loyal to the Union?" Janice asked when we arrived to check in.

"It was," I replied. "But we are just across the river from Robert E. Lee's Virginia."

The A-frames were only partially clean, and we found out later that the owner's teenage children were the cleaning crew. There were exposed pipes, and the toilet sat hard against the water heater, so you had to turn your legs sideways to use it. The beds sagged in the middle. All for the "special" rate of $150 a night. We lasted one night before retreating to a nearby bed and breakfast.

The Hayford side of the family didn't seem to mind the accommodations at all. They huddled around a campfire, drinking beer and smoking cigarettes, while their children roared by on ATVs up and down the dirt road, kicking up dust. Small children wearing only diapers wandered around aimlessly, playing in the dirt. Occasionally, a horseshoe game broke out, which required a fresh infusion of Miller Lite. I wondered how my mother had ever married into this family. But love can not only be blind but also stupid, and I suppose my sister and I wouldn't exist if she hadn't fallen for Billy Mathers.

The family reunion proved to be a stage for Janice at her finest.

"Aren't you being judgmental and looking down on people because they are different?" Janice asked me when we retreated to the A-frame for our one miserable night. "After all, you grew up in a double-wide."

I thought for a moment. "You are right. I am being judgmental," I conceded. I did, in fact, grow up with neighbors who weren't too much different from the Hayfords and Mathers. "I feel like I've checked into the Bates Motel with the Beverly Hillbillies."

Rather than keep her distance as I did, Janice set about meeting and talking to every single person at the reunion, especially the women whom she drew into long conversations about everything from babies to hairstyles – and eventually to talking about their troubled marriages and financial woes caused by their husbands' immaturity and addictions. Within a couple of hours, she was hugging an overweight woman who had lost her eldest son to an overdose in the OxyContin epidemic.

Janice nurtured everyone she met. It was part of her DNA to exude comfort. It flowed from her like a soft summer breeze. She was born to be a mother, yet she never got to be one. Instead, she mothered the weary and the burdened. By the end of the reunion, she had a circle of ten women huddled around her, bathing in what I called the "Janice effect."

"I am so sorry to hear about your wife," Cousin Jack said. "It's a terrible thing."

"Thank you," I replied. I wondered if he even remembered Janice's name. Jack had been the king of the reunion with his huge size and garrulous personality. Other people were merely an audience.

"Carolyn certainly was fond of her," he said. "She could talk about nothing else on the way home."

"Janice was a wonderful person," I said. I vaguely remembered Jack's wife, a petite blond with prematurely aging skin, chasing around a couple of small children.

Silence fell between us, something I didn't think was possible with Jack. Perhaps he was waiting for me to invite him in, which I wasn't going to do. I had plans for the rest of the day, and I might not be able to get him to leave once he was planted in my living room. I sensed a certain degree of awkwardness in him.

"You know we both lost our wives," he finally said sheepishly. "Carolyn left me."

"I didn't know that," I said. "I'm sorry."

"Took the kids and everything. Moved away."

"I am sorry."

"Sure, I blew it," he said. "I should never have done what I did with that waitress, but I was drunk."

I nodded.

"A man loses his job and he's looking for comfort somewhere, and she wouldn't…" he stopped. "You know what I mean."

I nodded again, though I could only guess at what he meant. If Janice were there, she would know and say the right thing.

"It's just that I don't make that much off the gun shows," he continued. "And with the child support payments the government squeezes out of me, I am stuck in a ditch. They are going to repossess my truck if they can find it."

Growing up in a double-wide, I knew what the loss of a man's truck would do to him in places like western Virginia. Take away his house, and that would be bad, but take away his truck and his pride would never recover. A man's identity was tied to his truck. A man was a Ford guy with an F-150 or a Chevy guy with a Silverado 1500.

"That's a tough situation," I said, for lack of anything better to say.

He paused and took a deep breath. "I was just wondering if I could get a loan from you to help me get past this," he said with a slight tremble in his voice, as though begging were something he had never done in his life.

Fortunately, Cecelia had seen this coming, and we had worked out a short-term strategy for dealing with the deluge of people we knew were heading my way. I would be the good cop, and she would be the bad cop.

"Well, that all depends on Cecelia," I said. "You see, I turned over everything to her to manage. She controls the money."

Jack looked at me incredulously. "You turned two billion dollars over to your sister?"

"It's what I did," I said flatly. "Every last dime."

"Why would you do that?" he blurted, once again loud enough for the entire street to hear.

I looked down at my feet sorrowfully. "With Janice dying, I'm not in the right state of mind to manage the money. Not right now at least."

This was a variation on what Janice and I had called the "Cancer Card." I used it often in dealing with medical bureaucracies and health insurance companies to get past gatekeepers and red tape that were keeping her from getting the treatment she needed. Who could turn away a distraught husband whose wife is dying? A few could, but most gave way and got her what she needed, whether getting in to see a specialist right away or access to a new drug.

Cousin Jack couldn't argue with a man's grief. What could he say? I could see him struggling to remember if and when he had met Cecelia. She had no reason to attend Janice's family reunion, so he might never have been introduced.

"Can you ask her?" he finally asked.

"You can ask her yourself," I said. "I will give you her phone number."

Jack's face fell. No doubt he sensed what I already knew. If he did call her, he would run into a stone wall. Cecelia was one of the most generous people I had ever met, both with her time and her money, far more generous than I ever was. If someone came to her in a crisis, she opened her wallet wide. However, she would not countenance excuses for irresponsible behavior and certainly not opportunism. If Jack came to her with tears of repentance for having ruined his marriage and drunk himself out of a job, she would help him even if I hadn't won the lottery, but if he justified himself, she would not. And I had a hard time seeing big Jack Hayford humbling himself before anyone, much less a woman.

I gave him Cecelia's number, and he drove off in his truck, the first of many opportunists who knocked on my door or called me on the phone. Some I knew; many I did not. The answer was always the same: talk to my sister. She has control of the money.

Almost no one did.

Chapter 3

Lionel Jackson

Brian had been strangely persuasive when we were sitting on the rock by Cascade Falls. We finally got to the topic I wanted to talk to him about. Or at least Cecelia had wanted me to talk to him about it.

"What do you think I should do with the money?" I had asked him. "The $2.8 billion."

"Or what's left of it after taxes."

"Well, that's a different story," he deadpanned. "Only a billion dollars, give or take a hundred million."

I laughed. It felt good. I hadn't laughed much in months. "I didn't ask for the money, and I don't know what to do with it. I didn't even buy the ticket. It was left in my home by someone, a volunteer with the hospice organization. I tried to return it, but the hospice organization didn't know anything about her. I am beginning to wonder if she even existed. Who would just walk into a stranger's home and sit with a sick woman the very moment she died?"

Brian took a moment to answer, a pensive look on his face. "That certainly is a mystery to be solved," he said. He paused for a moment. "Or revealed."

I shrugged my shoulders. "But that leaves me with a problem."

"Which wouldn't be a problem for most people," he said. "Millions of people in this country dream about winning the lottery. They stand in long lines to buy tickets when the jackpot gets high. They try to negotiate with God to win it. If you just let me win the lottery, God, I will give half the money to the poor."

"My negotiations with God are over," I said bluntly. "Besides, money doesn't mean much to me as long as I have enough to pay the bills."

"Then there must be another purpose."

"Or a strange twist of fate."

"If one believes in fate."

I remembered I was talking to a pastor. He was always going to lead the conversation back to God and to Jesus. There was no such thing as fate, only divine purpose, he would say. This was a topic I wanted to avoid. God, if he exists at all, failed me. Janice was gone.

"My life is a shambles," I said. "It's bad enough I lost my wife, but now it's apparent I can't keep my job. I am trying to act like everything is normal, but everyone treats me differently. When Janice died, everyone empathized with my sorrow and offered their condolences and support. Now it's as though she hadn't died. Everyone expects me to be happy, and most of them want something from me."

"People are thoughtless that way," Brian replied.

"One of the things I like about my job is talking to the players when they come in for treatment. It's sad, but most of these young men grew up without a father. They were blessed with great athletic ability but with no structure in their life outside of the football field or basketball court. Very few of them will be able to make their living as professional athletes, so the moment their college eligibility is over, they lose the only structure they have in their lives as well as the only father figures: the coaches. They go from being stars cheered on by tens of thousands of fans to being nobodies without a path forward and too often without an education. The university uses their talent but gives little in return."

"That's depressing."

"But I could talk to them. I might be stretching their muscles and their ligaments, but I also stretched their minds. I told them that this is their opportunity to be prepared for a job after football or basketball. I told them the importance of treating women properly and being committed to a good woman, of charting a path in life that will lead to good things, not bad things."

"Did they listen?"

"That's the strange thing," I said. "They did listen. Perhaps I am the only person who ever took the time to see them as more than athletes. I connected with them."

"And now?"

"And now the ticket has changed all that. They see me as the fulfillment of a fantasy – a man who got rich by picking the right six numbers. They are puzzled why I am still working and still talking to them. And they don't listen. All they do is gaze at me and see the illusion of millions of dollars. They fantasize about being me."

"So you care about these young men?"

I paused to think about the question. "Yes, I do," I said. "Perhaps while everyone else sees them as star athletes, I see them as victims, just as I was a victim of my father's addiction. And perhaps because Janice and I couldn't have our own children, I view them as my children."

Brian smiled broadly. "You know you are a good man. How many people would try to return a winning lottery ticket to its rightful owner or care what happens to star athletes when they are no longer stars?"

"No," I protested. "I am a lost man drifting at sea, trying to navigate by stars I cannot see. A storm is tossing my boat from wave to wave."

We fell silent, listening to the waterfall cascading into the pool with a roar. There is something about rushing water that soothes the soul. I remembered why Janice so much enjoyed this hike. She would sit for an hour or two on the rock, her eyes closed, absorbing the peacefulness of the place. I longed to put my arm around her and hold her close to me as I used to do, letting that peace pass through her soul to me. Without her, I could find no peace.

"What should I do?" I finally asked Brian. He had his eyes closed, and he opened them to look me squarely in the eye.

"Sometimes, Joe, you can't find the answer where you are," he said. "You need to go on a journey to find it. And only when you have traveled many, many miles does the storm pass and the clouds part so you can see the stars."

I contemplated his twist on my analogy. He was certainly right in one regard. I couldn't stay where I was with people treating me differently, laughing at my bad jokes, and wanting something from me. My life had died with Janice in more ways than one. I needed to leave Blacksburg.

"Are you suggesting a pilgrimage of some kind?"

"No, a pilgrimage has a known destination," he replied.

"But where should I go?"

"It doesn't matter where," he said. "What matters is that you go. It is only in going that you will arrive at your destination."

I gazed at the waterfall and thought again of Janice. What would she say? She would laugh at the irony that a man so unencumbered by the lure of riches would suddenly find himself a billionaire whose entire life had been turned upside down. Then she would say that there had to be a reason. She would tell me to go.

"You are right," I told him. "You are right."

That is how I landed a month later in an Alabama town I had never heard of before, home to a Piggly Wiggly, the J and V Smokehouse, and the Red Bay High School Tigers.

As it turned out, it was just the beginning.

——-

Cecelia came up with the idea of traveling in an RV rather than staying in hotels. To begin with, it would give me privacy. While every week put my 15 minutes of fame further in the past, there would always be someone who would recognize me as the winner of the largest Powerball jackpot in history. It would also allow me to sleep on my own bed every night and cook my own meals – RVs have microwaves, so the risk of starvation was minimal. Besides, she noted, I always loved the outdoors. While traveling in an RV, especially a big one, is not camping, or even glamping, it is out in nature.

Kevin, the salesman at the dealership in Suffolk, was a short, overweight man wearing too much Old Spice cologne. He didn't recognize me and immediately began sizing me up: a slightly balding middle-aged man in blue jeans and a Virginia Tech polo shirt trailed by an attractive blonde whom he wrongly assumed was my wife. I saw his eyes drift down not to her breasts or her legs but to her left hand, looking for a big diamond. The wives of real customers, as opposed to gawkers, always had big diamonds. There was no ring on Cecilia's finger, and I detected his disappointment. He would be wasting half an hour of his life with someone without the means to buy what he was selling.

Kevin was a salesman without a showroom. Rather, his products were parked outside, three brand new Prevosts, one of the most expensive luxury motor coaches available, at $2.5 million, plus whatever additional accessories the customer – or often the wife of the customer – wanted. Squeeze a jacuzzi into the 45-foot, 22-ton behemoth? It could be done. How about a subzero fridge or a wine cellar? Nothing was impossible. The people he sold to didn't quibble about costs. The old saying was true: "If you have to ask how much it costs, you can't afford it." His customers paid with a cash transfer from J P Morgan or Goldman Sachs and drove away, only to return for the inevitable repairs needed by a product with thousands of parts, many made in factories in rural China by people who had never seen an RV.

"Most RVs are built cheaply and made to look pretty, like lipstick on a pig," Kevin gave us his standard sales pitch. "But Prevosts are the Rolls-Royce of motor coaches, with the finest and safest chassis and the highest level of craftsmanship. To own one of these is not only a great investment but a statement that you have arrived. Just imagine showing up for a homecoming tailgate or a family reunion in one of our coaches."

"I don't need to make a statement," I replied. "I need a place to live while I travel."

Kevin frowned. "You do realize that these aren't ordinary motor coaches," he said. "They are top of the line. Our customers generally don't live in them, except perhaps for winter months in Florida or Arizona."

We both understood his message: you can't afford one of these. Cecilia smiled in that saccharine way she does when she feels she isn't getting proper respect from a man.

"We did look at the Volkner Performance S."

Kevin laughed. The Performance S, built by a German company, was the most expensive coach in the world at $7.7 million.

"I am sure you did," he said, his eyes drifting to another couple parking a Mercedes in the lot outside. "You are free to look at our coaches. And if you have any questions, just find me and I will answer them."

"We would actually like you to show us," Cecelia said.

Kevin gave us a slightly exasperated expression that said, "You are completely out of your league."

"Sure, I will be with you in a couple of minutes," he said, turning away. "In the meantime, look around."

We watched as he hastily crossed the parking lot in the direction of the Mercedes couple. Halfway there, he was intercepted by another man. An intense conversation followed, and Kevin looked over at us as the other man spoke.

"That's his boss," Cecelia speculated. "He recognized you."

Indeed, Kevin quickly reversed course and hurried – almost jogged – back to us. It was a whole new Kevin, a huge smile on his face. I suspected he would laugh at my bad jokes.

"Mr. Mathers," he said, holding out his hand, which I shook after some hesitation. "I didn't recognize you. Welcome! I would be very happy to show you our coaches."

New Kevin took us to see the Prevosts, focusing on me and not bothering to acknowledge Cecelia. They were beautiful machines, essentially luxury condominiums on wheels with a full kitchen, a living room area with leather couches and captain's chairs, heated ceramic floors, multiple televisions, one and a half baths with marble everywhere, and a king-sized Sleep Number bed adorned with no fewer than a dozen decorative pillows.

Cecelia was not impressed. "It looks like a madam decorated this to be a bordello on wheels," she told Kevin.

New Kevin frowned for a moment, but then put on his salesman smile. Cecelia had a point. The interior featured glitzy trinkets and sparkling pink designs completely out of place in the great outdoors but appropriate for an upscale brothel.

"We can custom-design a coach any way you want," he answered eagerly. "A lot of our customers like the Paris look, but we can give you a western look or any other look you want."

I thought Cecelia would bend over laughing at the words "Paris look," but she kept a straight face. I could not contain myself.

"Paris, Texas or Paris, Virginia?" I asked. New Kevin burst out laughing. Cecelia winked at me, one of the country's top new comedians.

It was at that moment that I had a revelation. I wasn't too much different from my sister, who returned the Lexus and kept the old Ford. I was uncomfortable with the over-the-top luxury that so many others crave. Rather than stirring longing within me, the sparkling $2.5 million motor coach made me queasy. I could afford it easily and pay for it with a few clicks on a smartphone, but I didn't want it.

New Kevin was sorely disappointed when we left. He tried every sales pitch he knew, every form of flattery possible, every appeal to vanity and pride. Nothing stuck. I am simply not wired that way.

"You knew I wasn't going to buy it," I told Cecelia as we turned onto the freeway home.

She nodded. "I knew."

"Why did we drive all the way here?"

"You needed to see it."

I pondered why I needed to see the Prevosts. I could think of no reason. In a few miles, Cecelia abruptly turned onto an exit ramp.

"Where are we going?" I asked.

"To buy an RV," she said. "The one you are going to travel in."

She was right. In two hours, I wired $400,000 to a dealer who agreed to drop off a lightly used Tiffin Allegro Bus at my doorstep the next week for one-sixth the price of the Prevost. The bus indeed was a bus, built on a Freightliner chassis, the same 45-feet long and 22 tons as the Prevosts, with largely the same features except the "Paris look" and the name on the front. The dealer also sold me a used Jeep that could be towed behind the bus using a Blue Ox hitch and an Air Force One braking system. The big question was whether I could learn to drive it.

I found out I had a lot to learn about RVs.

————

Two days before I left on my journey, I emptied my office at the gym. Brian showed up unexpectedly just as I was carrying the last cardboard box to my car. Co-workers had been dropping by all morning to say goodbye and wish me luck, although inwardly they all thought I had had my lifetime supply of luck already.

It was a sad day for me, yet an inevitable one. A billionaire can't live among normal people doing normal things. Even the university president and the head coach showed up to wish me off and to mention the need for the new weight room – casually, of course, because it happened to get jackhammered into the conversation so easily.

I suppose I should have asked Brian how he knew it was my last day and where to find me. The answer was obvious: Cecelia. What was less obvious was why he was there. He seemed to care about me, or maybe this was some ulterior way to talk to me about Jesus, which I wasn't going to do.

"So you are really doing it?" Brian asked. "Going on the journey?"

"What else am I going to do? Sit around the house ignoring knocks on the door from relatives I haven't seen in years?"

Brian looked in my box and picked out a photograph of the football team taken five years before, after they had won a bowl game. The quarterback stood in the middle holding the crystal trophy, the last victor to hold it since it was shattered the next year when a mascot accidentally dropped it. The photo was signed by the head coach: "To Joe, thanks for keeping our players on the field. Coach Adams."

"A lot of memories," he said.

"I don't remember anything about that game," I said. "I was back in the locker room taking care of a kid who tore his ACL on the first play."

"Where is that kid now?" Brian asked.

"He was one of my success stories," I said. "He now has an MBA and is working for a Fortune 500 company."

"So you made a difference?"

"I like to think I did."

"And now?"

Before I could reply, a faculty member who knew me happened by. He taught English literature and was doing his best to be the caricature of a college professor with a tweed jacket and bow tie. He shook my hand and said we should stay in touch and have lunch sometime. We both knew we wouldn't. I returned to the question.

"Now, I go."

Brian put his hand on my shoulder. "You are depressed, aren't you?"

"Mildly," I said.

"Do you know why?"

"I could venture a guess," I said. "My wife died of cancer, and my entire life has been upended by something everyone else wants but I don't."

"Could I venture a guess too?" he asked.

"Why not?"

"Why don't you let me buy you lunch and I will tell you," he said.

As a billionaire, I insisted on buying the $15.34 lunch at the college cafeteria. We sat in a corner by a window watching the students walking to class, leaning into a brisk breeze coming off the mountains. A few students eating their lunch recognized me and stared. One or two pulled out their smartphones and took photographs that would quickly be shared on social media.

"So why are you here? What is the guess you want to venture?" I finally asked him as we ate our food. "You came with a purpose in mind. A pastor doesn't just show up at someone's workplace, especially if he isn't part of his flock."

"Fair enough observation," he replied. "I didn't think we finished our conversation at the waterfall."

"You mean there is more?" I said. "You and Cecelia have already gotten me to buy an RV and head out on a journey to who knows where. Isn't that enough?"

"I thought so at the time, but now believe we have something else to discuss."

"And that is?"

"Your father."

"Is this some kind of therapy session?" I asked.

"No, I'm not a therapist."

"Isn't that what a therapist asks? Tell me about your relationship with your father?"

"It's often a good question when you are trying to figure out why someone is depressed."

"And you think I'm depressed because of my father, not because my wife died?"

"I would say that you lost more than Janice when she died, and you need to know what it is."

I liked Brian, and I was glad Cecelia had convinced me to talk to him. I appreciated his interest in me and that he didn't try to stuff Jesus down my throat. But my father was a bridge too far.

"He was a drunk," I said with finality. "And he is no longer around."

"Maybe he is still around more than you think."

"It's not something I want to talk about," I said firmly.

"Most people don't."

"Perhaps another time."

Brian smiled. "Feel free to call me from the road anytime," he said.

I nodded and changed the subject to the early spring snowstorm forecast for the coming weekend. Only later, when I began to pack up the Tiffin with food and clothes did I wonder why I had such a strong negative reaction to discussing my father. And what did Brian mean I had lost more than Janice when she died?

———

My mother was the last person I saw before I headed south on

Interstate 81 toward Alabama. She wore her Kroger's uniform with her nametag – "Dottie" – when I arrived at the million-dollar house I bought her the week after Cecelia and I returned from the lottery office in Richmond. It was in a gated community of luxury homes and expensive automobiles nestled in the mountains. Two large men were hauling new furniture out of a truck when I cautiously steered the Tiffin with the Jeep in tow onto the circular driveway and parked behind them. They momentarily gawked at the behemoth but then quickly returned to their work, carrying a dining room table through the double doors into the house.

"So you really are driving that thing?" she said, eyeing the Tiffin. "It's huge."

"It's not as hard as it looks," I said. "I'll be fine."

"And why are you doing this again?"

I thought about telling her about my conversations with Brian, but then decided against it. "I just need some time away," I said. "Some space."

"Why don't you just take a fancy vacation then?" she protested. "It's not like you can't afford it."

"You know that's not me," I said.

Over the years, Janice and I enjoyed backpacking and camping, not hotels and resorts. One of our most cherished memories was a two-week hiking expedition on the Appalachian Trail. In my favorite photograph, painful to look at now that she was gone, we stood arm-in-arm on Hawksbill Mountain with the sun setting behind us in a blaze of colors. We preferred the earth under our feet, and I couldn't remember us ever staying in a place fancier than a Holiday Inn.

"You have hardly spent any of the money, except on that beast," she pointed at the Tiffin. "You've spent more on me than on yourself."

It was true. The house and all the furnishings cost far more than the Tiffin. I hadn't bought anything else except the Lexus that Cecelia returned. The lottery payout was sitting in New York, earning 3 percent interest from the government bonds – a staggering $3 million a year, eclipsing my annual salary of $60,000 as a physical therapist.

"People think that's strange, don't they?" I mused. "I just need to figure out what it all means – losing Janice and then the ticket. Having to leave my job. Being rich all of a sudden."

"You grew up in a trailer park, Joe. You lost your wife to cancer. Can't you just take the money and enjoy yourself? Why are you agonizing over it?"

It was a good question. Perhaps I didn't think the money was really mine, and I had no right to spend it. Or perhaps I just didn't really want anything money could buy.

"I don't know," I said. "It just seems to have made things worse rather than better."

My mother embraced me. There was a wiry toughness in her body from a lifetime of struggle. What a remarkable woman she was, I thought. And yet there were millions of such women around the world, betrayed by the world, devalued by their cultures, abandoned by men, and yet still managing to survive and take care of their families.

"You know your sister and I are praying for you," she said.

"Prayer didn't help Janice," I replied.

"You don't know that," she said.

"I do know that," I said. "I buried her."

My mother took a deep breath, then reached down and took my hand. "You think that prayer is only answered when you get what you want," she said. "A lot of people think that way. But prayer is a lot deeper than that. God is not a cosmic vending machine where you push buttons and what you want comes out. The Bible says no matter how many promises God has made, they are all yes and amen in Jesus. I believe that. And I believe He said yes to Janice, even if we don't understand how at the moment."

"I think that's just a clever way of letting God off the hook," I retorted.

"He doesn't need to be let off the hook. All His ways are perfect."

"How can they be perfect when he let cancer strike down a beautiful young woman in the prime of her life? He had the power to stop it, but didn't. Maybe he doesn't have the power. Or maybe he doesn't care. Or perhaps he doesn't exist."

"He didn't stop it when His own son was brutally tortured and murdered for our salvation."

It was my mother's standard answer: the cross. I had heard this many times before. I really didn't want to get into the Jesus conversation again.

"How do you know that isn't simply a myth?" I replied. "Something made up by his followers who didn't want to admit they had followed a charlatan."

"They died horrible deaths rather than save themselves by admitting they made it up," she said.

"So they were delusional," I argued. "Like cult members who commit mass suicide because their leader told them to."

My mother let go of my hand and shook her head. "I know I can't convince you," she said. "I don't believe anyone ever debated anyone into the kingdom of God. I can see why Pastor Brian recommended you take a trip. God has provided the means, and you should go. Maybe he will reveal the truth to you."

"What is truth?" I asked, knowing that I was quoting Pontius Pilate.

My mother didn't respond. The conversation ended. I helped the workman maneuver a couch into the house. A few minutes later, I hugged her goodbye, started up the Tiffin, and headed south.

As I drove, I pondered her last words to me.

"You will find yourself where you don't expect," she said. "Know there is a reason."

—--

Two days later, my mother was proved right. I ended up in a place I would never have imagined: in an Alabama cave quaffing a Snake Handler Double IPA with a 75-year-old dog-loving R&B musician named Lionel Jackson.

I wouldn't have been there had I paid attention to the warning light on the Tiffin dashboard labeled DEF. I had an excuse. There were plenty of distractions, particularly keeping the Tiffin and tow car, or "toad" as I learned RVers call it, between the white lines of the interstate. The bus was so wide – some 11 feet from mirror to mirror – I had to straddle the line on the driver's side to keep the passenger side out of the shoulder. Then the GPS directed me to make a wrong turn in rural Alabama, leaving me completely lost.

Only when the Tiffin abruptly slowed down to five miles an hour and wouldn't go any faster, no matter how much I pumped the gas, did I wonder what the DEF light on the dashboard meant. I finally came to a stop on State Road 21, a two-lane road running through the remote backwoods.

With no other sign of civilization within miles and no cell phone signal, I hiked up a side road near where the Tiffin died. I soon came upon a grey-haired African-American man wearing an Alabama Crimson Tide jacket and holding a cane capped with a brass dog's head. He sat on a bench under a sign that read "Coon Dog Cemetery."

"You don't look like a man who has a dog here," he said. "You look like you need some help."

"My motorcoach stalled out on the road down there," I said, pointing down the hill.

"So you don't know where you are?"

I looked around. We were deep in the woods, and no one else was around. Just beyond the man was a carving of two dogs barking at a raccoon in a tree. Beyond that was the cemetery, a half acre of well-cared-for headstones and other markers.

"I know I am in Alabama," I replied. "I was heading for Red Bay until my coach suddenly slowed down to a crawl and wouldn't go any faster no matter how much I pumped the gas. Now it has died."

"A Tiffin, eh?"

"Yes, that's why I was going to Red Bay."

"And you have never owned a diesel pusher before?"

I didn't know what a diesel pusher was, but I wasn't going to admit it. "My first RV," I replied.

The man laughed. "I think I know your problem," he said. "This is quite a place to break down."

"What is this place?"

"It's the Coon Dog Memorial Cemetery," the man said.

I nodded with a puzzled expression. "That's what the sign says," I replied.

"Back in the 1930s, during the Great Depression, a man named Key Underwood buried his beloved coon dog here, and then other people started doing it. Pretty soon, people from all over the country were bringing their dogs here. Not any coon dog can be buried here. A dog has to be a purebred, and there have to be witnesses who saw it tree a raccoon. I am the first black man to ever have a dog here. I have two here, Fred and Doug."

"And you are out here to visit your dogs?"

"Last Sunday of every month," he answered. "They were family. Pretty much my only family left in this county."

"I am sorry," I said.

"No need to be," He said and abruptly stood up, leaning slightly on his cane. "Now let's go get your rig running again."

We slowly made our way down the hill to State Road 21, where the coach sat half on the shoulder and half on the road, the emergency lights blinking. Immediately, Lionel opened an outside storage area and found what he was looking for: a clear five-gallon jug labeled DEF. He carried the jug around the back of the coach, opened a small panel I hadn't noticed and poured the contents into a reservoir.

"The engine is designed to slow down when it runs out of DEF and ultimately shut down," he said. "But once you fill the reservoir, it will start right up." He explained that Diesel Exhaust Fluid, a combination of urea and deionized water, turns the pollutant nitrogen oxide from the Tiffin's 600 horsepower engine into a harmless combination of nitrogen and water.

I had taken one chemistry class in my life and got a "B" my freshman year in high school, my only grade below an A. I recalled that chemical reactions have something to do with electrons and that two hydrogen atoms and one oxygen atom form water, but not much more. I knew almost nothing about internal combustion engines.

"I guess I should have read the owner's manual," I said sheepishly.

Lionel looked up at me, his aging face crisscrossed with wrinkles. I recognized a pensive expression that seemed so much like Cecelia when she sees things I can't see.

"Everyone should read the owner's manual," he said. "It's written by the creator."

I had never thought of Tiffin Motorcoach Company as a creator. A manufacturer, yes. I was puzzled by his use of the word, but let it pass. It didn't dawn on me until much later in my journey that he might have been talking about another owner's manual.

"I was foolish not to," I said. "Can I buy you dinner as a way of saying thanks? I would like to hear about your dogs."

Lionel smiled. "I know just the place."

—--

"Have you ever heard of the Swampers?" Lionel asked me. We were riding down a steep slope sitting on chairs installed in the bed of a pickup truck. Below us was the Rattlesnake Saloon, a bar and restaurant built under the overhang of a cave. A waterfall flowed over the top of an overhang on the far side. There was no place for a car, much less a motorcoach, to park. The owners ferried their customers to the cave from a parking lot in a field above the cave.

"I can't say I have," I replied, clinging to my chair out of fear of falling out.

"They were a group of musicians north of here in Muscle Shoals who backed up many of the most famous singers and bands of the '60s, '70s and '80s – Aretha Franklin, the Rolling Stones, Bob Dylan, Paul Simon, and a lot of others," he said. "They created the Muscle Shoals Sound."

I nodded. I didn't know anything about music.

"I used to play with them when they needed an extra person," he said. "That makes me a minor celebrity around here."

"So you are a musician?"

"Much to my father's dismay. He wanted me to be an engineer or a doctor."

We arrived at the saloon, and immediately several customers and a waiter welcomed Lionel warmly. Only when we were seated and the waiter brought the IPAs did I notice that he was the only black person there. A man I guessed was the owner came over and greeted us, chatting briefly with Lionel about music. I didn't understand what they were talking about.

"So how did you end up owning coon dogs?" I asked when the man left.

Lionel took a sip of his beer and smiled. "It's a bit of a story," he said.

"I would like to hear it," I said.

"It's not an easy story to hear."

"That's all right," I said, my curiosity stirred. "I still would like to hear it."

Lionel hesitated and took another sip of his beer. I noticed a change in him, a raft of emotions rising from deep within. I sensed he didn't often tell the story.

"My grandfather was a remarkable man," he said. "He grew up here in Colbert County, the son of a sharecropper. It was not an easy life for a sharecropper in the 1920s, especially if you were a black man. His family barely survived, and the Klan made sure you stayed in your place. But my grandfather was not one to be kept down. He left home at 16 for Tuscaloosa and somehow managed to get an education. He graduated from Tuskegee Institute at 25 with a degree in agronomy. He was a genius, like Frederick Douglass."

"Hence the names of your dogs?" I interrupted.

"You picked up on that?"

"I did."

"Yes, like Frederick Douglass, a man born in slavery who ended up being one of the great orators and abolitionists of the 19th century. Except my grandfather never got to live long enough to make his mark in the world."

"What happened to him?"

"He came home and began to apply what he had learned to our farming practices. The yields went up. When his father died, he took over and managed to buy some land of his own, something unheard of for a black man in the 1930s in Alabama. He married my grandmother, and she gave birth to my father. Life was getting better. But that was the problem. Life was getting better for him than for his neighbors."

"The Klan?"

"He had a neighbor named Oswald Higgins, a nasty man who was the Grand Cyclops of the local KKK den. He did not take kindly to a black man getting educated and rising above his station."

Lionel paused, overcome momentarily with emotion. "They came in the middle of the night and lynched him. They didn't even bother to accuse him of anything, like looking at a white woman the wrong way. They simply murdered him – hanged him on a tree on his own property and left a burning cross on his lawn. No one was ever arrested. The sheriff and the local judge were both Klansmen. It was just another lynching out of thousands across the South in those days. His murderers all went to church together the next day. It's one of the reasons there are so few blacks left in Northwest Alabama. Everyone fled to the big cities up north."

"But your family didn't flee?"

"My grandmother was a strong woman. We were fortunate Higgins didn't burn down the house when the Klan murdered my grandfather. She persevered and, with the help of my father and a few friends, managed to keep the land and survive. When World War II came, my father enlisted and sent home his pay to keep us afloat."

A waiter interrupted the story, bringing fried catfish, hush puppies, and slaw. We ate in silence for a couple of minutes. A house band began to play nearby. I recognized the first chords of "Sweet Home Alabama."

Lionel smiled, "I worked with Lynyrd Skynyrd on that song," he said. "However, I wasn't on the final recording."

"Doesn't sound like Alabama was all that sweet for your family," I said.

"It wasn't," Lionel replied. "I love the state and I love the people – and I certainly love the Crimson Tide – but there was a deep evil that infected the land. And that evil killed my grandfather."

"You don't blame the people who did it? Just an evil in the land?"

"People are responsible for their actions, and they will be held accountable. But our struggle is not against people. It's against the forces of wickedness that take people captive and turn their hearts to do evil."

A Bible verse I had memorized as a teenager popped into my mind. "For our struggle is not against flesh and blood but against the powers, the principalities and the spiritual forces of wickedness in the heavenly realms," I recited.

Lionel's eyebrows rose. "So you know the scripture?"

"I was forced to memorize it," I replied.

Lionel reflected on this for a moment, and I was momentarily worried we were going to get into a discussion of the Bible. I was relieved when he said, "Let me continue my story."

"Please do," I replied.

"When my father came back from the war, the Klan was still very much active," he said. "It didn't matter that he fought for freedom; our country denied black people that freedom, especially here in the Jim Crow South. We had to step out of the way when we met a white person on the sidewalk and be off the streets at sundown. And every night there was the fear of robed men killing our sons and fathers or burning our homes. I was a boy, but I learned quickly to stay low and be deferential to white folks."

"And yet you don't seem bitter," I noted.

Lionel shook his head. "You need to hear the rest of the story. One day in 1946, a tornado came through the county. It mostly ripped up uninhabited areas, knocking down trees and a couple of barns, but it struck one house, the one owned by Oswald Higgins. A huge live oak fell and crushed the roof over the master bedroom where Oswald was sleeping. He was trapped and badly injured.

"My father was the only neighbor who realized what had happened. He showed up with a flashlight and climbed the stairs to the bedroom. Oswald recognized him and realized it was the perfect opportunity for my father to get his vengeance on him. He could easily pick up a two-by-four and finish him off. Everyone would blame the tornado. No one would know he was even there."

"What did he do?" I asked.

"My father went over to where Oswald was trapped and prayed for him. He forgave him for killing his father and prayed that God would have mercy on him. Then he set him free and drove him to the hospital for white people in Muscle Shoals."

"That's hard to believe," I interjected.

Lionel nodded. "What's harder to believe is that they became fast friends. The next year, my father baptized Oswald in Jackson Creek, just a few miles from here. Just the two of them. I'm sure it was the first time a black man had ever baptized a white man in Alabama."

"That's incredible."

"Miraculous," Lionel said. "But that isn't the end of the story."

"Go on."

"Oswald quit the Klan and lost just about every friend he had in the county. He was kicked out of his church and called all kinds of names that I won't repeat. No one would do business with him, so he suffered financially. Yet he was determined to ask forgiveness and make restitution to every family he had terrorized. My father sat with him in the back of our church every Sunday. He was the only white person ever to attend a service there. At first, people were scared of him, but gradually they understood that he was a changed man, like the Apostle Paul. God had gotten hold of him. It was a test of their faith to forgive him."

"Did they?"

"It wasn't easy," he replied. "But they did forgive him and they accepted him as a brother in the Lord."

"And what happened to him?"

Lionel smiled. "You may not believe this," he said. "But in 1965, Oswald Higgins, the former Grand Cyclops of the KKK in Colbert County, Alabama, marched with Dr. King across the Edmund Pettus Bridge in Selma. Later, an enraged mob beat him viciously, but he survived. My father nursed him back to health. He was fortunate. The Klan beat another white marcher, James Reeb, to death that day."

"That's incredible," I said. "It is hard to believe."

"The light shines in the darkness and the darkness has not overcome it," Lionel said.

At that moment, the man who appeared to be the owner came over to our table again and spoke quietly to Lionel, who nodded in agreement to what he was asking. When the man left, Lionel pointed at the band that was coming back from a break.

"Their saxophonist is not feeling well," he said. "He asked me to fill in. If you have to go, I understand."

"I should probably get going so I can make it to Red Bay before dark," I said. "Thank you so much again for rescuing me."

"One more thing. You asked about my dogs. Oswald Higgins was an avid hunter, and he often went hunting with my father. In the last week of his life, he gave his beloved coon dog, Nick, to my father. Nick sired my dogs, Fred and Doug. They are all buried together in the cemetery."

"Nick?" I asked.

"Nicodemus. The old Oswald died. A new Oswald was born."

"Born again?" I asked.

"From above," Lionel replied. "I figured you would get the reference."

"They made me memorize a lot of scripture," I said.

Lionel shook my hand and looked me in the eye with an expression that reminded me of Brian: disarmingly sincere and full of a deep calm.

"Joe," he asked as he left me. "My father forgave Oswald Higgins. Who do you need to forgive?"

As the pickup truck carried me out of the gully and towards the parking lot of the Rattlesnake Saloon, where the Tiffin awaited, I heard the smooth sounds of a saxophone solo floating through the trees.

The Swampers were right. Lionel Jackson could really blow.

———-

"Do you think there is a limit to forgiveness?" I asked Dr. Arlene Mathews two days later.

Dr. Matthews had ignored me for the previous 20 minutes while talking to Saul Weinstein, the man I had brought with me. I had barely spoken since we had arrived at her office at Tuskegee University, and I hadn't planned to ask such a question. It wasn't pertinent to the conversation. It just rose out of me, maybe because the woman didn't seem to be the kind who would forgive anyone.

Earlier that morning, I left the Allegro Bus in the Tiffin Motorhomes' parking lot and driven the Jeep four hours to Tuskegee. Saul, a short white man in a navy blue Armani suit who worked for Goldman Sachs, had flown on a corporate jet from La Guardia to Montgomery Airport. When I picked him up at the airport, I doubted he had ever ridden in any vehicle less expensive than a Mercedes, much less a Jeep.

I was wrong. As we drove, I learned a British man named Nicolas Winton had rescued Saul's father, along with 700 other children, from the Nazis in Czechoslovakia before the outbreak of World War II. The Nazis murdered the rest of his family in the concentration camps. A working-class Jewish couple in Brooklyn eventually adopted him, and he grew up to make his living as a subway conductor. Saul, the youngest of his five children, worked his way through NYU and eventually earned his MBA from Harvard.

When we arrived at Tuskegee, we found our way to the president's office. Dr. Matthews was a middle-aged African American woman who was at least two inches taller than my companion. She welcomed us with a handshake and ushered us to a small conference table. African pottery, masks, and other artifacts adorned shelves throughout the office. She focused her attention on Weinstein. I could hardly blame her. He was well-dressed, and I was wearing khaki pants, a polo shirt, and a light jacket.

"Thank you for seeing us on such short notice," Weinstein said as we sat down.

"I don't often get calls from Goldman Sachs, much less a visit, Mr. Weinstein," Dr. Matthews replied coolly. "You don't do much recruiting here."

Saul looked down at his briefcase to avoid her gaze. Goldman Sachs sent recruiters to the Ivy League and Stanford, not to historically black colleges, but he didn't rise to the top echelons of the nation's most prominent investment bank by being slow on his feet.

"I understand you got your degree from Princeton," he replied.

"My doctorate in economics. My undergraduate was right here at Tuskegee."

"Then clearly we made a mistake in not recruiting you."

"I would never have worked on Wall Street," she said. "My goal in life is to help the people here in Alabama. But I doubt you would have hired a black woman from the South in 1988."

"We weren't doing much hiring after the October crash in 1987," Weinstein replied awkwardly.

They both recognized this was a feeble response to what both knew was true, but she decided to move on.

"Tell me what brings you here, Mr. Weinstein?" Then she realized she had forgotten about me. "And Mr. Gathers."

"Mathers," I corrected.

"I'm sorry,' she said. "Mr. Mathers."

Weinstein opened his briefcase and searched through various documents. The receptionist reappeared with three cups of coffee and a plate of cookies. We all took a sip of coffee. I helped myself to a cookie, but the others were intent on each other.

"We have a client who wishes to remain anonymous who would like to make a substantial donation to your university," Weinstein said.

"What kind of donation?"

"$30 million," Weinstein replied. "More if needed."

Dr. Matthews sat up straight in her chair. She was not a woman who could easily be knocked off stride, but for a moment her face showed surprise. She quickly recovered her stern facade. "That would be the largest donation ever to our university. By far."

"We are aware of that," Weinstein said. "It is what our client desires."

"That is very generous," she replied cautiously. She clearly didn't trust a New York banker. "Is there a purpose behind it?"

"Yes," Weinstein replied. "My client wants the university to build a world-class performing arts venue and support musical education with a special focus on Alabama's musical tradition and African-American roots."

Dr. Matthews paused to take a sip of coffee and pick up a cookie before responding, giving her time to consider. "And why would this donor be interested in doing that?"

Weinstein was prepared for this. "The donor offers no reason. Just anonymity."

"It is strange to have such a large donation just land in our laps without any warning," Dr. Matthews replied. "But I am sure our board would be very interested. Are there any conditions on the gift?"

"Yes, one," Weinstein answered. "The naming of the venue."

"And what is that?"

Weinstein shot a quick glance at me, then closed his briefcase. Dr. Matthews hadn't inquired who I was or why I was in the meeting.

"Simon Jackson Hall," Weinstein replied.

Dr. Matthews took off her glasses and wiped them with the corner of her blouse. She made no effort to hide her dislike of Weinstein. "And who exactly is this Jackson?" she asked.

"Simon Jackson is the son of an alumnus of Tuskegee from the 1920s, and his son, Lionel, is a well-known musician in Muscle Shoals," Weinstein replied.

Dr. Matthews thought for a moment. "I believe I may have heard of Lionel," she said. "My father was a big R&B fan."

"He often played with the Swampers," I interjected.

For the first time, Dr. Matthews looked my way. "I am a bit uninformed," she said coolly. "Why are you here?"

"I am the anonymous donor," I said.

Once again, she was surprised but covered it up quickly. "You do realize the Swampers were a bunch of white men," she said.

I digested her meaning. "I can assure you Simon Jackson is a black man, if that is your concern."

She nodded. "Of course, his father graduated from Tuskegee in the 1920s," she said. "And you are going to honor this man with a check for $30 million to a university to which you have no connection?"

"Yes."

Dr. Matthews didn't respond, but studied us closely. This might have been some elaborate prank: two white men showing up at the office of the president of a famous historically black university promising the largest donation in its history. But Goldman Sachs is Goldman Sachs, and she had confirmed that Weinstein was a partner with the firm.

Before she said anything further, I broke the silence with my question: "Do you think there is a limit to forgiveness?"

"I don't understand the question," she replied. "What does this have to do with forgiveness?"

I recounted Lionel's story of Simon Jackson and Oswald Higgins: how Higgins had been the Grand Cyclops of the Klan in Colbert County and had lynched Simon's father. Yet according to Lionel, Simon had chosen forgiveness when he had the opportunity to exact vengeance. They had become fast friends, and Higgins had gone on to march with Dr. King in Selma.

When I was done, Dr. Matthews took another long sip of her coffee and looked me directly in the eye. "I don't believe that story," she said.

"Why not?"

"Simon Jackson was far from the only person to have a loved one lynched by the Klan in Alabama," she said. "Do you know what the Klan did to my people in this state? They lynched my uncle – my father's brother – after he was caught in town after sundown because he was taking care of his invalid mother and lost track of time. You wouldn't even ask that question if you knew what happened here."

I paused to consider my response. I thought about Saul Weinstein's grandparents and their families being marched to their deaths in concentration camps. Could there ever be true forgiveness?

"I didn't believe the story either," I finally said.

Dr. Matthews nodded, her eyes full of anger. "For some things, Mr. Mathers, there can never be forgiveness."

Chapter 4

Peter Flynn

Peter Flynn was my next improbable encounter. I met him on the fourth hole of one of the few golf courses in northwestern Alabama. Together, we faced the darkness.

Despite its name, the Redmont Country Club in Red Bay doesn't fit the popular image of a country club: well-dressed people dining next to large bay windows overlooking perfectly groomed fairways with tennis courts and two or three pools in the distance. Rather, like the town itself, it is a hard-scrabble facility, with only the course and a two-story building. It has no pro shop but only a counter for patrons to pay for their rounds and buy a beer. A skeletal maintenance crew mows the course regularly, but it is hardly manicured, carved into the woods at the edge of town.

The town of Red Bay is also a misnomer. It is nowhere near any major body of water, much less one that might have bays. Hard against the Mississippi border, Red Bay was named for its red soil and the native bay trees. It is also home to two industries that make it more prosperous than other towns in the area: a dog food plant that can be smelled for miles around, depending on the wind, and Tiffin Motorhomes.

As Lionel Jackson surmised, it was the latter that brought me to Red Bay to have my coach serviced and detailed, one of hundreds of big rigs parked in lots all over town as owners waited their turn. I blamed the Reverend Doctor Brian Cooper for my two-week stay in the town. Cecelia would say that I should credit him, not blame him. I eventually would have to agree, albeit reluctantly: my sister is rarely wrong.

I am not a golfer. Once a year, Coach Adams dragged me out to play in a charity golf event ostensibly to raise money for breast cancer research but in reality designed to get the team's boosters to donate more money to the football program. The biggest donors played with the coach. I invariably played in a foursome with the owner of the local pizzeria and other small businessmen who were enthusiastic Hokie fans without big bank accounts.

To keep from embarrassing myself completely, I once took a lesson from a golf pro, but after a half hour, he gave up on me. I figured he had reached the same conclusion my father had about my athletic ability. Teeing off in the charity event that year, I shanked a ball almost sideways into an adjacent parking lot. For a brief moment, every person in our group froze, waiting for the shattering of a windshield or the thunk of the ball striking someone's BMW or prized truck. Fortunately, it bounced twice on the pavement, struck the base of a Chevy Blazer tire, and rolled downhill along the asphalt until it came to a rest at the base of a stop sign 250 yards away. I had never hit a golf ball 250 yards before, so it was technically my longest drive ever.

There was, therefore, no chance I would play the Redmont Country Club course while the mechanics and detailers worked on the Allegro Bus. I am a hiker, however, and I took the opportunity to walk along the woods on the perimeter of the course.

On the fourth tee box, bordering a creek, I came across a lone golfer about to tee off. He was a younger man, I guessed in his mid-20s, slightly overweight on the way to being obese later in life, and attired in blue jeans, a shirt with a brown camouflage pattern, and an Auburn Tigers ball cap. This was pretty much the standard uniform for young men in Red Bay, except there were far more Crimson Tide caps than Auburn caps. I was mildly surprised when he hit a towering shot that landed softly on the green next to the flagstick 150 yards away. Despite his appearance, he knew what he was doing on a golf course.

I would have passed him by with a wave had he not abruptly reached into his golf bag and pulled out a Smith and Wesson 642. For a moment, I was concerned about his intentions, but he didn't even look at me. Instead, he walked over to the creek, took aim, and fired a single round. Apparently satisfied he had hit his mark, he quickly returned to his golf bag and stored his weapon.

"What are you shooting at?" I asked him.

For the first time, he took notice of me along the edge of the woods.

"Cottonmouth," he replied with a thick Alabama accent..

"Did you hit it?"

He nodded. "I don't miss."

It dawned on me that a golfer packing a firearm in his bag may not be all that unusual in Red Bay, Alabama.

"My father owned a Smith and Wesson," I said.

"The 642 is a good gun," he said. "Some people like the Glocks. I like Smith and Wesson."

I walked over to him and offered my hand. "I'm Joe Mathers."

"Peter Flynn," he replied, shaking my hand. "You must be one of the motor coach people."

I nodded. "Just here for a week or two," I said. "You work for Tiffin?"

"Dixie Diesel," he said. "Or at least used to."

When I arrived in town, I had learned that Dixie Diesel was one of many independent businesses in town run by people who had gotten their training working for Tiffin before branching out on their own. There were plenty of customers and RVs to repair to support them all.

"You don't like snakes, I assume?" I asked, simply to make conversation.

Peter's expression abruptly changed to what seemed like a combination of anger and sadness. "A cottonmouth bit my little boy," he said. "Killed him."

"I am sorry," I said quickly. There was nothing else to say. It dawned on me how easily we can step on another person's emotional landmine.

"Now I kill cottonmouths," he said. "I hunt them down in the swamps and creeks. That one makes 35."

"I understand," I said, not knowing how to respond. I waited to see if he would elaborate or change the subject. Perhaps he would go back to golf, and I would continue my walk.

Instead, a tear formed at the edge of his right eye. "I was supposed to be watching him," he said. "Our backyard bordered a creek. I was watching a race on television, and he wandered down there and got bit. It was my fault."

More tears leaked out of his eyes, and he wiped them away with the sleeve of his shirt. "My wife couldn't handle it," he continued. " I stopped going to work and spent all my time hunting cottonmouths. I was guilty, and she went to live with her parents. I stopped paying rent and moved out of our house. I'm living in my truck. Some man found me and served me with divorce papers."

"I am so sorry," I said. "That's terrible."

He buried his hands in his face and began to weep, a man overcome with grief and guilt with no one to pour it out on until I happened by. I put my hand on his shoulder, not knowing what to do. I wondered what Janice would do. Or Cecelia. Or Brian.

After a few moments, Peter straightened himself. "Mister, have you ever done anything that makes you feel so guilty you can't face it? All you can do is bury it in a place where you try not to think about it, but you can never escape it?"

The question pierced me. It was as though a wind had swept in and blown open the door to a buried vault, exposing the guilt hidden beneath Janice's death, the ticket, and the loss of my life in Blacksburg. Not even Cecelia and certainly not my mother would ever learn about it. I could never tell anyone. And yet now I felt exposed, compelled to confess it to a stranger.

"I have," I said. "I, too, failed my wife."

This time, my tears flowed. Peter waited patiently as I gathered myself. Was what he had done worse than what I had done? His failure was a matter of negligence. Mine was a decision I made. Perhaps someday he would realize that what happened to him could happen to anyone. He was distracted, and something tragic beyond understanding happened: a child had died. But I had an opportunity to think about what I had done, and yet I didn't stop.

"My wife was dying of cancer," I told him. "It was horrible. She was not herself for the last year, and finally she became comatose. I took care of her. I changed her diapers. I gave her morphine. She was still alive, but she was gone. I was exhausted mentally and physically. Mostly, I was drained from the day-to-day grind of taking care of a dying woman. I was alone in a way I cannot describe. I longed for human touch – for some kind of intimacy, even if it was an illusion.

"I am sorry," Peter said.

"There was a woman who went to our high school. I knew what she did for a living. I arranged to meet her. We were together for an hour. She held me while I wept. For a moment, I felt some relief, and then the guilt came crashing down on me."

Peter shook his head. "Your wife's cancer was not your fault," he said. "And you had a moment of weakness. It could happen to any man."

"No," I said. "I betrayed a woman who had done nothing but love me since the day I met her. I will live with it the rest of my life. It is beyond forgiveness."

———

A few minutes later, I carefully aimed the 642 and fired. I missed. The cottonmouth on the far bank slithered toward the water. Peter quickly took the weapon from me, aimed, and fired.

"Number 36," he announced as the bullet found the head of the snake.

"I'm sorry," I said. "I haven't fired a handgun since I was a boy. My father taught me to shoot, but I am out of practice."

"We will find another," Peter said. "This creek is full of them."

Peter reached into his golf bag and produced two Budweisers. We sat at the base of a live oak and began to drink, two men struggling with their guilt. But Peter had hope. I didn't. My sin was unforgivable.

"Would you like to get your wife back?" I asked.

Peter silently sipped his Budweiser. "I would, but I don't know how," he finally said. "Right now, I just come out here and hit golf balls and shoot snakes to forget about it all – to make the pain go away."

"I understand," I said.

"Would you like to get your job back, too?"

He nodded. "I would like that," he said. "But I don't know how. Everyone in town knows what happened. They know I am damaged goods: the crazy man out shooting snakes."

"You know that people wouldn't blame you for what happened? Everyone knows these things happen," I said.

"Sally blames me."

We both continued to drink our beer. In the distance, I saw a pair of golfers hitting tee shots on another hole.

"Women are a mystery to men," I finally said. "But I suspect what she really wants is for you to be there for her. She is a mother who lost a child, and that is a pain only those who have experienced it can grasp. I believe what she really needs is you. She will forgive you if you reach out to her."

Peter pondered this for a few moments. "And your wife? Would she forgive you?"

The question again conjured up the unbearable darkness, and I was afraid I would tear up again. But I collected myself, thinking about the kind, gentle soul who was Janice.

"She would forgive me," I said. "That was her nature."

"Then we are the only ones who won't forgive ourselves," Peter replied.

I took another swig of beer and watched the distant golfers hit their second shots over a pond and onto a narrow green. One missed, and the ball splashed into the water. "I don't think anyone can forgive themselves," I said. "At least for what we did. Our problem is I don't think we can accept forgiveness."

"How can we?"

"I don't know," I said. "I don't know."

———

The owner of Dixie Diesel, a huge man in his mid-40s wearing greasy blue overalls and smoking a cigarette, was incredulous. We stood just outside the single work bay, crammed into a Red Bay side street between a paint shop and a hair salon. Barrels and discarded parts of RVs lay all around us on broken asphalt. Everything seemed to be covered in a thick layer of grease and oil.

"A half million cash, Jake," I repeated, noting the nametag on his overalls.. "And I will hire you to run the place for $50,000 a year. But only if we complete the sale this week,"

Jake took a drag on his cigarette and continued to look at me as though I were crazy. "Why would you do that?"

"Maybe I don't like waiting in line to get my rig serviced when I come here," I said. "If I own the place, I can jump the line."

Jake shook his head until he figured out that I was making a joke. He took one last puff on his cigarette, then threw it on the ground and stepped on it. "If you are serious, mister, I would be a fool not to sell. But it doesn't make much sense."

"I've already set up an account at Valley State Bank and transferred the funds," I said. "I've hired a local lawyer to handle the paperwork. We can close on it tomorrow."

"I suppose you don't have to tell me why you would want my shop?"

I smiled. "Sometimes life doesn't make sense," I said. "But one more thing. You had a mechanic named Peter Flynn. I want you to hire him back at $25 an hour."

Jake stroked his chin and then lit another cigarette. "You know he's not in his right mind," he said. "His boy died, and he's out there playing golf and shooting snakes all day. He's a good old boy, but he stopped coming to work. You can't pay a man for not working."

"He will come to work," I said flatly.

"So you are going to buy my shop just so you can get this boy back to work?

I smiled. I was from Virginia, home to the capital of the Confederacy, but Jake thought of me as a Yankee: one of the rich motorcoach people who comprised a significant part of the population of Red Bay every day of the year except Christmas and Thanksgiving. I was simply a crazy Yankee.

"Trust me, Jake," I said. "This is the easy part."

Sally was the hard part.

"So you are trying to put this man's life back together?" Cecelia asked when I phoned her about Peter.

"I suppose," I said. "His wife is still alive. Maybe he can get her back. I certainly have the money, but is that enough? Will she be willing to take him back?"

There was a long silence on the phone. Sometimes Cecelia did this, and I figured she was praying, looking for answers that I never received – from the God who allowed Janice to die, the God who probably doesn't exist even if my sister says she hears his voice. She avoided the question. "Does he know what you are doing?" she asked.

"No," I replied. It hadn't dawned on me that Peter might not want his job back. I now owned a diesel engine repair shop, and all I could do was make the offer. Maybe he wanted to live in a truck and shoot snakes.

"So what are you going to do?"

"I have a plan," I said. "Or at least the beginning of a plan."

"Which is?"

"I contacted a real estate agent, and I have a contract on a nice house just outside of town. No contingencies. A quick settlement. All cash. To be titled in their names."

"So you are going to try to bribe Sally to come back to her husband with a nice house?"

Cecelia hadn't protested when I transferred $30 million to Tuskegee for the new music center, which the university board had voted to approve by teleconference within hours of my offer.

In fact, she hadn't commented one way or the other. I wondered why she was concerned about this.

"I wouldn't put it that way," I replied. "I just want to get Peter back on his feet so that she could at least consider it."

"I see," Cecelia replied.

Her failure to express an opinion frustrated me. "Tell me what to do," I said.

"Would Janice have taken you back if it were you?"

"Janice would never have left me." I felt a jab of pain. Janice wouldn't have left me even if she had learned my buried secret. That made the pain even worse: to betray someone who will forgive you.

"Then you don't know what will happen," she said. "And I don't either. It's always risky to interfere in other people's lives, especially their marriages."

"What is there to lose? She filed for divorce," I replied.

"Nothing, I suppose. But I doubt anything will happen quickly. A mother in that much pain needs time."

When we hung up, the vault deep inside opened again. I thought of Janice in bed, dying of cancer, while I was in bed with the woman from my high school. The worst part was that it wasn't just once. I went back week after week until Janice died, a drowning man grasping for a forbidden life buoy that was only an illusion. That was betrayal. That was contrary to everything I ever thought about myself – contrary to what I had vowed.

I was only able to stop myself when Janice died . I could not tolerate the thought of Janice in heaven, if such a place even exists, looking down to see me in the woman's bed. To know the truth.

Wiping tears from my face again, I struggled in vain to close the vault door. I wanted to go shoot some snakes.

———

The following afternoon, I watched from the safety of the Jeep parked at the end of a gravel driveway in Golden, Mississippi, five miles from Red Bay. To my left, across State Road 366, a liquor store was doing brisk business as residents of dry Franklin County crossed the state border to buy their beer and whiskey. To my right, Peter knocked on the front door of a small but tidy rambler. He carried a bouquet of roses in his right hand.

An attractive young woman answered, a middle-aged woman behind her. I held my breath waiting to see if she would slam the door in the face of the person responsible for the death of her child or listen to the plea of the husband she once vowed to love for better or worse.

I was relieved when Peter stepped inside, and she shut the door behind him. I wondered if she could see his pain through her own tears. Or did she just see the crazy man shooting snakes that everyone else in Red Bay saw? Minutes passed, and the front door opened. Peter came out, no longer holding the bouquet of roses. When he reached the car, he motioned to me.

"She wants to talk to you," he said.

I got out of the Jeep and followed him into the house. The living room was decorated in Laura Ashley style, warm and comfortable with calico everywhere – on the wallpaper, the cushions, and the curtains. Floral arrangements bloomed on window sills and side tables. I sat next to Peter on a sofa that invited an afternoon nap. Sally and her mother sat opposite us in chairs that thankfully were plain white, giving the eye a rest.

"Who are you, Mr. Mathers?" Sally asked. The tracks of her tears smeared her makeup.

It was a question I knew was coming, but I was surprised by the way she asked it. It was a good question, "Who are you?" I am not sure I could answer that question.

"Call me Joe," I said. "I am a man who lost his wife to cancer three months ago. I know what it is like to lose someone I love."

Sally buried her face in her hands. Her mother, a heavyset brunette with her hair tied in a bun, came over and wrapped an arm around her. We watched as she sobbed. I could see that Peter wanted to comfort her, but he had been admonished to stay away too many times.

"Why would you be interested in us?" the mother finally asked. "Did God send you? I've been praying He would help us."

I shook my head. "God doesn't talk to me," I answered. "And he doesn't listen to me." I would have added "if he even exists," but it was clear she was certain he did.

"Then why would you be here? Why would you spend all this money to buy a business and a house in Red Bay, Alabama, and then just give the house away to a stranger?"

I was ready for this with an explanation. "I won the Powerball lottery, the largest in history," I said. "I didn't ask for the money. It's turned my life upside down. I had to leave my job and leave town. I don't care if I ever spend a dime of it. I didn't even buy the ticket. I don't play the lottery. Someone left it in my house the day my wife died. Someone I can't find."

The mother digested this, crossing her arms. "An angel then?"

I am sure that was what Cecelia thought, even though she hadn't said it. I didn't believe in angels with harps or devils with pointy horns.

"She didn't have a halo," I said. "She was just a normal-looking woman."

The mother looked at me with that Cecelia expression of seeing something that can't be seen. I realized the God and angel explanation was the only one she would believe. I could reason all day, but unless a deity were involved she wouldn't accept that a Yankee would suddenly appear in Alabama to buy a house for her daughter.

Sally stopped crying and lifted her head. She looked at her mother, then at Peter. "I don't want a divorce," she said. "I never wanted a divorce. I just want the pain to go away, but it won't. I just wanted you to come home and comfort me. But you wouldn't. You went hunting snakes. You can't shoot the snake that killed Jason, and shooting every other snake in Alabama won't bring him back."

Peter took the admonishment in stride. "Would you forgive me, Sally?" he asked.

The question hung in the air for a long second. Then she nodded.

"Can I hold you?"

Tears began to flow again. "I would like that," she answered.

Peter cautiously left the couch and walked over to his wife. He wrapped his arms around her, and she buried her head in his shoulder. They wept together.

They were still in a teary embrace on the couch when I left ten minutes later. The mother stepped out onto the front porch with me.

"Mr. Mathers," she said. "You may not believe God sent you an angel with a winning lottery ticket when your wife died or that he guided you to my daughter, but I do."

I shook my head. "You don't understand. I am angry at God, if he exists."

The mother looked at me sternly. "And you don't think my daughter isn't? You don't think she isn't screaming at him in the middle of the night?"

"I am sure she is," I said. "I am sorry."

"Nothing will ever take away their pain," she said. "I lost my husband to a heart attack two years ago, and I am still grieving. Losing a child is worse. But your generosity means they won't lose each other and add sorrow to sorrow."

"I can't take any credit for that," I said. "I don't know why I do what I do anymore."

"He does," she said. "God did not give you all that money without a purpose."

I nodded. It was hard not to admire her faith, even if I didn't share it. Like Cecelia, she believed God could do no wrong. But I knew better. There would be no need for an angel with a lottery ticket if God had simply excised that first cancer cell from Janice's body or caused a cottonmouth to slither away from a little boy.

As I walked to my car after leaving her on the porch, one of the scripture verses I was forced to memorize as a child popped into my mind: "Blessed are those who mourn, for they will be comforted."

It was a lie, I told myself. There is no comfort in mourning.

Chapter 5

Lara

In the next week, Jake and Peter gave the Tiffin's 600-horsepower engine a thorough inspection and oil change. Peter and Sally moved into their new house after the trucks unloaded new furniture brought in from Birmingham. Then I left Red Bay. There was more gratitude than I wanted or deserved. There was also a lot of thanking God, even though I denied any divine intervention.

I had no destination. I drove west into Mississippi to Tupelo, where I made the snap decision to turn south on Route 45. Only then did it dawn on me that I would like to see the Gulf of Mexico. That led me to Foley, Alabama and the Frog Pond. And the Frog Pond was where I met Lara Miller.

When Route 45 dipped back into Alabama, I found an RV park just outside of Foley and drove the Jeep to Gulf Shores State Park. I sat on the beach and watched the fishing boats, tiny dots silhouetted against the horizon. I missed Janice.

I had learned that grief came in waves. It rose unexpectedly from deep places within me, sometimes when I rolled over in the middle of the night, sometimes in broad daylight, triggered by a smell or song or the sight of a couple holding hands. It brought up memories: a first encounter, a stolen kiss received with a burst of passion, or a time of lovemaking in a tent deep in the woods. With the memories came a longing to go back in time, to hold her once more, to tell her how much I loved her, which I never did enough.

Grief did not come alone, however. It brought with it loneliness. I was a man sitting on a beach watching the sun dip towards the horizon and boats returning to harbor with no one to share my life. I wanted to tell Janice about driving the RV, about Lionel Jackson and Peter Flynn, and about the billion dollars sitting in New York. But she was gone.

After a while, I began to walk the beach, letting the small waves engulf my feet at the edge of the water. A jogger passed me by, and then an older couple strolled by in the opposite direction. I imagined that could have been Janice and me in thirty years. Tears welled up in my eyes. I contemplated how the waves of the sea never cease but defy time hour by hour into all eternity. But not us. Our love is destined for tragedy. One day, the husband or the wife will bury the other and know grief and unbearable loneliness. Another scripture surfaced from the forced religion of my childhood and the "sword drills" at church. "All is vanity," said Solomon, supposedly the wisest man ever. "Chasing after the wind." Who could argue with that?

In a few minutes, I heard the gentle strumming of a guitar. A wiry, bearded young man wearing a Bob Marley tee-shirt sat on a large log that had washed up on shore, playing a familiar blues melody I couldn't quite identify. I stopped to listen, admiring his skill.

'You are very good," I told him. He thanked me, then played an Otis Redding song.

"Sitting by the dock of the bay, watching the tide roll away…"

he sang with a pure, baritone voice and continued with the lament of a man who left his home only to find himself lost and without purpose in life. When he reached the end of the last chorus, "Ooh, I am sitting on the dock of the bay, wasting time," I applauded.

"You must play professionally."

"Not exactly," he replied. "But I sometimes play at the Frog Pond."

"The Frog Pond?"

"It's a Sunday afternoon social on a farm near here. Local musicians get together and jam. Everyone sits on the lawn and chills out. Then there is a big potluck. Anyone is welcome to come, but you have to ask to get invited."

"How do you do that?"

"Just email the lady who runs it, and she will put you on the list. Bring some fried chicken or slaw or a bag of chips."

He produced a pen and a piece of paper from his guitar case and wrote down an email address. "You will really enjoy it."

I accepted the piece of paper. "I'm Joe Mathers," I said. "I'm just passing through."

The man nodded and stuck out his hand. "Will Skye."

I shook his hand. "I have a question for you, Will."

"Shoot."

"Why did you play that song just now?"

Will smiled. He projected an infectious warmth. I wondered what he did for a living and whether he had a wife and children. If he did, why was he out on the beach playing the guitar alone?

"I was a professional poker player before things changed for me one night," he said. "I got pretty good at reading people's faces."

"And?"

"In the words of Kenny Rogers. I can see you are out of aces."

I remembered the song. "You have to know when to hold them and know when to fold them."

"When to walk away and when to run," he continued. "And it looks like you are doing more than walking."

"My wife died of cancer," I said. "I am wandering."

Will nodded but didn't offer the usual condolences. Instead, he cocked his head slightly, "Come to the Frog Pond, Sunday," he said. "You might find someone there to talk to."

————

The Frog Pond at Blue Moon Farm might have had a pond, but I didn't see it. As far as I could tell, no one was doing any serious farming on the property. In fact, it was just someone's big backyard with a porch where local musicians jammed together.

I filed in with about 100 other people bearing lawn chairs and covered dishes. I had stopped by the local grocery store and bought some fried chicken, but I neglected to bring a lawn chair. I put the chicken on one of the picnic tables crammed with plates of cholesterol-laden southern comfort food and sat down on the lawn as the musicians warmed up. A woman nearby immediately called out to me, offering an extra chair she had brought.

"It's what we do," she said when I thanked her. "We bring more than we need and share. I always bring two chairs."

Her name was Lara – she only told me her last name later – and roughly my age with sandy hair, brown eyes, and one of those timeless complexions that seems as though it will never grow old. I was immediately attracted to her. It was clear to me that the feeling was mutual. We struck up an easy conversation that seemed as though we were old acquaintances.

It was the first time I had even thought about a woman – at least in that way – since Janice had died. It crossed my mind briefly that it was too early, that I had not waited the expected one year. I dismissed it. There would be time enough for guilt later. I was enjoying her company too much.

"What brings you to Alabama from Virginia?" she asked. "And how did you ever end up at the Frog Pond?"

I told her about Janice, about the cancer, and about the darkness of her last days. "I needed to get away after she died," I said. "To process what had happened. So I bought an RV. I drove to Alabama because that's where the RV was built and I wanted to have it serviced and detailed before I went anywhere else."

Lara nodded sympathetically. Then a quizzical expression crossed her face. "I think I recognize you," she said. "You are the one who won the Powerball the same week his wife died. I remember seeing it on the news."

"I had hoped people would have forgotten about that," I said, embarrassed that she knew I hadn't told her the whole story about why I left Blacksburg.

"I probably wouldn't have had I not been widowed myself," she said. "I wondered what it must have been like for you having all those cameras and reporters hounding you while you were trying to grieve."

I was startled. She was the first person who looked at winning the lottery as a bad thing rather than the greatest thing that could ever happen to someone. "You understand then?" I asked.

"I lost my husband five years ago," she said. "He went to work one day and died of a brain aneurysm. Just collapsed, dead before he hit the floor. I never got to say goodbye. I was suddenly a widow with teenage twin boys with no job and no marketable skills. I was fortunate that he had purchased a life insurance policy that paid off the house and made it so I didn't have to work right away. I was in no condition to work."

"I'm sorry," I said.

"It got worse every day," she said. "I soldiered on because of the boys and eventually got a job waiting tables. But both of them joined the Marines the moment they graduated from high school and I found myself completely alone. I descended into a dark place. I didn't know it at the time, but grief, which is normal and even healthy, transformed itself into self-pity. And self-pity is a poison. It kills you from the inside out."

At that moment, a trio of guitarists began to play, accompanied by a bass player at the far end of the porch. Two of them sang a song warning about a wild woman named Sugarcane Jane who had come into town. We settled down in our chairs and enjoyed the music and especially the impromptu jamming that went on for long stretches as the musicians showed off their talent. I pondered Lara's distinction between grief and self-pity. Was I, a man who won a billion dollars, feeling sorry for myself?

After forty minutes, the musicians took a break, and we resumed our conversation. "How did you escape it?" I asked. "The dark place."

Lara opened a soft drink and took a sip. " A friend called me out," she answered. "She grew weary of my complaining about my life: missing my husband, missing my sons, not having a social life, always being depressed. She invited me to go to church with her, and I went. The preacher quoted a verse from the scripture where Jesus said He had come that we might have life and life more abundantly. He was talking to me. I had no life, and in a strange way misery had become my identity. It was who I was: the poor widow whose husband died and was all alone. It was my default position, the place where I retreated because it didn't require me to do anything except to feel sorry for myself."

"What did you do?"

"I went up to the altar and asked Jesus into my life. Actually asked Him for life itself."

I cringed. How many times had I heard that in my youth? Ask Jesus into your heart. Plead the blood of Jesus. Jesus this. Jesus that. She saw my expression and waited. Finally, I asked, "And did Jesus answer you?"

Lara smiled at my vain attempt to hide the skeptical tone of my question. I am not even sure why I asked it. I didn't want a Jesus conversation.

"He did," she said. "He told me I had to give up my life if I was going to receive His."

"Jesus spoke to you?"

"Not audibly," she said. "He spoke to my spirit in His still small voice. That voice that penetrates your heart and you know it's from Him."

"How do you know it wasn't just your imagination?"

"You just do. It has a texture to it. A power. A warmth. A purity."

"I don't know if I can believe that," I replied. "I was dragged to church all through my childhood and I never heard any voice."

Lara paused for a few seconds as if contemplating sharing something more. Up on the porch, the musicians were getting ready to play again. I thought about Cecelia. Did she hear a still small voice? Did Brian? What about Lionel Jackson, whose father saved the life of the racist who murdered his grandfather?

"He showed me something at the same time," she said. " He put an image in my mind at the same time."

"An image?"

"A vision if you will, an image dropped into my mind," she said. "A vision of Him hanging on the cross. Of Him asking God why He had forsaken him. Of Him dying."

I frowned. It was like someone saying they saw a UFO. "Like one of those Renaissance paintings?" I finally asked.

"Not at all," she said. "There was nothing artistic about it. It was more like a videotape or a film. Stark. Brutal. Bloody. Pure agony."

"And the point was?"

"In your darkest moments, it all makes sense," she said. "If you want to see the cross, if you want to see God's love, find the place where people are suffering. Find your darkest place."

I did not know how to respond. Her words hung in the air between us. Janice had gone to the darkest place. She had suffered physically, and I had suffered emotionally. But I hadn't seen any image of Jesus on the cross. Had Janice seen something in her comatose state? Why would an all-powerful God, if he exists, choose to reveal himself in times of suffering, rather than simply remove the suffering? It made no sense.

The musicians started up again, and soon everyone was enraptured in a song about a man's broken heart being healed by the love of a new woman. I glanced at Lara and felt another surge of attraction for her. How badly I missed the love of a woman. The touch of a woman. Could she heal my heart?

Was it even allowed?

———-

Lara and I kissed four days later. If it were a Hollywood movie, we would have slept together, but that was not her way. I suppose I would have given in if she had suggested it, but she didn't. The desire was there for both of us. I had the strong physical longing a man experiences when a woman touches him. However, it really wasn't what I wanted either. In fact, the idea frightened me. I just wanted to be with her.

We spent each day together with picnics on the beach, long walks, and hours-long dinner conversations at a small restaurant downtown until the owner asked us to leave so he could close down. Lara told me about how she had made herself join a book club, volunteer at a food pantry, and take up hobbies such as crocheting and painting. Gradually, she had come back to life, and the fog of depression lifted. For my part, I told her everything about my life and how I had come to be a billionaire widower.

We fell in love. Or more accurately, we fell into that state of infatuation that people call "falling in love," but those who have been married a long time recognize as a fantasy. Real love, the love Janice and I had, takes years with many bumps and bruises along the way. There is no stardust in it. The real thing doesn't make for a good movie.

It was strange that Lara also wanted to know everything there was to know about Janice. If a woman is interested in a man, why would she want to hear about his late wife? Wouldn't she really want him to forget her, as if such a thing were possible?

"I can't know you without knowing her," she answered when I asked.

"Is that what you want?" I asked. "To know me?"

"It's what any honest woman wants."

"Perhaps I don't even know myself. Maybe I thought I did. But maybe I don't."

She laughed. "That's why you need us women."

We kissed at dusk while strolling by an old locomotive in a small park next to the Foley Railroad Museum. I didn't plan it. I didn't think about it in advance. It just happened spontaneously. Her body melded with my body, and we lingered for what seemed like minutes, enjoying the intertwining of our emotions.

I felt no guilt and no sense that I had betrayed Janice. Rather, I felt relief, a man dying of thirst in the desert finding an oasis and drinking deeply of its waters. I could not forgive myself for what I did with the woman from my high school. Yet four months after Janice's funeral, I kissed another woman with no regrets. I didn't just kiss her. I kissed her passionately.

It was the only time we kissed. I left town two days later.

———

I wanted Lara to go with me. Her sons were serving in Korea with the Marines, guarding the U.S. embassy in Seoul, so she had no family to keep her in Foley. I had $1 billion, so money was no issue. She could easily have gone with me. She wouldn't.

"You need to go by yourself," she said as we drank coffee in a small cafe near the train museum. After our kiss, we spent the next day together. But something had changed. I could see in her eyes that her feelings for me were still strong. She yearned to surrender, to jump off the jetty into a sea of passion, to give her whole self, even her body, to me. Yet there was something else. It was not fear nor even hesitation. We were both caught up in the flush of new love. She was seeing something bigger than I could see.

"I don't understand," I replied.

Lara reached out and took my hand. "You are the man I have prayed for for years," she said. "You are a good man, and I desperately want to be with you. But all these years have taught me to be patient. You need to go and then come back when the time is right."

"Are you afraid I am rebounding?" I asked. "That this isn't real?"

She shook her head. "This is real," she said. "But your pastor is right. You need to take a journey."

"He's not my pastor," I said quickly. "He's my sister's pastor." I had told her about my conversations with Brian. In fact, I had told her everything that had happened to me since Janice died.

"So be it," she replied. "He gave you the right advice. God doesn't give a grieving man $1 billion to stay where he is. He wanted you to go."

"God didn't have anything to do with this," I said softly. "And if he did, why would he want me to go?"

Lara stroked my hand lovingly. I sensed her need for me after years of being alone and of fighting her way out of the pit of depression.

"Because you don't know who he is," she said. "And you don't know who you are."

I did not respond for a while. We drank our coffee and gazed at each other. She was right, of course. I didn't really know myself. I didn't know why I did what I did. Why did I give $30 million to Tuskegee University? Why did I buy Peter Flynn and his wife a new house? Was that all there was to me: as Brian said, a good man? Yet one thing I knew. I didn't want Learjets or private islands. I wanted Lara. If I couldn't have Janice, I wanted Lara.

"Does anyone really know themselves?" I asked, then in a pleading voice. "I need you."

"You need God," she said. "And when you have found Him, then you can have me." She hesitated. I could see the conflict within her raging. "And I can have you."

"I don't understand women," I told Cecelia on the phone later.

"You don't," she said. "No man really does."

I certainly didn't understand Cecelia. I expected she would object to me being interested in another woman so soon after Jancie's death, much less falling in love with her overnight like a star-struck teenager. She didn't. In fact, she seemed to approve.

"Why would she want me to leave?" I asked for the third time in our conversation. It seemed so illogical to my male mind.

There was a problem: two widowed people in pain. There was a solution: a new relationship that would take away the loneliness. It was A plus B equals C. Besides, our loneliness would only get worse if I left because we had had a taste of love again.

"She told you," Cecelia said.

"Why would she reject me?"

"She didn't."

"But why would she try to force me to believe in God if I want to be with her?"

"She didn't. She told you to go find him."

"Isn't that the same thing?" I protested.

"No, it's not," Cecelia said.

"I don't understand."

"Jesus didn't force anyone to believe in him," Cecelia said. "But He did tell them to seek him. To knock on the door. He said only then would they find Him. The door would be opened."

"I did seek him," I said. "I did knock on the door. He didn't answer. Janice died."

There was a long pause. "Joe," she finally said. "You asked for a miracle. There is a difference between seeking the things of God and seeking God."

———

I met Will Skye again on the way out of Foley. I had driven the

Tiffin to a truck stop on Route 45 to fill it up with diesel and, having learned my lesson, to ensure the DEF reservoir was full. A couple of minutes later, Will pulled his truck into the island opposite me. After we greeted each other, I thanked him for letting me know about the Frog Pond and told him I enjoyed the music.

"Did you meet any of the locals?" he asked.

I figured he already knew the answer. He was the last musician to play, and he left quickly afterwards, but he certainly had seen Lara and me in the audience, enraptured with each other. Besides, in a small town, there are no secrets.

"I did," I said. I hesitated before continuing. "Lara Miller."

"I know her," he said. "I'm glad you met someone."

I briefly thought about sharing my pain and confusion at leaving town after falling in love – or infatuation – with Lara. She had given me relief, a ray of sunshine through the heavy fog of grief. Now she had sent me away, promising that I could return only when I found the God who let Janice die, the God who probably doesn't exist. I just didn't want to talk about it. I am sure he could see it.

"I especially liked your music," I said.

He nodded. "You know it's no accident that we ran into each other," he said. "I wanted to tell you something."

"What is that?" I asked.

"I haven't always been a musician. In fact, I didn't start playing guitar or any other musical instrument until I was 30 years old."

"You are very gifted," I said.

"I believe that is true," he said. "Music is a gift. I didn't have it as a child. It was given to me on my darkest night."

"I don't understand."

"I told you I was a gambler," he said. "A very good poker player. I dropped out of college to go to Las Vegas, and I was very successful. I could read people's faces. I don't know how. I just seemed to be able to do it."

"You certainly read my face," I interjected.

"You were easy to read," he said. "It's much harder to read a professional poker player's face and know whether he has a straight or whether he is bluffing. I could do it. I won lots of money in Las Vegas. And with the money came everything else: the parties, the drugs, and the women. Especially the women. I could sleep with a different woman every night if I wanted, and I often did."

"That's quite the life," I said.

"But that's not true. It wasn't life. At least a life worth living. It was completely empty. One morning, I woke up next to a naked woman I hadn't even known 12 hours before. We had sex, but I realized I couldn't even remember her name. I looked into her eyes and saw her soul the same way I could see another person's cards by looking at their face. It was empty. Desperate. Wanting some man to truly love and cherish her. I was the latest in a long series of men she had given her body to for the brief illusion of being loved. I had used her, and she had used me. Other than a brief moment of biological ecstasy, we had gotten nothing. No life. No love. Nothing."

He paused for a moment to put the diesel nozzle back onto the pump. Then he continued. "Men fantasize about the life I had. Not having to go to work. Not having a boss. Having plenty of

119

money. Lots of women. But that night, it came crashing down on me. I was in a high-stakes poker game. There was a huge stack of chips on the table, and I knew I had a winning hand: a flush. The man opposite had a straight at best. I knew how to milk the bet so that I could lure him into betting all his remaining chips. I could wipe him out."

He hesitated. "But as I began to push my chips to the middle of the table, something happened. Instead of seeing this man and the other gamblers at the table as human beings, I saw them as skeletons. I was surrounded by skeletons. And then I looked at my hand and I too was a skeleton. I heard a voice. I don't know if others could hear it or whether it was in my head."

"A voice?" I asked. What was it with these voices, I wondered? Cecelia, Lara, and now Will Skye all said they heard voices that no one else could hear. Insane asylums have long been filled with mentally ill people hearing voices.

"Yes, a voice in my head. It terrified me."

"I can imagine," I said, although I couldn't. "What did it say?

"The wages of sin are death. That was all. 'The wages of sin are death."

My childhood "sword drills" kicked in. "Romans 6:23," I said. I remembered obediently reciting the verse with a dozen other children in a Sunday School class when I was 12.

"Yes, but I didn't know that at the time," he said. "I had never been taken to church as a child, and I had never even picked up a Bible, much less read it. There was no way I knew that verse. Yet a voice in my head spoke it."

I contemplated this for a moment. Cecelia wouldn't have any difficulty believing him.

"So what happened?"

"I did the unthinkable. I folded a winning hand and left all that money on the table. I left the casino, not even bothering to cash my chips. I drove out into the desert and sat on the ground, gazing at the stars. What did it mean, the wages of sin are death? Was that all that lay in my future, to be a skeleton surrounded by other skeletons gambling for poker chips that could never be cashed? Was death the final destination of a long, empty road of gambling, drinking, drugs, and sex with women I would never see again? I had never felt so empty and desperate in my life. I was a man drowning in a sea of hopelessness. After a long time, maybe an hour or two – I lost track of time – the voice spoke again."

"Let me guess," I said. "'The gift of God is eternal life in Jesus Christ.'"

"Exactly," he said. "That's the rest of that verse."

"What did you do?" I asked.

"A hand reached down to pull me out of that sea of hopelessness. But I had to take that hand. I had to decide: the wages of sin or the gift of God."

"Sounds like an altar call," I said. I remembered responding to an altar call as a child because all my friends were doing it. One of the pastors told me about the four spiritual laws, and I said 'yes' when he asked me if I wanted Jesus to come into my heart. He told me I was saved. The box was checked. My mother took me out for ice cream afterwards. But I experienced nothing.

"I suppose it was," Will said. "And I took His hand – the hand of Jesus. And everything changed. Everything was made new. I never went back into a casino. I stopped taking drugs. I stopped sleeping with lonely women. I discovered I had a gift for music I didn't know about before. Most importantly, I had peace for the first time ever, a deep inner peace that is beyond understanding. I still had the ability to read people, but now I was using it to have compassion and to pray for them rather than to take their money."

I didn't know how to respond or how Will wanted me to respond. He gazed at me intently, perhaps expecting something or hoping for something. But what could I do? You can't tell someone they haven't had an experience they believe they had.

"So do you pray for me?" I finally asked.

"I do. I pray that you will choose the gift of life."

"I haven't had that experience," I said. "And I have never heard a voice."

"If you did, would you believe it?"

I thought of Lara and how much I ached to turn the Tiffin around and go back to Foley. If I just said 'yes,' pretending I heard voices and believed in a Jesus who changed a gambler into a musician, I could have her. However, I am not a liar, and I am sure she would see through me. Will told a great story, and part of me wanted to believe it. But the part of me that didn't believe it was stronger.

"I don't know," I said. "I doubt it."

Will nodded. "The real thing is not easy," he said. "The gate is narrow and the road difficult."

Somewhere in my mind, I knew he was quoting another verse that had been imprinted in my memory. I could not dredge it up. I wanted the conversation to end.

"I need to get back on the road," I said.

"Think about it," he said. "Or pray about it."

"I would if anyone were listening,"

I expected Will to be disappointed, but he didn't appear to be. He smiled broadly and wished me well on my journey. As we said goodbye, I wondered what he was seeing in me.

"Just remember one thing," he said as I fired up the Tiffin for my journey north to Memphis. "You have to know when to fold them."

I went looking for peace, but I could not find it.

Chapter 6

Mindy

During the seven-hour trip through Mississippi to Memphis, my mind and my emotions bounced between grieving for Janice and the pain of leaving Lara behind in Foley. Many times, I thought of turning the Tiffin around and heading back to plead with her, but I knew she would not budge. She didn't want to change me; she wanted me to change so she could have me. So I drove on.

Nature is my cathedral, my place of pilgrimage to escape the tangles of life. So when I reached Memphis, I left the Tiffin at a campground on the banks of the Mississippi and drove the Jeep through the hustle and bustle of the city to the Memphis Botanical Gardens, which advertised a "Garden of Tranquility." I sat at the edge of a serene Japanese pond crossed by a red bridge and waited for peace to descend as it had so often in the deep Appalachian woods. It did not. Not even the Garden of Tranquility could give me tranquility.

The next morning, I watched the barges passing by on the Mississippi on their way to New Orleans. I thought of the thousands of barges on the river at any moment. Each one has a cargo and a destination, a journey with a beginning and an end. A reason for being. Yet I was on a journey of pain with no idea where I was going or when it would end. Something had to change.

Then I remembered I was a billionaire. Perhaps I needed to act like one.

The Presidential Suite at the Peabody Hotel costs $1,400 a night, and I booked it. I arrived just in time to see a man dressed in a bellman's outfit herd a half dozen mallards out of the ornate fountain in the lobby, with a couple of hundred tourists snapping pictures with their phones. Even the ducks had a purpose and knew where they were going as the bellman guided them onto an elevator for a ride to their rooftop hutch.

The suite itself was luxurious with a sweeping view of Memphis. And yet after a few minutes, I again mourned Janice and craved Lara. Down below, the people in the cars and on the sidewalks had a destination and a purpose. I had lost both and received a fortune I didn't care about. I couldn't stay where I was, and I had nowhere to go. I took the elevator to the hotel bar.

When I squeezed through the crowd to an empty barstool, twenty members of the Minneapolis Chapter of the National Society of Optometrists were in full party mode. I don't drink much. In fact, I hadn't had any alcohol since the Snake Handler Double IPAs with Lionel Jackson at the Rattlesnake Saloon. I asked the bartender for a club soda.

"You can't order a club soda," a voice behind me said. "It's happy hour. Have a margarita."

I turned to face a woman named Mindy, according to her National Society of Optometrists nametag. She was a tall woman in her late 30s or early 40s with the slim, athletic figure of someone who spends a lot of time in the gym. She held up a half-full margarita glass and pointed to it. Other people in the crowd joined her in urging me to order one. I don't know why complete strangers would care what someone orders at a bar, but clearly tequila had a voice of its own and wanted everyone to join the party. So I changed my order to a margarita. Then, because I was a billionaire, I ordered a margarita for everyone. Immediately, the crowd bestowed on me an honorary degree in optometry and a membership in the society. I was relieved no one recognized me.

I discovered quickly Mindy was the unofficial leader of the party, and she had an interest in me. When she shepherded the party into taxis for ribs at The Rendezvous and then to a nearby nightclub to watch an Elvis impersonator, she stayed close. I continued to buy drinks for the group, and by the time we got back to the Peabody, we were well-oiled. We returned to the hotel bar for nightcaps.

I remember a time in college when a fraternity convinced me and other naive freshmen to chug Boilermakers, shots of whiskey dropped into glasses of beer. We quickly became dangerously drunk. It was mid-winter, and I was fortunate to make it across campus to my dorm room without passing out in a snowbank and freezing to death. I spent a miserable night bent over a toilet bowl, throwing up. I learned my lesson and never got drunk again. However, with the optometrist party still going full blast with peals of laughter at almost anything that was said and Mindy and the others egging me on, I kept drinking. What difference did it make? At least I was numb to the pain.

"I want to see the Presidential Suite," Mindy said as the party finally began to break up after midnight. "I want to see how the rich live."

I was two sheets to the wind, not quite three, and I missed her meaning. I took her up to the suite. Immediately, she wrapped her arms around me and kissed me. My body responded with intense desire for her, but I stepped back from her embrace.

"What's wrong?" she asked.

"You are wearing a wedding ring."

She laughed. "It's OK," she said. "Peter and I have an understanding. We are allowed when we are on business trips. I forgot to take it off."

Every cell in my body wanted her, lust pulsing through my veins screaming, "I must have her now." But even addled by alcohol, my mind resisted. Or perhaps it wasn't my mind but something else in me.

"I want to, but I can't."

"Why not? It's just some fun. No strings attached. You lost your wife. My husband doesn't care. What harm is there in it?"

What harm is there in it? Logically, she was right.

But what harm was there in being with the woman from my high school when Janice was comatose and dying? Then I simply craved to have someone hold me. Yet afterward it tormented me. This was different. This was pure lust, chum thrown into shark-infested waters. Who could blame a shark? Who could blame a man for giving in to an attractive woman kissing him?

Then in my mind's eye I saw Janice naked before me. This was not the Janice whose body cancer and chemotherapy had turned into an old woman, but young, healthy, vibrant Janice. Janice, whose body I wanted, but not just her body. All of her. Every molecule of who she was.

As much as I craved Mindy's body, I did not want all of her. "I'm sorry," I said. "You are beautiful and I want you, but I can't have you."

"Can't or won't."

"Can't," I replied. "I can't."

——-

I woke up the next morning with a massive hangover. My body felt like a city after urban warfare with bombshells and bullet holes in every door and window. I stumbled into the bathroom and downed four ibuprofen and a glass of water. Then I slept for another hour. When I woke up again, my head was still throbbing but not as badly as it had been. My body still resisted getting out of bed, but I needed coffee – not just a cup or two but a pot.

I arrived in the lobby just as the man in the bellman's outfit herded the ducks back into the fountain. They seemed content, swimming laps around the carved cherubs in a large centerpiece capped with flowers. I found a table in a corner far from the tourists and ordered coffee. The waiter brought me a pot along with copies of the Memphis Commercial Appeal and the Wall Street Journal. I ignored them while I sipped the coffee and tried to piece together what had happened the night before.

I was surprised when Mindy suddenly appeared out of the crowd of tourists and asked if she could sit with me. She had seemed hurt by my rejection when she had left my room the night before. Now she had a big smile on her face as she sat across from me.

"You aren't mad at me?" I asked.

She shook her head. "There is a first time for everything, and that is the first time that has ever happened to me. But I'm a big girl. No hard feelings. I misjudged you."

"In a good way or a bad way?"

"I think in a good way," she said. "I always figured no living, breathing man would ever do what you did."

"I can understand. You are beautiful and fun to be with. I wanted you badly."

"That's what I wanted to ask you," she said. "Why not?"

I paused to stir some sugar into my coffee and then take a sip while I pondered her question and whether I really wanted to talk about it. She waited patiently. After a few moments, I realized I, too, had questions for her.

"I was married to a good woman," I said. "Sex was not just sex for us. It was truly love-making. Yes, there were times when we were simply satisfying our appetites, kind of like stopping for fast food when you're hungry – which is OK, maybe even necessary when you are married to someone and life gets busy. But mostly it was five-star dining. Then she got sick and we couldn't do it anymore. In the end, a couple of months before she died, I lost her completely. But I never forgot what it was like to be one with her."

"I'm sorry," Mindy interjected. Her smile briefly turned to a frown. So I waited until she continued. "I've never known that. It's always been McDonalds or Burger King."

"Fast food can be tasty," I said. "But you can't live on it."

"I wanted some fast food last night," she smiled again.

"So did I."

"Then why not?"

Again, I considered her question. The thought struck me that it was hard to grasp how sex could be like playing tennis or bridge, and you could switch partners without a thought. Or what kind of marriage was it when a husband goes to bed knowing his wife likely was in the bed of another man? Or vice versa.

"It just seemed wrong," I said.

"Don't tell me you are religious and think God is going to punish you for a little fun?"

"God has already punished me," I said, "if he exists."

Mindy thought for a moment. Behind her, the crowd of tourists had dispersed. The ducks continued to swim in circles in the fountain. "But if he doesn't exist, why not?"

Was there even an answer to the question, I wondered. "Does God have to exist for it to be wrong?"

"Maybe we are our own gods and we can set the rules," she said. "And in my world, sex is nothing but sex."

"Like playing tennis?"

She laughed. "Yes, but not as much exercise."

A few minutes later, Mindy left to attend a session on the newest line of eyeglass frames while I caught a cab to the Memphis Pyramid, a large arena where both basketball teams and the Rolling Stones had once played. It was now a Bass Pro superstore. At the top of the pyramid, I ate lunch overlooking the city and, for the first time in 24 hours, thought about Lara. In the past week, I had met two women: one who wanted me for a night with no strings attached and one who wanted me permanently, but with one giant string attached. My emotions gyrated between grief for Janice, heart sickness for Lara, and lust for Mindy.

I spent the afternoon doing what tourists do in Memphis, engulfing myself in the pink Cadillac fantasy world that is Graceland. Elvis Presley took my mind off the three women, and

I returned to the Peabody with "You Ain't Nothing but a Hound Dog" as my earworm. I wondered if Lionel Jackson had ever backed up Elvis in Muscle Shoals and imagined him changing the words to "You Ain't Nothing but a Coon Dog."

The optometrist party was once again in full swing at the hotel bar. Mint juleps were the drink of the day, and the bartender was doing brisk business. After the previous night's bacchanalia, my body went into full-scale revolt at the thought of more alcohol. I was amazed that people could do it every day. I decided to skip the party and go straight to my room. I planned to order room service for dinner and spend a quiet night watching television.

As I walked to the elevators, I noticed Mindy in the crowd. She and a tall man sat at the bar, drinking and laughing. I had been replaced. She had her fun for the night. I noticed the man was wearing a wedding band.

She glanced up and saw me pass by. She smiled and waved. Desire for her arose in me again. In my mind, I could hear her question from the night before. "Why not?"

———

In the morning, I decided I had seen enough of Memphis. I planned to check out and retrieve the Tiffin from the campground, then drive in a direction yet to be determined. Somewhere to the north or the west.

Mindy was at a table in the dining room when I arrived for breakfast. She waved me over, and I sat with her, first looking around and not seeing the tall man from the night before. I wasn't quite sure what to say to her. Fortunately, she broke the ice.

"You didn't join us last night," she said. "You must have been tired."

"I was," I said. "I don't drink very often, and my body was in rebellion."

"It's my fault. You had ordered a club soda, and I got you to switch to a margarita. I corrupted you."

"I wasn't corrupted. I had a good time. It was fun to let loose a bit."

The waiter brought a pot of coffee and poured a cup for both of us. I ordered an Eggs Benedict from the menu, and he left. Mindy sipped her coffee and looked at me thoughtfully as though carefully considering what she might say next. Finally, she spoke in a soft voice.

"You know, you may have corrupted me," she said.

"How is that?"

"I decided not to have fun last night," she said. "I went to bed at midnight. Alone."

I nodded and said nothing. I didn't know how to respond.

"I don't believe in a God who punishes people and sends them to hell for…" she paused. "for having a little fast food with someone they aren't married to."

I nodded again. "But?"

"But when I thought about what you said, I realized I really don't like it when Peter goes on business trips."

"I understand that."

"So maybe he doesn't like it when I go on business trips."

"That could be."

"So maybe there is something there."

No one spoke for a while as we both pondered what the "something there" might be. The waiter brought my Eggs Benedict. I took a bite and then put my fork down.

"I don't think I believe in God," I said. "Maybe I believed before Janice died. I can't really say. I certainly said enough prayers. I guess I was talking to myself because she died. But when I married her, I made a commitment. I committed myself to her and her alone. Not to a marriage, but to her. And I think that was why we were able to enjoy five-star dining."

Mindy frowned. "I don't know that Peter and I are really committed to each other," she said. "We like being a couple, and I guess we are just using each other."

"So maybe that's the answer to your 'Why not' question."

We again fell silent. I tucked into the Eggs Benedict, and she sipped her coffee. I thought of Janice and Lara and wondered what they would say to Mindy. No doubt they would talk about God and Adam and Eve. Or what I had heard at so many weddings, including my own: "Therefore, a man shall leave his father and mother and be joined to his wife, and they shall become one flesh." That's what they would say.

"I would like five-star dining," Mindy said.

I smiled at her. "It's a lot better than a Happy Meal," I said. "And maybe a Happy Meal isn't so happy."

———

After breakfast, Mindy and I watched the mallards leave the

elevator and march past the sea of tourists to the fountain in the Peabody lobby again. Then she gave me a kiss on the cheek and we said goodbye.

I might see Lionel Jackson again. There would be a dedication of the new music hall at Tuskegee, and I would want to be there. I would probably see Peter Flynn again since he worked for a repair shop I owned, and the Tiffin would need servicing again in Red Bay. I would see Lara again, though I didn't know when. But I was certain I would never see Mindy again, except in the memory of her in the Presidential Suite, kissing me. A man can never erase such a memory or the desire that accompanies it. Cecelia would say that God can erase such things – the God who probably doesn't exist.

Later in the morning, I crossed the Memphis & Arkansas bridge on Route 55, still not knowing where I was going. Below, the mighty Mississippi continued to run peacefully towards the Gulf of Mexico. But I still had no peace. I called Lara and talked to her. She was interested in everything I did in Memphis. I told her about the optometrists, the Rendezvous, the Pyramid, Graceland, and even the Peabody ducks. I did not tell her about Mindy.

"Where are you going next?" she asked.

"I don't know," I said. "I'm just going to make decisions about what road to take on the spur of the moment."

I was hoping she would tell me to turn the Tiffin around. She didn't.

Chapter 7

Meadow

"The wind is the voice of Mother Earth," Meadow said as we sat around the campfire overlooking Cove Lake in Arkansas. She was a young woman in her early 20s wearing a faded floral maxi dress and a wreath of flowers in her hair. She took a drag of a reefer and then passed it to her companion, Mountain. "If you open your heart and your mind, you can hear her speaking to you."

"You know it's in the Bible," Mountain added. He was a lanky man wearing blue jeans and a paisley-patterned boho shirt. He took a hit on the reefer and passed it back to Meadow. "Did you know the Greek word for wind is the same word for spirit? The wind is the earth's spirit. Jesus was an ancient prophet who turned people on to Mother Earth."

"Interesting," I replied and offered them another piece from a bucket of fried chicken I had picked up on Route 22 during the four-hour drive from Memphis. It had been late in the afternoon, so I had turned the Tiffin onto Mount Magazine Scenic Highway and headed south. The panoramic views of the Ozarks proved a pleasant distraction from thinking about Janice and Lara. Soon, I saw signs for Cove Lake National Recreation Area.

When I arrived, I was fortunate to find a vacant site overlooking the lake. It had no electric hookup up but the Tiffin had a built-in generator if I needed it. I probably didn't. Since I didn't cook and the temperature was cool enough not to require air conditioning, the house batteries could handle my needs for a couple of days.

When I pulled the Tiffin into the campsite, I noticed Mountain in the adjacent site walking stiffly around their vehicle, an old yellow conversion van decorated with the words "Love Your Mother" under an image of the earth. Bright paintings of flowers, lakes, and streams covered the rest of the van.

I told him I was a physical therapist and offered to help him. He lay on the picnic table while I worked not only on his sore back but also the rest of his body. He was very thin, almost emaciated. So I retrieved the fried chicken from the Tiffin and offered it to them. In return, he offered to share their marijuana with me. I declined. I had tried marijuana once in high school, and the smoke made my lungs ache. Since I didn't get any of the mellow feelings others appeared to get, it seemed like much ado about nothing.

Meadow and Mountain eagerly took two pieces of chicken from the bucket. "We really are vegans," Meadow explained. "We are one spirit with animals, but we haven't eaten much the last couple of days."

"I understand," I said, "You can have as much as you want." Then I switched the subject. "How is your back feeling, Mountain?"

"Better, dude," he replied. "Much better."

We sat by the fire and chatted as they ate the chicken and got high. Mountain told me he had been born to a pair of carnies who worked with a traveling circus in Oklahoma and Texas. When he was three, his parents abandoned him. They took his older sister with them but left him behind in the care of "Uncle" Biff, a one-legged juggler. They never came back. His only memory came from a faded photograph of the troupe posing before a circus tent. The other carnies made him into a kind of mascot for the circus and watched out for him. He didn't attend school because the circus was always on the move, but Uncle Biff taught him to read and write and some basic math.

"I left the circus when I was 15 and hitchhiked across the country, just bumming. I panhandled to get money for food and weed, and I slept anywhere I could, mostly outdoors under bridges or on heating grates when it got cold. I would still be doing that if I hadn't met Meadow."

"How did you meet her?" I asked.

"I met her at the Slabs."

"The Slabs?"

Mountain looked puzzled, as though everyone should know what the Slabs were. "The Slabs in California. In the desert near Quartzsite."

I shrugged my shoulders.

"It's a cool place where people live off the grid," he continued. "It used to be a Marine base, but now the buildings are gone and all that is left are the concrete slabs. There's a whole community of people who live there. No police. No capitalism. We make our own rules. Everyone just gets along. A guy I bought weed from told me about it, and I hitchhiked there."

"So it's a commune?".

"Not exactly," he said. "But people share. Most people just live there during the winter. It's too hot in the summer."

I turned to Meadow. "How did you end up there?" I asked.

Meadow glanced at Mountain as if looking for permission. He nodded.

"My story is a lot different from Mountain's," she said. "I grew up on Long Island. My father was a partner in a big New York law firm. My mother didn't have a job. She spent her time planning parties and doing society stuff. I think I was an accident because I am an only child, an inconvenience. My parents didn't spend much time with me. Nannies raised me. As soon as he could, my father sent me off to an all-girls boarding school in Connecticut, and I spent the summers at an expensive camp in Nova Scotia. When I turned 18 at the end of my senior year of high school, I simply left. I jumped on a Greyhound bus and headed for the Slabs. I left a note with my friends telling my parents I hadn't been kidnapped, but I didn't tell them where I was going."

I thought for a moment. "So both of you were abandoned by your parents, but in different ways," I said. "Did they try to find you?"

Meadow nodded. "I am sure it was a huge embarrassment for my mother to have her daughter simply disappear. She bragged about me to her friends. My father hired detectives to find me. They almost did. One of them showed up at the Slabs, but Tree and the Clan protected me. I think they've given up. My father probably figured I would come home when I ran out of money."

"What is the Clan?"

"The Earth Clan. We worship Mother Earth. Tree is our prophet."

"Your prophet?"

"He's the Living Prophet," she said. "There are the Great Prophets. Whitman, Thoreau, and Jeffers, and the Ancient

Prophets like Buddha and Krishna. They have all been united with the spirit of Mother Earth. Tree communicates with them."

"Jesus was an Ancient Prophet too," Mountain interjected. "He said a seed must fall in the ground and die, and then it will produce many seeds. The Great Prophets – Whitman, Thoreau, and Jeffers – are in the ground. They have produced many seeds. Meadow and I are their seeds."

Meadow took another hit on the joint and began to recite. "I bequeath myself to the dirt to grow from the grass I love. If you want me again, look for me under your bootsoles."

"What's that?"

"Whitman," she said. "From Leaves of Grass."

"I see. And who is Jeffers?"

"Robinson Jeffers. He was a great poet who lived in a stone house on the Big Sur coast in California. He could hear the rocks talking to him."

"I see."

"Here is one of his prophecies," Meadow said. "It is time for us to kiss the earth again. It is time to let the leaves rain from the skies. Let the rich life run to the roots again."

"Interesting."

"I memorize the words of the Great Prophets. They show us the way." Then she paused. "Do you want to know the way?"

I didn't answer at first but stared at the fire. Did I want to know the way? Meadow and Mountain believed the wind was the voice of Mother Earth and that Jesus, some dead poets, and a man named Tree could hear her in the wind. Cecelia, Lara, and Will Skye all believed they heard the voice of the God of the Bible. What was it with all these voices? If God exists, why doesn't he just tell us he exists? Or if he happens to be a female, why doesn't she openly tell us?

"I'm not a very spiritual person," I finally said.

"But Tree says everyone has a spirit," Mountain jumped back into the conversation. "And we just need to connect with the Great Spirit, who is our mother. But instead of worshiping her, the greedy capitalists destroy her body with their machines so that they can make money."

"I see," I said. I briefly considered asking him about their conversion van, which was made from materials mined from the earth, but I resisted the temptation. Instead, I changed the subject.

"Where are you going from here?"

Meadow again looked at Mountain. I realized that even though she must have been far more educated, having attended what I assumed was an elite boarding school, he had the street smarts and was the decision maker. He thought for a moment and then nodded at her.

"Long Island," Meadow said.

"To see your parents?"

Meadow's face flushed. "Well, not really." I waited for her to continue, and she finally did. "Tree wants us to see if they will give me some money. My parents have lots of money."

"I see."

We fell silent again, watching the fire. Mountain threw another log on and then lit another joint, which he passed to Meadow. She inhaled deeply and then giggled lightly. I decided it was time to go to bed, so I excused myself.

As I left, I saw them remove the last piece of fried chicken from the bucket and place it on a small paper plate. Mountain took it into the nearby woods. When he returned, he didn't have it with him. I was puzzled for a moment, but then I figured it out. They were leaving an offering for Mother Earth.

———-

The next morning, I was surprised to see that Meadow and Mountain had not moved on. I found out they were out of money. Mountain made the rounds of the campground, knocking on the doors of RVs trying to sell marijuana, the one thing they seemed to have in great supply. But he came back with nothing but a couple of threats by fellow campers to call the police. I was glad no one did.

Later in the morning, a Ford 150 towing a Keystone Montana fifth wheel arrived and parked in a campsite on the other side of Meadow and Mountain's van. A couple in their 50s climbed out of the cab and began to set up camp. The man wore a T-shirt that said "America – Love It or Leave It" and a Kansas City Chiefs ball cap. On the rear window of the cab, there were stickers from the National Rifle Association, Ducks Unlimited, and the 82nd Airborne Veterans Association. One on the back of the fifth wheel read "I Stand for the Flag and Kneel before the Cross."

"I don't think you should offer to sell marijuana to that couple," I told Mountain when I brought donuts and orange juice to their campground.

"Why not?" He answered. "It might open their minds to Mother Earth."

"I just think it would be a bad idea," I said. "I would just leave them alone."

Mountain looked disappointed. "OK," he said. "But we need to get some money for gas. And no one else is buying. Would you be willing to lend us some money?"

Before I could answer, "Love it or Leave it" man appeared at the edge of their campsite. He was a large man with the body of an aging athlete, making some effort to stay in shape, but his belly hung slightly over his belt. He did not look happy.

"Is this your campsite?" he asked me.

"No, I have the Tiffin," I said, pointing at the Allegro Bus. I thought of the contrast between the Tiffin and the old conversion van and wondered what it must have looked like to the man as he pulled into his site.

"Well, I am not going to have some hippies smoking dope next to me," he said. "It's against the law in this state."

The man abruptly turned and went back to his campsite. Mountain frowned. "We get that sometimes," he said. "People don't understand that weed is the gift of Mother Earth to open our minds and to help us hear her voice. The capitalists hate it. They want everyone to be their slaves. They don't want us to be set free."

"Tree taught you that?" I asked.

"Yes, he is the Living Prophet," he replied. "He enlightened us."

I excused myself while Meadow and Mountain eagerly devoured the doughnuts. A few minutes later, I noticed them disappearing into the woods where they could get high without risking the ire of their new neighbor.

To my surprise, Cecelia arrived the next morning.

I had called her shortly after the "Love it or Leave it" man confronted Meadow and Mountain and told her all that had transpired. She was upset and had gone to DEFcon 1. She told me she was coming, and once she made up her mind to do something, there was no stopping her. Still, the speed with which she arrived caught me off guard. Later, I found out she had chartered a private jet to Fort Smith Municipal Airport and rented an SUV for the one-hour drive to Cove Lake.

"Where is she?" She asked after giving me a perfunctory hug and kiss on the cheek. I suppose it was the first clue to what was on her mind that she didn't ask, "Where are they?" But I missed it.

Cecelia hurried over to the neighboring campsite where Meadow sat at the picnic table, weaving long strands of grass together with a blank look on her face. Mountain was nowhere to be seen. I watched from the safety of the Tiffin as Cecelia sat down and began to talk to her in a soft voice. Meadow listened intently, and after a while, Cecelia reached out and held her hand.

Within five minutes, Meadow broke down in tears. I don't know if I have ever seen as much pain in a person's face as I saw at that moment. Cecilia wrapped an arm around her and held her close. No words were spoken. Meadow buried her face in Cecilia's shoulder and sobbed. I wondered what Mountain would think if he came back, but he didn't. Perhaps he was making the rounds again, trying to sell marijuana to the campers who had come in overnight.

A strange thing happened next. At least it was strange to me. Cecelia didn't seem to be surprised. The wife of "Love it or Leave It" man came out of the fifth wheel and sat down on the other side of Meadow. She placed a hand on her shoulder and began to speak. It took me a couple of moments to realize she was praying out loud.

When the prayer was over, Cecelia spent a long time talking to Meadow, who occasionally nodded but didn't say anything. When she was done, Cecelia and "Love It or Leave It's" wife helped Meadow to her feet and guided her to the conversion van. Meadow gathered clothing and a few personal items and then, led by Cecelia, climbed into the SUV. They drove off, and the neighbor's wife went back to the fifth wheel.

I would have to wait to find out what had happened.

———-

A half hour later, Mountain pounded on the door of the Tiffin. The mellow young man smoking a joint the night before had transformed into a raging maniac. I wondered whether he would assault me if I opened the door.

"Can I help you? I said loud enough for him to hear through the door.

"What did you do with Meadow?" He shouted angrily. "Is she in there with you?"

"I didn't do anything with her, and she's not in here," I replied, trying to project a calm tone. "What are you talking about?"

"She's gone. She took her stuff. Where is she?"

I suppose I could have dodged the question. I knew where she was – in a car with Cecelia – but I didn't know exactly where they were or where they were going. I decided to give him the truth, but not the whole truth.

"A couple of women were talking to her while you were gone," I said. "She got in a car with one of them and left."

Mountain pounded the door of the Tiffin again and let forth a volcanic eruption of profanity.

"Tree will kill me if the capitalists took her," he yelled. "Was it her mother?"

"I don't know what her mother looks like."

"I was supposed to protect her!" His anger seemed to have instantly morphed into panic.

I didn't know what to say. I was relieved when he left and went back to his site, where he sat by the fireplace and lit up a joint. I wondered if "Love It or Leave It" man would storm out of the fifth wheel the moment he caught a whiff. I was surprised when he didn't.

———

If I had any sense, I would have fired up the Tiffin and left. But life had ceased to make much sense. Ideas popped into my mind, and without much thought, I just barreled ahead. Give away $30 million to a university I had never attended? Sure. Buy a business just so I could hire back a man who was trying to kill every cottonmouth in Alabama? Sounds like a plan. Invite an angry and apparently panicked young man whose girlfriend had absconded with my sister to have pizza with me in the Tiffin? What could go wrong?

I rightly figured Mountain would accept my invitation because he was hungry and because it would give him a chance to make sure I wasn't hiding Meadow in the Tiffin. Still, he looked at me warily as I served up the pepperoni and sausage pizza hot out of the microwave.

"So what were you supposed to protect Meadow from?" I asked as we ate the pizza.

"The capitalists, of course," he said. "But especially from her parents."

"I thought Meadow said her parents had stopped looking for her."

Mountain hesitated, then answered in a quiet voice as though somehow Meadow might be overhearing. "She thinks they have, but Tree knows better. Her mother hired a man to put up flyers around the Slabs. We were able to take them all down before she saw them."

"Why would you do that?"

"We had to protect her."

"Why would you need to protect her from her own parents?"

"Because they are outsiders," he replied. "They would take her away from Mother Earth and make her a slave to the capitalists."

"Her mother would do that?"

"In a heartbeat."

In a heartbeat. I thought about my mother and the misery she had endured in life that would have crushed a lesser person. She had endured and given every beat of her heart to her children. She sacrificed to enable us to have a life far better than her own.

"Let me ask you a question, Mountain," I said. "What will Tree do when he finds out that you failed to protect Meadow? That she left when you weren't keeping an eye on her?"

Mountain frowned, and I saw fear in his eyes. "He will be very angry that I let Mother Earth down," he said. "I will be shunned when I get back. He will make me live in the desert alone with just a tent for days, maybe weeks. Mother Earth will freeze me at night and bake me during the day, and I will bow down before her and beg for forgiveness."

I thought for a moment. "But if Tree wanted to protect Meadow, why did he send her on this trip to see her parents? Isn't that the last thing he would do?"

"Tree told me not to take her home or anywhere near her mother. He said to go to her father's office on Wall Street and show up unexpectedly. I was to give him a note from her asking for money. I would tell him to look out his office window so he could see her on the street below. Tree said he would give us $100,000. "

"And if her father called the police?"

"It's not a crime for a daughter to ask her father for money."

"And you think he would write a $100,000 check?"

"It would be a wire transfer. Tree gave me a routing number and an account number."

I noted that Tree apparently knew a thing or two about the evil capitalists' banking system. "And then what would happen if he transferred the money?" I asked.

Mountain bit his lip and looked down at his pizza. "Tree said that Mother Earth told him I should leave her in New York."

"That makes no sense," I said. "Why would Mother Earth give up one of her daughters?"

"Tree says Mother Earth has her reasons. One of the Ancient Prophets said that her ways are not our ways and her thoughts are not our thoughts."

"That's Isaiah," I said, remembering the verse from the "Sword Drills. The one Brian had quoted to me. "Except Isaiah said 'His ways,' not 'her ways.'"

"You are right, it was Isaiah," Mountain said, impressed that I knew the reference. "He is one of the Ancient Prophets. Tree says his words have been mistranslated. It actually says 'her ways.' He meant Mother Earth.'"

"Tree studied ancient Hebrew?"

"Tree is the Living Prophet, the enlightened one."

We both fell silent and focused on our pizza. I retrieved two Mountain Dews from the refrigerator and gave him one. He eagerly opened it and took a long swig. We watched out the window as "Love or Leave It" man and his wife placed logs in their firepit. Finally, I spoke:

"You know it's all a lie, don't you, Mountain?"

"What do you mean?"

"You grew up around the circus," I said. "You know what a scam looks like."

Mountain stared at me intently. I didn't know what to expect. Would he argue with me and try to convert me? Would he get up and leave? Neither, it turned out.

"I know it's a lie," he sighed, "but I want it to be true. I have no other family. I have no place else to go."

An idea popped into my mind. I took a deep breath and wondered what I was about to get into. But as always, I plunged ahead.

"I have a place for you to go," I said.

——--

"Do you know what they did to that poor girl?" Cecelia asked when I called her after dinner.

"They passed her around like a box of candy. At least Tree and the other leaders did. They kept her stoned most of the time, and they all had their way with her, sometimes two or three at once."

"That's terrible."

"When she got pregnant, they made her get an abortion," Cecelia continued, barely containing her anger. "She's had three."

"Can they do that?"

"She's an adult, at least as far as the law is concerned. They had her doped up and brainwashed with all this Mother Earth nonsense, so she signed the right papers when they took her to the clinic."

"That's so wrong."

"My body, my choice," Cecelia said sarcastically, mimicking the abortion industry mantra. I didn't have an opinion about legalized abortion one way or the other, but she certainly did. Every year, she traveled to Washington for the March for Life on the anniversary of Roe v. Wade in January. She was so passionate and immovable in her opposition that I had stopped discussing the issue with her.

"Ironically, the only one who hasn't slept with her is Mountain," she continued. "He seems to genuinely care about her."

"He's not a bad young man," I said. "He's just lost."

"No kidding."

"But why would they send her back home?"

"They were bored with her, and they had plenty of other young converts to satisfy their appetites. So they figured they could sell her back to her parents," Cecelia replied. "They are smart enough to avoid an accusation of extortion. That's why they set it up the way they did, with Meadow asking her father for money."

"So where is she now?"

"Back with her parents. She was wrong about them. They may not have been the best parents, and they know they didn't get it right, but they do love her and care about her. They suffered a great deal through all this. Her mother scoured the country looking for her."

"And the Mother Earth stuff? How did you deal with that?"

Cecelia paused for a moment. "I told her a story," she said. "One that you have heard."

"A story?"

"From the Bible," she said. "When Jesus came upon a woman in Samaria who was getting water from a well."

"I remember." How many times had I been trapped in a pew listening to a pastor preach about the woman by the well!

"Joe, the woman by the well had been passed around from one man to the next. Five men had married and divorced her. She was sleeping with her sixth one, and he hadn't even married her. And who knows if there weren't others in between."

"I can see why you chose that story."

"The Samaritan woman tried to get into a religious debate with Jesus, but he wouldn't have it. He simply offered her living water. And when she finally drank that living water, she felt loved and valued for the first time in her life. She didn't have to surrender her body for the illusion of love. She was loved, not just by a man, but by the one who created her and breathed life into her soul. It was real love. Love that never fails."

"And that story caused Meadow to break down in tears and go with you?" I asked.

"The Holy Spirit used that story to set her free from the lie," Cecelia said. "She didn't need to give herself to a charlatan named Tree but to one who loves her and died for her."

"And she is now a Christian?"

"She is."

"That's quite a story."

"It is," she said. "What about you, Joe? Are you ready to take a sip of his living water?"

I hesitated. There was certainly an appeal to the story that I hadn't experienced in the past. An image flashed in my mind of Meadow, abused by so many men, taking a sip of a chalice offered by Jesus. I saw her face transformed with joy. But then I remembered Janice lying in our family room, semi-comatose and screaming in pain. Where was the living water for her?

"You mean the one who allowed Janice to die?"

"The one who allowed Janice to die," Cecelia repeated. She never defended her God no matter what he did or didn't do.

Neither of us said anything for a while. That's what usually happened when Cecelia pushed her beliefs on me. It was as if she were waiting for me to figure it out. To believe. I switched the topic.

"So how did you know to fly out to Arkansas?" I asked.

"I'm a woman," Cecelia answered. "I didn't have to be a brain surgeon to know what was going on when you told me about her. Then I prayed about it and God told me to go get her."

"The voice of God again."

"I heard right, didn't I?"

I laughed. It was 100 percent my sister.

"Cecelia, when was the last time you weren't right?"

——--

The next morning, "Love it or Leave it" man knocked on the door of the Tiffin. When I opened it, he introduced himself as Wyatt Samuel from Kansas City and apologized for being rude when he first arrived.

"I get frustrated when I get out into nature and have people camping next to me playing loud music or smoking dope," he said. "It defeats the whole purpose of camping. But I should have handled it better."

"I understand," I said. "It's no problem."

He waved at the campsite behind him. It was empty. Mountain had driven away an hour earlier.

"So where did that young man go?"

"Alabama, I hope."

"Alabama?"

"I own a diesel engine repair shop in Red Bay," I said. "I offered to have my manager train him to be a diesel mechanic. I gave him money for gas and food to get there. He can stay with a man and his wife I met there until he can get a place of his own. Maybe he will go, and maybe he won't. I would say it's 50/50."

Wyatt Samuels pondered this. "You gave him a choice then?"

"I did."

"Blessings or curses. Life or death."

"Some would say that," I said. "My sister says that."

"I will pray for him."

"Thank you," I replied. There was no harm in praying even if no one was listening.

When Wyatt went back to his campsite, I thought about Mountain and Meadow. Was this a turning point in their lives or just a short detour on the road to more chaos? They would decide.

Then I wondered what their real names were. I had never asked them.

Chapter 8

The Senator

Cecelia says there are no coincidences. In her view, the GPS again misrouting me, the senator taking his dogs on a walk, his dogs getting free, and my driving down the road at that exact moment were not accidents. It was planned. That it happened on a Sunday was just further proof. In fact, I think she believes everything that happened to me after I left Blacksburg was planned.

I can't argue that she isn't right.

I left Cove Lake at 8 a.m. on a Sunday morning, backtracked to Route 22, and headed west towards Fort Smith. When I reached Barling, the GPS directed me south on Route 49 when I should have stayed on 22. When I realized the mistake, I took an exit and then managed to get myself lost in rural Arkansas the same way I had gotten lost in rural Alabama. The GPS continued to be useless. I followed its instructions, and it repeatedly rerouted me in another direction.

I eventually turned right on an unnamed road and after a half mile came across two large red dogs running down the shoulder chased by an elderly man. The dogs were dragging their leashes, so it was obvious they had broken free from him. I drove well ahead of the dogs and pulled over just in time to grab the leashes as they ran by. The dogs jerked to a stop but still strained to get away. I was barely able to hold on but somehow managed to keep them in check. The old man came huffing up the road a minute later.

"Thank you!" he exclaimed. "Those mutts saw a deer crossing the road and took off. I couldn't hold on to them."

"It's no problem. I could barely hold them myself. They are beautiful dogs."

"They are not really mutts," he said. "I just call them that, especially when they misbehave." He leaned down to scratch one of the dogs behind its ears.

"Irish setters?"

"Yes. They're not the brightest dogs on the planet, but I love them," he replied, then pointed at the Tiffin. "That's a beautiful rig."

"Thank you, it's my home for a while," I said. "Maybe you can help me. I'm lost and trying to get back to Route 22."

The man chuckled. He seemed quite strong and vibrant for a man who appeared to be in his eighties. "You really must be lost to end up here," he said. Then he put out his hand. "Randall Farris."

"Joe Mathers," I said, shaking his hand. His name sounded familiar, but I couldn't place it.

"Ah," he said. "The same Joe Mathers who won the Powerball?"

"You recognize my name?"

"I am a bit of a news junkie and I don't forget faces," he said, then grinned a bit sheepishly. "Besides, I've been known to buy a Powerball ticket once in a while."

I nodded. Days had passed without anyone recognizing me. "And your name?" I asked. "It seems familiar to me."

"Ah, yes," he said. "I was a U.S. Senator at one time."

It was more of an admission than a boast. It made me suspect that Randall Farris and I had something in common: we didn't enjoy being recognized. Then again, who ever heard of a politician who didn't like attention?

"That must have been interesting," I said.

"A lot less than you think," he said. "I'd love to talk to you. I've never met anyone who won a lottery. Would you like to stop by my house for a cup of coffee? It's just up the road."

It didn't seem right to turn down an invitation from a former senator, especially in his home state, so I agreed. He walked the dogs, and I followed in the Tiffin. In a quarter of a mile, we turned onto a circular driveway leading to a well-kept house tucked into the woods. Beside the front door stood a life-sized wood carving of a grandmother hugging two small children with the words "Welcome to Our Home" at the base.

"That's beautiful," I said, admiring the artist's technique in carving the wood and capturing the emotions of the moment. "You can feel the love."

"It's my late wife and our grandchildren, and yes, the love is real," he said. "I carved it years ago when they were little. Now they have grown up."

I was impressed. "You were the artist?"

"Yes, it's a passion of mine," he said. "I'm an artist at heart. Come in and I will tell you about it."

The entrance of the house led to a large living area with cathedral ceilings and a western motif with distressed wood furniture and rustic light fixtures accented by warm shades of blue, brown, and red. Smaller wood carvings decorated the room: a dog and its master, a pair of galloping horses, a rodeo clown and a bull, and a cowboy with a lasso. On the walls were photographs of his late wife and grandchildren and block carvings of scriptures. The senator disappeared into the kitchen while I admired his artistry. He returned with two cups of coffee and bowls of creamer and sugar on a tray.

"So you were a senator, but you are also an artist," I said. "I would like to hear more about that."

"Ah, yes," he said, sitting down. "I was a senator. But the truth is I didn't have a heart for it. My father was a senator before me and a very powerful man in this state. He groomed me to follow in his footsteps, and I did. I went to the University of Arkansas and Harvard Law School. I only practiced for a few years before my father had me run for attorney general. There was no chance I was going to lose. The Farris name and my father's influence in Arkansas are what the Kennedys once were in Massachusetts."

"And from there you got elected to the Senate?"

"Yes. My father's plan worked perfectly. When he decided to retire, I was elected to take his place. He then got me on the right committees – agriculture, defense, and especially banking. Wall Street is where the money is, and he wanted me to eventually become chairman of the committee that oversees it."

"My father wanted me to be a football player," I interjected. "But that requires something I didn't have – talent."

The senator laughed. "If you had my father, you'd be a starting quarterback in the NFL, talent or no talent."

"So what happened?"

"I didn't like Washington at all, and neither did Carol. There is an atmosphere of self-importance that is infectious. Decent men and women get elected to Congress, and within a couple of years, they've caught Potomac Fever. They start to think of themselves as smarter and more important than they really are. Some get too cozy with the lobbyists and special interests. Frankly, a lot of them become insufferable. I suppose it's hard not to blame them. As a senator, I was treated like royalty. I had a staff that would take care of my every whim. I was invited to parties and dinners with world leaders, celebrities, and Fortune 500 big shots. All the young staff members running around the halls of Congress idolized us."

I nodded. "People treated you differently, I understand that. It happened to me when I won the Powerball and became a billionaire."

"I can imagine," the senator said. "I spent two terms following orders from my father and from party leaders. I had a couple of pet causes they let me pursue, such as supporting the arts, but on the important stuff, I just toed the line."

"So why did you leave?"

The senator paused for a moment to pet one of the Irish setters. "I woke up one morning and realized I was miserable," he said. "I wasn't born to be a senator. I was born to be an artist. So I quit and came home. My father had died by then, so there was no one to persuade me otherwise."

"I'm glad you did," I said, waving at the carvings in the room. "I see your talent,"

He stood up. "Come on," he said. " I'll show you my workshop."

We left our coffee and climbed down the stairs to his basement. He had a workbench equipped with a band saw, belt sander, drill press, mallets, knives, and other sculpting tools. Scattered around the room were various carvings, some completed and some works in progress. My eye caught one sculpture in particular, a fishing net overflowing with fish being hauled ashore by two pairs of hands.

The senator noticed my interest in the work. "153 fish," he said. "The miraculous catch when Jesus made breakfast for His disciples after His resurrection."

"It must take a lot of patience to carve 153 fish," I said.

He looked at me in a way that reminded me of Brian. It was a mysterious expression, as though he had retreated deep into his own soul for a moment.

"Not at all," he said. "It was worship."

The word "worship" conjured up painful memories of my childhood imprisonment in church. Before Janice died, Cecelia occasionally talked me into attending a service at my mother's church. I only went because I figured it might increase the odds of a miracle. Janice, of course, went every week until she became bedridden. At the end of one service, the pastor and elders gathered around her and laid hands on her, anointing her forehead with oil as they prayed for her healing. Their prayers were no better than my prayers. No one was listening. Since Janice's death, Cecelia hadn't been able to get me to go again, as hard as she tried.

When we went back upstairs and had a second cup of coffee, however, Randall Farris persuaded me to attend the 11 o'clock service at his church. Perhaps I agreed because of his stature as a former senator, but I don't think so. Titles have never impressed me much. Rather, he was simply convincing in an understated but compelling way. Plus, I was curious. He was an intriguing man who, despite having a domineering father, managed to find his identity – his true calling. Perhaps he could help me find mine.

After finishing our coffee, we climbed into this car and drove three miles on a winding road to the church. As I had before on my journey, I noted the juxtaposition of wealth and poverty in rural America. It was not like the cities where neighborhoods were either wealthy, middle-class or poor, and people lived with others in their socio-economic class. In the country, a beautiful, well-kept house with a manicured lawn might be next door to a weather-beaten mobile home on an overgrown lot. The rich and the poor knew each other. I wondered if that was true of his church.

On the way, I texted Lara with the news . "Hey, I'm going to church today."

She responded. "Let me know how it goes."

How it goes? I thought at least she would ask why I was going or express some happiness that I was willing to do it. Besides, how did she expect it to go? Maybe she hoped I would fall down on my knees, shouting "Hallelujah" to the God who probably does not exist.

As we drove, I told the Senator about Janice and how I won the Powerball even though I had never bought a ticket. I recounted my adventures in the Tiffin and meeting Lara. I didn't tell him the reason I left Foley without her. Even though we were on our way to church, I didn't want to start a Jesus conversation.

"I have had a couple of lady friends since Carol died," he said. "But no one I've fallen in love with yet."

"I didn't go looking for it," I said. "It just happened."

The senator chuckled. "Most of life just happens. It's like your trip in your RV. You cannot predict what is around the next corner."

I shook my head. "You're right. I certainly didn't expect to be going to church this morning."

The senator's church was a small building set on a knoll surrounded by woods. The white sign in front read simply "Christian Fellowship. Services at 11 on Sunday. Bible Study at 7 on Wednesday. Everyone is welcome!" There was no indication of a denomination and no pastor's name on it.

As we entered the church atrium, we passed a life-sized wooden carving of Jesus holding out his hands to a wounded man. The man was shackled hand and foot, but the shackles were broken and falling off. The two men looked into each other's eyes: Jesus with an expression of compassion and the man with gratitude and joy.

"You carved that?" I asked. "Is that how you see him?"

"It is who he is," the senator replied. "Pure love. Pure compassion. Pure holiness."

I felt a stirring in my heart I had never experienced before. As I leaned over to look at the carving, the eyes of Jesus seemed to penetrate into the depths of my soul. They were not eyes of judgment or eyes that threatened hellfire, although I remembered from my times of captivity in the pews of my youth that he taught about a lake of fire for the wicked. Rather, they were eyes of invitation that said, "Come to me!" Questions flooded my mind. Was I that wounded man, hobbled by the shackles of life and not even knowing it? Did the God who probably doesn't exist look at me like that? What would it be like for that man to have the shackles fall off?

I fought back in my mind. How many times had I been told to ask Jesus into my heart and I would be saved, yet it did not stir me at all? How many sermons and youth group meetings had failed to penetrate even an inch into my heart? And yet, suddenly, a sculpture of Jesus by a powerful man who had given up everything the world values to carve wood seemed to whisper in my mind, "I am the God who exists, and I know you and cherish you."

We moved into the sanctuary. It was a hall with chairs arranged in a semicircle around a wooden table covered with a colorful blue and purple tablecloth with the embroidered words, "Whom the Son Has Set Free is Free Indeed." A wooden cross stood on a base in the middle of the table. On the right side of the table, a lectern served as a pulpit.

About 20 people sat shoulder to shoulder in the front two rows of the semicircle while a handful of latecomers filed in and took the seats behind them. At first glance, they were a mixed lot: a man in overalls who certainly was a farmer; a teenage couple with a small child; an older woman with someone who by appearances certainly was her daughter; a man in a blazer and tie and his wife wearing a stylish blue wrap dress; an older man in blue jeans, a flannel logger shirt and a Vietnam Veterans cap; and an African-American couple with three daughters. Once again, I was relieved when no one recognized me.

When everyone was seated, the Vietnam veteran took a guitar out of a case at his feet and began to strum the chords of Amazing Grace. The congregation stood and began to sing at full throttle:

"Amazing Grace, how sweet the sound that saved a wretch like me. I once was lost but now am found, was blind but now I see."

I had heard that old hymn hundreds of times in my life – so many times that I had memorized the lyrics. Yet the people sang with a passion I had never heard before, as though they were actually singing about themselves. And it was the first time I ever thought about the words. Was the "wretch" the wounded man with the shackles? Was it me? Why was I even asking these questions?

The hymn continued:

"Twas grace that taught my heart to fear and grace my fears relieved."

The memory of the eyes of the carved Jesus continued to penetrate my defenses. A whisper again floated through my mind. "What are you afraid of, Joe?" I am not afraid of anything, I assured myself. I am angry. I am grieving. I am lonely. But I am not afraid.

I was relieved when the hymn ended. I fell back in my seat even while the others continued to stand. The guitarist switched chords, and the congregation launched into another familiar hymn. "Blessed assurance, Jesus is mine," they sang. I closed my eyes and tried to let my mind go blank, but the strange stirring in my heart would not be stilled.

Why didn't I want it to be true? Why didn't I want Jesus to be mine? I fought back again. He let Janice die. He healed others. Why not her?

The hymn ended, and the congregation sat down. The senator stepped to the pulpit. He apparently served as the pastor of the congregation. He opened a Bible lying and read a verse:

"Behold, I stand at the door and knock. If anyone hears my voice and opens the door, I will come in to him and dine with him, and he with me."

Then he began to speak. "Jesus stands at the door of our souls and He knocks," he said. "He knocks with blood-stained hands because Roman soldiers drove nails through His wrists when they crucified Him. He let them do it when He could have called legions of angels from heaven to destroy them. He let them do it out of a love that we can't fully comprehend. A love that surpasses knowledge. A love for us.

"Each of us hears the knocking of those blood-stained hands on the door of our souls. Some of us try to ignore it. We pretend we can't hear it. We might even argue that no one is there to knock on the door, so there can be no knocking. But everyone hears it. Everyone."

He paused and looked straight at me. "There is a reason we pretend not to hear the knocking," he said. "It's not because we are angry at God because He allowed something bad to happen in our lives. That's the lie we tell ourselves. No, the reason we pretend not to hear is that we don't want to give up control of our lives. If we open the door and let Him in, we give him control. And that is the last thing some of us want to do!"

I knew it was all true. I don't know how I knew it. I just did. My mind and my heart shouted in unison, "It is true!" Any suggestion that it wasn't true was simply foolishness, like denying the sky is blue or that the sun will rise in the morning. The God who probably didn't exist was knocking, waiting for an answer. Would I give him control?

I heard my sister's voice in my mind. "Blessings or curses." The choice was mine. He would not barge in uninvited.

I took a deep breath and looked to the ceiling. Then I opened the door.

Immediately, I fell to my knees on the hardwood of the church floor as his Spirit flooded my soul. I had been dead, not even knowing I was dead, sealed up in the coffin of my body. Only when he came in did I see my former state. The darkness of my tomb had been so normal – it was all I knew – until light came in both to expose it and overcome it. He brought with Him the gift of peace and joy. Everything I had been certain of in life became uncertain. Jesus, the one who came in when I opened the door, became my one true anchor, eternal and immovable.

My blessed assurance.

———

My younger self would never have opened the door. When I was in college, a philosophy professor taught the Marxist position that religion is the opiate of the masses. It had made sense at the time, and I had never really questioned it. Throughout history, the rich and powerful exploited the poor while threatening them with their religion. If they didn't behave, the jaws of hell opened wide, and their life in eternity would be unbearably worse. The well-behaved had the promise of heaven, but only if they were completely submissive sheep who didn't question and did everything they were told. I certainly understood why Marx, who lived in the misery of the London slums of the 1840s, would reach this conclusion. I could see why some of the most intelligent and accomplished people who have ever lived agreed with him.

When I opened the door of my soul that Sunday morning in Arkansas, however, I discovered Marx was wrong. What happened to me was no opiate. I did not fear hell or yearn for heaven, although in retrospect I should have. Like the wounded man in the senator's carving, I was already imprisoned and shackled on the doorstep of hell.

It was only later, when I read the scriptures, trying to fathom what had happened to me, that I learned I had been born into the lineage of the condemned, the lineage of rebellious Adam.

Jesus called the people who rejected Him children of hell. That was who I was, and I had no clue. The only way out was to be born again into a new lineage: Jesus' lineage. I had believed I was a good person, at least compared to other people. I gave $30 million to a university and rescued Peter Flynn from his grief, and helped save his marriage. Why would I deserve hell? No human being could convince me otherwise: not Cecelia, not my mother, not Brian, not Lara, not Will Skye. I was blind. Only amazing grace could open my eyes. Only Jesus could unlock the door of my prison and set me free – if I were willing to be set free.

After the service, I breathlessly told the senator how his carving of Jesus and the wounded man had stirred my heart and then how I knew beyond a doubt what he had said from the pulpit was true – so true at that moment that nothing could be more certain. We prayed together. I prayed. He prayed. And then the entire congregation laid hands on me and prayed. It was a moment of joy for them as it was for me.

"You may think that circumstances brought about your moment of faith," he said later. "But circumstances never created faith in anyone, only the opportunity for faith. Otherwise, everyone who saw Jesus' miracles would have followed Him as the Messiah. They did not. In fact, they crucified Him."

"I don't understand," I said.

"God may have engineered your meeting me and attending our church, but faith comes by hearing and hearing by the Word of God," he answered. "Your faith was born when you heard the scripture. You chose not just to believe it but to do something. You opened the door and surrendered yourself to it."

"And if I hadn't?"

"The moment of revelation would have passed," he said. "Many people hear the Word and know at that moment that it is true, as you did. But they choose to return to darkness, and the darkness swallows them again. "

"Blessings or curses?"

"Blessings or curses," he repeated. "There is always a choice."

I thought for a moment. "But I don't understand how I knew it was true with such certainty."

"Because Jesus Himself is the author of your faith," he said. "His Spirit, the Holy Spirit, testified with your spirit that the Word is true. His light shines in the darkness, and the darkness cannot overcome it."

"Then I was blind, but now I see?"

The senator nodded and put his hand on my shoulder. "We all are blind until He gives us eyes to see."

———

"So what happened?" Cecelia asked when I called and told her I had gone to church with a former U.S. senator. I suspect Will Skye would have picked her to be a good poker player. She was always hard to read, and I didn't know if I sensed hope or suspicion in her voice. No doubt she had prayed for me to go to church for years. Now she wanted to make sure she heard right. Besides, just attending a church meant nothing.

"You are right," I said. "God does exist."

"And?"

"Jesus knocked on my door," I said. "I opened it."

"And?

"He came in. He was so real. So present. So powerful."

"And?"

I was confused. I expected my sister to be shouting "Hallelujah!" into the phone. "What do you mean by 'And?'"

"And what happened?"

I took a deep breath. "I surrendered to Him. I have never felt so intimately known or so loved in my life. I didn't think it was possible. All I wanted to do was fall on the ground and..." I paused to find the right word.

"Worship?" Cecelia suggested.

Worship. To bow down. To honor. To glorify. To concede absolute superiority. To surrender all. Is this what I had done before the God whom I believed probably didn't exist but now I was certain did – the God of a reality greater than I ever imagined or could imagine?

"Worship," I said. "I worshiped Him."

As the words left my lips, an inexpressible joy rose within me. I heard my sister thanking God and praising Him on the other end of the line. What was so powerful about "worship?"

Then it struck me. I had humbled myself before the all-powerful and all-knowing God, and He had lifted me up to heights I never knew existed. Only later did I come across the Apostle Paul's description: "God raised us up with Christ and seated us with Him in the heavenly realms in Christ Jesus."

Seated in heavenly places. It was a glorious thought. At the same time, Cecelia knew, but I did not know, that there were still lower places I needed to go.

Much lower places.

Chapter 9

Dwight

Lara was delighted when I told her about my decision to follow Jesus, but she still wouldn't come visit me, even though I offered to send a private jet to pick her up. Nor did she want me to drive back to Foley.

"I don't understand," I said. "You said that when I found God, we could be together. I can pick you up at the Fort Smith airport this evening."

"It is wonderful that you found God," she replied. "But you also have to find yourself. And you haven't done that."

"Isn't it the same thing?"

"No," she said. "And you will find out it's not. You have a new identity. You have to find out what it is. And then you have to embrace it."

A rising tide of frustration and hurt flooded me. I felt rejected. "But don't you want to be with me?

"More than anything in the world," she said. "I ache to be with you. But we cannot stir up nor awaken love until it pleases."

"What?"

"It's a quote from the Song of Solomon," she said. "We can't let our desires hurry things faster than they should go. It's like picking fruit before it is ripe."

I was flustered and didn't know what to say. The God who exists had taken Janice away and given me Lara – except that I couldn't have her. At least not until I "found my new identity," whatever that meant. Why was Lara so much like Cecelia?

I couldn't disguise my exasperation. "What should I do?" I asked her.

"Ask the senator," she said. "He will tell you."

———-

"She sounds like a special lady," the senator said when I told him about my frustration. "How many middle-aged single women would tell an eligible billionaire to stay away until he figured out who he is?"

The senator had invited me to stay with him for a few days, and I eagerly accepted. I slept in the Tiffin in his driveway but otherwise spent all day with him, often watching him carve wood in his workshop. I was mesmerized. His hands caressed the wood, seemingly liberating a figure trapped inside it with each tap of his chisel.

There were many questions I wanted to ask him. First and foremost was about Lara. "I don't understand what she means that I have a new identity and I have to find it."

The senator looked up from the piece of wood he was carving

into the image of an angel. "A lot of people try to reduce the Gospel to the simplest construct: little more than a ticket to heaven," he said. "But what you experienced – and the choice you made to receive God's grace in the Person of Jesus – was infinitely more than a ticket to heaven. God translated you from this world, which is ruled by dark forces, into another kingdom, which the Apostle Paul called the kingdom of the Son of His love. You are now a citizen of that kingdom. And in that kingdom, you will find there are great mysteries."

I struggled to understand what he meant. "What are those mysteries?" I asked.

He put his chisel down and wiped a lock of gray hair back from his forehead. "That is a bit of a conundrum, Joe," he said. "Grab me an iced tea out of that fridge over there."

When I had retrieved the tea, he sat down on the bench next to me and took a swig before starting."I can name a few: the mystery of righteousness, the mystery of iniquity, the mystery of prayer, and the mystery of what we ultimately will be like when we are in heaven with Him.,

"I am not sure I understand," I said. "What do these mysteries have to do with Lara?"

The senator nodded. "There is another mystery," he said. "When you opened the door and surrendered yourself to Jesus, you were born again, not physically but spiritually. Your body remained the same, but in your spirit you became a new creation. The old Joe died, and a new Joe was born. You are on a journey to discover who that new Joe is."

"And if I discover who this new Joe is, what then?"

The Senator picked up a block of wood and examined it, then put it back on his workbench. He took another sip of tea, then continued. "You won't, at least completely this side of heaven. Who you have become is too great for you to comprehend. Or for any of us to comprehend fully."

"I still don't get it."

The Senator thought for a moment while petting one of his dogs that had rubbed against his thigh seeking attention.

"They need to be walked," he said. "I will answer your question when we are outside."

Once we left the house, the dogs immediately strained at the leashes, trying to bolt into the woods. The senator handed me one of the leashes. In that way, we could keep them under control. Then he began to talk.

"Imagine an oak seedling planted in the ground," he said. "If you could ask that seedling what it is, it would answer that it is a seedling because that is all it can see. But in the eyes of heaven and in the eyes of the enemies of heaven, the seedling is already a towering 200-foot-high oak. God sees who you will become, not just who you are."

"So I am a giant oak, not a seedling?"

"You are," he said. "But you need to grow into it."

I frowned. "And how do I do that?"

"By discovering who He is."

"That makes no sense."

The senator chuckled. "I told you it was a mystery," he said.

"I just don't understand."

He reached out and touched me tenderly on the shoulder like a father instructing a child. My father had never touched me that way. "Joe, you died, and your life is now hidden in Jesus. It is His life that flows through you, the very life of the Creator of the Universe. When you learn to live by faith in Him – and in nothing else – then you will know who you are."

I scratched my head. "That is confusing."

"It certainly is, but it is true," he said. "It is a narrow path. The only way to navigate it is to keep your eyes on Him."

He didn't seem phased at all by the puzzled look on my face. In fact, he seemed to expect it.

"And will Lara then have me?" I asked

The senator took a deep breath and smiled. "How could a woman like Lara ever say no to a towering oak who truly knows who he is in Jesus?"

––-

On Tuesday, my third day with the senator, he took me to visit the Vietnam veteran who had played the guitar during the church service. The man, whose name was Dwight Moore, lived off a dirt road atop a mountain in the Ozarks. It took a good half hour to wind our way up the mountain in my Jeep until we finally came to a clearing where Dwight had built a small log cabin home. An American flag and a "POW-MIA" banner bracketed the stairs to the front door.

Dwight showed us his cabin, which had a single bedroom, a bathroom, and a combination living room and kitchen. The floors, wall paneling, vaulted ceiling, and furniture were all made of pine. He had done all the work himself, including designing and building the furniture. In one corner was one of the senator's wood carvings: a soldier on his knees praying. A large stone fireplace was the most prominent feature of the cabin. On its mantle, Dwight displayed a variety of 19th-century pistols, including two Derringers. Mounted on the wall above the fireplace were a flintlock musket and an Enfield rifle.

"I did two tours in 'Nam," he said when we sat down on his front porch with a sweeping view of the valley below. "I was a forward observer for the Army, and I was involved in more firefights than I can count. I was lucky to live through it. Many of my friends didn't come home."

"Dwight won the Congressional Medal of Honor," the senator interjected. "I was honored to attend the ceremony when President Nixon presented it to him."

I was impressed. "What did you do to earn it?" I asked.

"Dwight is much too modest to talk about it," the senator answered. "He single-handedly rescued a platoon that had been pinned down by the Viet Cong in a swamp. He outflanked the enemy and routed them with grenades and gunfire. They thought they were being attacked by a large force and retreated, leaving behind a half dozen dead. He followed them through the jungle and continued to attack until he ran out of ammunition."

"I was just trying to help my buddies," Dwight said. "Any one of us would have done the same thing."

"Tell him what happened when you came home, Dwight," the senator said. It dawned on me that he had brought me to the cabin specifically for the purpose of hearing the story.

Dwight sighed and stared off into the distance. I sensed that he had told this story many times before, and it was still painful for him.

"When I came home from 'Nam and went back to Detroit, where I grew up, America wasn't in much of a welcoming mood," he said. "People spat on me and called me a 'baby killer.' I learned it was a mistake to wear my uniform in public. I had thought about making the Army a career, but when all that happened, I quit as soon as my hitch was over. There was a girl I was interested in, and she was interested in me, but then she got caught up in the anti-war movement and dumped me. I had trouble getting a job, and I started taking drugs. I had done some hashish with my buddies in 'Nam, but not that much. When I came home, I became a full-blown addict. Mostly heroin."

Dwight hesitated as if conjuring up memories that were too painful to bear. I noticed the deep lines on his face that made him seem older than he was. War and drugs had left their mark on him.

"You see, I had left Vietnam, but Vietnam hadn't left me," he continued. "I had nightmares and I woke up screaming in the middle of the night, bothering my neighbors. I went to the VA, but they hadn't quite caught on to what PTSD is. Nobody knew what to do with me except give me the last thing I needed, which was more drugs. I was a mess, heading for homelessness and an early grave."

"That's horrible," I said. My own trauma of watching Janice die paled in comparison.

"I hung out in an abandoned old house in a rough neighborhood in downtown Detroit. They called it a "shooting gallery" because that's what a group of us did: help each other do drugs. A lot of us were vets, and we had a kind of band of brothers, except we were a band of junkie brothers.

"There was a street preacher on a corner nearby. He was a vet too, and we thought he was crazy. He would be there every day with a big sign that said, "Repent and be saved." He used a megaphone to preach at people walking by and at drivers stopped for a red light in front of him. Almost everyone ignored him. Some people mocked him. He didn't care. He just kept preaching.

"One day, I was walking by him, heading for a convenience store where I was going to shoplift some candy and chips. He turned to me and said, 'God knows you, Dwight. He knows you are pinned down and you need someone to save you. He sent someone. His name is Jesus. Just say the word and He will save you.'

"I didn't know how this man even knew my name. At the time, I didn't know anything about the gift of knowledge that the Holy Spirit gives people at times. But his words penetrated me, especially the last words, "Just say the word and He will save you.'

As he spoke, tears began to run down his weathered face. I imagined a man hanging over a cliff, holding onto a single thread with nothing but an abyss below him. Another man leaned over the cliff, offering his hand, but the hanging man needed to take hold of it.

"The question was 'Did I even want to be saved?'" Dwight finally continued. "Did I want to risk being saved from heroin, from Vietnam, and from the soul-sapping rejection of a country that called me a murderer for donning its uniform and putting my life at risk? It took me three days, but when I woke up shaking all over in the middle of the third night as my body craved heroin, I decided I did want to be saved. I said three words, 'Jesus save me!'"

"What happened?" I asked.

Dwight wiped the tears off his face. "I was instantly swept up and taken to another place – I don't know if in the body or not," he said. "It was on the side of a hill next to a road that ran by a rock formation that looked like a human skull. There were three men being crucified and a Roman soldier guarding them.

I was deposited on the ground in front of the middle one, just below his feet. A single drop of blood from the man's pierced feet dripped on my forehead. It was like an explosion in my soul. Not of TNT or gunpowder but of light. Warm, soothing, healing light. And then instantly, I was back in the shooting gallery.

"My body wasn't shaking, my craving for heroin was gone, and even more so, the PTSD was gone. I could still remember the firefights and the deaths of my friends, but it no longer had power over me. I lay there the rest of the night experiencing a peace I had never known before and didn't think was possible. The apostle Paul described it as the peace that passes all understanding.

"The next morning, I found the street preacher, and he spent all day telling me about Jesus. He took me down to the Detroit River and baptized me. The river was polluted in those days, but the pollution didn't seem to touch me. It was as if it were pure water, and now I know it probably was."

"You were baptized in a polluted river?" I marveled.

"Just wait until you hear the rest of his story," the senator said.

"It was about that time that the paperwork for the Congressional Medal of Honor finally made its way through the military bureaucracy," Dwight continued. "I had no idea I had been put up for it, and I didn't think I deserved it. The men who gave their lives deserved it. I got a call from the White House asking me to come to a ceremony. So, in their memory, I agreed to go. A veterans group paid for my airfare and even bought me a suit. President Nixon himself put the medal around my neck. He invited me to sit in the gallery at the State of the Union address. I was shocked when generals and admirals saluted me. I had been just an enlisted man, but I wore that medal.

"Afterwards, I suddenly found myself employable. Defense

contractors and other companies wanted to hire me. They offered me generous salaries to do public relations and lobbying. But I turned them all down. I was employed by someone else: Jesus. I spent the next year in the underbelly of our society, spreading the gospel to the lost, especially the veterans whom our country seemed to have forgotten. I tracked down every surviving member of my platoon and led most of them to Jesus. I went to shooting galleries, homeless encampments, open-air drug markets, food kitchens, and anywhere else the destitute and downtrodden hung out. Almost every night, I came home with someone who had been delivered from drugs and despair by Jesus. Many of them are living good lives now: they have homes, jobs, wives, and children."

"Many but not all?" I asked.

"Not all," he said. "And that is something I will tell you about in a moment, but I need to finish the story."

"Go ahead," I said.

"Eventually, I sensed there was something more God wanted from me. Then one night, I was praying and he told me to take the gospel to the very people who had spat upon us when we came home from war and called us murderers. I told him I didn't want to do that. But then I did."

"Why did you change your mind?" I asked.

He chuckled lightly. "Jesus can be very persuasive," he said, then continued his story. "I started in the Haight-Ashbury section of San Francisco, where the hippie movement had flourished, and what I found shocked me. Many of the same young people who had been so vocal and even violent in protesting the war and condemning anyone associated with it were now broken and hooked on drugs. The free love they proclaimed was just an excuse to use other people for their pleasure and gratify the lusts that war against the soul. They were lost children. I especially remember the empty, lonely eyes of the young women who had allowed men to use their bodies, mistaking "free love" for the real thing. Those eyes haunt me to this day.

"Before I could do anything else, however, I found I had to forgive them and all the other people who had treated us so poorly when we came home. That was not easy to do, but I remembered what Jesus had done on the cross when He asked His Father to forgive those who were torturing Him because they did not know what they were doing. How could I do otherwise to these naive young people?

"Then I went out to the coffee houses, the parks, and the flop houses and preached Jesus to them. The Lord sent others to do the same thing, and pretty soon we had a revival. They called themselves "Jesus Freaks" and were full of excitement and passion. The Lord even sent me out to reach a small community of hippies living in the desert."

"The Slabs?" I interjected.

"Why yes," Dwight said with surprise. "That's what they called it. Have you been there?"

"No," I said. "But I know some people who used to live there. One of them is an employee of mine in a small repair shop in Alabama."

"It's a small world," Dwight mused.

"So what happened next?" I asked.

"That's the sad part," he said. "Many Jesus Freaks ended up drifting away from him. They couldn't sustain the intense emotion and excitement, and when following the Lord became difficult, which it always does, they lost interest and went back to chasing the things of this world. One even went on to become a top Wall Street banker. He told the New York Times he was a dedicated atheist."

"So were they ever really saved?"

"That's a good question, Joe, and I can't say I know the answer. But I can tell you that if they don't confess Jesus as Lord, they don't belong to Him."

We fell silent. My heart had warmed when I listened to Dwight tell his story. It reminded me of Will Skye's story. But now I felt a different emotion: fear. If people could hear about Jesus and experience his presence but then drift away, could that happen to me? Would I wake up one morning and decide it all didn't really happen? Was this the reason Lara was making me wait?

We spent the afternoon with Dwight, and he shared how he had spent decades traveling the country seeking out destitute people, especially homeless veterans, to share the gospel. He lived off the monthly stipend the government gives to Medal of Honor recipients and flew free on military flights with priority even over active duty personnel. Veterans organizations supported him generously and, when he became too old to travel, gave him money to build the cabin on the mountaintop.

God had sent an angel with a lottery ticket to make me a billionaire, but he had made Dwight far richer. I wanted to be like Dwight. But deep down, I wondered about the cost of such riches.

————

After five days, the senator told me to leave. In fact, he arranged for a place for me to go, a remote cabin on Lake Eufaula in Oklahoma, two hours to the west on I-40. He didn't ask me before he made the reservation and paid up front for a week in the cabin. He simply did it and then presented it to me as what I was going to do, whether I liked it or not.

"You need to go on a retreat by yourself and learn to pray," he told me over a spaghetti and meatballs dinner at his house. "And when you learn to pray, the Holy Spirit will show you things you need to know and tell you things you need to do."

I knew he was right. So much had happened to me, it seemed like yarn tangled in a giant knot, and I had to pull on the strings until I figured out how to unravel it. I had tried to imitate the members of his church and the way I had heard them pray, but my words seemed wooden and contrived, as though I were trying different combinations of a lock, hoping to find one that worked. My heart still warmed at the remembrance of opening the door for Jesus the previous Sunday and the rush of peace and power that flooded me, but I found myself puzzled, unable to fully understand what had happened, except I had no doubt it was real. So I agreed to go.

Before I left the next morning, the senator made coffee for us. He presented me with a gift of a carving for the Tiffin, a smaller version of the one in the atrium of the church that had moved me so deeply. He also gave me a leatherbound version of the New King James Bible. I felt regretted that I had no gift for him, even if he seemed to be a man who didn't need or want anything more than what he had.

"I have something to share with you before you go," he said. "You asked Dwight whether the Jesus Freaks who later stopped following Jesus were ever saved to begin with?"

"Yes."

"I could tell the question bothered you."

"It did."

"Jesus gave us an answer to that question. Do you know the parable of the sower?"

I vaguely remembered the story. "Tell me," I said.

"Jesus told his disciples about a farmer who sowed seed that fell on various kinds of soil. Some of it fell on thin soil. The plants grew up quickly, but when the sun rose, it scorched them because they didn't have deep roots. The soil was too thin."

"So those who drift away are the thin soil?"

"Exactly. Jesus knew what was going to happen to those who professed to follow him. It wasn't going to be easy. A lot of people would start, but not everyone would finish. In fact, He said most wouldn't. But at the same time, He assured us that seeds sown on good soil would produce an abundant harvest."

"What does that mean for me?"

"Don't be the thin soil. Be the good soil."

"How do I do that?"

"The answer is in your will and not your emotions," he said. "Your journey will take you to towering mountaintops and lush green fields, but it will also take you to vast deserts and barren wildernesses. You will find yourself among friends who will build your faith up, but also among enemies who will try to tear it down. You won't always recognize these enemies until later. Do not be deceived by your emotions. God knows where you are. He led you there. Worship. Pray. Read the Word. Every day when you wake up, turn the rudder of your soul in the direction of Jesus."

I nodded, although only later would I begin to understand what he meant. Even then, I found it puzzling. "If I had opened the door and let Jesus in, why would I ever be in a barren wilderness?"

"The Holy Spirit drove Jesus into the wilderness to face the enemy," the senator said. "We are no different, except for one thing."

"What is that?"

"We will never be alone."

———

I was surprised when Dwight showed up as I was hooking the Jeep up to the Tiffin just before I left. He and the senator laid hands on me and prayed for me that I would be safe in my travels and grow in the knowledge and love of Jesus.

"We haven't talked about my money," I told them. "I see that some of the people in your church appear to be poor, or at least poorer than most people. I would like to help them."

The senator shook his head. "You could easily make them all millionaires," he said. "And I know that you would do it in a heartbeat. But if you did, you would take something more valuable away from them. Right now, they take care of each other. They are a family. If you gave them each a million dollars, they would stop needing each other. They would stop making sacrifices for each other. They would drift apart."

"But surely they don't need to be living in old mobile homes or struggling to pay their bills," I protested.

"They don't. And our church has a fund that helps them when they need it," Dwight answered. "There is a box in the back of the church for donations. Everyone knows it's there, and no one talks about it. But every week, I find money in that box. Honestly, I think God multiplies it because I don't see how people who don't have much can give that much. We use that to help our people through the hard times."

"Can I make a donation?" I asked.

"You can," the senator said. "But I think it would be better if you held onto your money. If we believe God has told us someone needs it, we will call you."

As I drove off, this time with clear directions to Route 22, I pondered one thing: why did I keep meeting people who had no interest in a billion dollars?

Chapter 10

John Demas

The senator's handwritten inscription on the title page of the Bible he had given me read:

"Call to me and I will answer you and tell you great and unsearchable things you do not know." Jeremiah 33:3

I pondered the verse as I sat on the front porch of the cabin overlooking Lake Eufaula. The cabin was indeed remote. It had no wifi and there was no cell service, only a landline with a rotary phone from the 1960s. If the senator intended for it to be just me and God, he certainly succeeded. I would be by myself for the week. I didn't even have the luxuries of the Tiffin. The steep driveway was too narrow for a 22-ton bus, so I parked it a half mile away in a clearing on a dirt road and drove the Jeep to the cabin.

So what now? I wondered. It was a beautiful morning. I noticed for the first time a canoe sitting on a dock that jutted into the water. I decided I would take it out on the lake in the afternoon, but in the meantime, I would do what the senator had told me to do: seek God.

A light breeze drifted across the lake in front of me and ascended the hill to where I was sitting. It felt like an invitation. I left the porch and strolled towards the lake, passing under a towering red maple. Another breeze, somewhat stronger, wrapped itself around me as though embracing me. I stopped and scanned the landscape in front of me, sensing a powerful presence. Then I did something I had not done since I was a child in church, imitating the adults. I fell on my knees. I prayed by myself.

"God, I don't know how to pray," I said. "But you are the God who exists, and I opened the door and surrendered myself to Jesus. Teach me to pray the way Cecelia prays, the way Brian prays, the way Lara prays. Let me hear Your voice."

Another breeze, still stronger, swept across the lake. There is no way to adequately describe what I experienced when it engulfed me. Calling it unspeakable joy would not do it justice. Calling it a peace deeper than the oceans would not suffice. Calling it a flame of pure holiness that filled my heart with love would be inadequate. Later, when I tried to tell Cecelia about it, I could only use the words of Jeremiah that the Senator had written in the Bible he gave me: great and unsearchable. Unknowable yet somehow knowable.

Cecelia understood. As we talked on the landline, the spirit of the God who exists also touched her deeply. We stayed on the phone, saying nothing, basking in His love. We were beyond the boundaries of time, swept up in an eternal Now that has neither past nor future but only an endless present.

We both fell asleep without hanging up and without another word, wrapped in His arms.

———

I woke up the next morning filled with the presence of God and a sudden hunger to read the Bible. With a cup of coffee in hand, I sat on the front porch and dove into the New Testament, starting with Mark, the shortest gospel. By lunchtime, I had finished both Mark and Matthew. I had no desire to eat, so I just kept reading, finishing Luke – and therefore all three synoptic gospels – by mid-afternoon.

The book, which I had found dreadfully boring all my life, suddenly transformed into the most fascinating book I had ever read. It was like switching from watching a movie on an old black-and-white television set to seeing it 3D on a three-story IMAX screen. Mary, Peter, Mary Magdalene, and others in the gospel stories were no longer distant figures on stained glass windows but real people with real struggles who walked with Jesus and marveled at His miracles and teachings. In the end, when He rose from the grave, He transformed them the same way He had transformed me.

It was in John's gospel, however, where I truly met Jesus the Person, and I understood why it is different from the first three. I sat with Nicodemus as Jesus told him he must be born again to enter the kingdom of God. I drank living water with the Samaritan woman by the well and could say as she did, "Here is a man who told me everything I ever did." I marveled as Jesus called Lazarus out of the tomb and then felt His callused carpenter's hands wash my feet at the Last Supper. I stood with John as He watched Him suffer on the cross and commit His spirit to His Father. And like Mary Magdalene, I heard Him call my name at the empty tomb and open my eyes to see Him clearly. I, too, longed to take hold of Him and never let Him go.

When I finished, the sun was just dipping below the horizon. I walked down to the dock and sat on the end, dangling my feet in the water. I wanted to read on, but I was tired. Out on the lake were men fishing from boats. I thought of the 153 fish the apostles had pulled in when the resurrected Jesus made them breakfast on the beach, and how the senator had patiently carved 153 fish to express his love for Him.

In my heart, I did something I had never truly done before. I worshiped Him.

———

I floated on a high spiritual plane for the next three days, filled with the Holy Spirit and immersing myself in prayer, worship, and the Bible. I began to memorize scripture again, and the verses I was required to learn as a child came back to me filled with life and light. Moreover, I began to hear the still small voice of the Holy Spirit speaking to me through the scriptures. I lay face down on the cabin floor, worshiping God and came to understand that since we are material beings, the position of our bodies as we approach Him can reflect our submission and obedience. It was glorious. I desired more. I wanted to be closer to Him, more surrendered.

And then it ended.

I woke up on the fifth day, and there was nothing. No sense of God. No spotlight from heaven illuminating verses in the Bible. It was as though a faucet had been shut off, an umbilical cord severed.

My reaction, of course, was to try to get it back. I fell on my face. I read the Word. I recited scriptures. I prayed. I wondered what I had done or thought to cause the Holy Spirit to withdraw from me. I wanted to fix what was wrong, but I couldn't. I pleaded with God, but my prayers seemed to hit the ceiling and go no further.

Then the thought began to creep into my mind: was it real? If my sense of His presence could disappear so quickly, was it just an illusion, a trick of the human mind? Or something like "falling in love," a temporary state of infatuation that is mistaken for real love but fades away? Had I "fallen in love" with the idea of God?

I sat under the red maple and read the Bible and prayed to no avail until I finally became frustrated and stopped. I ate lunch and then decided to go out in the canoe. The water was calm as I paddled to the middle of the lake. From that vantage point, I could see other cabins and lake houses. I was surprised no other boats were on the water. In fact, I saw no one on the shore. I kept paddling, hoping for a light breeze to come across the water and embrace me as on the first day. Nothing happened. The lake was still.

I continued to paddle to the far shore and then skirted it, passing cabins and docks. Ultimately, I went around a bend and came upon a tall, thin elderly man fishing off the end of a dock. I would have passed him by to avoid disturbing him or the fish he was trying to catch, but he called out to me.

"Hello," he said. "Beautiful morning, isn't it?"

"It is," I replied. "Are you having any luck?

"None so far," he replied. "Do you live here or are you just visiting?"

"Just visiting. I'm in a cabin around the bend."

"All by yourself?"

"Yes. I'm on a retreat."

The man smiled. "Who are you retreating from?"

I laughed. "It's nothing like that," I said. "I'm just reading the Bible and praying."

"The Bible, eh?"

I couldn't figure out from the man's tone of voice or his expression what he thought about reading the Bible.

"You've read it?" I asked. "I'm pretty new to it. At least I'm new to believing it."

"I've read it very carefully," he said. "I'm a professor of philosophy at the University of Oklahoma. I've studied all the religions."

I considered this a stroke of luck. Perhaps this highly educated man could help guide me. Surely he had read the Bible more studiously than I had.

"I would love to talk to you about it," I said.

"Dock your canoe and we can have a cup of coffee," he said. "I am John Demas."

"Joe Mathers," I replied as I paddled to the dock, where he helped me out and tied up the canoe.

As we climbed a staircase to the lake house, John told me it had been in his family for three generations and that he had inherited it from his parents. It was a Cape Cod design, unusual for Oklahoma, but he explained that his grandfather had originally been from Boston before moving west to cash in on the wheat frenzy of the 1920s.

"Wheat prices were high, and it was a get-rich-quick idea," he said. "People came from everywhere until it seemed every square inch of the prairie was plowed and planted, often by weekend farmers who paid others to do the work. Unfortunately, it turned out to be one of the greatest man-made natural disasters in history. There was nothing to hold the soil in place, and when a drought came, the wind swept it into massive clouds that buried the whole state in dust."

"The Dust Bowl?"

'Yes, the Dust Bowl."

"I've read Steinbeck."

"My grandfather had the wisdom to get out of farming before the market collapsed and the dust clouds came. He got into the oil business and became rich. That's how he could afford to build the lake house in the middle of the Great Depression. Being from Massachusetts, he built a Cape Cod. It's also how I ended up at Harvard."

"You attended Harvard?"

"I did. A lot of people claim their family goes back to the Mayflower. Mine actually does. Generations of men in my family line attended Harvard, and it was unthinkable that I wouldn't."

"I went to Virginia Tech," I said with a smile.

"A fine school," John replied without a hint of irony. "Great football team."

When we entered his house, I immediately noted how immaculate it was. I wondered if he had a wife, but suspected he didn't because I saw no feminine touches. Rather, the living room had a fishing theme, much the same as Dwight's had a hunting theme. That made sense, I supposed. After all, it was a lake house.

John went to the kitchen to make coffee. I thought about telling him about being the physical therapist for the Hokies and spending Saturday afternoons on the sidelines of football games, but then decided that would probably raise questions that would lead to the Powerball ticket. Besides, I was interested in what John had to say about the Bible.

"So what got you interested in philosophy?" I asked when he brought a tray with two cups of coffee and a plate of biscuits.

195

"I was not a very energetic student in college, at least when it came to academics," he said, again with a broad smile. "I preferred to study young women and new concoctions of alcoholic beverages, if you know what I mean. There is an old expression that wealthy legacies like me often receive what is known as a Gentleman's C in our courses. I got a lot of Gentleman's Cs. But I did have one philosophy professor, Professor Skinner, who fascinated me. He raised questions about what we know and what we think we know, who we are and who we think we are, and especially what we do and why we do it."

"B.F. Skinner?" I interjected.

"Why yes," he replied, clearly surprised I recognized the name. "Are you familiar with him?"

"Not really," I said. "We read some of his writings in a class I took. He was a behaviorist, as I recall."

"Precisely. Ironically, I didn't end up agreeing with him about behaviorism, but he did launch me down the path toward a career in philosophy. I discovered that once motivated, I was a very good student. I stayed at Harvard for both my master's and PhD. "

"Impressive." I tipped my coffee cup towards him in salute.

"Skinner was an atheist, but I found I was not," he continued. "I came to believe there was some power or mystical reality that people experience and call God or Allah or Vishnu or any of a thousand other names. In that respect, I became a disciple of sorts of a Harvard professor from the 19th century, William James. James concluded that if there is such a thing as 'truth,' it is entirely personal and dependent upon its use to the person who holds it."

"And you pursued this?"

"Yes, I risk oversimplifying James' theories, but he believed that mystical experiences are a result of a Darwinian evolutionary process and could serve as a doorway to explore the subconscious. I was intrigued by this. I wrote my dissertation as a continuation of James' 'Varieties of Religious Experience,' exploring the various ways different people and groups of people develop their 'truth' based upon their own mystical experiences and how that truth is useful to them in an evolutionary sense – thereby making it 'true' for them."

"Wow," I said. I wasn't quite sure I fully understood what he meant. "But what do you think of the Bible?"

"Ah, the Bible," he replied. "No one worth his or her salt could claim to be a philosopher if they hadn't read and studied the Bible, if for no other reason than its impact on philosophy. It expresses truths that are useful – and therefore true – for many people. Jesus and Paul were able philosophers. Certainly, their ideas helped shape Western civilization."

I tried to digest what he had said. "So you have studied it a great deal?"

"In the original languages," he said. "I wasn't content to simply read a translation. I studied Hebrew and Koine Greek. I also spent a sabbatical studying Sanskrit and Classical Arabic so I could read the Bagavagita and the Koran in their original languages."

"That's pretty humbling," I said. "I have trouble even understanding Shakespeare."

He chuckled. "I discovered I have a gift for languages. It's easy for me to learn them."

"So what do you think about the Bible? I think you said it was mythology."

"Of course it is," he replied. "Who could say otherwise?"

"How so?"

"Well, no serious scientist, or scholar for that matter, would actually believe its stories, especially in the Old Testament. Who could believe that a man named Noah actually existed and that he managed to save two of every kind of animal in a wooden ark while the entire world was flooded?"

I thought for a moment. "Jesus seemed to believe he existed," I said. "I just read the verses this week where He warned that His Second Coming will be like the days when Noah prepared the ark."

"Ah, yes, Jesus," John said. He paused for a moment to reflect. "You really can't take everything Jesus said literally. Otherwise, we would all have to cut off our hands or pluck out our eyes when we do bad things. He was just using the myth of Noah to make a point."

"And what was that point?" I asked.

John hesitated. "That's a very good question," he said. "A very good question. But you can't really believe that the world was created on October 22, 4004 BCE, as Bishop Ussher calculated in the 17th Century. We have found pottery older than that."

I noted that he hadn't answered my question but had changed the subject. I let it go. "I suppose that depends on whether you believe that time is immutable," I said. I was surprised I had used the word "immutable" or that I had even had a thought about time as anything but a constant. It just popped into my mind. "But I am interested that you believe Jesus was a philosopher. Do you think he would agree with William James?"

"Oh no, William James was a giant," John exclaimed. "We know that Jesus existed because Josephus wrote about him, but he was just a peasant from a remote corner of the Roman Empire. The great philosophers of his day were in Athens. His ideas are quaint and certainly worthy of consideration, but completely impractical, like the poor in spirit being blessed and turning the other cheek. The whole story of his rising from the dead was clearly invented by his followers, who probably were embarrassed that their rabbi had gotten himself killed."

"They certainly convinced a lot of people it was true," I noted.

"And if it was useful to them, then it was true for them."

"Even if they were persecuted and killed for it?"

John stroked his chin and took a sip of coffee. "I have noticed over the years that people believe what they want to believe. Do you remember the cult members who committed suicide because their leader had convinced them an alien ship was trailing the Hale-Bopp comet and they would all be transported by it to heaven if they killed themselves?"

I vaguely remembered the strange case of the members of the Heaven's Gate cult who committed suicide in matching outfits in a mansion in California in the 1990s. "So western civilization is rooted in a delusion similar to the Heaven's Gate cult?"

John laughed. "I wish you were in one of my philosophy classes," he said. "We would have some fun discussions. Jesus was a teacher who had some good ideas about loving our neighbors and doing good – being a good person. But I wouldn't take the Bible too seriously if I were you."

"And what about God?"

"If you want to believe in God and that is useful, then it is true for you," he said. "But I am more of a transcendentalist. There are mystical forces in the universe that we can experience, but they are not personal. They don't have a material form or even self-consciousness. Perhaps as evolution continues, we will one day be united with them."

Once again, the question penetrated my mind: was what I experienced real? Or was John right that all that had happened to me was the result of an evolutionary process? In his view, the supernatural was not actually supernatural. It was mystical, yes, but ultimately it was part of the warp and woof of the universe, like gravity, rather than set apart from it.

"But I have seen Jesus," I protested. "According to the Bible, His spirit abides in me. I have sensed His presence, and He has spoken to me. He has testified to me that the Bible is indeed true as it is written."

John chuckled. "William James interviewed many people like yourself who reported remarkable experiences," he said. "In following up on his research, I've met people who said they have seen angels. I talked to a mother who believes the deity of the Bible cured her child of leukemia after she prayed. I met someone who said she had been transported up to heaven and experienced a joy beyond description. It's all fascinating. As James noted, it is a door to explore the human mind, especially the subconscious."

"But I've met people who were delivered from addictions and had their whole lives changed in an instant," I said. "I even met someone whose father was able to rescue and forgive the man who brutally murdered his grandfather. And that murderer was transformed from a bitter racist to a friend and advocate for those he had persecuted."

"Fascinating," John said. "I would like to interview that man. It sounds like the Road to Damascus myth. It's simply remarkable what the human mind can do."

I grew irritated. John had stirred up a crisis. The day before, I was absolutely certain of God and everything the Bible says about him. Yet I had awakened with no sense whatsoever of His presence – it was completely gone. I was in a spiritual wilderness. Now John was saying that it was all in my mind. How could I prove it wasn't?

"So in a sense, evolution is your god?" I asked.

"That's an interesting way to put it, although evolution is a process, not a person," John replied. "But you have to admit it makes more sense than believing a man defied the laws of physics by walking on water or feeding 5,000 people with five loaves of bread and two fish."

I didn't respond for a while, and I suspect John believed he had won the debate. I wondered how many students he had persuaded with the same reasoning: young people who had grown up in church and professed a faith in God only to be convinced that their experience of God was simply a product of millions of years of evolution. Furthermore, he taught them a 2,000-year-old book that had shaped the course of human history was not true unless they decided it was – but only if their belief was useful to them. There was no objective truth outside of themselves and, therefore, all truth was subjective.

I again searched inside myself for an emotion – any sense of God's presence – but I found none. Then I remembered what the senator had told me about finding myself in a barren wilderness at times surrounded by enemies, some of whom I would not recognize. What mattered was the will, not the emotions.

"I might have agreed with you a month ago," I finally said. "But in recent days I have read the Bible and believe that Jesus Himself is the truth. When we know Him – not just about Him – and surrender ourselves to Him, then we know the truth. And the truth sets us free."

An angry expression crossed John's face. "That is nonsense," he snapped. "Do you think a mythical figure is the truth? You may as well believe in Zeus and Jupiter. You are defying all reason. You are being willfully blind."

"I apologize for offending you," I said.

Immediately, John's expression changed back to that of the patient professor tutoring a student. "That is all right," he said. "I just don't like seeing people deceived."

"What would you have me do?" I asked.

"It is simple," he said. "Trust your mind. Use your reason. Do not let yourself be fooled."

I nodded and changed the subject, which he didn't seem to mind. We talked about the beauty of Lake Eufaula, which led to a discussion of the Appalachian Mountains and the scenic Skyline Drive that runs down its spine in Virginia. We eventually discussed my travels in the Tiffin. John had traveled far and wide and seemed to have visited every place I had been. He even knew about the Coon Dog Cemetery, although he said he had never been there.

A half hour later, as I boarded my canoe to paddle back to my cabin, he added one more thought. "You have lost your wife, and that can cloud any man's judgment, Joe," he said. "Not even a billion dollars can change that. Trust yourself to find the truth. Your mind will show you the way."

As I paddled off, I realized I had never told him about Janice or the lottery ticket.

Later that night, I came across a scripture that caught my attention: "Satan transforms himself into an angel of light." Ironically, these were the words of Paul of Tarsus, the one who met Jesus on the road to Damascus, which John had called a myth.

It didn't surprise me when I found out the University of Oklahoma had no record of a professor of philosophy named John Demas.

Chapter 11

Gaylord and Sarah

Three days later, I was lost in Oklahoma, just as I had been in Alabama and Arkansas. But this time I knew it wasn't the GPS that got me lost. It was God. And I wasn't lost to him.

When I left the cabin, I intended to backtrack to Interstate 40 and head west. But when I reached Route 69, I had a strong sense I should turn south rather than north. I stopped by the side of the road and contemplated it. Was this the still small voice of the Holy Spirit that Cecelia and Brian talked about, or was it my own idea? I decided to head south towards Dallas.

I never made it. When I reached Durant, I sensed I was supposed to go west on Route 70 towards Lake Texoma. Again, I pulled over to think. I remembered the times in my life I had had a hunch something was going to happen, and then it didn't. The only time I had ever been to horse races, I was certain a filly called. "Cotton Candy Dandy" was going to win the next race. I bet $20 on her only to watch the horse fade in the stretch and finish fifth. How could one discern the difference between a hunch and the still small voice of God? I decided I would ask Brian whenever I got back to Blacksburg. In the meantime, I decided no harm would be done if I went west again instead of south. After all, since I left Red Bay, I had no fixed destination.

I kept driving west on Route 70 until I reached the lake, thinking that might be my next stop. But when I crossed the bridge over the lake, I didn't turn on the exit to Texoma Lake State Park or any of the lakeside RV parks. It seemed as though a voice was saying "keep going," just outside the range of my hearing, like a whistle that only dogs can hear. Something in my spirit could discern it even if my ears could not. It had a texture and a peaceful certainty that warmed my heart, the same as when a scripture verse had jumped off a page as I read the gospels at Lake Eufaula.

As I drove, I noticed the afternoon sky was growing darker on the horizon as thunderheads began to stack on top of each other. I turned on the radio. The National Weather Service had issued a tornado watch for the counties along the Texas/Oklahoma border. I had never seen a tornado in person, only the photographs of the massive destruction they left in their wake, turning neighborhoods into rubble. I decided to take my chances and keep driving towards the town of Kingston, where Route 70 abruptly veered north.

I traveled only a few more miles when the inaudible voice within me nudged me to take an exit into the Oklahoma countryside. By then, the storm on the horizon was closing in. The wind picked up, and rain began to pelt the Tiffin as lightning lit the clouds and thunder rolled across the plains. The radio crackled. The National Weather Service had upgraded its alert to a tornado warning. I pulled the Tiffin onto a shoulder opposite a farmhouse and waited, my heart pounding.

Soon, hail the size of pigeon eggs pinged on the roof. The clouds and sky turned an eerie shade of green, and a long horizontal cloud descended from the towering thunderheads. I didn't recognize the violent drafts of hot and cold air rising and falling in the clouds, rotating faster and faster because of wind shear. The storm was in the labor pains of birthing a tornado.

I looked around, desperate for a place of refuge, but there was none. The landscape around me was flat. There were no overpasses where I could park the Tiffin. If I had known better, I would have left the Tiffin and lain low in the drainage ditch next to the road. It dawned on me that if a tornado struck the Tiffin, I would not survive. I considered running to the small farmhouse, but I didn't think I would make it in time. Besides, I probably wouldn't be any safer.

So I did the only thing I could think of. I prayed harder than I ever had in my life: five alarm prayers, fueled by terror and adrenaline. I pleaded with God to keep any tornado from forming. I asked Him to calm the storm the way Jesus had on the Sea of Galilee. If a tornado was going to drop out of the sky, I begged Him to guide it out into the fields and away from the Tiffin and the farmhouse.

A quarter mile in front of me, a funnel descended out of the horizontal cloud and reached the ground with an explosion of dirt and debris. It moved quickly towards me, obliterating a portion of a fence, roaring like a giant jet engine. I braced myself for its impact, but then 100 feet in front of the Tiffin, it abruptly turned and headed towards the farmhouse.

"Lord, let it miss the house," I prayed desperately. "Please God! Let it miss the house."

It did not. The twister needed no more than five seconds to swallow the house, blasting debris in all directions. Within 15 seconds, all that was left was the foundation and piles of twisted rubble. Nothing else. The tornado continued across the fields and then abruptly dissipated. I tried to call 911, but the storm had knocked out cell service, so I left the relative safety of the Tiffin and ran towards the house, hoping no one had been inside.

Rain was still falling hard and immediately soaked me. However, the storm line had passed overhead, and there were clear skies behind it. I circled the rubble but saw no one. It was an eerie feeling being in the middle of such destruction all by myself. No cars on the road. No sirens blaring. It was a post-apocalyptic landscape, as though a nuclear bomb had been dropped and I was the only survivor.

Yet I wasn't. As I circled the house a second time, I heard a creaking sound behind me. A manhole-sized lid buried in the ground a few feet from the foundation opened. A wiry man in his late 50s or early 60s emerged. He surveyed the destruction with a pained but stoic expression. Then he reached down and helped a petite woman out of the manhole. She looked around, tears flowing from her eyes. She leaned over and picked up an item out of the rubble on the ground. It was a small porcelain dish that remarkably hadn't broken. She held it close to her heart while the man put his arm around her and comforted her. They didn't notice me behind them as together they surveyed the ruins of their house.

After a few moments, the man whispered something in the woman's ear. She nodded. Together they knelt on the wet ground. I heard the man's voice in prayer.

"Heavenly Father, thank you for hearing our prayers and sparing our lives from this storm," he said. "Thank you for this home that you gave us to live in and raise our children. It was Yours and not ours. You have been faithful to provide for us all the days of our life, and we know that You will continue to provide for us."

The man stopped, and the woman continued the prayer. "We trust in all your promises, Father, for they are all 'Yes' and 'Amen' in Jesus. You have promised that all things work for good for those who love you and are called according to your purpose. We love you, Lord, and You have called us to your purpose. Therefore, we know that even this tornado will work for good in our lives and in the lives of others. So we give You all praise and all glory in Jesus' name."

They said 'Amen' together. They didn't get up immediately but held hands and silently continued to pray. Finally, the man stood up and helped the woman up.

"Are you all right?" I asked. "I tried to call 911, but the cell service is out."

They both turned towards me. If they were surprised by my presence, they didn't show it. "We are OK," the man said. "We were in the storm shelter."

"This is terrible," I said, pointing at the twisted remains of the house. "I am so sorry."

The man shook his head. "Houses can be rebuilt," he said. "We are thanking God that He protected us. We are in His hands. He already knows how He will provide for us."

Later, I learned that Gaylord Norris and his wife Sarah had lived in the small farmhouse for 40 years, scratching a living out of the Oklahoma soil. I marveled at their deep sense of calm as I helped them sift through the rubble looking for items that had survived the tornado. They didn't question why a stranger was doing this. Nor did they seem intent on sending for help.

Sarah found a framed photograph of their family in a broken pile of what had been roof trusses. Remarkably, the glass hadn't shattered. The family, younger versions of themselves with two teenage children, stood in their Sunday best outfits in front of a wooden church with a steeple that reminded me of Brian's church near Radford.

Sarah began to cry again, and Gaylord held her close again. I tried to imagine what it must be like to lose everything in just a few seconds: not just the material items but the place of so many memories. Somewhere in the twisted and broken ruins was the table where the young family ate together, welcomed guests, did homework, and sat around talking about the day-to-day events of life. Perhaps there was a cradle being stored for grandchildren or great-grandchildren. Or a silver service handed down as an heirloom from past generations, now scattered somewhere in the fields.

"Would you like me to drive somewhere where there is cell service and call anyone?" I asked.

"No need," Gaylord said. "They will be here soon."

Sure enough, five minutes later, a car appeared and parked behind the Tiffin. The driver, a heavyset balding man with a slight limp, navigated the debris in the driveway. He gave Gaylord and Sarah a hug. Soon, a half dozen other cars lined up behind the Tiffin, and a crowd of people surrounded them, talking in whispered voices.

No one seemed to notice me. I drifted in the direction of the Tiffin. There seemed to be nothing I could do to help them.

———-

As I drove westward, I pondered what had made me leave. It was hard to get my head around my own motives. I was willing to help anyone – I had gone out of my way to help Peter Flynn – but for some reason this time I didn't want to interject myself into someone else's tragedy. So I called Lara. She straightened me out.

She was alarmed when I told her about the tornado and relieved it had turned away from the Tiffin at the last minute. But when I told her about the farmhouse and my decision to drive west until I found an RV park for the night, she challenged me.

"You left?" she asked incredulously. "Why did you leave?"

"A lot of people showed up and I didn't see anything I could do to help," I said.

"God had you drive a couple of hundred miles out of your way to a farmhouse in the middle of nowhere just as a tornado touched down and destroyed it, leaving a couple homeless," Lara said. "And you left?"

"What was I supposed to do?" I replied defensively.

"I don't know," she said. "But you'd better go back and find out."

I didn't like the idea of going back, but I couldn't think of a good reason for not doing so. Or at least a reason that would be accepted by Lara. Or Cecelia, for that matter. She would certainly have scolded me and told me to hightail it back to the farmhouse.

"Suppose I just imagined that God was telling me to make all those turns and I just happened to be there by coincidence," I protested.

"You weren't there by coincidence, Joe," Lara said. "There are no coincidences."

Duly chastened, I hung up the phone. It was too late in the day to return, but I decided I would go back in the morning.

——-

As soon as the sun rose, I unhooked the Jeep and drove back to the farmhouse. It was still early morning, and no one was there. The devastation shocked me even more than it had the day before. I had seen videos of the damage left by tornadoes on newscasts, but they could not adequately convey the level of destruction. I felt small and powerless. It was a beautiful morning with dazzling sunlight and a light breeze dancing through the nearby wheat fields. It was hard to comprehend that the same natural forces that delighted the senses could suddenly rise up as a hammer of ruin.

I wondered why God spared me but allowed the tornado to destroy the farmhouse. Did he not hear my prayers? Were his ears closed to the prayers Gaylord and Sarah most certainly prayed when they were in the storm shelter? What good could come from allowing the forces of nature to destroy their home? Didn't the Bible say he is the God who is love? How was what I saw before me "love?"

When no one came for a few minutes, I continued down the road. I wondered where Gaylord and Sarah had spent the night and imagined the emptiness they felt as they fell asleep with all their possessions destroyed or scattered over the landscape. I pondered how anyone could immediately fall on their knees in thanksgiving when their home was destroyed and their lives upended.

The road led to an intersection where I came across the country church from Gaylord and Sarah's family photograph. There was a car in the parking lot. I pulled in just as the heavyset man with the slight limp from the day before came out the front door.

"You are the guy at the Norris place yesterday," he said when I got out of the Jeep. "Thank you for stopping to help."

"I just happened to be there when the storm hit," I said, extending my hand. "I'm Joe Mathers."

"Reggie Wilson. I'm their pastor," he said as he shook my hand. He had a soothing bass voice. It was easy to imagine him preaching in a country church. "Did you see the tornado strike their house?"

"I did. It almost hit my motorcoach, but then it veered off and struck the farmhouse. It would have killed me."

"I saw your rig and I wondered about that," he said. "I am thankful no one was hurt and there was only property damage. Five years ago, Gaylord said the Lord told him to build a storm shelter. It didn't surprise me." He smiled and shook his head. "If Gaylord and Sarah say the Lord told them something, he certainly did. It had sat there unused since he built it, and some people might wonder why he went to all that effort. Now they know."

We fell silent for a moment. He cocked his head and studied me. "If you don't mind me asking, why did you come back here today?" he asked.

I shrugged my shoulders. I wasn't going to tell him about being admonished by Lara. "It just didn't seem right to leave things the way I did. I wanted to know if they were going to be OK. Or if there was something I could do to help."

"I suppose if you were Bill Gates," he said with a frown. "They lost everything. They've always just scraped by and couldn't afford homeowners' insurance, which can be expensive here because of the storms. So it's a total loss. They trusted God. They have always trusted God. They have been the most generous people I have ever known. They never had much, but anything extra they gave away to others who needed it. We will all rally around them and help them, but it's going to be tough. They may have to sell their farm."

So there was the answer. Of course, it was obvious. With one phone call, I could solve their problem. I could never replace their home, but I could replace their house. And I would. I would build them a better house than they ever imagined and not even blink at the cost.

"I have a question since you are a pastor."

"What is that?"

"I am new to truly believing in God and giving my life to Jesus," I said. "When Gaylord and Sarah came out of their shelter and saw their home had been destroyed, the first thing they did was get on their knees and thank God not just for sparing their lives but for giving them the house to live in for so many years – the house that had just been destroyed."

"That sounds like them," he nodded..

"I lost my wife to breast cancer a few months ago," I said. "I didn't thank God for her life. I was angry at God for not healing her when I prayed. I decided God did not exist. Or at least a loving God did not exist."

He nodded. "A lot of people feel that way when something tragic happens."

"So how can Gaylord and Sarah do that? How can they give thanks when something tragic just happened to them?"

He thought for a few seconds. "You have to understand something about Gaylord and Sarah," he replied. "Every moment of their life, they walk with God. Not just on Sunday mornings or at times during the day when they remember to pray or read the Bible. Every breath is a prayer. They see the world through God's lens in a way that I don't yet, even though I am a pastor."

I took a few seconds to digest what he was saying. I looked at the church and thought of Brian giving up his religious career to serve poor people in West Virginia. Reggie seemed to grasp this and waited patiently. "I don't understand what that means," I finally said.

"Try to imagine you could see every person you meet or everything that happens to you in life from God's perspective. We aren't God, so we aren't omniscient, but he abides in us, and he invites us to be filled with his Spirit. So we can have perfect confidence in his love for us, in his power, and in his control of what happens to us. Gaylord and Sarah live that way."

"So when a tornado destroys their home?"

"They give thanks. They trust in his promises. His peace and his word reign in their hearts."

"And if Sarah died of breast cancer?

"Gaylord would give thanks to God for her life."

"That is hard to grasp," I said. "It almost seems like they are in denial."

"Maybe we are the ones who are in denial," he replied. "We are in denial about the reality of who God is. Paul wrote that we should rejoice always, pray without ceasing, and give thanks in all things. The key words are always, without ceasing, and in all things."

I shook my head with a sigh. "I would like to believe that," I said.

"Let me ask you a question," Reggie said. "Why are you here? Did you get yourself to this exact place at this exact moment to have this exact conversation?"

I pondered this while Reggie waited patiently. "I didn't have to be here," I finally said. "I am not a fatalist. Each step of the way, I could have turned in a different direction."

"It is true you had choices," he said. "But why are you here?"

I thought about everything that had happened: the directions from the inaudible voice to stopping the Tiffin opposite the farmhouse as the tornado struck to the conversation with Lara.

"Okay, okay!" I said, throwing up my hands. "You got me! God got me here!" I finally said.

Reggie slapped me on the back, a big smile on his face. "And why did God get you here?"

"Because God made me a billionaire and he sent me to help two people who trust him completely."

Reggie stepped back in shock, raising his eyebrows. "Come on! You are a billionaire? I was kidding about Bill Gates."

"I am," I said with a shrug. "I didn't ask to be. A hospice volunteer left a winning lottery ticket in my house the day my wife died of cancer. I tried to find her, but I couldn't. No one at the hospice organization had ever heard of her. No one had seen her but me. Who knows if she even exists or whether she was an angel? In any event, I have a billion dollars sitting in New York that has completely upended my life. My sister convinced me to take a journey across the country in an RV."

Reggie looked at me quizzically. I didn't know if he believed me or not. "And you ended up here?"

"I ended up here," I said, wondering how much I should share about my trip. "I guess God sent me here to help them. I will rebuild their house and take care of whatever else they need."

Reggie smiled broadly, a thoughtful expression on his face. There was something about him that reminded me of Brian. I wondered if he, too, had left a promising career in a mega church to serve in a small congregation in the middle of nowhere. "I don't think God sent you here just to spend money," he said.

I shrugged my shoulders. "Then why did he send me here? What else do I have to offer Gaylord and Sarah?"

Reggie chuckled. "Perhaps they have something to offer you," he said.

———-

It is remarkable the power having a billion dollars can give a person. I just say the word, and people get busy. No one makes me wait. I go straight to the head of the line.

Later in the day, a real estate agent quickly found a three-bedroom house for Gaylord and Sarah to live in while their new farmhouse was under construction. I could have rented it, but I just went ahead and bought it. It only took a week to settle since it was an all-cash offer with no contingencies. In the meantime, I rented a deluxe cabin on Lake Texoma for them with room enough for their two adult children when they arrived. I would have had food delivered, but the church members descended on the cabin with a dozen casseroles and other dishes.

The following morning, I flew in a well-known architect from St. Louis on a private jet to meet with them. A local builder arranged for the lot to be quickly cleared, setting aside any undamaged or personal items found in the rubble. I gave Gaylord and Sarah free license to build whatever they wanted on the property. Normally, it would take at least six to eight months to build a new house. The builder promised it in four months when I offered him a 20 percent bonus for meeting the deadline.

The neighbors and other church members were amazed at the speed with which everything happened. Even Reggie said he was dumbstruck, especially that I had gotten the architect to fly out on a moment's notice.

"Money will do that," I said. "Their farmhouse will be in

Architectural Digest when he is finished."

Gaylord and Sarah were grateful, of course, but they were not surprised, especially when I told them about Janice's death and everything that had happened during my journey.

"The Lord did not allow a tornado to destroy our home for no reason," Gaylord said when Reggie and I met them at the ruined farmhouse after the meeting with the architect.

"He sent you here, and he will glorify his name. "

"I suspect most people don't have that much confidence in God," I said. "They might say they do in church, but they struggle when faced with life's problems."

"That is true," Gaylord replied. "It is not easy to believe, especially when bad things happen like an illness or the death of a child, or losing a job. Faith takes work."

We continued to walk around the ruins of the house. I bent over to pick up a broken teacup wedged under several books in the dirt. It had a floral design with sunflowers, roses, and daisies intertwined. I noticed one of the books was Pilgrim's Progress. Gaylord picked it up and brushed it off, then handed it to Sarah.

"You mean faith doesn't simply happen?" I asked him. "You have to work at it?"

Then Sarah answered. "Jesus is the author and finisher of our faith," she said. "But we have to work out our salvation. And that means working to surrender to Him."

"An army doesn't work to surrender," I protested. "It stops fighting and lays down its arms."

"Precisely," Gaylord said. "Except our surrender is not to an enemy. It is to one who loves us and wants nothing but the best for us. "

I gave them a puzzled look and shrugged my shoulders. Gaylord continued: "The crowd that Jesus fed loaves and fishes asked Jesus what they had to do to do the work of God. He told them that the work of God is to believe in the one he has sent. He said faith is a work. And if you work at it, it gradually requires less and less effort. It becomes a reflex. But if you don't work at it, you can shipwreck your faith."

"That makes no sense to me," I said. "Isn't salvation a gift?"

"100 percent," Gaylord answered. "But even though it is completely ours, we don't immediately embrace it 100 percent. Our faith has to be worked out through patience and endurance and a lot of worship and prayer."

I thought of Gaylord and Sarah immediately falling to their knees in prayer when they saw the destruction of their home. It did appear to be a reflex. Their eyes were on God. They saw the ruin of their home through his eyes. Deep inside, I desired to be like them: totally at peace and totally confident in God's guidance and provision, no matter the circumstances.

"Explain it to me some more," I said.

"Think of it this way, Joe," Sarah said. "We belong to a God who is all-powerful, all-knowing, and ever-present. Furthermore, he loves us so much that he was willing to hand his own son over to something far worse than a tornado destroying a house. In fact, the cross was the most horrible thing that has ever happened to anyone in the history of the world. Yet he turned the cross into the greatest thing that ever happened: an eternal victory over death itself."

"I believe that."

"Don't you think he can do the same thing in our lives? Why would any of us ever be anxious about anything?"

I thought for a moment. "I don't know," I said.

"You see why we have work to do," she said. "It isn't just believing. It's knowing. We have to come to know who we are dealing with and what he has done and what he is capable of doing. We need to know him not just in our minds but in the depths of our hearts and our souls. And that is work."

I scanned the piles of rubble before us. A water heater lay on its side in front of me, sliced open and nearly cut in half. "When do I do this work?" I asked.

Gaylord took his wife's hand and spoke softly, reverently. "Every day," he said. "Every moment. Every breath."

Chapter 12

Cornelius

I wanted to leave that evening. God would not let me. Or more precisely, Reggie would not let me. He couldn't have stopped me, of course. But it was Saturday night, and he invited me to church the next day. What was I going to say? I had no place to go and no excuse. I would have liked to have told him the truth: I didn't want to stay because I didn't want to be looked at as a hero or, worse still, a solution to people's money problems. Instead, I accepted his invitation.

When I arrived at the church the next morning, I expected people to be curious about me, and they clearly were. The parishioners, about 100 in all, were polite enough not to stare when I sat down next to Gaylord and Sarah and their two adult children, Grace and Cornelius, but they were sneaking peeks. Some, I am sure, whispered to their neighbors that they saw me at the Norris place just after the tornado struck. I felt as though I were on stage, exactly the reason I had wanted to get out of town as quickly as I could. If there was one thing I was certain of, I deserved no credit for helping Gaylord and Sarah. I made no sacrifice. I had only given to them what had been given to me.

The congregation sang three songs, led by a pianist accompanied by a gray-haired woman playing an acoustic guitar. If the people had been focused on me when we came in, they were no longer. A spirit of reverence fell upon the congregation, like the dove descending on Jesus after His baptism. More than that, there was another spirit that I struggled to identify until it finally dawned on me. It was a spirit of unity. The people were not 100 individuals; they were one. This spirit drew me in, inviting me to join the worship, to be part of one body lifting hands in praise to God.

As we sang, a vision filled my mind. I was kneeling before the cross of Jesus with a multitude of people behind me, also on their knees in humble worship. I saw the nails in His wrists and feet, the crown of thorns on His head, and the drops of His blood dripping onto the ground. I heard His groans of pain as He pulled himself up to take a laborious breath. I witnessed the price He paid for me: not just for sinfully embracing the woman in Blacksburg when Janice was dying but for every self-centered and mean-spirited thought and action that rose from my heart – a darkness infinitely more destructive than the twister that destroyed the Norris' house. It was a darkness that swallows life itself. Yet in that moment, kneeling before Him, I knew peace. I knew joy. I knew I was loved.

Then all at once, the vision changed. I was no longer right in front of Jesus but in the last row of the great multitude. I could still see Jesus on the cross, but He was far away, a small figure like an airplane at 30,000 feet seen from the ground.

"Wait!" I cried out. "I don't want to be here. I want to be where I was. I want to be up front with Jesus, not just one of thousands upon thousands of people in the crowd. Why does everyone else get to be in front of me?"

Then I was ashamed. I understood. God didn't want me to worship my experience of Jesus. He wanted me to worship Jesus. And the only way to worship Jesus was to humble myself as He humbled himself – to take the lowest place. To find His peace and His joy in the last row, letting others go first.

I opened my eyes and, as if on cue, the congregation began to sing an old hymn I had heard as a child, except now the words caught fire in my heart because I grasped what they meant.

Tis the gift to be simple, 'tis the gift to be free,
'Tis the gift to come down where we ought to be,
And when we find ourselves in the place just right,
'Twill be in the valley of love and delight.
When true simplicity is gain'd,
To bow and to bend we will not be asham'd,
To turn, turn will be our delight,
Till by turning, turning we come round right.

I could not help myself, but fell on my knees, my eyes full of tears. "Lord, let me come down to where I ought to be," I prayed. "Let me know the valley of love and delight. Let me make my home in the last row and worship You forever."

I don't know what the congregation thought of a billionaire stranger collapsing in tears in their church, but Gaylord understood. When the hymn ended, he lifted me from my knees and gave me a long embrace: two men united as could never happen anywhere else but in the presence of God.

Sarah produced a handkerchief, and I wiped the tears from my face, as Reggie rose from the first row to preach. It was then that I saw Cornelius – or Neil, as I found out they called him for short – sitting at the far end of the pew with his arms crossed and a scowl on his face.

Reggie read two passages of scripture. The first was from Luke's gospel.

Now Jesus sat opposite the treasury and saw how the people put money into the treasury. And many who were rich put in much. Then one poor widow came and threw in two mites, which make a quadrans. So He called His disciples to Himself and said to them, "Assuredly, I say to you that this poor widow has put in more than all those who have given to the treasury; for they all put in out of their abundance, but she out of her poverty put in all that she had, her whole livelihood."

The second was from the Sermon on the Mount:

Take heed that you do not do your charitable deeds before men, to be seen by them. Otherwise, you have no reward from your Father in heaven. Therefore, when you do a charitable deed, do not sound a trumpet before you as the hypocrites do in the synagogues and in the streets, that they may have glory from men. Assuredly, I say to you, they have their reward. But when you do a charitable deed, do not let your left hand know what your right hand is doing, that your charitable deed may be in secret; and your Father who sees in secret will Himself reward you openly.

Then, after an opening prayer asking God to open our minds and write his word on our hearts, he began to preach.

"I want to preface my message today by telling you I decided to preach on these verses five days ago, before any of the events of this week happened. But as the Holy Spirit always does, He prepared this message in advance for me to give to you.

"In the first scripture, Jesus describes a woman who gave herself completely to God, even her last tiny bit of money – what she might have spent on food to keep herself alive for another day. She put her very life in God's hands. He would either provide for her or she would starve.

"I don't need to tell any of you that we have in our congregation a couple who have lived their lives as this widow did. On countless occasions, Gaylord and Sarah have given their last two mites to others, trusting that God would provide for them. He always has. And this week, when a tornado destroyed their home, He did it again. As with today's sermon, He planned it well in advance. We can only stand in awe at what He has done.

"The second scripture speaks to the man whom God chose to carry out his plan. God made him rich beyond asking or imagining at a time of great loss and sorrow. He didn't ask to be rich. He is puzzled by it, and he has been on a journey to find out what it means. Step by step, God is showing him. In the meantime, he blows no trumpets. He wants no glory for himself. His right hand doesn't know what his left hand is doing. If I hadn't invited him to church this morning, he would be well on his way to Colorado by now.

"What does this mean to us? It means God can be trusted. He is trustworthy. He has counted every hair on your head. Not a bird falls to the ground without Him knowing it. And He is on your side."

Reggie paused and scanned the congregation as if looking at each person individually. Finally, he spoke. His smooth bass voice seemed to contain both reassurance and a hint of challenge.

"He loves you enough to die for you," he said. "To die for you."

——-

Reggie and his wife Lucy invited me to lunch after the service at the parsonage a mile from the church, a tidy rambler that backed up to a creek. We were joined by the Norrises and their two children. I appreciated a home-cooked meal that didn't involve a microwave. While clearly thankful, Gaylord and Sarah did not over-express their gratitude to the point where it would have been awkward. They sensed I didn't want thanks for having done nothing but be an intermediary – a go-between if you will – between God and themselves.

As we chatted around their dining room table, I learned a bit about their life stories. Gaylord had a difficult childhood as the son of a roughneck who moved around in the oil fields of Texas and Oklahoma, always looking for work. His father was a hard-working, hard-drinking man who cheated frequently with bar flies in the sawdust-on-the-floor, shot-of-Jack-Daniels-with-a-beer-chaser honkytonks along the Red River. His mother was a beaten-down woman who put up with it because she had nowhere else to go. At least his father didn't physically hurt her and usually kept food on the table.

The last of four children, Gaylord effectively raised himself. When his oldest brother died after a "widow maker" line on an oil rig snapped and nearly decapitated him, he decided he wanted nothing to do with the oil fields. He focused on agriculture, spending as much time as he could on his maternal grandfather's farm. His grandmother introduced him to Jesus and taught him a deep love for the Bible.

"My grandmother walked as closely to the Lord as any person I have ever met," he said as he cut into a thick slice of ham. "She used to ask me, 'What is the point of saying you believe in God, if you act like He doesn't exist? '"

It was a good question, of course, and I wondered if I had already built a "God shelf" where I could store Him until I needed Him.

Gaylord inherited his grandparents' farm and never lived anywhere else. He had only joined one church in his life and married the daughter of one of Reggie's predecessors, the Rev. Maxwell Mills. He rarely ever missed a Sunday, and when the pastor was sick or had to be away, he took over the pulpit. Yet he never felt called to be a preacher or a pastor. God made him to be a farmer, and he was going to do what God made him to do.

For her part, Sarah could not remember a time when she hadn't known God intimately. She had no "God shelf." Jesus walked with her the way He walked with the two disciples on the road to Emmaus, except she recognized Him when her heart burned within her at the sound of his voice. She had no use for popular culture that says a woman can't be fulfilled in life unless she has a career. She believed her calling was to be a farmer's wife and a mother.

"When I was a teenager, the devil started to convince women that having a job was their identity and women who supported their husbands and raised their children were victims of oppression," she said. "I don't doubt some women are born to be plastic surgeons and lawyers, and there are lots of women who have to work outside the home to support themselves, but some women are born to be wives and mothers. It is a noble, God-breathed calling. I am saddened so many women have missed their calling and are living empty, miserable lives trying to climb a mountain they were never intended to climb."

As Gaylord and Sarah talked about their lives, I noticed Cornelius glumly pushing his food around his plate at the far end of the table, occasionally taking a bite. I guessed his age at 35, but at that moment, he had the demeanor of a surly boy. I decided to engage him.

"Neil, where do you live?" I asked.

He looked up from his plate with an expression that said, "Leave me alone."

"Oklahoma City," he replied, then looked back down at his food.

I wondered if this was exactly how he had been as a teenager and, due to some strange psychological machination, being with his parents had taken him back in time.

"What do you do for a living?" I asked.

"Lawyer."

I am not easily deterred by one-word answers. Otherwise, I would never have been able to have conversations with the Hokie football players as I treated their injuries. I found that if I kept at it, eventually they opened up. Many of them didn't have fathers in their lives, and, once they felt safe, they told me about their childhoods, their mothers, their girlfriends, and their hopes for the future, which usually centered on the fantasy of playing in the NFL.

"What kind of law do you practice?"

"First amendment."

"That's interesting," I said. "Who do you work for?"

"ACLU," he said, punctuating each letter as if firing bullets from a gun. I had no difficulty figuring out the target. I glanced at Gaylord and Sarah. They had no reaction. Maybe I should have let it drop at that point, but I didn't.

"What kinds of cases do you work on?"

"Separation of church and state," he answered, again punctuating each word. "Keeping religion out of schools. Out of the government."

Reggie decided to step in at this point and suggested everyone adjourn to the living room for coffee and dessert. Sarah seized the moment and quickly jumped up to collect the dishes. Grace gave an angry glance at her brother and then rose to help her mother. Cornelius rolled his eyes and stood up. I noticed that he favored his right side as he walked to the bathroom at the far end of the house. When he returned, I pulled him aside.

"Old injury?" I asked.

"Football."

"Does it hurt?"

"Every day."

"I was the trainer for the Virginia Tech football team for many years. Would you like me to see if I can do something to make it better?"

For the first time, Cornelius looked directly at me. His demeanor radically changed. "I thought you were some rich guy. Some billionaire. What were you doing at Virginia Tech? Did you know Michael Vick?"

"Before my time," I said. "It's a long story. Let me see what I can do to ease your pain."

"Sure," he said with a newfound respect. "I would like that."

———

Cornelius had an untreated case of spondylolysis, a small crack between vertebrae in the lower back, common among athletes. He told me the pain came and went over the years after he injured his knee in a football game in high school. The knee was fine, but his back still hurt at times, and I suspected he had repeatedly reinjured it.

I laid him across a picnic table in the backyard and was able to relieve some of the pain, but what he really needed was time off from playing basketball with his friends. As I stretched his back muscles, we talked, first about Virginia Tech football and then about his parents. The man who had given one-word responses at the dining room table now rattled on about his childhood. It didn't surprise me. I had seen it before.

"Football was my life when I was a kid, but my father had no interest in it," he said. "His interests were Jesus and farming, in that order. I was a farm kid, so I learned how to get up early and work hard, but it was never in my blood. I couldn't wait to go to college. I desperately wanted to get a football scholarship to the University of Oklahoma or Oklahoma State. I was good enough, too, until I got hurt."

"What happened?"

"It was in the state quarterfinals in Norman against the defending champions," he said. "It was pouring rain, and the field was sloppy. We were beating them in the third quarter. I was a linebacker and tackled their running back at the line of scrimmage. But a 280-pound tackle rolled on my leg and twisted it under the pile. I tore my ACL, and that was it for my football career. Colleges lost interest."

He was animated as though he were reliving the moment, and his whole body tensed up. I sensed there was more to the story than a football injury.

"So does this have something to do with your father?" I ventured.

His face flushed. "You're damn straight it does."

"Tell me about it."

"He wasn't there. He was going to come, but the creek overflowed its banks because of the rain, and some woman's house was flooding. He went to help her instead of coming to my game. I had no one with me when they carted me off the field and took me to the hospital."

"So he chose someone else over you?"

"You are damn straight. And that wasn't the first time or the last time."

I paused to give him a few moments to calm down. In the meantime, I did more stretching and massaging of his back than was actually needed.

"You and I had opposite childhoods," I finally said. "My father wanted me to be a football star the way he was in high school, but I had no athletic ability and didn't like the game. He ended up drinking himself to death, completely ignoring me in my teenage years."

"Are you angry at him?"

"In a way, yes. But mostly I feel sorry for a man whose identity was tied up in something he couldn't have and ended up destroying himself."

"My father's identity is tied up in Jesus," he sighed.

"Did he ever come to your games?"

Cornelius nodded. "He rarely missed one. And he took me to practice. But his heart wasn't in it. I think he wanted me to be a pastor."

"So you never felt his approval?"

"Not for what was important to me."

I had noticed that the Virginia Tech football players rarely talked to me about their mothers except to express glowing praise. On the other hand, the fathers – or lack of fathers – were Ground Zero for trauma and pain. I decided it was time to take a chance, as I had done with so many players when I drilled down into their past. Sometimes it worked. Sometimes they shut down.

"So you rebelled?" I asked.

"I suppose I did," he conceded.

"You purposely chose a career that would upset him? You became the opposite of what he wanted you to be?"

"I did," he said. "And I married a woman who would be the opposite of someone they hoped I would marry."

"Tell me about that."

"She was a nurse in a family planning center," he said. "Otherwise known as an abortion clinic."

"You really did stick the knife in," I said. "Is that why she didn't come down with you?"

"Oh no," he said. "We got divorced two years ago. It was ironic. We were fine until she couldn't get pregnant. We tried everything. Fertility treatments. IVF. Nothing worked. Every day she went to work to treat pregnant women who didn't want their babies, and she wanted a baby and couldn't get pregnant. It tore her apart. Eventually, it tore us apart."

"And how did your parents react to her?"

"They were who they are," he said. "They never said a negative word about her. They always welcomed her. I know they prayed for her. I think it bothered them a lot more that we got divorced than what she did for a living. They believed she would eventually see the evil and turn to the Lord."

"So you couldn't get under their skin no matter how much you rebelled?"

"I am sure I did, but they never let on."

We fell silent. I began to massage and stretch other parts of his body unrelated to his back pain. The inaudible voice I had heard on the road began softly speaking. Again, I wondered if I was conjuring it up or whether it truly was from God. It's one thing to take a turn on a road because God told you. It's quite another to believe God is telling you to speak words to another person. Yet the texture of the voice was comforting, reassuring, and conveyed a sense of certainty. I couldn't dismiss it as my own imagination.

"Neil," I said. "Most of us fall into the trap of looking to other people for things that only God can give us."

"I don't understand," he said.

"'We all have a need to be loved and approved unconditionally, and it's natural we look to our parents, especially our fathers, to fill that need. If we don't look to our parents, we look to our spouses or our friends. But no matter how good our parents are or how loving our spouse is or how caring our friends are, they are still flawed human beings. They cannot meet that need."

"But my father could have been at that game," he protested.

"He could have been," I said. "But even if he had been there, he would have fallen short at other times. And he probably did."

"Many times. Everyone says how great a man my father is and what a great example of a Christian he is, but I know better. He let me down."

"I am sure he would agree with you."

Cornelius shrugged his shoulders. "Who knows?"

The voice whispered again. I hesitated, then plunged forward. "There is only one who can love you the way you crave to be loved – the way you need to be loved," I said. "That is God. He is the only one who made you and knows you for who you really are. He is the only one who will love you perfectly. If you look elsewhere, you become bitter. A bitter root will grow inside of you."

Cornelius pondered what I had said as I massaged his shoulders. "Do you think I have a bitter root?"

"You turned your back on the God your father loves and serves with all his heart and embraced a career that stands in opposition to everything he holds dear."

"That is true," he said. "But what should I do?"

I waited for the voice to whisper again before I answered. "Forgive your father for falling short," I finally said. "Set yourself free from the bitter root that is poisoning your soul. Turn to God. Ask him to forgive you for putting expectations on your father that he cannot possibly meet. And then look to God for the love and approval you crave."

"I don't know if I can do that."

I nodded. The voice spoke to me again. "With God all things are possible," I said. "But it is you who need to decide."

Cornelius bowed his head and looked at the ground with a frown on his face. I sensed a battle going on, not in the physical realm but the spiritual: a fortress of pain nurtured over years suddenly under assault not by an earthly army but by heavenly arrows of pure light. The walls, seemingly a defense, were in fact a prison. His choice, faced by countless prisoners over the centuries, was simple: freedom or slavery, blessings or curses.

"Can you lead me?" he finally whispered, looking up at me.

I put my hand on his shoulder. "Are you willing to kneel?" I asked.

He nodded. Together we lowered ourselves into the dirt. He prayed the first real prayer of his life: a prayer to forgive and be forgiven that brought tears to both of our eyes. The walls of the fortress tumbled down. The light overshadowed him.

It dawned on me how strange it was that two devout and loving parents raised a boy to manhood, immersed in the Bible, church and service to God. Yet all they received in return was resentment. Then God gave a wandering widower in an RV the words to speak that brought a stubborn young man to his knees before his Creator and to the forgiveness that set him free.

"What do I do now?" he asked afterward, wiping the tears from his face.

I put my arm around him the way my father had never put his arm around me. "I have an idea," I said.

———

The following week, the American Civil Liberties Union in Oklahoma City had a vacancy in its law staff. Meanwhile, Marshall County, Oklahoma, welcomed a new law firm with one very wealthy client. Its mission was to provide legal services to poor Oklahomans free of charge, whatever their need. The only restriction was no divorce cases. The firm would pay for marital counseling if the clients couldn't afford it.

"That's pretty amazing," Cecelia said when I told her about the sudden change in Cornelius and how he asked his parents' forgiveness for how he had treated them. His father, in turn, asked forgiveness for the times he had failed him when he was a boy.

"It's not really," I said. "A lot of times, people are trapped in a bad relationship that could be easily fixed. Often, they are just too proud to admit they are wrong, but sometimes the inertia of a bad relationship just keeps pushing people along until something stops it. I think that was what happened with Cornelius."

"And you were the one who stopped it?"

"I just pointed out that he was looking to a flawed man – a good man but a flawed man – to give him something that only God can give: unconditional love and approval."

"That's pretty deep, Joe," Cecelia said. "Have you told Lara about this?"

"Not yet," I said. "But I will."

"I think she would like to hear about it."

"I would like to see her again," I said.

"You will," Cecelia said. "At the right time."

I smelled a conspiracy. Had Cecelia been in contact with Lara? Had they talked about me? Had Cecelia flown to Alabama to see her?

"Are you two plotting something?" I asked.

"Not at all," she said. "You just met her."

I'm not sure if I believed Cecelia. She was a thoroughly honest woman, but when it comes to love and romance, the rules can be bent, if not broken.

"I wouldn't put it past you," I said.

Cecelia ignored what I said and changed the subject. "What did Gaylord and Sarah say about the change in Cornelius?"

"They told me that these past few years had been deeply painful for them. In fact, it was hard for them to put into words how heartbreaking and soul-wrenching it was to see their son go astray and then express such anger and bitterness towards them. Yet they had confidence that God would straighten him out and bring him home. They fasted and prayed many times. They were upset when his marriage failed, and they still pray daily for his ex-wife. After all is said and done, they said that having their son back was worth much, much more than the price of a tornado destroying their home."

"So all things do work for good for those who love the Lord and are called according to his purpose?" Cecelia asked.

I thought for a moment. "That is certainly true if your son has an old football injury and God sends a billionaire physical therapist into your lives."

Cecelia laughed and then spoke in that mysterious voice she used when she sees something no one else can see.

"Perhaps you haven't seen anything yet, Joe," she said. "Perhaps you haven't seen anything?"

Chapter 13

The Dream

The dream came in vivid colors four days later.

Perhaps it was spurred by spending time with Gaylord and Sarah and observing the deep intimacy shared by a couple who had walked hand in hand with the Lord for decades. They were unique individuals, Gaylord a quiet soul while Sarah was a fireball of spunk and enthusiasm, but they complemented each other. At the deepest level where true love abides, they were united in their faith and obedience to Jesus.

"The German theologian Dietrich Bonhoeffer wrote that it is impossible for two people to have a real relationship apart from Jesus," Reggie told me when I asked him about Gaylord and Sarah. "They are living evidence of the truth of what he said. A couple can grow old and learn to tolerate each other without ever truly knowing what intimacy is. But the moment a couple bows down together before Jesus, He becomes the mediator in their marriage. And when Jesus joins two people together, there is a love the world can't comprehend."

Immediately, a fresh wave of grief washed over me as I missed Janice and desired to be conveyed back in time to when we were young and healthy. We could have built a marriage with Jesus as the mediator had we only known. Instead, we tried our best to love each other in our own strength. We succeeded far more than other couples we knew, but we still fell far short of Gaylord and Sarah.

I tried to bury my grief under hard work. I helped Cornelius lease office space in Kingston for his new practice and interview candidates to be his secretary. Later in the day, I met with Gaylord and Sarah and the builder on their property, which had been cleared, any salvageable furniture and household items put in storage. The county government was eager to help them expedite all the permits needed to start rebuilding as soon as possible.

Reggie and Lucy gave me a standing invitation to dinner that I accepted, but I also insisted on taking them out to dinner with the Norrises. There are no five-star restaurants in that part of Oklahoma, so we ended up at BJ's World's Best BBQ on the lake. The ribs were tasty, but "World's Best" might have been an exaggeration.

As always, grief arrived with its first cousin in tow: loneliness. When I turned off the light above the king-sized bed in the Tiffin, I was alone in the dark. I did not hear Janice's childlike breathing or feel the furnace-like heat that came off her body when she was asleep, forcing me to the far side of the bed until I couldn't stand not having my arm draped over her and snuggled close again. I desperately wanted to talk to her the way we did every night just before we drifted off, sharing things that we hadn't been able to during the day when we were working our jobs. I wished we could pray together the way Gaylord and Sarah prayed.

As I lay in bed In the dark, I also thought of Lara. I relived the emotions of our only kiss and longed for her. I wondered when she would join me on my journey. Or if she ever would. There was a deep fear in me that as real as our kiss had been for me, it hadn't been as real for her. Lara could never take away the grief – I would never stop mourning Janice – but she could take away the loneliness and let me know again the soft touch of a woman that even the strongest man needs, even if he does not admit it.

Of course, I questioned whether it was wrong to simultaneously mourn my late wife and long for another woman to fill the void left by her death. Did I need to complete my sentence in the purgatory of grief before I let my mind even consider what it would be like to love someone else? Would others conclude that I really didn't love Janice because I moved on with my life after our marriage covenant ended when, as the wedding vows proclaimed, "death did us part?"

I wanted to ask Reggie, but I was afraid of what the answer might be. So I went to sleep, holding a pillow instead of Janice. In my imagination, I kissed Lara in the park in Foley.

Then the dream came.

———

The forest bustled with birds, squirrels and other animals enjoying a perfect spring morning with sunlight glistening through the leaves of the maples, elms and giant oaks. Janice and I sat on a blanket in a glade next to a chattering brook. A gentle breeze rippled through the treetops full of springtime renewal of life and hope. Before us lay a picnic basket and a bottle of wine.

Janice leaned into me, resting her head on my shoulder. She was not the Janice of the last days when cancer and death relished their victory over her body. No, this was Janice more beautiful than I had ever seen her. Everything about her was perfect – her eyes bluer than I had remembered, her skin radiant and every curve of her body flowing together in harmony. She was Eve before the fall, what God envisioned when He created the first woman as the image of all that is feminine to complement and complete the man He had fashioned out of the dirt of the earth. It dawned on me how much money and effort women expend to recreate that image in themselves, and yet they fall short. No woman on earth could match the beauty I saw in Janice.

"Is this heaven?" I asked her.

"It is," she said.

"It is beautiful," I said. "You are beautiful."

"Everything in heaven is beautiful," she said. "Yet this is but one atom in a vast universe that never ends. You can only handle this tiny sliver because it is familiar to you on earth, but some day, you will see beauty no one can comprehend, not even the angels."

At once, we were transported to a mountain top in the middle of the Alps with seemingly endless snow-capped peaks before us in all directions. The air was cool and crisp but the sun warmed us. I pulled her closer to my body. In the distance, I saw two crystal blue lakes that met in a valley connected by a small river. I rejoiced that Janice and I were at that moment like those two lakes, a river of love flowing between us and connecting us.

"Anything that is lovely on earth is even more lovely here," she said. "And you have all eternity to enjoy it. Our joy is His joy, and His joy is our joy."

In the next moment we sat on a tropical beach with pure white sand stretching out for miles to a headland where waves crashed into the rocky shore, sending geysers into the air. Macaws and parrots flew overhead while a pair of humpback whales breached playfully just beyond the surfline. Calypso music drifted through the palm trees.

"We keep moving from one place to another," I said.

"Yes, and this is just the perfection of what is on earth but there is infinitely more," she said. "There are heavenly delights you cannot imagine, where living light bathes your soul in unspeakable joy and where choirs of angels sing heavenly music far more sublime than anything ever composed on earth. As the psalm says, 'Delight yourself in the Lord and he will give you the desires of your heart.'"

"So he enables us to enjoy whatever our heart desires?" I asked.

"Yes, but we don't know the desire of our hearts," she replied. "It is his Spirit that reveals our true desires to us."

I looked deeply into her eyes. She was so lovely. Joy and longing danced together within me. Yet I also felt a sharp guilt. "You are the desire of my heart," I said. "But I failed you when you were dying. I embraced another woman."

"I know about that," she said matter-of-factly as though we were discussing the previous day's weather. "God has forgiven you and so have I. The penalty of sin has been paid. What you did is cast into the sea as far as the east is from the west. Likewise, you will someday know how I failed you and you will forgive me."

"You never failed me," I said. "And even if you did, I love you and want you."

"And you will have me for all eternity and I will have you, but not as we had each other on earth. There is no marriage in heaven, except our marriage to Him. We are the bride and he is the bridegroom. It will be unimaginably greater than anything on earth."

"Can I stay here with you?"

"No," she said. "You are here so I can talk to you. But then you must go back."

"What must I do?"

"You have found God but you need to find yourself. And then you must marry Lara."

"But I am married to you."

"Our marriage covenant ended when the Lord brought me here," she said. "You must enter a new marriage covenant with Lara."

"But doesn't that bother you?"

"There is no jealousy here," she said. "There are no tears. No pain. No betrayal. No selfishness. No darkness."

"But I will feel guilty," I protested.

"There is no guilt here."

"But…" I started but I couldn't think how to finish the sentence.

"God has given her to you for a purpose," Janice said. "And he has given you to her for a purpose. Enjoy her and let her enjoy you. But remember there is a purpose. God never allows his children to endure suffering and loss without a purpose."

"I don't want to leave you."

I leaned over to kiss her. But at that moment the dream ended. I woke up to sunlight shining through the bedroom window of the Tiffin, bathing my face.

———

"That's quite a dream. What do you make of it?" Sarah asked.

We sat on chairs on the small dock overlooking Lake Texoma. I had pondered all day who, if anyone, I would tell about the dream. I decided it needed to be a woman since the dream was about two women. The choices were limited. Cecelia had never been married. Other than Lara, I didn't know any other woman well enough to share something so intimate. Then I thought of Sarah, who was not only someone who had decades of experience as a married woman but also someone who might understand a dream. I found her at the rented house alone as Gaylord had gone with Reggie to attend to some church matters.

"I am not sure," I answered. "Can you imagine telling Gaylord he can marry another woman if you die?"

"Of course. I have many times," she said with a smile. "But only if God sent her to him."

"How would he know?"

"Gaylord would know," she said. "The Lord would tell him."

"I am not as experienced as you or Gaylord in hearing his voice?"

Sarah laughed. "Hearing God is not a skill set one develops," she said. "A child can hear the voice of God just as well as a pastor. It just involves shutting up and listening. If he has something to tell you, he will tell you. Once in a while, he will use a bullhorn to get your attention, but most of the time you just have to have your ears open."

I shrugged my shoulders. "Most people would say I would be an idiot to marry someone, especially so quickly, and effectively give her half my money, $500 million."

"Do you care about $500 million?"

"Not really."

"That's why God gave it to you," she said. "Does Lara care about $500 million?"

"She doesn't seem to."

"That's why God sent her a man who is a billionaire."

I paused and watched the Boston Whalers and other fishing boats on the lake. The sun was beginning to go down, and one by one they were returning to shore. I wondered what the anglers would say if I took a poll. I figured "forget getting married and buy a private island" would be high on the list.

"Most people would say I am just rebounding and would regret it," I said. "You know, 'Marry in haste, regret at leisure.'"

"Are you rebounding?"

"I've been lonely."

"That's understandable," she said. "Men need women more than they realize. Widowers tend to get remarried much faster than widows."

"That doesn't mean it's a wise thing to do," I said. "Janice has only been gone a few months, and Lara and I have only spent a few days together. Most people would say it's reckless.'"

"Most people?" Sarah asked. "Who are most people? You've mentioned them three times."

"I guess the average person."

"Would the average person have done what you did when you won the lottery? Would they have bought an RV and hit the road?"

"Probably not."

"Then clearly you are not 'most people,'" she said. "You can't live your life by what you think other people would do. Peter and Andrew left their fishing boats to follow an itinerant rabbi from a remote town. So did James and John. Matthew left his lucrative tax business. Would most people do that?"

"I suppose not," I conceded. "I guess I'm not most people."

Sarah left to get us drinks and a snack from the house. The sun dipped below the horizon and dusk settled in. I realized I was no closer to an answer. Loneliness was a bad reason to get married. Yet in the dream Janice had told me to marry Lara. But was the dream real?

"There is one thing you haven't considered," Sarah said when she came back with two glasses of lemonade and a plate of macaroons.

"What is that?"

"You are not the only one with a choice."

I thought for a moment. "Of course, you are right."

"If God actually told you in a dream to marry Lara, He would certainly tell her too. And she doesn't sound like the kind of woman who would rush off and marry someone on a whim, even someone with a billion dollars."

"She wouldn't or she would be here already."

Sarah shook her head with a big smile. "Why don't you ask her?"

—--

I didn't ask Lara to marry me. If I were going to do that, I would do it face to face. I also didn't tell her about my dream: what could she possibly say to "my late wife came to me in a dream and told me to marry you?" Perhaps someday I would tell her. In the meantime, I merely asked her to come visit again. There was a pregnant pause while she considered her answer.

"I have to pray about it," she finally said.

I was relieved she hadn't said 'No' right away as she had every other time I asked. "How long will that take?"

"I have no idea," she said. "I will let you know."

"But if you love me…." I started and then stopped. I had tried that argument before. It didn't work. "This is all very confusing."

"God is not the author of confusion, Joe," she said. "Trust the Lord with all your heart and stop leaning on your own understanding. Or your own feelings."

"How can I not trust my feelings?" I retorted. "I love you and want to see you. I want to be with you. I am afraid you will never come."

"God is not the God of fear."

"You are spiritualizing everything," I protested. "Can't we just be a man and woman in love with each other?"

"That's what the world does, Joe," she said. "I did love and marriage the world's way.

I'm going to do it God's way this time."

—--

Cecelia and Sarah both said the same thing when I told them about my conversation with Lara.

"She's the real deal," Cecelia said. "You better not blow it."

"You won't find many women like that," Sarah said. "She's a keeper."

Lara was only a keeper if she allowed herself to be kept, I thought. In the meantime, I decided to continue on my journey. Cecelia was overseeing the finances for the diesel shop in Red Bay, and she could do the same for the new law firm. She also could authorize the payments for the new farmhouse.

Reggie, Gaylord, Sarah, and especially Cornelius were sad to see me go. They were thankful I had given them so much. I assured them that they had given me far more than I had given them.

I had not told Reggie about the dream. Yet just before I drove off, he leaned over the driver's side window and whispered to me the same words Janice had said to me.

"Joe, you have found God," he said. "Now you must find yourself."

Chapter 14

Gabe Remiel

When I left Texoma Lake and Kingston, I didn't need to pull over to the side of the road to contemplate whether I was hearing my own thoughts or the still small voice of the Holy Spirit. I knew where I was supposed to go. In fact, I sensed I was being intensely directed each mile and each turn. The word "driven" came to mind.

I traveled north past Oklahoma City to Wichita, where I spent the night in a Walmart parking lot, the Tiffin lined up with a half dozen other RVs. In the morning, before anyone else was awake, I continued northwest through Nebraska to the Dakotas, passing through the Rosebud Sioux reservation into the Badlands. I did not check into an RV park but turned onto a side road into the bleak, rocky, disturbingly beautiful landscape.

I was utterly alone in the shadow of multi-layered rock formations rising into a bright blue sky, guarding the land like medieval castles. There was no cell service. I fired up the Tiffin's generator to run the three rooftop air conditioners as the sun rose higher in the sky and the temperature soared. I dug my Bible out of the closet and turned to Genesis.

"In the beginning God created the heavens and the earth," it began, and then over 11 chapters recounted a fantastic story of how God created everything that is, including one creature made in His own image, endowed with free will. It told of fruit trees with the power of life and death; a garden where the first two people walked and talked with God until they declared their independence from Him; a holy cherubim with a flaming sword; evil angels who mated with women and produced a hybrid race of giants; men who lived hundreds of years before dying; a worldwide flood that destroyed all humans except one man and his family who survived in a massive ship loaded with animals; and a tower built by proud men seeking to reach the heavens and make a name for themselves.

When I was done, I knelt by the side of my bed and prayed. The voice spoke to me and challenged me: "You must decide if it is true. If it is not, nothing that follows can be true."

———

Two men came to me that day. I recognized the first man from a distance. He wore hiking gear, including a broad-brimmed hat to protect against the sun, and carried a walking stick. I had no doubt who he was and why he had come. Yet, I also knew I had to talk to him.

"You know this all began 75 million years ago," John Demas said when he approached me as I waited for him on an outcropping behind the Tiffin. "The buttes are made of sandstone, limestone, and other sedimentary rock. The Cheyenne and White rivers eroded them over millions of years to what you see today. A haunting landscape, isn't it?"

"Are you now a geology professor?" I asked.

John laughed. "Oh, that?" he said as he climbed up onto the outcropping. "It was a bit of dissembling, I admit. I suppose I tell people that so they take me seriously. I do like to be taken seriously."

"And you just happened to be wandering through South Dakota?"

"Oh, you know why I am here," he said. "Someone has to enlighten you. You are a smart man, but there are questions that need to be answered."

"And a fake philosophy professor from the University of Oklahoma is here to answer them?"

"Well, I admit the bit about being a professor was an exaggeration, of course, but the philosophy itself was quite on point. Did you know the native tribes include these buttes in their creation stories?"

"And you are going to tell me about them?"

"Only if you want," he said. "The ancient peoples believed the Great Spirit created a beautiful land for humans to live in, but when they forgot about him and began to kill each other, he destroyed all the plants and animals with a great flood. Then he swallowed the land with a massive earthquake and vomited these lifeless buttes as a reminder to them of their disobedience."

"A little bit like Genesis," I said. "Disobedience and a great flood."

"The creation myths of people around the world are often similar," he said. "People need a myth. Now we know better."

"We do?" I asked. "Isn't the fact that you are here proof that Genesis isn't a myth?"

John smiled knowingly. "When we talked last, I conceded there is a spiritual realm. Every civilization in the history of the world has recognized this. Almost all of them have a myth about some variety of Great Spirit and a creation story. But now we know Genesis is just one of those myths, and these buttes aren't 6,000 years old."

"I can't say I know that," I protested.

"Oh, please, Joe, I thought we covered this last time we talked," he said, reaching out to pat me on the back. "Back in medieval times, people believed in all these things. You know, demons and devils and the serpent in the Garden of Eden. Then fortunately, the Enlightenment and the scientific revolution came along and we realized it was all a myth. Do you really believe there are angels from heaven who mated with women and produced evil giants who roamed the earth? You might as well believe the Great Spirit vomited up these buttes."

I didn't answer him for a few moments, wondering if I should simply leave. But the still small voice clearly had directed me to this wilderness. Then John Demas, who was a spiritual being or perhaps a human controlled by a spiritual being, showed up. I might have just happened upon John at Lake Eufaula – although I suspect not – but this clearly was a divine appointment.

"So how should we read Genesis?" I asked.

"As I said, it is a myth, and myths can be useful. If you go into most churches in America, the preachers don't really worry about Genesis. Sure, the kids learn about Noah and the flood, but that's just a cute story. Otherwise, it's kind of an awkward subject that's best to avoid. If Genesis is a myth, then surely one could wonder if the story of Jesus is a myth."

"And you believe the story of Jesus is a myth?"

"Well, not exactly a myth," John replied. "We know that Jesus was a historical figure. Of course, most myths are rooted in something that actually happened. Crucifixion is a historical fact, but resurrection is not."

"So you are saying that if we can't trust Genesis to be actual history, we can't trust the resurrection either?"

"Lots of people try," he said. "But it's impossible. The Bible doesn't make sense unless you treat all of it as a kind of mythology."

"Or all of it as historical fact," I countered.

"You know in your heart, you can't do that, Joe. You are too smart a man to bury your disbelief," John replied. "There is too much science and too many questions. Haven't archeologists found pottery and cave paintings dating back 20,000 years? Where did the Neanderthals come from, and where did they go? Why does Genesis say plants were created before there was a sun and a moon? Don't plants need sunlight to live? I could go on all day."

I paused to consider his questions. Above our heads, a vulture circled. I wondered how any animal could survive in such a harsh place to provide a meal for the bird.

"I will answer you," I finally said. "But I need to pray about it first."

"Why would you need to do that?" John replied quickly. I sensed a hint of alarm in his voice.

"And read the Bible."

"But isn't the Bible the question at hand?" he retorted. "Whether it is a myth or not? Especially when you know in your heart that it is."

"I don't see how it could hurt," I said. "If this were a court of law, the jury would want to review the evidence."

John folded his arms. "That is fine," he said. "I will come back tomorrow and we will continue this discussion. I am sure you will conclude that angels, even if they exist, couldn't possibly mate with women and that no ship would ever be big enough to hold two of every animal in the world."

He abruptly walked away, eventually disappearing behind an outcropping.

—--

The second man came at night, just before midnight when the sky dazzled with a million stars. He didn't approach the Tiffin. Rather, I saw his outline in the bright moonlight, standing atop a small butte a hundred yards away. Flashlight in hand, I left the Tiffin and climbed a slope to the top of the butte. When I drew near, I realized the man was gazing through a telescope.

"It's a clear night," he said as I approached, as though he were expecting me and there was nothing unusual about a stranger approaching in the middle of the night. "Perfect for stargazing."

"I can see," I said.

He was a large man, but it was so dark I couldn't make out much else about him. It would have been rude to shine the flashlight in his face.

"I saw your RV," he said. "I figured you would come out to see what I was doing. Would you like to take a look?"

"I would like that," I said, holding out my hand. "Joe Mathers."

"Gabe Remiel," he shook my hand. "Have a look."

The telescope was extremely powerful. When I peered through it, I saw the planet Saturn and its rings in remarkable detail.

"That's mesmerizing."

"Saturn is 900 million miles away," he said. "The light you are seeing left the planet three and a half hours ago. And that's not even the end of our solar system. Let me show you another."

He adjusted the telescope to a different direction and gestured that I should look. I saw a bright diamond-shaped star.

"That's Proxima Centauri, the closest star to Earth," he said. "The light you are seeing left the star four and a half years ago."

"Remarkable," I replied.

He adjusted the telescope again and beckoned me to look. This time, I saw a circular pattern of stars with a bright center.

"That's the Andromeda Galaxy. It's the closest galaxy to ours. The light you are seeing left the galaxy 152,000 years ago. That's roughly the time evolutionary scientists say modern human beings began to dwell in Israel."

Up to that moment, I thought it was possible, although unlikely, that the man simply showed up with a telescope in the Badlands at the very spot where I had been directed to camp because it was a good place to stargaze. But as Cecelia had noted, there are no coincidences. The mention of Israel confirmed it.

"So do you know John Demas?" I asked.

"I do," he said. "I've known him for a very long time."

"And did he send you out here with a telescope to prove to me that the universe can't be 6,000 years old?"

"Not at all. John probably knows I'm here, but he didn't send me."

"Then what is the point of showing me a galaxy that was emitting light 152,000 years ago? Wouldn't that contradict Genesis and prove it is a myth?"

Gabe chuckled softly. "That is certainly what John would tell you."

"What would you say?" I asked.

"I would say that there are mysteries."

"Mysteries?"

"Take another look through the telescope," he said. "And tell me what you see."

I looked through the telescope again and saw the same galaxy. Nothing was different. "I see the galaxy."

"True. Yet astronomers will say that between us and that galaxy are vast quantities of matter that you can't see. This matter doesn't emit light. It doesn't produce radiation. You cannot detect it with your eyes. In fact, to date, no one has ever been able to detect it at all. Scientists have created elaborate experiments to detect it and have not succeeded. Yet it is there."

"How do they know it is there?"

"Because it has a gravitational pull. They call it dark matter because they can't explain it. Yet, they believe that 85 percent of the matter in the universe is dark matter, and its gravitational pull keeps the universe from flying apart."

"Why would the universe fly apart?"

"That's the interesting part," Gabe said. "You would think with all that gravitational pull, the universe would eventually collapse on itself. But it doesn't. In fact, it's expanding."

"So there is another force at work?"

"There you go. Astronomers call it dark energy. Einstein originally came up with the concept. But no one knows what it is except that it is pushing the universe ever outward. Dark energy is forcing the universe to expand while dark matter is resisting its expansion."

"So scientists are befuddled?"

"It makes no sense, does it? How can we live in a universe that is largely made up of matter we can't detect and ruled by forces we can't explain? And suppose some day we could detect dark matter or explain dark energy, don't you think there might be more mysteries we haven't even contemplated?"

"I imagine that is true."

"So perhaps the myth is not in Genesis but in ourselves," he said. "The myth is that we have the ability to grasp what is real and what is not."

"I can see that."

"But therein lies another mystery," Gabe said. "In fact, we do have the capacity to grasp the reality of the universe. Not scientifically, of course, and not with our minds. But spiritually. Because as Genesis says, we are spiritually designed to be in relationship with the One who created the universe."

I didn't respond as I struggled to understand his meaning.

"What does the Bible say?" he continued. "In Ecclesiastes,

Solomon, the wisest man who ever lived, declared God 'has put eternity in our hearts, except that no one can find out the work that God does from beginning to end.'"

"So we already have access to the reality of the universe?"

"Yes and no. The Apostle Paul wrote that now we see in a mirror dimly, but someday all things will be revealed to us."

I took a couple of moments to contemplate the paradox of being one with the Creator of the Universe and yet being so limited in our understanding.

"How does that explain Genesis?"

"A good question," Gabe answered. "John Demas wants you to focus on angels mating with humans and Noah's ark, but humans can't get past the third verse of the Bible without running into a scientific enigma – an impossibility more perplexing than a great flood."

"What is that?"

"'Then God said, 'Let there be light'; and there was light.'"

"And?"

"Einstein made a befuddling discovery," Gabe said. "Light is both a particle and a wave. That's seemingly impossible according to classical physics. The scientific world was amazed at the time, and many scientists had trouble agreeing with it. But then over the decades, everyone accepted it as the way light is."

A thought dropped into my mind. "And Jesus is the light of the world," I said. "He is both 100 percent human and 100 percent God. That's impossible."

"Exactly. You don't need angels mating with women to dismiss the Bible. Just start with that paradox. It required a new way of thinking about the universe and the advent of quantum physics. But even quantum physics can't explain it."

"Then some things are inexplicable, at least to our minds, but true."

"Exactly," Gabe said. "It's impossible that the universe is 6,000 years old while the light you are seeing in my telescope was emitted 152,000 years ago from a distant galaxy. But it's true."

"I don't think John would agree with that," I said.

"He wouldn't admit to it," Gabe said. "But that's not the important question."

"What is the important question?"

Gabe let a few seconds pass and then waved his hand across the sky with its millions, maybe trillions, of stars. "The important question is 'Does Joe Mathers think what's impossible is possible?'"

———

A half hour later, Gabe departed with his telescope and left me sitting atop the butte gazing at the stars, pondering the light that traveled over vast expanses of empty space to reach my retinas – except the space was filled with unseen matter that no one could explain. Then again, I couldn't explain Gabe Remiel or John Demas.

When I returned to the Tiffin, I had trouble sleeping as the conversations with the two men swirled in my mind. I spent an hour reading Genesis, and then just before dawn, I brewed some coffee and took a short hike. As the sun rose and the stars disappeared, I examined the nearby buttes. While they mostly consisted of horizontal layers of sedimentary rock, there were also veins of harder rock that cut vertically across the layers.

"Clastic dikes," a voice behind me said. I turned to see John. He had somehow come up behind me undetected. "They provide support for the buttes like tent poles. Some geologists believe that sedimentary rock flowed down from the surface into cracks, while others believe it rose from below. There is no consensus."

"Another mystery," I noted.

"Mysteries are simply things we haven't yet figured out," he said. "Everything can be explained."

"Dark matter?" I suggested.

John chuckled. "I see you have been talking to Gabe," he replied. "Two hundred years ago, scientists didn't even know bacteria and viruses existed. Our world is full of them, yet they were invisible to us. Now we can decipher their DNA."

"How about a virgin having a baby?"

"Impossible. Clearly a myth."

"With God, nothing is impossible."

"Something Gabe would say."

"It seems you've had this argument with him before."

John smiled in a way that seemed condescending to me. "A few times," he said. "A few times."

"I agree with Gabe," I replied. "And scripture."

"Then you are a fool," he replied sharply. "A fool indeed."

A gentle breeze drifted across the Badlands. I looked away, scanning the landscape, and briefly pondered how a place so desolate and seemingly lifeless could be so hauntingly breathtaking. John said it took the impersonal forces of nature 75 million years to create it, but I saw the hand of an artist who could take dirt and mud and miraculously create beauty – the same hand that could take the dust of the earth and create a man in his own image.

"In the beginning was the Word," I spoke to the landscape, quoting John's prologue. "And the Word was with God, and the Word was God. All things were made through Him, and without Him nothing was made that was made."

When I looked back, John Demas was gone.

———

"Science is a useful servant but a terrible god," Reggie said when I called him later that day from a diner ten miles away that had Wifi. "And John Demas wants you to make science your god. In the end, it is just another way of making ourselves our own god."

"So you've met him?"

"I've met John," he said. "He showed up at a Wednesday night Bible study at the church when we had a young couple who had just been baptized. He had all kinds of questions and was trying to get them to doubt their faith. As I recall, he said he graduated from Yale Divinity School but hadn't decided whether to be ordained as a pastor. He said he was seeking God while staying at his parents' lake house."

I laughed. "He told me he was a professor of philosophy at the University of Oklahoma," I said. "Did you ever meet Gabe

Remiel?"

"I haven't. It sounds like you are the current battleground in a cosmic debate that has been going on since the dawn of time."

Behind me, a waitress dropped a plate of scrambled eggs and sausage. Embarrassed, she apologized to her customer, an elderly man, profusely. He told her it was all right. He often dropped things. She went off to get a mop to clean up the mess.

"Do you think they are angels?" I asked when the commotion ended.

Reggie thought for a moment before answering. "It's possible," he said. "Angels are simply messengers. They can take human form. Paul wrote that people have unwittingly welcomed angels into their homes. He also warned that Satan masquerades as an angel of light."

"But why would God put me in that situation?"

"Why would the Holy Spirit drive Jesus into the wilderness to be tempted by Satan?" Reggie said. "At some point, we have to face the enemy of our souls head-to-head."

"And Genesis is the issue?"

"It is for you. The enemy attacks the place of weakness."

I paused to consider why Genesis would be my place of weakness. "I have decided Genesis is a historical fact," I said with more confidence than I felt.

"Then you have answered your question why God sent you into the Badlands," he said. "It won't be the last time you have to deal with John Demas or someone like him."

"That's not something to look forward to."

"No one does," he said. "But be aware of one thing."

"What is that?"

Reggie hesitated for a moment before answering. "It may not be so obvious next time," he said.

Chapter 15

Saints and Sinners

"Try Saints and Sinners, darling," the middle-aged woman with green hair and tattoos running up her arms said as she ran my credit card at a truck stop on Route 217. "They have an RV park."

"Saints and Sinners?"

"It's just down the road, sweetie, you can't miss it."

I thanked her and a minute later fired up the Tiffin, hoping she was right. I had passed a number of RV parks on the highway, but either they couldn't handle a 45-foot rig or they didn't have the 50-amp hookups required to run everything on the bus, including the air conditioners. After three days in the Badlands, I also needed to recharge the house batteries, and 30 amps would not do that.

Down the road, there was no sign saying "Saints and Sinners." I found out later that it was the locals' description of two large buildings on either side of the highway: one was the Revival Christian Church and the other the Firebird Resort and Casino. Hence, the saints on one side and the sinners on the other. The sinners had built a luxurious RV park specifically designed for large, expensive motor coaches owned by their target clientele, people who could afford to gamble and lose a lot of money.

I had only been in a casino once in my life, and then only briefly when I attended an old friend's wedding in Las Vegas. I didn't have a moral problem with gambling. It just never interested me. Besides, it seemed fruitless. You are wagering against a mathematical equation that assures the more you play, the more likely you are to lose. Obviously, no one builds big, expensive casinos to give you money. The irony, of course, was that state-sponsored gambling was the reason I was on the road in an RV rather than stretching and massaging football players. The winner of the largest Powerball lottery in history didn't gamble and had never bought a lottery ticket.

While I hooked up the Tiffin, the Saturday night crowds descended on the casino, and its parking lot filled up. While I had no intention of placing any bets, I found myself strangely curious to look inside. I didn't feel driven by the Holy Spirit, as I had when I had camped in the Badlands. In fact, I was surprised I had any interest at all. I could have easily camped for the night and hit the road in the morning on my journey westward. Instead, I crossed the parking lot and passed under the enormous mythical bird in flight over the entrance, lit up not by fire but by neon lights.

A man in a well-tailored suit immediately greeted me when I came through the revolving door into the lobby.

"Mr. Mathers," he said, offering his hand. "I'm Dan Wilson, the general manager of the resort. It is great to have you with us."

"Hi," I replied, instinctively shaking his hand. "How did you know my name?"

"The manager of the RV park let us know you had checked in," he said. "We are delighted to have you with us."

Of course, an RV park owned by a casino would do an internet search on anyone checking in. My Powerball win would have popped right up. The clerk quickly passed the word up the line that a billionaire was on the premises. I made a tactical mistake by registering in my real name. Then again, I'm sure they would check the license plate numbers on the Tiffin and the Jeep.

"I'm just having a look around," I said. "I'm not a gambler."

If Dan Wilson was disappointed, his face didn't show it. It struck me he had heard that line before from people who later cheered on a pair of dice as they tumbled across a craps table.

"I will give you a tour if you would like," he offered.

I agreed, and we soon were weaving through hundreds of slot machines, each with flashing lights and exotic themes. Most of the gamblers were older people, many of whom seemed mesmerized by the spinning symbols in front of them. No one was smiling or talking; all their concentration was on the screens. No sooner had the symbols stopped than the gamblers pushed a button and they started spinning again. It was hard to figure out if they were winning or losing on each spin.

"You get a lot of senior citizens here?" I asked.

"We send buses to retirement communities," Dan said. "It gives them something to do."

I pondered the entertainment value of betting with a computer programmed to take your money but didn't say anything. The zombie-like expressions on the faces disturbed me. I resisted the urge to grab the old woman nearest to me, shake her out of her trance, and tell her to go home before she blew away her monthly Social Security check.

Dan chatted me up as we passed the blackjack tables, the craps tables, and the roulette wheels, all rapidly filling up with the Saturday night crowd. Attractive waitresses in revealing outfits carried trays of drinks to the tables, while stern pit bosses behind the croupiers and dealers watched the action. A noisy crowd of young men surrounded one of the craps tables, chugging beer, ogling the waitresses, and yelling at the dice. It was an intoxicating fantasy world with no clocks or sense of time, divorced from sunlight, wind, or anything natural.

Eventually, we came to a side room that was roped off and guarded by a large man who looked like he might have been an NFL lineman. Seeing Dan, he quickly unhooked the rope and we entered the room, where there were a half dozen tables with gamblers – almost all men – hunched over stacks of chips on green felt. I immediately noticed a different atmosphere, far more serious and, as strange as it seemed, cerebral.

"This is where the higher-end games are," Dan said. "We have two baccarat tables, two blackjack tables, and two poker tables."

"What are the stakes?"

"Buy-in for Texas Hold'em is $5,000," he answered. "I can get you a seat at the table if you are interested."

I shrugged my shoulders and laughed. "I don't even know what Texas Hold'em is."

"We can get one of our dealers to teach you," he said hopefully.

I glanced at a nearby table where eight stone-faced men locked their gaze on a dealer turning cards over on the table. Three of them were wearing sunglasses even though we were indoors.

"It seems pretty intense," I said. Then I thought of something. "Do you happen to know a man named Will Skye?"

"Everyone knows Will Skye," he said. "One of the best Texas Hold'em players in the world. Then he simply disappeared. They say he became a musician of some kind. I guess the pressure got to him."

"Or something else," I mused. "I think I've seen enough. I appreciate your giving me the tour."

"Would you like to have dinner in our restaurant? Of course, we would 'comp' it."

"Comp it?"

Dan looked at me quizzically. "You know, complementary."

"Ah," I said, wondering why a billionaire would need a free dinner. I thought of the microwave pizza in my freezer. While a dinner made by an actual chef would have been nice, I had had enough of the casino. On one level, the atmosphere was infatuating, but I sensed it was unhealthy. Something about it seemed to war against my soul. "I appreciate it, but I have dinner ready for me back at the RV park."

Dan continued to chat with me as though we were old friends as we walked back through the main casino floor to the entrance. More and more people flooded in, and there were people waiting for seats at the blackjack tables. When we reached the revolving doors, he handed me an envelope.

"Just a present from the casino in case you are looking to kill some time later tonight," he said. I thanked him and put it in my pocket, then we shook hands and I left.

I opened the envelope when I got back to the Tiffin. Inside were two $500 chips imprinted with the casino's firebird logo.

I woke up early Sunday morning. The casino parking lot had emptied out almost completely, while across the street, Revival Christian Church's parking lot was filling up. Since I had been among the sinners the night before, I decided to hang out with the saints.

As I walked across the casino parking lot, I came upon a lone blue sedan parked under an elm. The driver's side window was open, and I saw a red-headed young man about 30 years old with his head in his hands, leaning forward against the steering wheel. He was crying.

When he saw me, he immediately sat up straight and wiped away his tears. "Mister, would you like to buy a watch?" he asked, sniffling as he spoke.

"Let me take a look at it," I answered and drew near to him. Still seated in his car, he showed me a beautifully crafted gold watch.

"It's a Rolex Bubble Back," he said. "My granddad bought it in Europe when he was a soldier in World War II. It's worth $4,000, but I'll give it to you for $1,000."

"Why would you sell your grandfather's watch?"

"I need the money," he said desperately. "I'm broke."

"Does that have something to do with where we are?"

The floodgates opened. Between sobs, he told me he had been up all night playing blackjack. At first, he did well playing for $10 a hand, but once he had a pile of chips in front of him, he upped his bets to $50 a hand. Then his luck changed, and soon all his chips were gone. He went to an ATM at a nearby convenience store and maxed out his credit card to get cash. That lasted until 6 a.m. when he doubled down on a hand and the dealer pulled a 21 that cleaned him out.

"I need to win the money back," he said. "My wife said she would divorce me and take the kids with her if I went back to the casino again. She took them to see her parents for a week. I couldn't help myself."

"Sounds like you are addicted to it."

"I don't know, man," he said. "Can you please buy the watch?"

It dawned on me to do something I hadn't done before, something I had seen Gaylord and Sarah do when the tornado destroyed their home: pray on the go. Not just to pray when I was alone at home or when I turned the lights out before falling to sleep. No, to pray at the moment. The man waited expectantly while I closed my eyes and asked God to tell me what I should do. Immediately, I knew.

"I will make you a deal," I said. "I have two $500 chips in my pocket. If you go to church with me, I will give them to you afterwards. You can keep your grandfather's watch."

"Go to church?"

"Yes, across the street. Right now."

The man hesitated. "I don't know if I want to face God right now."

"Do you think he will condemn you?"

"That's what I've been told all my life."

"At the church you grew up in, did you ever hear Jesus called the Condemner?"

"No."

"What is he called then?"

"Our church was called The Church of the Redeemer."

"Then why don't we go find out if he really is the Redeemer?"

The man opened his car door. "If you promise to give me the two chips."

I smiled and nodded. "I promise."

————

We arrived in the atrium of Revival Christian Church ten minutes before the service. The church had a coffee station near the entrance where I ordered a French Roast and the young man, whose name was Kiff Bellingham, a latte. He told me he had been married six years and had two daughters aged four and two. His marriage had been going well until a group of men from his softball team introduced him to the casino. He was immediately hooked and sometimes slipped out at night after his wife had gone to bed to gamble. The loss of sleep had begun to affect his job as an accountant, and he was afraid he was going to be fired. Then there was the lost money: he had secretly raided the account they had set aside for a down payment for a house, and it was gone.

"It's an evil place," he said, pointing at the casino. "It pulls me in like a magnet. I love my wife and my kids, but the blackjack table owns me."

"Then perhaps you need a change of ownership," I said as we entered the sanctuary, a large arena with stadium seating and a stage backed by massive video screens.

The church was almost completely full with what I estimated to be two thousand people. An usher immediately guided us to a section near the front that was roped off. By the look on the man's face, I realized someone had recognized me. Apparently, saints and sinners both had their eyes open for billionaires. In the back of my mind, I recalled there was a Bible verse about that, but I couldn't recall what it was. Soon, a well-dressed couple sat down next to us. The man introduced himself and said he was the congressman from that district. It was obvious someone had told him about me. He had no interest in Kiff Bellingham.

A group of musicians came on stage, and the service started with upbeat music accompanied by a kaleidoscope of video effects on the screens behind them. In the middle of the first song, which repeated the same lyric "You are love" at least a dozen times, the guitars and keyboard fell silent, and a saxophonist delivered a lively solo. Behind us, much of the congregation had its hands in the air and was attempting to sing along, although the amplified instruments on stage drowned out their voices.

"This isn't like the church my parents took me to," Kiff whispered when the song ended.

"It's new to me too," I said. I couldn't think of how it could be more different than the quiet reverence of the small churches led by Reggie and the Senator.

After three songs, the music ended, and the pastor came on stage to preach. He was a man about my age in his late 30s or early 40s with prematurely graying hair wearing blue jeans and a button-down red shirt. He spoke for about 20 minutes, a sermon about God providing for those who trust Him just as He clothes the flowers of the field and feeds the birds of the air. At the end, he talked about money.

"You may invest your money in an IRA," he said. "But God wants you to invest in a spiritual IRA. The more you invest in what we are doing at Revival Christian Church, the more God will give you back."

I glanced over at Kiff. He had a perplexed expression on his face, and I didn't blame him. What would God give back? Spiritual blessings? Money? What was the pastor's meaning?

The musicians returned to the stage and began to play another lively praise song while the ushers prepared to take the offering. I prayed again for guidance. Then I dug the two $500 chips out of my pocket and offered them to Kiff. He stared at the chips, the firebird logo seemingly looking up at him, taunting him. The congressman's jaw dropped, and I sensed he wanted the chips himself.

Kiff took the chips. He hesitated for a moment and then deposited them in the offering plate held out by one of the ushers.

He looked up at me, tears again forming in his eyes. "I need to be set free," he said.

—--

After the final "Amen", the congregation began to file out. The usher who had directed us to our seats approached me and said the pastor would like to greet me personally. He told Kiff that he could have a cup of coffee and wait for me in the atrium. Apparently, the pastor didn't want to meet him, just me. I told Kiff not to leave but that I would find him. We had things to talk about.

Dr. Brantley Clay had a corner office with a view of the casino across the street. He welcomed me with a hearty handshake and directed me to a sitting area across from his desk. An assistant brought a tray with two cups of coffee and cream and sugar. A framed diploma from Dallas Theological Seminary hung on the wall.

"I am so sorry to hear about the loss of your wife," he said. "What brings you to our church today?"

"A strange thing happened," I said. "The day Janice died, I won the largest Powerball jackpot in history. That made me an instant billionaire. Not everyone knows what to do with a billion dollars, and I didn't. So I bought a motor coach and started a journey across the country. Today, I'm here."

"I heard about that," he said with a smile. "Have you figured out what you are going to do with it?"

"Not exactly. But I have met some interesting people. One in particular."

"Who is that?"

"Jesus."

It would seem unusual for the mention of Jesus to create an awkward moment in a pastor's office, but there it was. Dr. Brantley Clay, D.Div., a man I sensed was rarely at a loss for words, seemed momentarily off balance. He recovered quickly.

"That's wonderful," he said. "Everything we do is about Jesus."

"So you know Him then?" I quipped. We both laughed. The man had a diploma from Dallas Theological Seminary on his wall.

We took a sip of our coffee, and then he spoke in a quiet, soothing pastoral voice:

"What can we do to help you?"

I resisted the temptation to ask what a man who is a child of the Creator of the universe and has a billion dollars might need. Instead, I pointed at the degree on the wall. "I see you went to Dallas Theological Seminary," I said. "Do you know Brian

Cooper?"

Dr. Clay raised his eyebrows. "Brian Cooper? He was a classmate of mine. A brilliant guy. I don't know what happened to him. We all thought he would be leading a big church by now."

"He's pastoring a small country church in southwestern Virginia."

"Wow, that's certainly not where I thought he would end up."

"He didn't either," I said. "But the Lord sent him there."

Dr. Clay pondered this as we both sipped our coffee. Then he sighed deeply. "Mr. Mathers," he said. "I will be candid with you. Our church looks like it's doing well, but it's not. We fill the place up on Sunday, but the money is just not coming in. We are running a deficit of $30,000 a month, and it's getting worse. We really need some help."

"It must be hard to pastor a church this big."

"To be honest, it's brutal," he said. "There are so many balls in the air and so many expenses. I have trouble sleeping some nights."

"I can imagine," I said, barely restraining myself from reminding him of the sermon he had just preached to his congregation about the flowers of the field and the birds of the air. "So it must have seemed to be good fortune when a billionaire wandered into your church this morning?"

"I have to concede that word got around that you were at the RV park," he said. "I was glad to hear you came to worship this morning."

"Dan Wilson told you?"

Dr. Clay grinned. "You got me," he said. "Dan's in my golf

group."

Most people I know would describe me as a calm man who avoids confrontation and especially doesn't like to upset other people. However, something happened to me at that moment. I was angry. I had not gotten upset with John Demas when he had lied to me and tried to confuse me with his sophistry. Yet for some inexplicable reason, Dr. Clay filled me with ire bordering on rage.

"Let me get this straight," I said. "When I walked into the casino last night, Dan Wilson immediately met me because I am a billionaire. When I walked into your church today, the usher took me to a special roped-off section because I'm a billionaire. So what is the difference between a casino and a church?"

Dr. Clay hadn't seen this coming. He shrugged his shoulders with a startled expression and didn't respond. I continued. "I came in today with a young man in desperate need of God, a man caught in the evil vortex of a casino that you can see from your office window. It is destroying his family and his life. Yet not a soul paid attention to him. You invited me to your office, but you left the man who really needs pastoring drinking coffee by himself in the lobby."

"Well, I...."

"I'm not finished," I said. "How many people come out of that casino on Sunday morning, having spent the night losing the mortgage money, and stumble across the parking lot into this church? You see it every week, don't you? What do you do with these people? They don't even have two mites left to put in the collection plate."

"We welcome everyone," Dr. Clay protested feebly.

"You treat this church like any other business. You are the

CEO, and you want to make a profit. But you don't work for shareholders. You work for a King. And He doesn't care about how much money you get in the collection plate. He cares about that bleary-eyed guy coming out of the casino with a hangover and no money."

Dr. Clay glanced at the door, no doubt wondering how to get me to leave. "I don't know what to say."

I was still not done. "Do you know what your classmate Brian Cooper is doing today? He's probably in a hospital, pastoring a gas station attendant or factory worker who overdosed on OxyContin last night. Or taking food to a teenage mother whose boyfriend is in prison. Why aren't you doing that? Why don't you go out into that parking lot on Sunday morning and invite people to church?"

"Well, I have to get ready to preach. I'm the pastor."

I wound up to deliver the final blow. "You have forgotten who you work for, Dr. Clay," I said with a raised voice.

I had had my say. Neither of us spoke for a few moments. Dr. Clay sipped his coffee slowly and stared out the window in the direction of the casino. It was almost 11 o'clock, and the casino parking lot was beginning to fill up as the church parking lot emptied. Finally, he spoke, not with his soothing pastoral voice but as a normal person one might meet on the streets or at the grocery store.

"He sent you, didn't he?"

"He?"

"God," he said. "I thought he might have sent you to solve our financial problems. But that wasn't it. He sent you to remind me why I went to seminary in the first place. Day by day, I've gotten more and more wrapped up in building a career, and that meant building a bigger and fancier church. I lost my first love."

"He seems to be sending me to lots of places these days. And I'm pretty sure what I just told you didn't come from me."

"What do I do now?:

"There is a young man in your lobby who just put two $500 chips in your collection plate and badly needs pastoring," I said. "Go find him."

———-

I figured Will Skye would come, and I was right. I had to wait until evening to call him since he was playing at the Frog Pond in the afternoon, but he instantly agreed. I arranged for a private jet to meet him at Foley Municipal Airport at dawn, and he arrived by mid-morning.

Dr. Clay met us at a local diner for lunch. "I spent most of the afternoon with Kiff," he said after we ordered our food. "He is a mess, but the Holy Spirit touched him during the service. And you are right, we had two $500 chips in the collection plate. That's the first time that's ever happened."

"Thank you for doing that," I said.

"Thank you for calling me out," he replied. "It was the most alive I have felt in years. I have spent years counseling people because it is part of my job. Yesterday I sensed the power of the Holy Spirit working through me. It was like I was a young pastor again."

"You never know with addicts," Will interjected. " Gambling addiction is especially tough to beat. Some say it's worse than opioid addiction."

"I think he's going to be fine. I believe God truly did set him free," Dr. Clay said. "No thanks to my sermon."

The waitress brought our drinks and an appetizer of Buffalo wings. A couple recognized the pastor and stopped by to say hello. They were part of his congregation, but I could tell he was struggling to remember their names. I wondered what it was like to be a celebrity in town with 2,000 people who look to you as their spiritual leader: people who might have been sitting 20 feet in front of you on Sunday buttonhole you, yet you don't know their names, much less anything about them. Like a good politician, Dr. Clay engaged them graciously, and they left happy with the encounter.

When the main course arrived, we talked about the plans for the future. Revival Christian Fellowship would make helping gambling addicts a major focus of its ministries. Will Skye, who arguably knew more about gamblers and their psychology than anyone on the planet, would advise Dr. Clay in establishing a new program. I would fund the hiring of two new pastors trained in addiction recovery. A team of volunteers would patrol the parking lot on weekend mornings looking for broken gamblers. Dr. Clay promised he would join them before services.

"Dan Wilson's not going to like that," he mused. "He may never play golf again with me."

"Maybe it will get him thinking about how his line of work affects families," Will said.

"He's especially not going to like the sign," I added.

The sign was my idea. At 80 feet tall, it would be higher than the Firebird Resort and Casino sign at the entrance to its parking lot. It would feature a dove perched on top that would be larger than the huge firebird atop the casino sign. People visiting the casino certainly would see it, but it would be especially visible to anyone coming out of the front entrance. In bold letters that lit up at night, the sign would say:

"Lost everything? God Gives You Grace. Inquire Here."

———-

"You went into the senior pastor's office after a Sunday service and told him he wasn't doing his job?" Lara asked incredulously. It was the first time in two days I had talked to her. She heard that Will Skye had flown out to be with me and wanted to know what was going on. At the sound of her voice, my heart ached to see her.

"I was invited," I said. "I told him he had forgotten who he worked for."

"And he listened to you?"

"He listened to God," I said. "It wasn't me."

"What about the young man, Biff?"

"Kiff," I corrected her. "I am going to help him out. His marriage is hanging by a thread."

"Aren't you worried about enabling him?"

"It's a chance I'll take," I said. "I think God gave him amazing grace. I don't think he will go back into that casino again."

"What did he say happened to him?"

"He told me he grew up in a legalistic church where God was depicted as a stern taskmaster and judge," I said. "But during the church service yesterday, he felt God reach down and embrace him, not condemning him but loving him. He actually could feel the arms of Jesus holding him. His despair evaporated, replaced by a deep peace. And most importantly, the prison doors flew open, and he was set free from his addiction."

Lara didn't say anything for a few moments. I hoped she would announce that she was ready to come be with me – that whatever she was waiting to be changed in me had happened. When she arrived, I could ask her to marry me, just as Janice had told me to do in the dream.

"Joe, you are on an incredible journey," she finally said. "These things aren't happening by accident."

"I know," I said. "It would be nice if you were with me."

"I would love to be," she said. "But I can't. It's not time."

"Will it ever be time?"

There was silence on the line. She was struggling with the question. "That's not for me to decide," she finally said.

When we hung up, I fell on my knees at the edge of my bed and prayed. God did not warn me what was about to happen next.

Chapter 16

Bayou Thunder

Darkness came in one of the most beautiful places in the world. Soul sucking darkness. "All is vanity" darkness. Condemning darkness. Utter darkness.

After two days staying in the casino RV park, I left Dr. Clay and Will Skye to work on the new recovery program for gambling addicts and drove west on Interstate 90 for eight hours to Cody, Wyoming, at the border of Yellowstone National Park. The town, which advertises itself as the World Capital of Rodeo, overflowed with visitors for its annual Cody Stampede, the biggest rodeo of the year. When I pulled into an RV park just outside of town, the clerk said there was a space open for the Tiffin in the otherwise packed campground. Someone canceled just before I arrived. I was not surprised. There are no coincidences.

I had never been to a rodeo until a second "coincidence" landed me a scarce ticket to the next day's Xtreme Bulls event at the town's rodeo arena. The owner of the RV park came into the office as I was registering. He asked the clerk if he would like his tickets to the event because his son's Little League team had unexpectedly qualified for the state championships, and he had to drive him to Cheyenne for the first round.

"No one saw that coming," he said. "The team isn't very good, but somehow they managed to win their last two games and take their division. I don't know what got into those boys. They played way over their heads."

The clerk had other plans for the following day, so the owner offered the tickets to me free of charge. I took them but insisted on paying. After all, I was a billionaire.

In the morning, I played tourist, wandering the streets of Cody decorated with countless flags for the Fourth of July. I basked in the mythology of the American West at the Buffalo Bill Museum, which celebrated the life of William Cody, one of the town's founders. In the afternoon, I toured the Buffalo Bill Dam just west of town on the Shoshone River, the largest dam in the world when completed in 1910.

Late in the afternoon, I embraced the cowboy culture and bought a Cattleman hat at a local haberdashery. They say a real cowboy can tell a dimestore cowboy by the way he wears his hat. I am sure everyone in town knew I put the "dime" in "dimestore." I didn't care. A lot of little boys dream of being a cowboy, and I was once a little boy. I liked the feeling of being a true westerner, even if it was an illusion.

When I took my seat in the grandstand overlooking Cody's rodeo arena, however, it didn't take long to figure out that insanity also wears a cowboy hat. From the program handed out at the entrance, I learned that Xtreme Bulls is the top rung of professional bull riding. The best cowboys in the country climb atop 2,000-pound bulls s in a narrow, fenced-in area called the chute where the animal is immobilized. holding on with one hand to a "bull rope" looped around the animal's torso.

As soon as the cowboy is ready, he nods. The gate swings open and the bull launches itself into the arena, bucking wildling while spinning right or left, sometimes changing directions in an instant. If the cowboy can stay on the bull for eight seconds, he gets a judge's score for the quality of the ride and might get a paycheck depending on how the other cowboys fare. If he gets bucked off, he doesn't get paid.

Even if many of the cowboys didn't make any money, the local doctors clearly did. The sheer violence of a man attempting to ride a bull was mesmerizing. A bull named "Killer Kong" whipsawed the first contestant and tossed him into the dirt like a rag doll, then tried to gore him. The man scrambled away while two men dressed up as clowns, called bullfighters, distracted the animal. The second contestant wasn't as fortunate. A bull named "Big Daddy" threw him off and then stepped on his foot. The bullfighters helped the man hobble on one foot out of the arena. I suspected the other foot had multiple broken bones from the weight of the animal.

On and on it went. Some cowboys managed to last eight seconds, and the crowd roared its approval. Even then, they had to find a way to get off the animal without getting stepped on or gored. It was not surprising that a local chiropractor was the lead sponsor of the event with a full-page advertisement on the back of the program.

"This is nuts!" I said to a large man seated next to me. "Whoever thought of trying to ride a bull?"

"It's part of the culture," the man said. "They start riding sheep when they are little boys and then eventually graduate to bigger animals. Finally, they start riding full-grown bulls."

I immediately recognized the voice of Gabe Remiel. I had not been able to see him in the dark when I gazed at the universe through his telescope in the Badlands. Now I saw that he was not just a large man but one powerfully built, with a square jaw and chiseled muscles. He was wearing a cowboy hat, blue jeans with a large Ford F-150 belt buckle, and boots. He fit in well in Cody,

Wyoming. Nobody would call him a dimestore cowboy.

"Are you an angel?" I asked.

"Angel is simply a job description for a messenger," he said. "So yes, I'm a messenger."

"From whom?"

"From the one who loves you."

I looked Gabe in the eye and grappled with the reality that he truly was a heavenly being. I had abandoned the idea that I was randomly wandering the country in an RV when the tornado destroyed Gaylord and Sarah's farmhouse. God had taken away Janice, given me a billion dollars, and had directed my path. Now he had sent an angel in human form to give me a message. I reached out and touched Gabe's arm. My hand didn't pass through his skin. He certainly seemed to be flesh and blood. I should have been amazed or alarmed, but I noticed in the Badlands that Gabe had an aura about him. I recalled the Hebrew word for it used by Jewish friends in Blacksburg: "Shalom."

"What message?" I asked.

Gabe nodded towards the chute below, where a young cowboy climbed atop a bull.

"That cowboy is attempting to ride 'Bayou Thunder,' the No. 1 bull in the world," he said. "Forty cowboys have tried to ride him. None has succeeded. Three had to go to the hospital. He gored one so badly that he spent a week in intensive care. Most of the time, he will spin clockwise at first, then switch to counterclockwise. But sometimes he reverses it. When he bucks, his hooves will be five feet in the air. And if he throws a cowboy off, he comes after him with his horns. He is a terrifying animal, and that young cowboy shouldn't be on him. But these cowboys have no fear. It takes a special kind of man to ride bulls."

"The kind found in insane asylums," I suggested.

Gabe smiled and shook his head. "Fear is a strange thing," he said. "A man who can climb on a 2,000-pound beast might be frightened to death of telling a woman he loves her. It's one of the things that makes human beings so interesting."

The announcer on the loudspeaker told the crowd that Bayou Thunder was in the chute. There was a murmur, and every eye was on the young cowboy wrapping the bull rope around his hand.

"So what's the message?" I asked again.

"Just watch," Gabe said. He extended his arm and pointed at Bayou Thunder at the exact moment the cowboy nodded and the gate swung open. The bull did not move for a couple of seconds. Then it stepped out of the chute and calmly began to walk around the circumference of the arena, the confused cowboy gripping the bull rope tightly, waiting for an explosion that never came. It reminded me of a pony ride at a carnival.

Chaos did break out, not from the arena but from the crowd. The people were stunned for a few moments, then began to laugh and boo wildly. The cowboy hopped off the animal, shaking his head. The bullfighters guided Bayou Thunder out of the arena towards the bullpens outside.

"I have never seen anything like that," the announcer said over the loudspeaker. "Bayou Thunder has decided to take the day off. We will find another bull for Luke Jackson to ride."

I looked at Gabe. "What did you do? What's the message in that?" I asked.

Gabe smiled, then spoke to me in a soft voice. "You see, Joe," he said. "You have that bull inside of you. Nobody has ever ridden that bull, and you can't. Everyone looks at you and sees a good man with a big heart for people. Nobody has opened the gate yet and let that bull loose. Maybe no one will. Yet Bayou Thunder is still there. Still inside of you."

"That's hard to fathom," I said. "I have a raging bull inside of me?"

"You don't know it's there because you don't know yourself yet."

"Yet?"

The crowd suddenly roared as the chute gate swung open and a red and white bull launched a cowboy into the air within two seconds. The man landed on the bull's rump and then toppled to the ground. The bullfighters rushed in before the animal could gore him.

"Joe, you have figured out that nothing that has happened to you since you left Blacksburg has been an accident. The One who loves you has given you the gift of salvation, and you have received it. He has delivered you from the power of darkness and conveyed you into the kingdom of the Son of His Love. He sent his Spirit to abide in you and to comfort and guide you. You have proved yourself obedient to His voice. You have discovered that you have spiritual enemies who will attempt to deceive you, and you have learned that the One who loves you will never leave you but watch over you like a shepherd."

He paused to let me digest what he had said. I saw how each point was true. I nodded. "I can see all that," I said.

"Good," he continued. "But there is more. The One who loves you said that the path to eternal life would be difficult and few would travel it."

"Difficult?"

"More than you can imagine," he said. "You have to deal with Bayou Thunder."

I thought of the mighty bull and the damage it did to cowboys who tried to ride it. "How do I do that?" I asked.

"There is a place you will go," he said. "Be obedient to the voice of the Spirit, and He will lead you. But remember, you still have a will, and the one who loves you will not violate it. No matter how painful it is, do not turn back. Remember the one who loves you is greater than the one who is in the world."

At that moment, the crowd erupted again. Down in the arena, a cowboy managed to ride an enormous bull for eight seconds and then dismounted the animal without getting hurt. He flung his hat in the air in celebration as the bullfighters guided the animal to the chute leading to the bullpens.

"Well done, Garvey Johnson," the announcer said. "That is a 92-point ride, good for first place so far."

When I looked back, Gabe was gone. I realized the extra ticket I had bought from the RV owner was for the seat he had occupied.

The One who loves me had thought of everything.

———

A storm rolled in overnight, and I awoke to heavy rain pounding the roof of the Tiffin. I brewed a cup of coffee and stared at the weather out the windshield. A torrent of water raced down the road towards Cody under leaden clouds that offered little hope of a break. A strong wind buffeted the trees, and large puddles began to flood nearby campsites.

I was not surprised when the Holy Spirit spoke to me. Gabe had said He would guide me. I had learned to recognize His inaudible voice without any of the inner questioning of just a few weeks before. I immediately put on my rain gear, fought through the wind and the rain to the Jeep, and drove west towards Yellowstone National Park.

Normally, Yellowstone would be packed during the Fourth of July week, but because of the sheer intensity of the rain and the wind, the roads were nearly empty. The ranger at the gate told me she had never seen anything like it. She asked me where I was going. I shrugged my shoulders and said I didn't know. She suggested I might want to hunker down like everyone else and wait for the next day when the forecast predicted clear skies and sunshine. I wished I had had that option.

I continued driving through the park, at one point slowing down to see a black bear with two cubs enduring the rain in a meadow next to the road. Wildlife near a road usually causes a massive traffic jam, but there were only two other cars stopped. Nobody was getting out.

After an hour, I pulled over to a trailhead. When I got out of the Jeep, the rain was coming in sideways. It lashed me and soaked my face. Fortunately, I had bought top-of-the-line rain gear before I left Blacksburg that kept the rest of me dry. The trail was a sea of mud, but the still small voice pushed me onward through the pines, birches, and aspens. Occasionally, I had to leave the trail to avoid muddy quagmires or duck under branches weighed down by water.

I hiked well over a mile and perhaps two miles when the trail broke into a clearing. The moment I stepped out of the forest, the rain stopped, the wind ceased, the storm clouds disappeared, and bright sunshine poured down on me. The grass below my feet was completely dry. At the far end of the clearing, there was an opening where a sheer cliff face plunged to the Yellowstone River.

In the distance, the rain-swollen river fell several hundred feet in a thundering waterfall. Sunlight refracting through the mist cast a rainbow over the watery chaos of the raging cataract.

As I marveled at the sight, I heard footsteps behind me. I turned to see a very old Chinese man wearing a traditional Kung Fu robe and embroidered slippers approaching me.

"Joe Mathers," he said with a Mandarin accent. "You must come."

He pointed to the other side of the clearing, where two other people were seated on logs next to a roaring fire. I was certain no one had been in the clearing when I came out of the forest, and I wouldn't have missed the fire. I threw up my hands. If an angel can show up at a rodeo dressed like a cowboy, why wouldn't an ancient Chinese man show up in the middle of a storm on a hiking trail deep in Yellowstone?

I followed him across the clearing. The other two were a young Arab man wearing a traditional Bedouin thawb and shemagh and a Native American woman in a knee-length sheepskin dress with a deer-skin cloak. The three seemed as though they had been transported through time from the 19th century.

"Sit here," the Chinese man said, pointing to a log on the opposite side of the fire from the Arab and the Native American woman.

As I sat down, I realized there was no wood fueling the fire. It was a six-foot flame rising directly out of the earth. When I first sat down, it emitted a comforting warmth, but then the heat faded, and it became cool. A minute later, it was warm again, and this pattern continued the entire time I was there.

"What is this about?" I asked.

"Gabe Remiel has told you that the gate is narrow and the way is difficult," the Arab man said. "This is the narrow gate."

"The flame?"

"The warmth you feel is the Spirit of the One who loves you, but because you are human and not yet glorified, you can only sense a tiny fraction of the power of His presence and then only at certain times," the Native American woman said. "You couldn't bear it otherwise."

As she spoke, the warmth of the fire abruptly turned cool again. The woman told me it was not the fire that was changing but my capacity to receive its warmth.

"What must I do?" I asked.

"You must pass through the gate to the difficult path," the Asian man said.

"What if I don't?"

"There are only two paths," the Arab said. "The one that is difficult and painful leads to eternal life; the other, which is wide and easy to travel but leads to destruction."

"But I have bowed down before the Son," I said. "I have received His life."

"This is true," the Asian man answered. "But you still have your free will that the one who loves you gave you when He made you to bear his image. He will never take away your free will."

"So I must decide again?"

"Eternal life is free," the Arab said. "It is given to you by grace. You did not earn it. You could not earn it. It had to be paid for by the Son and given to you. But it is costly. It costs you your life.

You must use your free will to take up your cross."

A thought fell into my mind, another scripture from the Sword Drills of my childhood.. "I must be a living sacrifice then?"

"You will see what that means if you pass through the gate," the Native American woman said.

"I need to walk through the flame?"

"It is the way," the Asian man said.

The other two nodded in agreement. They waited patiently as I gazed at the flame, which was warm again. Or more precisely, at that moment I could perceive its warmth, whereas a moment before I couldn't. I wondered if I could overcome the primal fear of walking into a fire. The Native American woman had said that this was the presence of the Holy Spirit, but could I believe that? And even if I did believe it, could I risk being consumed by a holiness and power beyond my imagining? The more I thought about it, the more I realized this was the real question.

I stood up and took a step forward. A blast of heat forced me to step back. I looked at the others.

"Remember, he gave you free will," the Arab man said. "Use your will."

No one warned me it would be like this: not Cecelia or Brian or Will Skye or the Senator or Reggie. I wanted to flee to the trail, to my car, to the Tiffin, and then far from Cody and Yellowstone. Then I remembered how Gaylord and Sarah had fallen on their knees after the tornado destroyed their home and offered a prayer of thanksgiving. I took a deep breath and gave thanks for all that happened to me that day and for the gate of fire before me. I closed my eyes and prayed God would drive out my fear.

When I opened my eyes, I didn't hesitate but boldly lunged into the heart of the fire. A blaze of dazzling light and intense heat engulfed me.

Then the darkness came.

—--

There was no light. Or perhaps I was blind. I couldn't tell which. The air lacked oxygen, and I labored to breathe. The ground under my feet was rough, pockmarked, and littered with what felt like boulders. I reached into the inky blackness but could feel nothing. I waited.

Soon, the sound of footsteps came rapidly towards me out of the darkness. Only when a huge body brushed by me with a foul stench did I realize they were not footsteps but the hooves of a large animal. It thundered off into the dark.

Then the voice came. "You are nothing," it said. "You are a fraud. Everything is meaningless. Go back."

It was the voice of John Demas.

"Where am I?" I asked, but my words didn't penetrate the darkness. They echoed through my head.

The sound of the hooves grew louder. The beast returned, moving quickly. This time, its horns slammed into my body and launched me into the air. As I fell, my head struck a boulder. I cried out in pain, but again the sound did not penetrate the darkness.

As I lay on the ground, the animal stood over me, its putrid breath on my face. I quickly realized my body had not been hurt by the animal's horns or even the fall. The darkness was the source of my agony. It had invaded my soul, spewing a poisonous elixir of accusation and hopelessness.

"All you have trusted in is an illusion, a trick of your mind," John Demas spoke again. "You have failed to justify your existence. You are condemned."

With each word, the animal's tongue touched my face. I realized the beast itself was speaking to me with John Demas' voice. I scrambled to my feet to get away, but it lunged forward and threw me through the darkness again. I landed hard on a boulder and curled up into the fetal position to protect myself.

"Go away!" I cried out. The words again went nowhere. The torment became a choking vine engulfing my soul.

The animal hovered over me. "Who are you, Joe Mathers?" it asked. "A speck of dust. You are nothing more. It is all a lie. No one loves you. No one cares about you. You have failed. You will be forgotten. There is no meaning to your life."

The beast abruptly moved away, the sound of its hooves gradually fading, and I was alone. The darkness metastasized within me. My mind began to echo the words. You are useless. Nothing. A hollow shell of a man. Condemned.

Desperate to get away from the raging animal, I struggled to my feet and took a step into the dark. I heard the hooves again. I braced myself, and its horns drove into my body and lifted me high in the air. When I fell, I heard its voice, taunting me.

"You have not justified your existence," it said. "It's all a lie. You do not deserve to live. Turn around. Go back"

This time, it was not John Demas' voice. It was my own voice. The beast spoke with my voice. As the words pierced me, the despair morphed into something greater and more toxic. It was no longer a choking vine. It was a tsunami flooding every millimeter of my soul, eroding the last remnants of my will.

My will.

The revelation came as a distant, tiny light in the darkness. I was not blind after all. I could see. At once, I knew what John Demas wanted, what the darkness craved. The beast, a creature of the darkness, spoke with both his voice and my voice, pushing me to surrender it.

What had the Asian man said? "He gave you free will. Use it."

I rose to my feet and stepped towards the light. The animal immediately rushed me again, throwing me into the air with its horns. When I fell to the ground, it spoke to me again in my own voice.

"It is a lie. You have not justified your existence. It is useless."

A second tsunami of despair, even more toxic than the first, flooded my soul. Yet I rose again and moved towards the light, stumbling at times over the boulders. The beast again attacked. Once more, the waves of despair mounted higher, but I stood again. Over and over, the animal rushed me, punishing me with its horns. Over and over, I rose.

As I drew nearer the light, the beast's attacks became more desperate and more violent. Yet at the same time, the growing light allowed me to see my tormentor. It was Bayou Thunder, the terrifying bull that could not be ridden. The great animal positioned itself between me and the light, daring me to risk its horns again.

At that moment, the light grew brighter. Its rays formed the shape of a sword. It stood upright on a platform I recognized to be an altar of some kind. I understood what I needed to do.

Bayou Thunder seemed to be aware of what I had seen. It snorted and charged, burying its horns under my ribs and tossing me to the ground. "It is no use," it said with my voice as it stood over me. "It is an illusion. A myth. A fairy tale. You have not justified your existence. Go back!"

A final wave of despair, greater than all that had come before, washed over me. The accusation crushed the last measure of my will with its truth. I had not justified my existence. I could not go on. I did not deserve to go on.

I rose again, this time to go back. Yet as I turned, in my peripheral vision, I saw the light sword again. I remembered how easily Gabe Remiel had tamed Bayou Thunder in the arena. The great animal was not all-powerful. The cowboy had ridden him.

I pivoted back towards the light. At once, it gave me strength greater than I had ever known. I ran past the bull's horns to the altar and seized the hilt of the sword. When I turned towards the animal, the great beast no longer snorted and no longer charged. It cowered before the sword.

"If you kill me, you will kill yourself," it said, still with my voice. "You will no longer have an identity. You will be no more."

"Come," I commanded. My voice rumbled through the darkness like thunder.

"But you will surely die," the bull protested, now with John Demas' voice. "You will surely be no more."

"Come," I repeated.

Bayou Thunder, the great and unconquerable bull, obeyed the command. It walked forward as peacefully as it had when the cowboy in the arena had ridden it. When it reached the altar, I swung the sword. A flame rose from the altar and consumed the animal

The sacrifice was offered.

————

Where there was darkness, now there was light. The altar, covered in ashes, stood at the edge of a vast, barren plain covered in the boulders that I had been thrown against by the bull and stumbled over when I walked in the dark. Behind the altar a garden climbed up a hillside, with flowers, trees, and bushes blooming in an array of vibrant colors.

Two men came out of the garden. As they drew near, I saw that they were dressed as Roman soldiers. They did not speak to me but instead gestured for me to follow them. When I hesitated, each grabbed an elbow and firmly guided me. We passed through the gates of the garden and ascended to the top of the hill.

I was shocked. On the other side of the brow of the hill, stood a line of crosses as far as the eye could see. On them, men and women of all ages and colors hung crucified, their bodies contorted and blood flowing from their wounds. They were in the process of dying. However, they were not crying out in pain. Rather, they sang a hymn together in perfect harmony.

When fear falls like rain
When my heart is sore afraid
In dark and deepest pain
And no one comes to aid
Oh Father, hear my cry
Lead me to the Rock who is higher than I

Lead me to the Rock! Lead me to the Rock!
Lead me to the Rock who is higher than I!

When storms rage around me
And waves come crashing down
When sadness is all I see

And sorrow the only sound
Oh Father, hear my cry
Lead me to the Rock who is higher than I

Lead me to the Rock! Lead me to the Rock!
Lead me to the Rock who is higher than I!

"How can they sing when they are being crucified?" I asked the soldiers.

"Death has no sting here," one replied. "You are invited to join them. Then you will know who you are."

The soldier pointed at a wooden cross at our feet I hadn't noticed before. It seemed to have appeared at that moment. I didn't hesitate but lay down on it. The soldiers pounded iron nails through my wrists and ankle bones, then hoisted the cross from the earth and placed it in a hole along the line of crosses. I hung there, crucified and bleeding, yet an unspeakable joy eclipsed whatever physical pain there might have been.

I began to sing.

Then I died.

———-

I was somehow alive. I found myself on my knees in a grassy field with a bright blue sky above, dotted with enormous cumulus clouds. I did not know how or when I arrived there. Time and space seemed to have no meaning.

In the distance, a man crossed the field, striding towards me. As he drew near, I recognized him. Although Gabe Remiel still appeared in the form of a large, muscular man, he was no longer dressed as a cowboy. Rather, he wore a white linen robe that flowed down to the ground with a gold sash around his waist.

"Now you look like an angel," I said when he was near enough to hear me.

"I am a messenger and my appearance is part of the message," he said, kneeling beside me.

"I am not sure I can handle another message," I replied. "No more bulls, please."

Gabe chuckled, and I noted that angels can laugh. I wondered if they could weep as well. There was so much I didn't know.

"Bayou Thunder is dead," he said. "You will never have to face a bull again."

"That is a relief."

"I told you the path would be difficult and few would endure it. But you have persevered. You have made the sacrifice."

I bowed my head. "I cannot take credit," I said. "I would have turned back except for the light."

"It is in your weakness that the one who loves you makes you strong," he said.

I didn't understand what he meant. It was a paradox. I let it pass. "So what is the message?"

his

"When we last met, I told you that you did not know who you were yet."

"I remember."

"Now I will show you who you are," he said. "Your true identity."

He pointed across the field. At once, the earth shook with a deafening rumble. A blazing ring of fire appeared just above the grass. A man appeared, rising from the middle of the ring, a hundred times larger than Gabe. As the man ascended, Gabe bowed his head, and I realized this was Jesus, or at least a vision of Jesus, for His body was not what I expected. It was formed not of bones and flesh but of people of all ages and colors, clothed in white robes. Each connected to the others to form His hands, His torso, His legs, and is feet. At the sight, I fell on my face and worshiped.

I don't know how long I lay there, immersed in what seemed like a vast ocean of peace. Again, time seemed to have ceased to exist. Or at least time, as I understood it. But when I finally looked up, the fiery ring and the vision of Jesus were gone. Gabe stood over me, waiting patiently.

"Do you know what you saw?" he asked.

"I am not sure," I said. "I saw Jesus and many people who were part of Him."

"Now you know who you are," Gabe said. "In their fallen state, people are separated from their Creator and from each other. They are isolated individuals, competing with each other and seeking to use each other. Even those whom they would call good cannot help but ultimately be isolated in themselves, for being good is their identity. But the ones you saw in His body are those who entered through the narrow gate. They persevered on the difficult path. They sacrificed their own Bayou Thunder, which is their old identity, on His altar. They were crucified with Him and raised with HIm. They have a new identity as part of His body – not their own identity but His identity that they share with everyone else who is part of Him."

"And that is my identity?"

"That is your new identity, the identity you were created for," Gabe said. "And when you go back, you will recognize those who share your identity."

I thought for a moment. "But why must I go back?"

Gabe smiled. "There is a woman who is waiting for you," he said. "It is part of His plan."

———

I awoke at sunset in the clearing. Birds sang in the trees, and the last rays of the sun created a golden glow on the Yellowstone waterfall. The Asian man, the Native American woman, and the Arab man were gone. There was no fire and no sign that there had been a fire.

I enjoyed the beauty of the river for a couple of minutes and then crossed to the trail. The moment I stepped across its threshold, a sheet of rain drenched my face. I looked at my watch. It was still morning. Not a minute had passed from the time I had entered the clearing. I slogged down the trail toward the trailhead and the Jeep.

Nothing had changed, but everything had changed.

Chapter 17

Mount Moriah

"You can't expect other people to understand your spiritual experiences," Cecelia told me when I called her that night. "God reveals Himself to each person in a unique way perfectly designed for them. If you try to tell others what you experienced, you usually will get a blank expression in return."

"But my heart is burning within me," I said. "It was so real."

"That is between you and Him," she said. "If you tell others that you had to sacrifice a raging bull on an altar or that you were crucified while singing hymns, they aren't going to get it. At best, they will nod their heads and change the subject. At worst, they will think you are delusional."

"Have you had experiences like that?"

"I have, but I'm not going to tell you about them," she replied. "You wouldn't get them."

"But what do I do now?" I said. "I tried to call Lara, but she isn't picking up. The angel told me she was waiting for me. I want to ask her to come out here. I want to marry her."

Cecelia let a few seconds pass before answering. "Joe, if you read the Scripture, you will see that God makes promises He intends to fulfill, but then makes people wait, sometimes a long time. Abraham had to wait 25 years for the child of promise, Isaac. Israel had to wait 700 years after Isaiah prophesied God would send a child who would be the Messiah."

"I don't have 25 years to wait," I said. "I want Lara to come now."

"She will come when God tells her to come."

"You have talked to her, haven't you?"

Cecelia hesitated again, which was itself an answer to my question. Finally, she spoke: "Joe, I will not lie. Lara and I prayed together on the phone. I visited her in Alabama. God has put a remarkable woman in your path. I don't know that I've met many people who have as close a walk with Jesus. We both love you, but she wants to be obedient to God."

"So I was right," I said. "It's a conspiracy."

"Perhaps. But a divine conspiracy."

"I don't understand it," I said, flustered. "We are both lonely. I love her and I think she loves me, even though we have only known each other for a little while. I have a billion dollars. There is no reason we can't be together."

"Perhaps there is no earthly reason," Cecelia said. "But His ways are not our ways. As the heavens are higher than the earth, so are His ways higher than our ways and His thoughts higher than our thoughts."

"I am in a lot of pain over this," I said. "And you are quoting a scripture verse?"

I sensed Cecelia was smiling and, if I had been with her, I would have seen that otherworldly expression I had seen so many times before.

"That's the best time to quote scriptures," she said.

———

The next day, the weather was perfect, 75 degrees with blue skies. The clerk at the RV park was surprised when I checked out. Cody buzzed with anticipation for the Fourth of July celebrations. It was an odd time to leave and miss the festivities, but I felt compelled to continue westward.

I could have driven through Yellowstone, but I would have been snarled in traffic the whole way, so I went north to I-90, then turned west. As usual, I had no destination in mind. After an overnight stay in Butte, I continued on the interstate to Missoula. It was there that I saw signs for Travelers Rest, where Lewis and Clark spent two days in the fall of 1805 before embarking up the Lolo Pass through the Bitterroot Mountains.

The idea of following the path of Lewis and Clark appealed to me. I had something in common with the great explorers: we both headed west, not knowing where the path would lead, albeit they did it on foot, guided by local Native Americans, and I was doing it in a luxury motor coach using a sometimes faulty GPS. I decided to do the same thing, taking a couple of days off on my journey to relax and then drive the Tiffin over the breathtakingly beautiful mile-high pass to the town of Kooskia in Idaho, hard against the picturesque Clearwater River.

My next divine appointment occurred in a grocery store outside town, where I encountered Lizzy Miller. A small African American woman in her 60s, Lizzy was an unusual sight in that part of Idaho with its tiny black population. She was stocking up on supplies when I first encountered her. She stopped and stared at me while I was perusing the varieties of ice cream in the freezer.

"You are Joe?" she asked.

I am," I said, figuring she had recognized me as the winner of the Powerball Lottery.

"I am Lizzy," she said. "You are supposed to have lunch with me at my house."

"I am?"

"Yes, you are," she said. "He told me. I didn't know who you were until I saw you here. Then He told me."

The logical response would be "Who is He?" But I had traveled beyond the realm of human reasoning. I thought of Cecelia's quotation from Isaiah, which Brian had also quoted to me. His ways are not our ways. There was no question who "He" was.

"Should I drive my motor coach?" I asked.

"Leave it here in the parking lot. Follow me in your Jeep."

Lizzy drove a Datsun. The Japanese company Nissan hadn't manufactured a Datsun since the 1980s, and I hadn't seen one in years. Still, it seemed to work fine as we climbed a steep road out of Kooskia and then turned onto a dirt road cut through the maples, firs, and lodgepole pines. Eventually, we came to a small compound consisting of a Craftsman house and several smaller outbuildings. A woman I guessed was Lizzy's daughter opened the gate, and we parked next to the house. She didn't seem to be surprised that a white man in a Jeep was following her mother.

Lizzy and I hadn't spoken a word to each other since our brief introduction. Whatever needed to be said would be said, and there was no need for small talk. As I helped her carry her groceries, I noted another compound next door surrounded by a high fence topped with barbed wire.

"Good fences make good neighbors," I quipped,

"Not in this case," Lizzy responded. "That's why you are here."

———

As taciturn as Lizzy had seemed in the store, she was garrulous over a lunch of homemade chicken pot pie and biscuits. Her daughter, Lucy, and her son in a wheelchair, Gerard, ate with us at her kitchen table. The house was immaculate, but the decor was hardly Western. Lizzy had decorated her living room with pictures and framed posters of Thelonious Monk, Louis Armstrong, John Coltrane and other jazz greats.

"We are a southern family, from just outside of New Orleans," she said. "My father was a drummer."

"A jazz musician?"

"He backed up Monk and Coltrane," she said. "He played at Preservation Hall in the 1960s before he died. Both my brothers took after him and are jazz musicians in New Orleans."

"How did you end up here?" I asked.

Lizzy laughed. "You mean 'how did a black girl from New Orleans end up living in Idaho County, Idaho, where less than one out of a thousand people is black?' I get that question all the time."

"And the answer is?"

"The same reason you are here," she said. "God sent me. This is my Mount Moriah. And it's going to be yours as well."

I glanced at Lucy and Gerard, who didn't seem at all confused by what their mother had said. I was sure they had heard it before.

"You are going to have to explain that to me," I said.

"Of course," Lizzy said. "I was not raised in a godly environment. As I said, my daddy was a jazz musician, and my mama occasionally was a jazz singer. They had a sometimes good, sometimes bad relationship for many years and had three children. But they never married. I grew up with parties and jam sessions lasting late into the night and strangers sleeping on the couch. Booze and drugs were everywhere. You know the deal. I didn't even know there was a God until I was 10 years old. No one told me. I figured "Jesus" was a swear word and 'damn' was the word you said after 'God.'

"When I was 10 and I was in the fourth grade, a teacher pulled me aside and told me about Jesus. She wasn't allowed to do that, but she did it anyway. I'm sure she saw this little girl who wasn't being raised proper. She led me in a prayer asking Jesus to come into my heart. And He did. After that, I never doubted. I may be confused by many things in life, and I've made a lot of mistakes, but I have never been confused about Jesus.

"A few days later, a Christian lady next door took me to an African Methodist Episcopal Church down the street. My mama and daddy didn't care. They were sleeping off hangovers on Sunday morning. The people in the church helped me stay straight and graduate from high school. I was the top student in my class and got a scholarship to LSU. But I drifted away and didn't graduate. I had my two children with a man who later died of a heroin overdose. I never lost my faith in Jesus. I just put Him on a shelf and did what I wanted to do.

"But Jesus is the Good Shepherd. He doesn't forget His lost

sheep. Eventually, I became desperate. I was a single mother of two teenage children, barely making it. I worked as an aide in a retirement community for rich white people. One of those people was a woman in her late 80s. One day, she asked me if I wanted to hear her story. I said I did, and she told me a story that broke my heart.

"I didn't know white people, especially rich white people, could have lives like that. Her father was a drunk, and her mother was too busy chasing other men to be a mama. They sent her to boarding school, and she tried to kill herself twice. She flunked out of college. Then she got hooked on cocaine and slept around. She had three abortions, trying to find someone to love her.

"A rehab counselor shared Jesus with her, and she said the sinner's prayer, but it didn't stick. She just continued to slide downhill. She never ended up in the gutter because her father would rescue her. She got arrested selling drugs, and he hired a lawyer to keep her out of prison. But by the time she was 30, her life was over. Everyone had given up on her. They were waiting for the phone call that she had died from an overdose.

"But Jesus did not give up on her. Just like He did with me, he sent someone. Believe it or not, it was a woman ringing the bell for the Salvation Army at Christmas. This time, she really did get saved. She was delivered from drugs. She got married to a good man and had four children. But her trials weren't over. One of her children came down with meningitis and died suddenly. She got ovarian cancer and had to go through chemo three times when it kept coming back. Finally, her husband died, her children moved away, and she was alone again."

"That's sad," I said.

"But you know what, Joe? She had peace and joy. I could see it in her face. She said she knew who she belonged to and where she was going. I wanted that. This rich white woman got me back to Jesus. And I learned something. You never know who God is going to send to you. It might be the last person you expect."

Lizzy paused her story to clear the dishes off the table. She brought back cups of coffee and slices of pecan pie for us.

"So what about Mount Moriah?" I asked.

Lizzy sat down at the table again and took a bite of pie before answering. Lucy and Gerard listened with interest, even though I suspected they had heard the story many times before.

"Once I got right with Jesus, I began to enjoy life. Sure, there were challenges, but I had my children and my church, which I rejoined. I was active in the prayer ministry and growing spiritually. Every day, I was moving closer to Jesus. Eventually, I began to become a kind of mother figure to the younger women. I led Bible studies in my home. And then…." she hesitated. "And then I started to really hear the voice of the Holy Spirit. He told me to do something I didn't want to do."

"What was that?"

"Move," she said. "Not just move. But move to lily-white Idaho. Move to a place where a lot of people are stuck in time before the Civil Rights movement. A place where I would not feel welcome."

"I can see how that would be a shock."

"Not only that, but He told me He already had a place for me to live. A house he would give me, even though I had never owned a house and didn't have much money."

"What did you do?"

"I stalled, of course. That's what most people do when God tells them to do something they don't want to do."

"So what happened?"

She chuckled. "God has a way of getting His point across," she said. "One day I went to work and that rich white woman told me she had been praying and the Holy Spirit gave her a message for me."

"Oh?"

"She told me God said I needed to move to a place called Kooskia, Idaho, to a Craftsman house that he had arranged for me to buy. I was shocked. I fell on my knees in tears. I hadn't told anyone about what the Holy Spirit had told me to do. There is no way she could have known about it."

"Amazing," I interjected.

"And then she said the Holy Spirit had told her to pay for the move. She told me she was going to be obedient and do it. So that was my Mount Moriah moment. God sent Abraham on a three-day journey to sacrifice his son on Mount Moriah. He sent me across the country to sacrifice everything that was familiar and comfortable to me and live in a place where I would be an unwelcome stranger. I didn't even know what a Craftsman house was. He sent me blindly out here. I arrived in town with a moving van, not knowing what I was going to do when I got here. But there was a Craftsman house for sale. This house. And that rich white woman bought it for me."

"That's incredible," I said. "But you said this was my Mount Moriah moment. What did you mean by that?"

Lizzy took a deep breath. Then she stood up and began to collect the dessert plates. "Give me a couple of minutes," she said. "Then we can go onto the back porch and I will tell you about it."

———

Lizzy's house featured a deck with a spectacular view of the
Clearwater River and the Heart of the Monster, a geological
mound that is part of the creation story of the Nez Perce people.
As she and I sat down and Lucy wheeled Gerard onto the deck,
I noted again the adjacent compound with its high fence topped
with barbed wire, and I wondered what Lizzy meant when she
said it was the reason God had directed my path to her house.
Before I could ask, however, a man began shouting on the other
side of the fence. I couldn't quite understand what he was yelling,
but he was clearly in a rage.

"That's Buster," Lizzy said. "He is your Mount Moriah."

"I don't understand," I said.

"He is the reason God sent you here."

I shrugged my shoulders. "I think I need some explanation."

Lizzy took a deep breath. Her expression suggested whatever she
told me wouldn't be easy for her.

"Buster Blanchard lives in that house with his wife and their two
sons. They were here when we moved in. He doesn't like people.
He especially doesn't like Indians and black people, so we do our
best to avoid him. Not a day goes by that he isn't yelling at his
wife and kids. He has two pit bulls and a lot of guns. When he
is drunk, he shoots them late at night out the back window of
his house. Fortunately, he doesn't shoot in our direction, but I
wouldn't put it past him."

"Sounds like the neighbor from hell," I said.

"That's not all," Lizzy said. "I have never seen his wife or his sons
leave the compound. In fact, the only time I've seen her is when
one of the dogs got out of the front gate and she and the boys
had to chase it down. She is a haggard woman, and her sons look

like stray dogs. It was obvious they weren't getting enough to eat. Buster leaves every day – I guess he has a job somewhere – so we started to leave bags of food outside the gate for them."

"That was kind."

"It was risky. If Buster had found out that black folks were giving his family food, who knows what he might have done? But I think his wife managed to keep it a secret."

"This man sounds like pure evil."

Lizzy frowned. "One night, Gerard went out front to look at the stars. There is a place down the road where you can get a good view. As he walked down there, someone came out of the shadows and attacked him. He beat him badly and left him on the road. When he didn't come home, we went out and found him. He spent a month in the hospital, but the damage was too much. He will never walk again. We knew who did it, but we didn't have any proof. Like everyone else, the sheriff is scared of Buster. He refused to knock on his door to ask him questions. Said he didn't want to get shot."

"So he got away with it?"

"Nobody ever gets away with anything," Lizzy said flatly.

I wasn't sure what she meant. "So what did you do?"

Lizzy looked at Gerard, who had hardly said a word since I arrived. He was a handsome man who looked like he might have been a good athlete when he was younger, but his legs were atrophied. I tried to imagine what it was like to be a young black man in rural Idaho with a disability. Why would God put him in this situation?

"I forgave him," Gerard said.

"We all did," Lizzy added. "We all forgave him."

I dropped my fork on the plate. "You forgave him?"

"If we don't forgive others, God won't forgive us," Lizzy said.

I remembered what Tuskegee University President Arelene Mathews said when I told her about Simon Jackson's forgiveness of Oswald Higgins: "For some things, there is no forgiveness." Surely, there could be no forgiveness for the brutality of Buster Blanchard.

"Certainly he didn't mean someone like Buster?" I protested.

"I don't recall him making any exceptions," she replied. "He forgave those who were crucifying Him."

At that moment, Buster began yelling again. This time, I could hear his words. "You are a dirty whore," he shouted. "You cheat on me when I'm at work, don't you, you whore?" There was no response, and I could imagine his wife cowering, hoping the storm would pass.

"Does he hit her?" I asked.

"What do you think?" Lizzy asked.

"Then how can anyone forgive him? He paralyzed your son. He abuses his family."

Lizzy closed her eyes for a moment as though she were praying. When she opened them, she pointed at the Heart of the Monster across the valley.

"The Nez Perce believe Coyote destroyed a great monster who was killing all the animals and scattered its remains across the landscape. That mound is its heart," she said. "We, too, have monsters in our lives. But Jesus doesn't tell us to destroy them. He tells us to forgive them."

Buster began to yell again, something about his lunch not being ready. I felt my anger rising. "He is the last person on earth who deserves forgiveness," I said.

"Joe, you haven't learned the power of forgiveness," she said. "But once you do, you will touch the face of God."

———-–

We switched topics. For the next half hour, I shared my journey from the day Janice died. Lizzy and her children were dumbfounded when I told them about the lottery ticket and how I had become a billionaire in the middle of my grief. However, they weren't surprised when I told them I had never bought a lottery ticket. They knew what it took me weeks on the road to grasp: the hospice volunteer was either someone sent by God or an angel. We would not know which one on this side of heaven.

Lizzy was especially interested in the story of Lionel Jackson's father, Simon, and how he forgave the man who lynched his father and then baptized him.

"The power of forgiveness," she said. "It changes everything."

I didn't tell the entire story of my journey. I skipped the donation to Tuskegee University and meeting Lara in Foley, but I did tell them about Peter Flynn and his wife and about Gaylord and Sarah losing their farmhouse to the tornado. I also told them about the Senator's carving of Jesus and how I had come to finally know him for who he is in a rural church in Arkansas. I didn't mention anything about John Demas or Gabe Remiel. Cecilia was right. Some things you shouldn't share with other people.

"God has sent you to bless people," Lizzy said. "He knew who to give the lottery ticket to."

"Yes, but I realize that nothing I did on this journey cost me anything. I gave away money I hadn't earned. It was a gift and I simply passed it along."

"But now you are here."

"What am I supposed to do?"

Lizzie took a deep breath. "Knock on his door," she said. "The Holy Spirit will tell you what to say."

"He might shoot me."

"That's a possibility. Even the cops are scared to knock on his door."

"Then why do it?"

"Because God sent you here to do it."

"But the man is a monster."

"That's not the way God sees him. He sees him as someone made in His image. Perfectly designed to be in intimate fellowship with Him. God hates his sin just as he hates our sin. Jesus wept over Jerusalem, and I often wonder if God weeps over Buster. But He loves him."

"But I could die."

"Isaac could have died. Isn't that the point? Abraham had to be willing to sacrifice the most precious thing in his life."

"So it's not just about Buster. It's about me."

Lizzy nodded. "And the power of forgiveness."

"I don't understand that," I said. "How can forgiveness have power?"

"It's not something most people understand, Joe," Lizzy said. "I didn't until I came here and God showed me. When someone hurts you or takes something from you, you have a case against them. You think about it a lot. You stay up all night. You think of ways to get that person back and to teach them a lesson. Eventually, it becomes poison to you. The person might not even know about it, or they might not care. They aren't staying up all night thinking about it. You are. And maybe you do something bad to get them back. But that doesn't make you feel any better. You still have that poison in you. And that person isn't going to suddenly say, 'I was wrong and ask you to forgive them.' They probably will think of ways to get you back for getting them back."

"Like the Hatfields and the McCoys," I interjected. "I'm from West Virginia."

"That's right," she said. "But when you forgive somebody before God, He sucks the poison right out of you. It may not feel that way right at that moment. A lot of things Jesus said don't feel true when we obey them. But over time, you will see how you have been set free from it. That's part of the power of forgiveness."

"Part of the power?"

"Oh, there is a lot more," she said. "When you forgive someone before God, even if they don't ask you to forgive them, your case becomes God's case. You turn it over to Him to deal with that person. And He will do it, especially if you pray for the person. His Spirit will convict their hearts. He won't give them a moment's peace until they admit what they have done and come to Him for forgiveness. And if they refuse to repent when God comes after them, then they will never have peace. Never."

"So God is after Buster?"

"God is after Buster."

"But I don't understand why I am here? Why am I part of this?"

"It's too much for Buster to ask anyone for forgiveness, especially a black family from Louisiana. You are God's final plea to him. You stand between Buster and an eternity in hell."

"And God wants me to offer my life the way Abraham offered Isaac?"

"If it's the most precious thing to you."

"Do I get a choice?"

"You always have a choice."

I hesitated and gazed out at the Heart of the Monster. Buster Blanchard was the true monster. I didn't want anything to do with him, but was I going to say 'no' to God? "I don't know what I should do," I said.

Lizzy smiled. "That's easy," she said. "We need to pray."

———

Buster Blanchard arrived home at precisely 5:15. I watched out the window as he opened the gate to his compound and parked his Dodge Ram 3500 truck in his driveway. He was a short man wearing work overalls with a crew cut and a chunky build. The two pitbulls ran over to greet him, but he ignored them as he quickly entered the house. Within 30 seconds, he was yelling at someone, maybe his wife, maybe his sons.

Lizzy and I had spent much of the afternoon praying with Lucy
and Gerard. They prayed prayers I had never heard before: intense
prayers, spiritual warfare prayers, prayers of binding enemies and
commanding them off the battlefield in the name of Jesus. When
I asked her about them, she quoted Jesus telling His disciples that
He had given them authority over serpents and scorpions and all
the powers of hell.

"It is not our authority," she said. "It is His authority given to us."
I wondered if Brian and Cecelia prayed such prayers. They had
never mentioned it.

Then the three of them laid hands on me and prayed I would
be dressed with the full armor of God, the same list of items I
had been forced to memorize as a child: the belt of truth, the
breastplate of righteousness, the footwear of the Gospel, the
helmet of salvation, the shield of faith and the sword of the Spirit,
which is the Word of God.

When they were done, something changed inside of me. I had
been terrified about knocking on Buster's door, but at once the
fear was gone. I had no hesitation walking over to his front gate
and knocking loudly on the metal frame. I expected his dogs
to bark and perhaps rush the gate, but they stayed out of sight
behind the truck.

It took a few minutes either for Buster to hear me or to get the
shotgun that he carried with him. He had no qualms about
pointing it directly at me. I remembered one of the mantras my
father repeated over and over again when he trained me to shoot
as a child: never point a gun at someone unless you intend to
shoot them.

"What do you want?" he demanded. His finger was on the
trigger. Another mantra: Don't put your finger on the trigger

until you are ready to shoot.

The inaudible voice of the Holy Spirit began to tell me what I should say. I had no fear. Buster might as well have been pointing a child's squirt gun at me. "You know why I am here," I said.

Buster glared at me spitefully. Yet there was something in his expression other than rage. I realized he was the one who was filled with fear, not me. He was a man seeing something that terrified him. He was trying to hide it, but it was unmistakable.

"Who are you?" he asked.

"You know who I am."

"I should shoot you."

"You won't."

"Get on your knees," he shouted.

"No," I said. "You come with me."

"Get on your knees!" He yelled again, this time with desperation.

"Put the gun down, Buster. Come with me."

He didn't lower the shotgun and continued to glare at me. I imagined few people had ever looked him in the eye without some fear, but I had none. Then he thought of an idea. Keeping the gun pointed at me, he unlatched the gate and called for his two dogs. They came running, but instead of attacking me, they jumped up playfully on me and licked my hands.

"You need to come with me, Buster."

The rage disappeared from his face. He was petrified. "What are you going to show me?" he asked pitifully. "You are the man in the dreams. You look just like him. He kept telling me he was going to show me something."

"Come," I said. "And I will show you."

———-

The clearing was on a bend in the road, a quarter mile from Buster's compound. We did not speak as we walked to it, trailed by the two pitbulls who were still playfully jumping up on me and licking me. Eventually, we came to a place in the clearing where the voice of the Spirit told me to stop. If Buster Blanchard had been terrified before, he was now visibly trembling, like a small animal caught in a trap.

"The man in your dreams has brought you here, hasn't he?" I asked.

He hesitated, then nodded.

"Close your eyes," I said. "God will show you."

We both closed our eyes. Immediately, we were walking together in a dark place, as though transported through space and time. A voice cried out. "Help me!" It was Buster's voice. At once, animal sounds filled the dark – lions and hyenas fighting over prey. The lions roared, and the hyenas yapped. The prey called out, "Help me! Please help me!" Then there were cries of pain as the animals tore into the man.

"Why won't someone help him?" Buster asked.

"There is no help," I said. "There is no hope. Your tormentor is a roaring lion who will devour you, and no one will come to save you. He will consume you, but not consume you for all eternity. Over and over again, you will be consumed. Your cries for mercy will never be answered. There is no mercy."

Buster fell on his knees in the dark and grabbed hold of my legs. "I wanted to beat him up, teach him his place," he whimpered. "I didn't mean to cripple him."

The lions roared again, and the man being devoured cried out again for help.

"There is no mercy here, Buster."

"What can I do to be saved?" he cried out in terror.

I made him wait a few beats, letting the full impact of his situation sink down into his heart. Then I replied: "Open your eyes, Buster, and I will tell you."

———-

I did not need to stay long, and I left before the sun went down. I had only been there six hours. I doubt Abraham dawdled on Mount Moriah.

Before I left, Buster Blanchard – violent racist, bully, and abuser – fell on his knees in the living room of his black neighbor begging forgiveness not only from her and her crippled son but also from his wife and two sons. He listed everything the Holy Spirit convicted him of having done and asked to be forgiven. It was a long list.

"You have already been forgiven for what you did to me," Gerard, the man who would never walk again, told him.

Buster nodded, but he did not understand. He did not yet grasp that Gerard's forgiveness had opened the door for his dreams and the arrival of a West Virginia physical therapist at the gate of his compound that afternoon. Maybe he would never understand.

Or maybe he would only understand when God gave him his own Mount Moriah moment.

He did understand what I had told him he had to do if he were going to be saved from the darkness and devouring lions. He had to ask for and receive the forgiveness of God given by the One who bore God's wrath for his sins in his place on the cross. He had to humble himself to ask for the forgiveness of those he had harmed in life. And finally, he had to ask Lizzy Miller to baptize him in the Clearwater River, not in some remote location but in the middle of town, witnessed by the small fellowship of believers that had welcomed Lizzy and her children as part of the body of Christ.

"One more thing," I told him. "Lizzy Miller will teach you and your family the Word of God. You will sit under her teaching."

When I hooked up the Tiffin and drove west out of town on Route 12, I passed the Heart of the Monster. God had not destroyed the monster named Buster Blanchard. He had taken away his heart of stone and given him a new heart.

Such is the power of forgiveness.

Chapter 18

Dr. Decker

Three days later, I met Dr. Mel Decker on a trailhead just south of the quirky town of Wallace on I-90 deep in the heart of the Idaho panhandle. He may have saved my life, although I am still not quite sure what would have happened to me had he not been there. He definitely saved the life of a miner named Travis Maynard.

A century ago, Wallace was a boom town, fueled by silver mining and timber harvests. The silver petered out, and with the town in decline in the 1970s, the federal government planned to run the interstate through the middle of it. However, the mayor and other leaders outmaneuvered the bureaucrats by having the downtown designated as a National Historic Landmark. As a result, the federal government was forced to build the interstate over the town rather than through it.

A subsequent mayor declared Wallace to be the "Center of the Universe" and commissioned a manhole cover in the middle of town as the absolute center. The Flat Earth Society peer-reviewed and approved the designation. Who could prove it wrong?

I parked the Tiffin under the towering 100-foot overpass the government had built over the town and decided to go for a hike in the surrounding forest. I found a trail that runs two miles to the entrance of an abandoned silver mine that itself is now a National Historic Landmark. It is where a 6'4" forest ranger named Ed Pulaski fearlessly guided 43 men to safety in 1910 when they were about to be overtaken by the "Big Blowup," the largest forest fire in the history of the country, burning three million acres in Idaho and Washington.

As I put on my hiking boots at the trailhead, I was overcome with yet another wave of mourning for Janice and began to weep.

"You look pretty upset for a man about to go on a hike," a voice said.

I looked around and saw a thin man in hiking attire next to the trailhead carrying a walking stick. I had not seen him before, and there were no other cars in the parking lot. No doubt he had walked the mile from the town.

"I'm sorry," I said, although there was no reason for an apology. "My late wife and I used to love to hike in the Appalachians. Coming here to hike without her stirred up some emotions."

"I understand," he said in a soft manner that made me believe he really did understand. Perhaps he, too, knew what it was like to weep over the death of a loved one. I had a strange feeling I knew him from somewhere, although it was improbable someone from West Virginia would know anyone in rural Idaho and not remember it.

"I am going to hike the trail," I said. "Would you like to join me?

He smiled broadly and nodded. "I always enjoy company."

He introduced himself as Dr. Mel Decker. It turned out he knew far more about Ed Pulaski and the great fire than was written on the interpretative signs along the way. He gave me a history lesson as we hiked.

"Wallace was a hotbed of silver mining in 1910," he told me. "In fact, the mines in this area produced more silver than any other place in the world. The town was a wild place then, with saloons, bordellos, and gambling dens to satisfy the appetites of the miners. But Ed Pulaski was a different sort of man. When the great fire swept through this area, he could have escaped it, but instead, he left home, telling his wife he might never return. He hiked right into the path of the inferno to rescue his men."

"Greater love has no one than this, than to lay down one's life for his friends,' I said.

Dr. Decker was impressed. "You know that verse?"

"I was required as a child to memorize a lot of scripture," I said. "I don't know why it popped into my head just now."

"It applies perfectly," he said. "Ed was willing to lay down his life for his friends. He cared about them more than he cared about his own safety. That is the true definition of love."

We hiked silently for a few minutes, crossing a bridge over a lovely waterfall. The trail ran through a forest of pines, firs, and spruce that had regenerated itself in the century since the fire scorched the mountains. I relished the rich scents and oxygen produced by the trees and imagined what it must have been like for an entire forest to become a raging inferno.

"When Ed reached his men, the fire had completely engulfed them," Dr. Decker continued his narrative. "They were effectively dead men except that Ed had explored every inch of the forest. He knew about the Nicholson mine. It wasn't much of a mine, just an exploratory tunnel to see if there were silver deposits. When none were found, they stopped working on it. But he knew it was there."

"I can't imagine what that was like for them," I interjected.

"It was terrifying. The wind was howling, driving the fire closer and closer to them. They were choking on the smoke, and the heat was oppressive. A lot of men wanted to quit and simply die, but he wouldn't let them. He even pulled out his pistol and threatened to shoot one man if he didn't get up and keep going. It was strange that a man would rather burn to death than be shot, but it worked. The man got up and pushed on.

"Meanwhile, men were crying out in despair. A lot of men who hadn't said a prayer in years called out to God to save them. The further they went, the worse it got. Men were coughing and could barely breathe. It was like a Biblical description of hell: a lake of fire."

Dr. Decker continued to recount each man's experience, even using their names. I was mesmerized by his descriptions. It was as though he knew each one personally and shared in their ordeal.

"A burning tree fell on Bill Pullman and killed him," he continued. "They couldn't stop. They had to go on. He left behind a widow and two small children. Others were on the verge of panic by then. But Ed himself kept a cool demeanor throughout, and that helped the men keep going."

"A true hero," I said.

"A man of deep faith," Dr. Decker said. "As he hiked, he recited the words of Isaiah: 'When you walk through the fire, you shall not be burned, nor shall the flame scorch you. For I am the Lord your God.' I am sure as a firefighter that was a verse he had memorized."

"One might imagine," I said, wondering how he knew all of this.

"When you are in crisis, it is always good to remember God's promises," he said. "Don't hesitate to remind God of them, too, not that He would forget them."

Eventually, we came to the mine tunnel. It was not much to look at, just a hole in the hillside, the entrance framed by wooden posts. A metal grill prevented anyone from entering. I could imagine Ed Pulasaki finding it as a boy wandering the woods and even exploring its depths.

"The mining company dug in only a couple of hundred feet before giving up," Dr. Decker said. "Ed took his men to the furthest point and had them lie down. One man, Noah Pickens, wanted to leave, but Ed again pulled out his pistol and told him he would shoot him before he let him go. Noah survived the fire and went on to have 10 grandchildren and 24 great-grandchildren. One of his grandsons was elected mayor of Wallace.

"At one point, the entrance beams caught fire, and smoke began pouring in. There were puddles in the mine, and Ed scooped the water up in his hat to put out the fire. The smoke knocked him unconscious, and the men had to carry him back to the end of the tunnel. He suffered lung damage, loss of sight in one eye, and burns that plagued him the rest of his life, but he saved the lives of 38 men. When they managed to get back to town the next morning, Ed and his wife spent their savings to pay for hospital care for the men. The government never reimbursed him and even refused his request to put up a plaque honoring the men who died."

"So what happened to him?" I asked as we turned around to hike back to the trailhead.

"The Forest Service may not have rewarded Ed or even recognized his heroism during his lifetime, but he received his reward," he replied. "A man's willingness to sacrifice his life for others resonates through the universe."

———-

When we reached the trailhead on our return trip, my brain shut down. Or at least that is what I was told. I have no memory of anything after we came down the trail and I saw the Jeep parked where I had left it. I woke up in a Spokane hospital room. Ten hours of my life were a complete blank.

"Where am I?" I asked a heavyset nurse leaning over me, taking my vital signs. Her name tag said her name was Delores.

"You are in Spokane General Hospital," she replied in the clipped voice of someone who has dealt with too many difficult patients in her career. "We don't know what happened to you. We are awaiting an MRI."

I glanced around the room. It was a typical hospital room with monitors displaying various vital signs on a stand between two beds. A bearded man about my age with multiple tattoos on his arms lay sleeping in the other bed. "How did I get here?"

"By ambulance," she said. She abruptly turned and left the room.

I took an inventory of my mind and body. Everything seemed fine. I could move my hands and feet, and I could remember details of my life, including Dr. Decker and the hike to the mine. It seemed strange to me that a nurse left so quickly without offering more details to a patient waking up. Later, I learned that I had been conscious the entire 10 hours but had no short-term memory. I had been peppering the nurses with the same questions over and over again.

The nurses had taken off my hiking clothes and replaced them with a hospital gown. I would have gotten out of bed were it not for the IV hooked up to my arm. I racked my brain for memories of an ambulance ride and, I assumed, being treated by doctors and nurses in the emergency room. It was all a blank. I was growing frustrated and looking for the call button to summon a nurse when a doctor came in.

"Mr. Mathers," she said. "I am Dr. Putnam. I am a neurologist. Do you understand me?"

"I understand," I replied. "Dr. Putnam. Neurologist. Apparently, I have been out of it for a while, but I'm back now. Can you tell me why I am here?"

"I am told you were out hiking and got disoriented," she said. "The person you were hiking with called an ambulance. The local doctor in Wallace had you transported here because you need an MRI, and they don't have a machine."

"I don't remember any of that."

"You were conscious the entire time," she said. "You were talking to people but not remembering anything. It's possible you had a stroke. Or it is possible you have a tumor. Or it could be something else. We are waiting for the MRI machine to be free. We will know more then. But in the meantime, I would like to do some cognitive tests."

For the next 10 minutes, Dr. Putnam quizzed me about what month it was, who was the president of the United States, where I lived, and other questions. She gave me words to remember, then distracted me with questions before asking me to recall them. She made me follow her finger in different directions and then touch my nose. Then she tested my limbs to see if I had lost any strength. I passed everything with flying colors.

As she finished up, the other man in the room woke up moaning in pain, holding his head. "I will come see you when we have the MRI results," Dr. Putnam said and left.

Almost immediately, a hospital clerk came in to ask me about my health insurance. Hospitals need to be paid, of course, and I had no insurance card in my wallet. The MRI alone would cost more than $5,000. I gave her Cecelia's number with strict instructions that Cecelia was to wait for a diagnosis before flying out. I didn't want everyone to go to DEFCON 1 until we knew exactly what had happened.

As the clerk was about to leave, I mentioned that I was a billionaire and would be able to pay whatever the hospital and the doctors charged. She was taken aback, not sure whether to believe me, but then offered to have me moved to a private room. I declined. I was fine where I was.

Dr. Putnam had instructed the nurse to give the man across the room pain medication, and after a few minutes, he was well enough to talk to me.

"Why are you in this little corner of hell?" the man asked.

"I wish I could tell you," I said. "I woke up here. They say I've been out of it for 10 hours. They don't know why yet. Why are you here?"

"Brain cancer," he said. "I've been in remission for two years, but this morning I woke up dizzy with a terrible headache. They think it might have come back. I know it has."

"I'm sorry."

"It's a death sentence," he said. "We all know that. Glioblastoma. That's a fancy word for it. I'm just a miner. All this doctor talk doesn't mean anything to me. But I know when things are bad. They are going to put me through this machine, but I already know what they are going to find."

We talked for a while as we waited for the orderlies to take us to the MRI. Travis Maynard had grown up in rural Idaho, the son of a miner who never thought of doing anything else besides following his father's footsteps. He married a local woman who worked as the assistant manager of a fast food franchise, and they had two children, a girl and a boy. They were doing fine, living the middle-class life, when he fell unconscious deep in the mines one afternoon. Since then, it had been a long, hard slog fighting the cancer with surgery, radiation, and chemotherapy, draining their savings and straining their marriage. His wife would come over to be with him as soon as her shift ended, and she arranged for the children to stay with a neighbor. They needed the money more than he needed the company.

"Don't worry about the money," I told him. "I have more than I will ever need and will pay your hospital bills. And whatever else you need to get back on your feet."

"Seriously? I heard you tell the clerk that you were a billionaire. I thought you were joking."

"It's a long story," I said.

"If you are serious, thank you so much. It would be a huge relief. I worry about them when I am gone."

"I am serious," I said. "It is no coincidence I'm here now in the same room you are. There are no coincidences."

"That's what my wife believes," he said. "She believes no matter what happens, God works it for good. I'm not so sure about that."

"I imagine she prays a lot."

"Endlessly. I'm not sure why. If God was going to heal me, He would have done it by now."

I thought of Janice and how God had not healed her despite all my prayers. I could identify with his wife pleading for a miracle. Now he was back in the hospital with a severe headache, certain he was going to die. I didn't need to imagine what she was thinking and feeling. I had lived it.

"You just focus on your health and stop worrying about paying for things," I said.

——-

The MRI machine reminded me of a coffin.

I lay in the same position as a corpse at a funeral, my hands folded over my chest. I wore headphones to protect my hearing from the deafening sound of the machine. The headphones also allowed the technician to play music and talk to me. As the Eagles sang "Hotel California," he broke in to remind me to remain perfectly still. Then the machine beeped loudly and the magnets began to spin.

A gnawing fear rose somewhere deep inside of me. Or so it seemed. Maybe they were a primal response to a perceived threat of being suffocated in a confined space. Or maybe I was terrified of what the terrible, deafening machine would detect in my brain. I always assumed I would live a normal life and death was decades away. But suppose this was it? Freud said our unconscious does not believe in its own death and acts as though we are immortal. Freud had never been in the high-tech coffin of an MRI machine.

Immediately, I thought of my faith in God and felt ashamed that I would ever fear dying. What would Brian or the Senator or Gaylord think of a man who professed that Jesus had conquered death and yet found himself nervous when the prospect of dying actually loomed before him? Cecelia said that when Janice died, Jesus was there to hold her hand and take her to the place He had prepared for her in heaven. I wondered if that was true. Was

Janice at perfect peace in her semi-conscious state as the cancer finally won its battle over her body?

I certainly was not at perfect peace as the heavy magnets whirled noisily around me. A battle raged between faith and fear. I realized there were places inside of me that had not surrendered to the Gospel. A scripture planted in my childhood mind surfaced about the inner conflict between the Holy Spirit and our flesh. But what did it mean? Another verse arose where Paul asked, "Who will deliver me from this body of death?" As the law of Moses tempted Paul to despair, the MRI machine could only diagnose my disease. It could not cure me. It could only give me the sentence of death. Paul gave thanks to God through Jesus Christ. Could I do the same?

"You are a fraud and a fool," Bruce Springsteen sang to the tune of "Born to Run." Your faith is wishful thinking? A fantasy."

It wasn't Springsteen's voice. It was John Demas. "Where is your Jesus now?" he sang. "You are doomed to hell."

"Shut up!" I barked. The sound of my voice echoed inside the coffin. The music stopped.

"Is everything all right, Mr. Mathers?" the technician asked.

"I'm OK," I replied, my heart pounding. "I just had a moment."

"If you want to stop the test, just push the button in your right hand."

"I'm OK."

John Demas had overplayed his hand. His very existence reminded me that there was a spiritual battle going on. I had an enemy, but I also had a savior. Another scripture from the sword drills of my youth came into my mind. "I am the resurrection and the life," Jesus said just before weeping at the tomb of His best friend. "Whoever believes in me will live even if he dies, and whoever lives and believes in Me will never die."

Peace flooded my heart, the peace that defies understanding. Yes, Jesus had been there holding Janice's hand as her body died. And yes, He would be at my side when I died.

But that day had not yet come.

——-

When the orderlies pushed me back to the room, the clerk appeared again, along with a nurse and another man wearing a suit, who turned out to be the CEO of the hospital. They had discovered that indeed I was a billionaire. The CEO offered to move me again to a private room and to provide my own full-time nurse during my stay. I assured him I was fine where I was and told him to assign the nurse to Travis, who was still waiting for his turn in the MRI machine. I told him I would pay for it.

"Do you know Mr. Maynard?" the CEO asked.

"No," I said. "I just met him. But he needs a nurse more than I do. And if you could have someone bring us both some sandwiches, that would be great. I think we both are hungry."

"We will do that," he said, waving at the clerk. "We are a non-profit hospital and depend a lot on charitable donations, but we will do our best to take care of both of you."

I was impressed at how cleverly he slipped the possibility of a donation into the conversation. We chatted for a few minutes about how I ended up in Idaho and the story of Ed Pulaski before he wished me well and left. He did not say a word to Travis. The nurse, however, hovered over Travis, checking his blood pressure, then retreated to a corner of the room. There was nothing for her to do until the neurologist returned with the MRI results.

Shortly after, Travis' wife, Clara, showed up in full panic mode. She rushed to her husband's side and embraced him, tears flowing. What they had feared most had happened. They could hope the MRI came back with good news, but they knew better. I had a flashback to the two times Janice's cancer had returned. The first time it was visible, a lump was growing through her sternum. The second time, a PET scan had revealed tumors in her lungs that ultimately spread to her liver and her brain. Both were soul-crushing.

A fresh wave of grief flooded me, and I said a quiet prayer for them. "Lord, please spare them what Janice and I went through." It was a simple prayer, and I wondered if it was enough. It was all I could muster. It dawned on me that the quality, not quantity, was the true measure of prayer: that all the "thees" and "thous" of my childhood church paled before a simple plea from the heart. "Help them," I whispered.

A couple of minutes passed, the air filled with Clara's sobs as she buried her head into Travis' chest. He rubbed her back to comfort her. Even the nurse, a middle-aged woman who had had a stern, clinical countenance, dabbed the corner of her eye. My heart ached at the remembrance of holding Janice's body after she died, not wanting to let go of her even though she was gone.

Then there was a mild commotion in the hallway outside. "Only family are allowed in, sir," a nurse said sternly.

"He is part of my family," came the reply.

I recognized the voice of Dr. Decker. He appeared at the door still dressed in his hiking outfit. I wondered why a doctor would have to lie to a nurse to see a patient.

"There you are," he said as he crossed the room to my bed. "I hope you don't mind, but I took your car keys from your pocket and drove your Jeep up here. I don't have privileges at this hospital, so it took me a bit of effort to get to see you as a visitor."

"Thank you," I said. "That was very kind of you. Can you tell me what happened to me?"

"When we got to the trailhead, you became disoriented. You didn't know where you were. I told you where we were, but you forgot immediately and asked again. I examined you and was worried you might have had a stroke, so I called an ambulance."

"It is a good thing you were there," I said. "I could have gotten lost in the forest."

"You seemed to recognize your Jeep and could tell me your name. You knew you were from West Virginia, and your sister's name is Cecelia. But you couldn't remember what happened 30 seconds before."

"But I'm fine now," I said. "What do you think happened, doctor?"

"I'm not a neurologist. Unfortunately, you are going to have to wait for the MRI results."

"How concerned should I be?" I said. "I feel fine."

"Anytime someone becomes disoriented for no apparent reason, it's a concern."

For the first time, he took note of Travis and Clara still in a silent embrace across the room. He crossed over to them and whispered something in Clara's ear. She pulled away from her husband and looked at him with a puzzled expression, tears still streaming down her cheek. He leaned forward and put his hand on Travis' forehead, looked up to the ceiling, and mouthed words silently.

When he was finished, he abruptly turned towards me. "I'm afraid I can't stay, Joe," he said. "I have other people I need to see. I wouldn't worry about the MRI results. I'm sure they will be fine."

I again thanked him for coming and bringing the Jeep. Then he left just as the orderlies came to take Travis for his MRI.

"Do you know that man?" Clara asked me.

"I just met him today," I said. "But he seems familiar to me. Like I've met him before. I just can't place him."

"Me too," she said quietly, then turned back to her husband. "Me too."

An hour later, Dr. Putnam returned carrying a clipboard and an Apple tablet, trailed by three other doctors and a nurse. Clara stepped back, and they huddled around Travis, alternatively examining his head and the Apple screen. They seemed perplexed.

"How is the headache?" Dr. Putnam finally asked.

"Completely gone," Travis replied. "I feel so much better. Thank you for whatever you gave me."

Dr. Putnam nodded and glanced at her colleagues. Two of them shook their heads. The other, a large man wearing a surgical cap, intently scrutinized the tablet and looked dumbfounded.

"Mr. Maynard," she finally said. "Can you confirm that you had surgery to remove a glioblastoma 18 months ago."

"Yes, ma'am. Dr. Williams here took it out," he pointed to the large doctor.

Dr. Williams shook his head. "This is impossible," he said to Dr. Putnam. "Are you sure this is the right MRI?"

"We triple-checked it," she replied. "It's his."

"I don't believe it," one of the other two doctors said. "Let's not get our hopes up."

Dr. Putnam gave a stern look at the doctor. Then she turned to the large doctor. "Dr. Williams, Mr. Maynard is my patient, but you were his surgeon. Would you tell him what the MRI shows?"

Dr. Williams stepped forward. "I do not believe in miracles, Mr. Maynard," he said. "But if I did, I would say I am witnessing one. I performed surgery on your brain 18 months ago and removed a tumor the size of a pigeon egg. In the process, I was able to remove some surrounding tissue that was not essential to your brain function. Your MRI today, which I will insist that we repeat, showed a perfectly healthy brain with no sign of any surgery." He paused, brushed back Travis's hair, and then exhaled loudly. "And there is no scar."

The room fell silent as Travis and Clara digested what he had said. "Then the cancer didn't come back?" Clara finally asked breathlessly.

Dr. Williams hesitated before responding. "There is no cancer," he finally said. "There was a tumor. I removed it. I can show you the pathology slides. But there is no tumor now. According to this MRI, there never has been one. In fact, I never performed surgery."

―--

Dr. Ethan Williams buttonholed me the next morning as I

checked out of the hospital. He was an intimidating man, both physically and intellectually. I learned later that he was a former All-State linebacker in high school. He made second team All-American at Washington State, then graduated at the top of his class at Johns Hopkins Medical School. He completed his surgery residency with a fellowship in neurosurgery at Mass General before returning home to Spokane. He did not strike me as a man who suffered fools or wasted time on idle conversation. Nor was he a man used to taking "No" for an answer.

"Mr. Mathers," he said with a bass voice matching his large, athletic body.. "Would you allow me to buy you lunch?"

"That would be fine," I replied. "But I will buy. Not in the cafeteria. Let's go to a decent restaurant."

As we drove in his Lexus to a small bistro near the hospital, I wondered if Dr. Williams had invited me to lunch to ask what had happened in the hospital room with Dr. Decker. Then again, he might also have been looking for a donation to the hospital.

On the way, he said he was pleased my MRI revealed no strokes and no tumors. My brain was perfectly healthy. He had seen several cases of Transient Global Amnesia, a puzzling but rare event where a person loses short-term memory for a few hours with no permanent damage. It was a medical mystery. He said no one knows what causes it, and it rarely happens twice.

The previous night, I had talked at length to my mother, Cecelia, and Lara, and they all gushed with relief and praise to God for the diagnosis. None were surprised when I told them about Travis. They were interested in Dr. Decker, but I couldn't tell them much except that I went on a hike with him and he called the ambulance when I became disoriented. They were highly amused when I told them about the puzzled looks on the doctors' faces when they saw Travis's MRI results.

"I've seen that look before during my career," Cecelia said.

When Dr. Williams and I sat down at the bistro, we briefly discussed football, especially how my father would have loved to have had a star linebacker as a son. Dr. Williams said that ironically, his parents, both musicians, had no interest in football, and he had no idea where in his family lineage the genes had been passed down for him to be a star athlete. He had always wanted to be a doctor, and he made it clear to the NFL scouts that he would be going to medical school. As a result, no team drafted him. The ESPN talking heads were aghast that anyone would give up the millions he would have earned tackling running backs on Sundays. No one had ever done that before.

"I understand a family member of yours was in the room before you were both taken for an MRI," he said after we had ordered sandwiches.

"Not a family member," I replied. "The man who joined me for a hike near Wallace and then called the ambulance. Dr. Mel Decker."

"A doctor?"

"Yes, but he said he didn't have privileges at Spokane General."

Dr. Williams pondered this for a moment as the waitress brought glasses of lemonade. "I have never heard of him, but there are lots of doctors in Spokane," he said. "It's strange that he would lie to get to see you. If he had identified himself as a local doctor, we would have made an exception."

"I guess it was just a way to get past the nurses quickly."

"What exactly did he do while he was there?"

I briefly recounted what had happened in the five minutes Dr.

Decker had been in the room. He was especially interested in what he had said when he touched Travis on the forehead, but I was too far away to hear it.

The waitress brought our sandwiches, and we both tucked in. After a couple of bites, Dr. Williams wiped his mouth with a napkin and spoke softly.

"Mr. Mathers," he said. "I would like this conversation to be confidential. It would be inappropriate for a doctor to talk about a patient's case to someone who is not specifically authorized by the patient. But I think you would agree this is an exceptional case."

"My lips are sealed."

"Good," he said. "Let me tell you a little bit about myself. I am a man of science. In science, things that happen have explanations, even if we haven't discovered them yet. The universe operates on immutable physical laws. If I drop my fork, it will end up on the floor, not the ceiling, because of the law of gravity. I could do it a million times, and a million times it would end up on the floor. I do not believe these laws can be suspended or manipulated. That is why I reject religion. I am an educated man, and educated people read the Bible because of its importance to Western civilization. I have also read the Buddhist, Islamic, and Hindu scriptures. I reject them all. A man cannot walk on water. A person dead for three days cannot be brought back to life.

"I have had several moments in my medical career when something unexplained happened. A woman patient of mine had an aneurysm in an artery in her brain stem that would kill her almost instantly if it burst. We admitted her the night before, and I was scheduled to do surgery at 7 a.m. the next morning. When I cut into her in the operating room, there was no aneurysm. It had disappeared overnight. I had the MRI and the CT right in front of me that showed the aneurysm, but it wasn't there. She claimed it was because her pastor and two elders of her church had anointed her with oil and prayed for her. I decided that as unlikely as it was, the artery had somehow fixed itself overnight."

"Is that possible?"

'Highly unlikely, but it happened."

"But now…"

Dr. Williams took a long swig of his lemonade. It was clear he was carefully editing what he would say next.

"There is no possible explanation for what I saw on Mr. Maynard's MRI and when I examined him. It is not a matter of not yet knowing the explanation. There is no explanation. He has the healthy brain of a 38-year-old man who has never had brain cancer or surgery to remove a tumor. He doesn't even have scars where I cut into him."

"And that leaves you where?"

"There is no explanation except the explanation that I have rejected as unscientific."

"That God healed him and Dr. Decker had something to do with that?"

"That is hard for me to accept."

I thought for a moment. "And the reason you invited me to lunch was not to ask for a donation to the hospital but to give you an explanation that you could accept."

Dr. Williams nodded. "I read about you on the internet late last night," he said. "I am sorry about the loss of your wife, so please accept my condolences. I thought about the infinitely minute chance that a man could lose his wife on the same day he defied billion-to-one odds to win a lottery. No doubt you have pondered the same thing."

"I have," I said. "Especially when you consider what the newspapers never found out. I have never bought a lottery ticket in my life. It was left by a hospice volunteer at my house. A volunteer who can't be found and apparently doesn't exist in anyone's records."

"That's unbelievable," Dr. Williams gasped.

"Not as unbelievable as what happened to Travis Maynard," I said. "Dr. Williams, you have entered into the realm of the divine. Perhaps dragged kicking and screaming, but that is where you are. It is a realm I have lived in for the past few months since Janice died. This is about God. I don't know who Dr. Decker is, but he certainly has something to do with God."

"I have a hard time accepting that."

"So did I," I said. "When Janice died, I was done with God. My first conclusion was he didn't exist. My second conclusion was that if he did exist, He either wasn't all-powerful or he wasn't good. We prayed and prayed, and yet Janice died. I figured I had just been talking to myself. No one was out there listening."

"So what changed?"

I finished my sandwich, took a last sip of lemonade, and launched into my story of traveling the country in the Tiffin until God used a wooden sculpture of Jesus carved by a former U.S. Senator in the Ozark Mountains to penetrate my hardened heart.

"That's a remarkable story," Dr. Williams said when I finished.

"I have seen too much along the way to have any doubts," I said.

"And what happened to Travis Maynard no longer surprises me."

Dr. Williams looked up at the ceiling. "I don't know if I could come to that point."

"That is understandable," I said. "I've had a lot of time driving across the country to think about what leads people to faith in an unseen God. I find there is usually one of four scenarios, although sometimes a combination of them."

"And they are?"

"The first is a crisis. Something threatening happens outside their control, like a health issue, a wayward child, or loss of a job. They have ignored God all their lives, but then they cry out to Him for help or even a miracle."

Dr. Williams nodded. "I have seen that many times with patients and their families," he said. "It's understandable, but I have dismissed it as inventing hope when there is no hope."

"Second, they reach a point where they are sick of themselves. They are suddenly faced with their self-centeredness, their selfishness, and the terrible things they have said and done to other people. They know there will be a price to be paid. They reach the point of despair and cry out to God for mercy."

Dr. Williams frowned. "If one doesn't believe in God, why would one worry about sin and judgment?"

"Exactly," I said. "But people know deep in their hearts that there will be a judgment day. They will be accountable. They simply deny it until they can't deny it anymore."

"I have to think about that."

"The third reason people turn to God is mostly true of children,"

I continued. "God gives a child a glimpse of His love, perhaps in a dream. It is so intoxicating and so wonderful that the person spends the rest of their lives seeking im. I believe this is true of my sister, Cecelia."

"Nothing like that ever happened to me. And I am not sure I would have believed it anyway."

"Me neither," I said. "But then there is the fourth reason. A person reaches a point in their life when everything seems meaningless. They may have been successful in getting what they want in life, or they may not have, but they are overcome by a sense of futility. Every day they are nearer to death, and they are not content. It is a quiet despair, and I think it is the reason a lot of people commit suicide."

Dr. Williams glanced away, scanning the bistro with a blank expression. He took a sip of his lemonade and coughed lightly. Finally, he looked back at me, no longer with the appearance of a confident neurosurgeon but of a perplexed man.

"Mr. Mathers," he said. "I have heard 60,000 people in a stadium cheer me wildly because I sacked a quarterback. I have been applauded as valedictorian of my high school class, and newspapers have published glowing articles about me. I have been interviewed on ESPN. I have been hailed by medical school professors and seen my name on the lists of the top neurosurgeons in the country. I have become rich and attracted beautiful women, two of whom married me. I've had mothers and fathers thanking me profusely for saving the lives of their children. When I walk into the hospital, I am treated like royalty by the nurses, the staff, and even the other doctors. I have lived the dream.

"Yet when I turn out the lights at night, I am lonely. I have gone through two divorces. My last wife said it was impossible to be married to a man who was in love with himself. But I am not in love with myself, Mr. Mathers. I am frustrated with myself. I have worked hard and had huge success in everything I have done. But all of it has left me dissatisfied and lonely."

"Chasing after the wind," I interjected.

"Solomon in Ecclesiastes," he replied. "It is the one book in the Bible that is completely honest."

"Good memory."

"When I read something, I don't forget it. That is how I finished at the top of my class everywhere I went."

I got the attention of the waitress and ordered more lemonade and a slice of chocolate cake for dessert. Dr. Williams skipped the cake and asked for a latte. The waitress scurried off.

"Dr. Williams, forgive me if I speak too bluntly. I don't know you, and you are a far more accomplished man than a physical therapist for the Virginia Tech football team who won a billion dollars in a lottery he didn't enter. But I assume you didn't ask me to lunch to flatter you. You want the truth and, for some reason, you believe I can give it to you. So to the best of my ability, I will.

"The challenge you face…the choice you face…is ultimately not about science versus religion. That is a red herring. It is about identity. You are an extraordinarily gifted man. Stitch by stitch, you have woven an identity for yourself that is admired by the world. Every day you put it on like your lab coat, and other people admire the name on it, Dr. Ethan Williams, Neurosurgeon.

"The reason we are sitting here is because you know that is not your true identity. You weren't made to be a linebacker or a neurosurgeon. You were made to be in an intimate relationship with the God who created you. You were made to bear His image.

When a man becomes what he is intended to be, he has peace. He is never lonely."

"And where is that identity found?"

"In Jesus."

"I have trouble believing in Jesus."

"Faith ultimately is a choice, a matter of the will. Choose to give Him your life, and He will give you a new identity."

"I am not sure I am ready to make that choice. It's not rational."

"Neither is a man with brain cancer being instantly healed and restored, even to the point of a scar disappearing."

Dr. Williams took a deep breath. "What then would you have me do?"

I paused to consider what I would say next. "There is someone I want you to meet, but it will require you to take some time off from your work and go on a trip. I haven't asked him yet, but I am quite certain he will agree to have you come visit."

"Who would that be?"

"The man I told you about in my story, Randall Farris, the former senator from Arkansas. I think you should meet him."

Dr. Williams looked dubious. "You think I should go to the backwoods of Arkansas on some kind of spiritual quest?"

I thought for a moment, then looked straight into the eyes of a man not used to being challenged by other people.

"That all depends on how badly you want it."

Lara called me when I got back to the Tiffin in Wallace later that afternoon, but I did most of the talking. She listened patiently while I told her about my meeting with Dr. Williams and his decision to visit Randall Farris in Arkansas the following week. The Senator had been more than willing to host him.

"I've figured it out," she said when I had given her an opening.

"What did you figure out?"

"Dr. Decker."

"Oh?"

"His first name is Mel, right?"

"Yes."

"Mel Decker?"

"Yes. What are you getting at?"

Lara laughed. "Do you remember the mysterious figure who met Abraham when he returned from rescuing Lot and gave him a blessing? The Bible says he was the king and priest of a place called Salem."

"I can't say I know that."

"Salem later was called Jerusalem."

"And?"

"Many theologians believe this king and priest was Jesus. In fact,

Paul wrote that Jesus was part of the same order of priesthood – a priesthood not based on ancestry but on the power of an endless life."

"And?"

"His name was Melchizedek."

Chapter 19

An Eye Dropper by the Ocean

When I left the hospital, I discovered something about God. Sometimes He is too much for me.

He is 10,000 volts coursing through a device designed for 120 volts. Except His voltage is infinite. Somehow, He limits Himself and only gives us what won't short-circuit us. It's what He did when He became a man. The disciples walked and talked to the Creator of the universe day by day for over three years. They ate with Him and even saw Him weary and thirsty under the hot Middle Eastern sun. But when He went up the Mount of Transfiguration and Peter, James, and John saw Him for who He is, they couldn't handle it. They fell asleep. They shut down.

In Wallace, Idaho, I shut down. After hiking with Dr. Mel Becker, aka Melchizedek, aka Jesus, my brain went blank for 10 hours. The doctors diagnosed Transient Global Amnesia, but who knows? Maybe there was too much voltage, and my brain shorted out for a while.

When I returned to the Tiffin, my emotions flatlined. I awoke depressed for no reason. The opposite should have been the case. I had walked with Jesus and witnessed a miracle. I should have been dancing on air. Yet inside, I felt like a runner completing a marathon and collapsing on the ground, every bit of emotional energy expended just to reach the finish line. Lying in my bed staring at the ceiling of the Tiffin, all I could do was ask, "What is wrong with me?"

———-

"I am too small and God is too big," I told Lara when I awoke her at 6 a.m. "I am on the shore of a vast ocean holding an eye dropper. It is overwhelming."

She seemed to understand. "When you come down from the mountaintop, you usually have to go to a valley," she said. "Sometimes you go into the wilderness. It is painful, and you are tempted to flee. To go hide somewhere."

"I don't know what to say or what to do," I replied.

"Think of what the Apostle Paul wrote in his letter to the Corinthians," she answered. "He said he was struck down but not destroyed. He was perplexed but not in despair. He always carried around the death of Jesus that the life of Jesus would be revealed in him."

"But I question myself whether I even have faith at all. How can a man have faith and feel depressed?"

"It is the way God works in us. Paul was given a vision of heaven so fantastic he couldn't even speak of it, but then God allowed Satan to strike him with a thorn in the flesh to keep him from being puffed up," Lara said. "He performed miracles during his ministry, but there were also times when he felt abandoned in a Roman prison. He was so alone that he wanted to die and be with Jesus. But weak and weary in that dank, dirty prison cell, he wrote some of the most powerful scriptures of the New Testament."

"But I should feel exalted, yet I feel deflated."

"Oh, Joe," she said. "God plants the seed of His Word in us. But humility is the soil where it grows. And God is simply humbling you."

It took a tunnel and a funeral to lift me out of the valley of my depression.

The tunnel was more than a mile and a half long on the Trail of the Hiawatha, a former railroad line converted into a bike and hiking path with scenic views of the Bitterroots. It was something Janice and I would have done together, and I wanted a distraction from the heaviness and disconnection from God that weighed on me. I rented a bike and soon rode deep into the heart of the mountains. As I pedaled, the light from the tunnel entrance gradually disappeared, and I found myself in a cold, murky underworld with only dim bulbs mounted on the sides of the tunnel to keep me from utter darkness.

I moved slowly, and other bikers sped by me, splashing water from puddles in the darkness. Eventually, I came to a stop and moved to the side. It occurred to me that the tunnel represented my current state. On both ends, there was bright light and beautiful scenery. If I kept pedaling, I would eventually come out of the tunnel back into the sunshine. But where I was, there was nothing but dank gloom that oppressed my soul.

"Is anything real?" I asked myself. I had seen a miracle with my own eyes. At that moment, I could not have denied the love of God. As I told Dr. Williams, I had seen too much traveling across the country to doubt. Yet in the tunnel, the doubts arose. Why could I no longer feel the presence of God? What was wrong with me that my soul would be so cast down?

Eventually, I pedaled on. After a few minutes, the light at the exit to the tunnel appeared as a pinprick. It gradually grew larger and larger until at once I burst into the fullness of an Idaho summer day and the vast beauty of the Bitterroots.

One of the scriptures I was required to learn as a child rose in my mind. "The path of the righteous is like the light of dawn, which shines brighter and brighter until full day." Yet I questioned whether the light of dawn would ever come again for me, much less the full day.

———

The following day, still oppressed, I had dinner with Travis and Clara in their log cabin home deep in the Bitterroots. They had invited a few friends to celebrate the miracle of his healing with a meal and a time of prayer: a fellow miner and his wife, an ambulance driver, and their pastor, Bill Mitchell.

When the main course was finished, I asked a question. "What does a man do with a billion dollars?"

It was a strange question, and I don't know why I asked it. The average job in Idaho paid $33,000 a year. At that rate, it would take any of the people around the table 30,000 years to earn a billion dollars. Like Travis and Clara, they probably lived paycheck to paycheck, maybe setting aside a little for a rainy day. They may never have traveled outside of Idaho on a vacation. Yet they didn't seem shocked. I was not Marie Antoinette looking down on the Sans-Culottes of the French Revolution – literally the ones "without underwear" – saying, "let them eat cake." I was simply a depressed man asking what to do with a fortune he never sought.

"Have you prayed about it?" Clara asked from the kitchen where she was scrubbing the dinner dishes.

Clara reminded me of Cecelia. She had only a high school education, but she was naturally intelligent and perceptive. I could easily imagine her as a doctor or university professor if she had been born into a different family in a different place. Even the intensity and purposefulness of the way she moved around the kitchen reminded me of my sister. I imagined that she, too, was a truth teller. Maybe that is why I asked the question.

"I have," I said. "At least I have since I became a believer. I didn't pray to anybody after Janice died."

"I'm sorry," she said. "It must be hard to celebrate a miracle of healing."

"I would be lying if I said I hadn't questioned why God healed Travis and not Jance or told you it isn't painful," I said. "I wonder where Dr. Decker was when Janice needed him."

Pastor Bill looked up from his plate. "What did Dr. Decker talk to you about when you were with him?" he asked.

The pastor was a slim man with gray hair. He wore thick eyeglasses that reminded me of a caricature of an accountant. I learned his church was not large enough to support a full-time pastor, nor was it likely to ever be because of the sparse population in the Bitterroots. Like thousands of pastors across the country, he worked – as a roofer in his case – to pay the bills but otherwise dedicated his life to ministry. Clara said he was well-respected and other pastors looked to him as an authority on the Bible.

"We didn't talk about Janice," I answered. "There was no reason to. He talked about Ed Pulaski and his men. He knew everything about them and what they experienced during that terrifying ordeal."

"He was with them," Travis said matter-of-factly. He was sitting next to the pastor at the head of the table and had been quiet most of the evening. I realized that was his personality. I could see why he and Clara were a well-matched couple, but even a strong marriage can be tested by a crisis like brain cancer. "He was also with Janice."

I looked at Pastor Bill. "So do you think it was really Jesus, pastor?"

Pastor Bill hesitated, and I could tell he was thinking hard about how to answer the question. The Bible foretells Jesus' return in glory to destroy Satan and eventually create a new heaven and a new earth where all who give their lives to Him will reign forever with Him. But would Jesus actually appear in bodily form before then?

"If you had told me he talked to you about theology, I would answer 'No,'" he said. "We have the Bible. God has given us all the theology we ever need. He has revealed Himself for who he is. He has nothing more to say on that matter. But you said he talked about those poor men trapped in an inferno. He knew their names. He experienced their terror and their despair with them. He mourned with those who died and celebrated with those who survived. So I will answer yes, that is what I believe."

"I don't understand."

Pastor Bill looked at me inquisitively. I realized he could sense the dark cloud that had enveloped my soul and the doubts it had conjured up.

"Think about it," he said. "When John the Baptist was in prison, he sent a messenger asking Jesus if He truly was the Messiah. In the darkness of Herod's prison, he was probably depressed and having doubts. How did Jesus respond? He said the blind receive their sight, the lame walk, lepers are cleansed, the deaf hear, the dead are raised up, and the poor have good news preached to them."

"Which means?"

"If you want to know if Jesus is real, you need to do what He said."

"Which is?"

"He said, 'Where I am, there my servant will be.'"

"And where is that?"

"With people who need Him. That's where He is."

"I am not sure I understand."

Pastor Bill smiled. "Come with me tomorrow. I will show you."

———-

Before I left the hospital, I asked Cecelia to create the Decker Medical Relief Foundation to provide assistance to people in the Bitterroots and Spokane who were struggling to pay medical bills or otherwise couldn't get care. The afternoon after our dinner with Travis and Clara, Pastor Bill took me to the funeral of its first beneficiary, Melissa Shoemaker.

Melissa had just turned 65 when she passed away from an acute case of pneumonia that had gone untreated because she had no health insurance and didn't trust doctors in any event. All the new foundation could do for Melissa was to hire a nurse to attend to her in her last hours of life and then take care of her disabled daughter, Mary.

"Melissa had a tough life," Pastor Bill told me as we drove to the funeral. "Her father was an alcoholic who barely kept food on the table. She dropped out of high school to help support the family. Then she married an abusive man who beat her regularly. She had two sons and then Mary with him. She refused to leave him, but then he left her for a younger woman. One of the sons died in a car crash when he was a teenager. After that, she had a lump in her breast that was probably breast cancer, but she refused to go to a doctor. She just prayed, and whether it was cancer or not, it never spread.

"About that time, her other son was killed in a logging accident. All this happened while she took care of Mary, who was born with spina bifida. Mary needs a wheelchair, but she is able to work as a cashier at a local convenience store where Melissa also worked. They somehow scraped together enough money to survive, but every day was hard. Mary will not be able to live by herself."

"Of course, the foundation will take care of Mary," I said.

"God provides," Pastor Bill said.

"Indeed," I said. I had no illusion that I was providing for her. God was.

"Melissa lived an invisible life in a remote corner of Idaho," Pastor Bill continued, "Sometimes, I am driving in the mountains and I find an old graveyard from the 19th century on a dirt road that nobody has visited in a long time. As I read the headstones, I try to imagine what life was like for the people buried there.

"Sometimes, there will be three or four little headstones next to a big one. Those are the babies and little children who died. It was very common then. Many children didn't survive to adulthood. You can imagine the sorrow of each death. You can also imagine how perilous life was living off the land on the frontier. There was no safety net. All you had was your neighbors to help you. If they could."

"They lived unknown to the world, and they died," I said. "Then they were forgotten."

"They certainly are not forgotten by God," Pastor Bill replied.

We fell silent for a few moments, and I thought about the celebrated Dr. Ethan Williams, who was well known to the world. He was the opposite of Melissa Shoemaker. One day, he would have an elaborate headstone in a cemetery somewhere. Then, a century or two from now, someone like Pastor Bill will read his epitaph and wonder what his life was like. At that point, what ultimately was the difference between Dr. Williams and Melissa Shoemaker?

We arrived at Pastor Bill's church, which stood along a creek in the mountains. It reminded me of Brian's church in Radford with its steeple and white clapboard sides. The parking lot overflowed with trucks and cars, and people were filing into the church. These were working people, and some had come from their jobs in blue jeans or overalls. By the time we entered the church, nearly all the pews were full. Melissa's body lay in an open coffin in the front.

Pastor Bill welcomed everyone, and the congregation sang "Fairest Lord Jesus," one of Melissa's favorite hymns. He gave a short eulogy focused on Melissa's unwavering faith amid a life of continual struggles and crises. Then he led the congregation in another hymn, "It Is Well with My Soul," which was appropriate to her life. Its 19th-century author, Horatio Spafford, penned it following the death of his four daughters in a shipwreck.

When sorrows like sea billows roll
Whatever my lot, Thou has taught me to say
It is well, it is well, with my soul.

How much comfort Spafford's hymn must have given to Melissa and many others struggling with tragedy and loss in the 150 years since he had written it. I could not have said "It is well with my soul" after Janice died. But could I now? In the strange darkness that had overcome me, could I believe that Dr. Decker was with me just as he was with Ed Pulaski's men?

If anything, seeing Melissa's lifeless body in her coffin and her daughter Mary in a wheelchair sobbing as the congregation sang the hymn only deepened my depression. These working-class people of the Bitterroots no doubt struggled under the burdens and trials of their own lives. Now they were witnessing where it all ended for one of their own. Life offered no apologies for its difficulties.

Death did not have the final word, however. The miners, loggers, store clerks, and mechanics of the Bitterroots did. Pastor Bill opened the floor for them to share memories of Melissa, and one by one, they made an invisible woman visible if only for those who had eyes to see and ears to hear.

It started with a neighbor who spoke about the time her child was desperately ill with meningitis. Melissa stayed with her every moment the child was in danger, fasting and praying without ceasing until he recovered. Then an older man stood up and told of Melissa nursing his late wife in her final days when he couldn't afford any help. On and on it went, story after story of a woman struggling with her own trials who nevertheless poured herself out into the lives of others.

Finally, a petite teenager who had been standing in the back came forward holding a sleeping baby. She gazed at Melissa's body for a few seconds, then turned towards the congregation with tears in her eyes.

"A year ago, I was going to kill myself," she said in a breaking voice. "I discovered I was pregnant. When my boyfriend found out, he broke up with me and wouldn't return my calls. My parents threw me out of the house. I dropped out of school. I slept in the basement of a friend's house. Her parents were friends of my parents, so she had to sneak me into the house after they had gone to bed. I had to leave before they woke up. I had nowhere to go.

"But on the day I planned to jump off a bridge, I stopped by the convenience store where Melissa and Mary work. Melissa knew what I was going to do just by looking at me. They pulled me aside and talked to me about Jesus. For the first time in my life, I felt truly loved. In fact, Jesus was there. Right there with us. I could see Him. Not with my physical eyes but with my spiritual eyes. Instead of throwing my life away off a bridge, I gave my life to Him."

The congregation broke into applause with shouts of "Hallelujah" and "Praise God!" "Melissa and Mary invited me to stay with them until Ray was born," she continued. "They got me a job at the convenience store and helped me find a place to live. They watched Ray so I could work the night shift. And most importantly, she brought me here to meet Pastor Bill and all of you. You haven't judged me. You have loved me."

She paused for a moment and then began to sing Amazing Grace over Melissa's body in a beautiful soprano voice, tears still streaking down her cheeks. Enraptured, the congregation joined in on the second verse.

At once, I was aware of the presence of Jesus in the church. It was not with my eyes, as the woman had said. This was not Dr. Decker in bodily form. Rather, He came as light. More than light, in fact – radiance. The face of the young woman glowed, and as I looked around, I saw other faces seemingly bathed with a spotlight of soft, comforting light. I felt a warmth in my own countenance. The dark cloud that had weighed on me evaporated, replaced with a sense of otherworldly love, a love beyond knowing.

When the congregation had sung the last verse, Pastor Bill stood behind Melissa's coffin. He seemed to look straight at me. "Jesus said 'Where I am, my servant will also be'," he said. "Melissa was where Jesus was, and Jesus was where Melissa was. Melissa's life teaches us that if you want to find Jesus, don't go to a seminary. Go to where He is. Go to the people He loves."

—--

Before I left Wallace, the Decker Medical Relief Foundation had a new chairman. Dr. Ethan Williams returned from Arkansas and immediately agreed to oversee the foundation when I met him for lunch at a diner near the "Center of the Universe" with a 1950s decor much like the rest of the downtown. He had been eager to talk to me and drove the 90 minutes from Spokane to meet me.

"You were right," he said as we sat down and a waiter scurried over with menus. "I entered into the realm of the divine. But it might not have been what you expected."

"I am not sure I know what to expect anymore," I said. "What happened?"

He took a deep breath. He was dressed casually and seemed much more relaxed than at our last lunch. "I was impressed with Senator Farris. It takes a lot of self-awareness and conviction to turn your back on fame and power and move to the backwoods to live among people the world has no interest in."

"Indeed," I said, remembering how Dr. Williams had described being treated as royalty by the hospital staff and other doctors in Spokane. He could more easily imagine than I could leaving behind the prestige of walking the halls of Congress as a U.S. Senator. I had only left behind the sidelines of a college football stadium and countless spools of athletic tape.

"I enjoyed his church service and his preaching," he continued. "He gave a great message on the power of forgiveness. It got me thinking quite a bit about the people I need to forgive. And those who need to forgive me."

"We don't realize how important forgiveness is or how powerful," I said. I was going to tell him about Lizzy Miller and Buster Blanchard and how one woman's determined forgiveness changed the life of a hateful racist, but we were interrupted by the waiter. After we ordered our food, Dr. Williams continued his story.

"I have lived my life around some of the smartest and accomplished people in the country," he said. "And while I recognized Senator Farris as one of these people and spending time with him was enjoyable, it did nothing to move the needle."

"Move the needle?"

"I still felt unsettled and dissatisfied, desperately trying to explain away what happened to Travis Maynard so I wouldn't have to confront what I didn't want to confront."

"Chasing after the wind?"

"Chasing after the wind," he said. "And as fine a man as Senator Farris is, he could not help me catch the wind."

I shrugged my shoulders. I had expected the Senator to have more of an impact on him. "So what happened?" I asked.

Dr. Williams leaned forward as if to share a secret. "It was the mountain man," he said. "The Vietnam Vet named Dwight. He was the one who moved the needle."

"You visited him?"

"Senator Farris took me to his place," he said. "I was skeptical.

You've been there and you know what I mean. I half expected Jed Clampett to come out of the cabin when we drove up."

I laughed. "I get that," I said.

"He told me his story. I was, of course, impressed that he had been awarded the Congressional Medal of Honor. They don't give those to just anyone. But it was what he said next about his addiction and the street preacher that reached my heart. I had seen a miracle with Travis Maynard, although I tried to deny it. But when I heard Dwight tell of being instantly delivered from addiction and his willingness to reach out to the very people who had derided him when he came back from Vietnam, I knew it was a miracle. I have worked with addicts, and I can tell you what he said is as unlikely as what happened with Travis. Drugs and PTSD change a person's brain chemistry. It can't be fixed in an instant, if it ever can be fixed."

He hesitated, then continued. "But more important than the miracle, I sensed the presence…." he paused again for a moment. "I sensed the presence of God when he told me his story. I heard God speak. It wasn't audible, but it was clear. He said 'Don't harden your heart, Ethan. Listen to this man, he is telling you the truth.'"

"What did you do?"

Dr. Williams looked up at the ceiling to reflect on what he would say next. The waiter arrived with a tray of food, but he raised his hand to tell him to wait a moment.

"I fell on my knees and wept," he said softly. "The distinguished Dr. Ethan Williams, MD, put his head in the lap of a mountain man from Arkansas and asked God to deliver him from the loneliness and despair of this world. To deliver him from himself. And that, Joe, is a miracle."

"Wow," I said. It was hard to imagine such an imposing man on his knees in tears.

"Dwight and the Senator baptized me in the creek behind his house," he said. "I was not just baptized in water. I was baptized in the Spirit of God. I was overwhelmed. It was more than I could handle. More joyful than can be imagined. I had a vision of myself as a small, helpless child held in the arms of a loving Father. He whispered in my ear 'Stop striving, Ethan, you are home.'"

I instinctively reached out and put my hand on top of his hand: a hand that had brought healing to so many people through surgery, and yet the hand of a man who desperately needed to be healed himself.

"Praise God!" I said.

"Praise God," he repeated. It was genuine, but it was strange hearing those words from an accomplished man of science and medicine who just a few days before had rejected any notion of God or the divine.

I thought of Pastor Bill, Melissa, and the young woman who sang Amazing Grace at her funeral. "Sometimes," I said. "We can be too smart for our own good. When he was bemoaning that life is vanity and chasing the wind, Solomon also noted that in much wisdom is much grief. The person who increases knowledge increases sorrow. We try to find God with our minds, and we fail. He is too big. Or we try to avoid God with our minds, and we end up chasing the wind."

"I certainly didn't find God with my mind," Dr. Williams said. "God found me through the last person I would have expected."

"If you want to find Jesus," I said. "Go to where he is."

"What do you mean?"

"With people. That is where you will find Him. Travis' Maynard's pastor told me that recently."

Dr. Williams reflected for a moment. "I suppose that is true," he said. "No one could have ever debated me into the kingdom of God. Something about Dwight bypassed my mind and gave me eyes to see."

I nodded. Then a thought struck me.

"Dr. Williams," I said. "I bet when you got back to the Senator's house, you took a long nap."

He raised his eyebrows. "How would you know that?" he asked. "Yes, I was utterly exhausted."

I smiled. "Because as great an athlete and surgeon as you are, you are still only a man with an eye dropper," I said, "And you are standing on the shore of a vast ocean."

———

When I returned to the Tiffin after lunch, I found a note taped to the door. In neat block letters, it simply said. "Camp Misery. Jewel Basin. Meet me."

It was not signed. I looked around, but no one was in the adjacent RV sites. Wherever Camp Misery was, it was my next destination.

Chapter 20

The Lake

Camp Misery is a misnomer. There is nothing miserable about it. Rather, it is a hub for hiking trails leading from the Jewel Basin high into the Swan Mountains with stunning views overlooking Flathead Lake in Montana. After a three-hour drive from Wallace, I left the Tiffin in an RV park at the south end of the lake and drove to the trailhead near the north end.

According to the note, someone was supposed to meet me. The lot was almost full as hikers were just returning to their cars, but no one approached me. The note hadn't specified a time, so I had no idea when I was supposed to meet this mystery person – if indeed it was a person.

After a half hour with no one even making eye contact with me, I thought about what Cecelia would do. She was never one to sit around. She would tell me to do something. So I put on my boots, grabbed my hiking stick, and set out on one of the trails. Whoever left the note would have to find me. If they didn't find me, then the note was a prank. A random prank for sure, but a prank.

I climbed the steep trail along switchbacks cutting through the spruces, pines, and larches. A few hikers passed me coming from the other direction, perhaps surprised someone would be starting out so late in the day. I didn't know where I was actually going, so I didn't want to venture too far and risk being far from the trailhead as night fell. I didn't bring a flashlight, but I did remember my bear spray. I might surprise a grizzly bear – or even worse, a grizzly bear with her cubs – coming around any corner.

After a half hour – just about the time I was going to turn around – I came to a clearing on a ridge. Stretching out before me was the breathtaking vista of Flathead Lake, bordered on the east by the Swan Mountains and the southwest by the Mission Mountains. No one else was visible except for three mountain goats grazing just below the ridge line.

I sat down on a large flat rock by the trail and soaked up the unspeakable beauty of the landscape. I wondered how anyone could look upon such glory and not recognize the hand of an Artist. Yet just a few months before, I would have been one of those people. Janice and I loved nature, and hiking refreshed my spirit, but I would never have believed the Sunday School God of my childhood – the rules-obsessed God who didn't heal Janice — would manifest Himself in rocks and trees and lakes. Now I saw His hand everywhere.

"The heavens declare the glory of God," a familiar voice said. I turned to see Gabe Remiel standing behind me on the flat rock. He wore hiking attire and gazed through binoculars at a distant bird soaring above the lake. "What a beautiful bird He designed when He created bald eagles. But if you really want to be awestruck, watch a condor on the wing. They are ugly on the ground because they are vultures, but when they are soaring, they are ballerinas in the air."

"I figured it might be you who left the note," I said. "I never thought I would see you again after Bayou Thunder."

"We are always around, even if you don't see us, Joe."

"I'm sure you didn't call me here to talk about birds," I said.

"Not at all," he said. "In fact, you didn't come here to meet me. I have a task for you. A divine appointment, if you will. They will be here in about 30 seconds. Keep your eyes on the lake."

"What am I looking for?"

"Don't worry, you won't miss it."

———

Just as Gabe had predicted, a couple appeared along the ridge from the opposite direction, a tall man and a petite woman in their late 60s or early 70s. They had the appearance of experienced hikers, well-equipped and physically fit. The man wore a small backpack with bear spray in one side pouch and a bottle of Gatorade in the other. We exchanged greetings, and they sat down near me on the flat rock. The woman dug a bag of trail mix out of the backpack and offered me some, which I declined.

As they tucked into the trail mix, we silently enjoyed the magnificent view. After a couple of minutes, the woman asked the universal question strangers ask each other: "Where are you from?"

"West Virginia," I answered. "But my wife passed away, and now I am a wanderer. I live in a Tiffin Allegro Bus and travel the country."

"A full-timer!" She exclaimed. "So are we. And we have an Allegro Bus as well. We are from Missouri, but we've been on the road for two years."

We dove into a conversation I had had many times. Where have you been? Where are you going? Have you been to Red Bay? Did you meet Bob Tiffin? What did you do for a living? I was glad they didn't recognize me. It was unlikely someone living in an RV and moving from place to place would be keeping a close watch on the Powerball lottery, but one never knows. The typical small talk rattled on and usually ended with shaking hands and never seeing the other people again. But I had to figure Gabe hadn't brought me to this place simply to chat with strangers.

Little did I know that this would be the pivotal moment in the lives of Baron and Phoebe Hurtz – and in the end, both joyful and tragic. In fact, I wondered afterwards how much Baron remembered it. For some people, the curtain falls, and there is no remembrance.

The view became even more spectacular when the sun dipped below the distant mountain, birthing a magnificent sunset as its light refracted through the atmosphere and lit up the clouds. The water of Flathead Lake came to life with a variety of shades of green and blue and even pink near the far shore. The entire valley morphed into a kaleidoscope of color as though O'Keefe or Turner had painted it.

"Mother Nature is quite an artist," Phoebe said. "These are the moments we live for. It makes all the travel worth it."

"Do you think nature is really a mother?" I asked tongue in cheek. "Couldn't she be a he, a father?"

Phoebe smiled. "Well, I never thought about that," she said. "I suppose Father Time could be Mother Time."

"I don't have experience being a mother," I replied. "But it seems to me that mothers don't have any time. So it must be Father Time."

We laughed. "You are right," she said. "I raised two boys. I had no time. It must be Father Time and Mother Nature."

Baron hadn't said a word up to this point except to shake my hand and introduce himself. He seemed distracted, glancing at his watch and standing up. "Speaking of time," he said. "We'd better get going or it's going to get dark on us."

At that moment, however, Flathead Lake caught fire. At first, I thought it was just an optical illusion, and I am sure Baron and Phoebe figured the same. But then flames began rising into the air off its surface, and we could hear the crackling sounds of a great inferno. A wave of heat accompanied by the smell of smoke rolled over us.

"What the...?" Baron exclaimed, sitting down again – in fact, almost falling backwards on the flat rock.

"What is that?" Phoebe gasped.

"It must be some kind of illusion," Baron said. "The lake seems to be on fire!"

"How beautiful!" Phoebe said excitedly. "Nature is so awesome. I've never seen anything like that."

I didn't say anything. Clearly, this was the reason Gabe had guided me to this place. When you've slain Bayou Thunder and hiked with a doctor who turned out to be Jesus, nothing completely surprises you, even a lake on fire.

Phoebe fished a smartphone out of the backpack and started to take pictures of the lake. But when she looked at the photos on the phone, there was no fire, only a lake in the fading light of dusk. She took several more photos with the same result.

"I wonder why my camera is not working," she said.

"Perhaps it is something that only we are given eyes to see," I suggested. "And a camera lens can't detect it."

Baron took his eyes off the lake for a moment to look at me doubtfully. "You mean you think it's just a hallucination? A trick of the mind?"

I shook my head. "I doubt three people would have the same hallucination at once, not to mention feel heat and smell smoke," I said. "I think God is showing this to us for a reason."

Both Baron and Phoebe stiffened at the mention of the word "God," then glanced at each other. "It's very interesting," Baron said, beginning to stand up again. "But I think we need to be going."

Before he could get to his feet completely, Phoebe gasped again and pointed at the lake. "Look, there are people walking on the lake!" she exclaimed.

Baron and I both followed the path of her finger, and indeed, there were outlines of people among the flames. They trudged slowly forward toward the lakeshore as though battling against some kind of force, like people trying to walk against hurricane winds. When they reached the edge of the lake, they could go no further because the force against them was too great. After trying to step onto shore for a few moments, they turned around and headed toward the other side of the lake. The force switched directions and continued to press against them while the flames leaped around them.

"It's definitely a hallucination," Baron said. "People can't walk on water."

"You are right, Baron," Phoebe said. "It must be our imagination."

"Or it could be God showing us something," I said. "You do believe in God, don't you?"

Baron glanced at me with a scowl on his face. "Absolutely not," he said angrily. "And it's offensive to me that you would even suggest it."

"Now, Baron," Phoebe quickly jumped in. "I don't think he intended to offend us. He probably believes it." I got the impression that Phoebe often had to intercede with others for her husband's quick temper and sharp tongue.

"Well, I don't," Baron said. "And I don't like it when idiots try to force their superstitions and fairy tales down my throat."

Phoebe looked at me apologetically. "I'm sorry, Joe," she said. "We tried religion once. A neighbor convinced us to go to church with them, and we even went to a Bible study for a few weeks. But then Baron realized that a man who had cheated him in his business was an elder in the church. We stopped going, and now he gets angry anytime someone mentions God."

"With good reason," Baron said. "They are a bunch of self-righteous hypocrites. It's all a scam to get your money and tell you how to live your life."

"You are right about one thing," I conceded. "Churches are full of sinners."

"Exactly right," Baron said. "Except that's not the word I would use. They think they are better than we are and look down their noses at us because we don't believe their fantasy."

"Well, the man did come to you and apologize. And he wrote you a check," Phoebe said.

Baron gave his wife another hard look. "I didn't want his apology, and I turned down the check. I didn't want that man's money."

Phoebe shrugged her shoulders and sighed. "I'm sorry," she said to me. "Baron does feel strongly about it."

"You are damn straight," Baron barked as he started to stand up again. "We need to be going."

Before he could get to his feet, however, the lake erupted with a geyser of fire that rained down embers on the people struggling to cross it. It reminded me of the finale at a Fourth of July fireworks celebration. The people on the lake cried out in agony. Their screams echoed through the valley. Baron plopped down on the flat rock again.

"What is that about?" he pointed at the geyser, which continued to erupt.. "That is like Old Faithful except it is fire, not water."

I turned to him. "Do you suppose it is a picture of hell?" I asked.

"Could it be?" Phoebe asked, her eyes wide open in amazement. "Didn't the pastor at that church we went to talk about a lake of fire?"

"That's nonsense, Phoebe," Baron retorted loudly. I detected a hint of uncertainty in his voice.

Phoebe cringed, then forced the smile of a woman dominated by her husband, who wants to keep the peace at all costs and doesn't want other people to notice, even though it is obvious.

We fell silent for a few moments, watching the people in the lake struggle. Finally, I asked, "What do you think it means that three people would have the same hallucination, smell the same smoke, and hear the same screams?"

Baron harrumphed, then stuck his finger in my face. "All that heaven and hell stuff," he said. "I've heard it. It's just a way to control people through fear."

"But suppose it isn't?" Phoebe asked.

"Shut up, Phoebe!" Baron barked. "Don't let this man deceive you."

Phoebe cowered at his rebuke, looking down at her lap. "I'm sorry," she said.

Baron ignored her. He pulled his finger away from my face and picked up his backpack. "Now we do need to get going," he said. "This man is infuriating me with his religious foolishness."

Once again, a geyser of fire erupted in the lake, and the embers fell on the people, now in the middle of the lake. They screamed in pain again. Baron unleashed a string of expletives and didn't get up.

"Why do you suppose they can't get out of the lake?' I asked.

"Why don't you go ask them?" he responded sarcastically.

I raised my eyebrows. "That place is not for me," I said. "But let me suggest a reason that they can't get out of the lake."

"What do you think it is?" Phoebe asked.

Baron didn't rebuke her this time, much to my relief. I suspected he was curious about what I would say.

"It is their ego that keeps them trapped – or at least what people call ego these days. I would call it 'self.' If this is indeed a picture of hell, and I believe it is, then the force that pushes against them is their obsession with themselves. I might say self-adoration, but it wouldn't be true. In reality, deep down, they hate themselves.

They struggle to reach the edge of the lake where they could escape from the agony of the fire by climbing on the shore, but they can't do it because self stops them. So they turn around and cross the lake, hoping they can get out on the other side."

"But wouldn't they learn and then get out?" Phoebe asked.

"That's impossible," I said. "While they were alive on earth, it was possible. They had a choice. They could repent. In other words, they could literally turn away from self and surrender themselves to God. And God would deliver them from their slavery. But once they died, the choice they made while they were alive was cemented in place. There is no possibility of repentance in that lake. They are permanently slaves to their own self – the self they actually hate. And as you saw a moment ago, self won't let them out of the lake."

"That's a bunch of gibberish," Baron said softly, his voice betraying increasing uncertainty.

I pointed at the people in the lake as another geyser rained down fiery embers on them. They were elbowing and pushing each other, trying to get to the front of the pack. "That's what they said when they were alive. Although I'm not sure they believed it. I think everyone knows in their heart that they will face a judgment day."

"I don't want to end up in that lake," Phoebe said with a tremble in her voice.

Baron gave his wife another nasty look. "Even if it were true, which it is not, you don't have to worry about that, Phoebe. We have lived a good life. We are good people."

Phoebe looked at me rather than her husband. "But why would God show us this if He didn't want to warn us?"

"Don't you start that God stuff on me now," Baron snapped. "We settled that years ago."

"You settled it. I didn't. I don't want to end up in that lake."

I sensed she had surprised herself with her boldness. She tensed up, waiting for an explosion from her husband. Baron hesitated, however. His wife questioning what he said seemed to have thrown him off balance. "It's just a hallucination," he replied quietly.

Phoebe leaned towards me. "You don't seem to be scared, Joe," she said. "Doesn't it frighten you? Would God send good people to that lake?"

I could not have responded to her question very well, except that the answer simply dropped into my head. I realized it was the still small voice of the Holy Spirit speaking to her through me.

"It isn't God who sends people to that lake," I said. "They made a choice to go there. Scripture says God desires all people to be saved and come to a knowledge of the truth, but He leaves the choice to us."

"Why would anyone choose to go there?"

I remembered what Gabe Remiel had told me when I faced Bayou Thunder. "Because even though being saved from that lake is free, it is also costly," I said.

"What do you mean?"

"God's salvation is a gift. You can't earn it by being a good person or doing good deeds. His standard is complete holiness, and none of us can reach that standard by our own efforts. You either receive God's holiness as a gift or you don't receive it. The people in the lake rejected the gift. The cost was too high for them."

'What is the cost?" Phoebe asked with a worried expression.

"Your life," I replied. "Not your physical life but your soul. You can't bow down before the God of the Universe and continue to be the god of your own life. Many people try to do it. They go to church and profess beliefs, but they don't surrender to Him. They are never set free and end up in the lake buffeted by the very identity they refused to surrender. Sometimes, tragically enough, it is a religious identity they cling to."

Baron scoffed loudly. "That's a bunch of nonsense," he said. "Not that I wouldn't like to see the guy who cheated me suffering in that lake."

"I don't want to end up in that lake," Phoebe repeated.

"God doesn't exist," Baron said loudly. "Don't let this man fool you."

I ignored Baron's outburst and turned to Phoebe. "There is only one way to be saved from this lake. Someone else had to pay the penalty for your rebellion against God – for making yourself your own god. Someone had to give you God's holiness."

"Jesus?"

"Yes, Jesus," I replied. "There is no other way. Would you like to receive God's gift?"

"Nonsense," Baron shouted. "Phoebe, he just wants our money. This is all a trick of some kind. We need to go."

Phoebe ignored her husband. "I would," she said.

"That's it," Baron barked, standing up. "We are going." He grabbed Phoebe's wrist and tugged her to her feet. She didn't have the strength to resist him. He pulled her onto the path and dragged her along behind him.

"What do I do?" She cried out to me.

"Just talk to Him," I called out. "He will hear you. He will answer."

"Shut up!" Baron shouted. "Shut up!"

The flames on the lake disappeared. Baron and Phoebe turned a bend in the trail. Then they were gone.

———--

Gabe was waiting for me when I returned to the trailhead just as darkness fell. We were alone in the parking lot. He was leaning against the hood of the Jeep, still dressed in hiking attire.

"I see you have the bear spray ready," he noted as I reached the Jeep. Indeed, I was holding the bear spray with a death grip, my finger on the trigger.

"You are an angel and don't have to worry about grizzlies in the dark," I said. "But we mere mortals need to be prepared."

"No one is a mere mortal," he replied slyly. "That was one of today's messages."

"I got that," I said with a smile. "I'm not sure it was received, at least by the husband."

He frowned. "It wasn't," he said. "Maybe it will be."

"What about Phoebe?" I asked.

Gabe nodded, a smile on his face. "We often don't let people know what happens to others they share the good news with," he said. "They don't find out until they are in heaven, and then it is a joyful surprise. But in this case, I can tell you she started talking to Jesus as they hiked to their car."

"And?"

"She belongs to Him now," he said. "She is no longer afraid. His perfect love has driven out all fear of that lake. It won't be easy for her. The gate is narrow and the way is difficult. Baron will bully her and try to make her turn back. But light overcomes darkness. She will find in herself a strength far greater than his. In the end, maybe she will influence him in the time they have left."

I thought about Phoebe being in heaven, in the place where I met Janice in my dream. Then I thought of Baron trapped in the lake of fire. "I am both delighted and grieved at the same time," I said.

"It is the price of freedom," he said cryptically. "Not just for you but for God."

"Where do I go next?"

"Stay in this area," he said as he turned and walked into the darkness of the forest. "The next lesson is for you."

Chapter 21

The Forest

Dr. Arlene Mathews knocked on the door of the Tiffin at 9 a.m. the next morning. I had just gotten out of bed after a long night's sleep and opened it with uncombed hair and a cup of coffee in one hand. To say I was startled to see the president of Tuskegee University seeking me out in Polson, Montana, would be an understatement, but as noted before, I was learning not to be surprised by anything that happened to me. I immediately wondered if she was part of the "next lesson" Gabe had mentioned – the one for me.

"Dr. Matthews," I exclaimed. She was meticulously dressed in a blue dress and high heels with a stylish saffron scarf around her neck, not the attire one normally saw in an RV park in Montana.

"I am sorry to show up unexpectedly, Mr. Mathers," she said. "But my secretary could not reach you. I found out where you were through Goldman Sachs and then your sister, Cecelia. May I come in?"

I glanced at the interior of the Tiffin. It was not picked up. Dishes lay in the sink. It was an unwritten rule among full-time RVers that the inside of a coach was a private space unless specifically invited in. Most socializing occurred outside around a campfire.

"Sure, but it's a mess," I said.

Dr. Matthews was simultaneously awed by the luxurious inside of the Tiffin and repelled by my dirty dishes and clothes draped over the corner of the sofa. I remembered her office: she was a meticulous person. I cleared some space on the captain's chair for her to sit and sat on the couch opposite her. I offered her some coffee, but she declined. I noticed she sat upright with perfect posture and speculated that she had had ballet lessons as a child and a grandmother who insisted on ladylike behavior.

"This is my first time in Montana," she said. " In fact, other than Denver and California, I haven't spent much time in the West. There is a lot of America I need to see, but I have never been an outdoors girl. I preferred studying in libraries and visiting big cities."

"Then welcome to the wilderness," I replied with a chuckle. I noted her demeanor was completely different than when I met her in her office. She had been stiff and cautious then. Now she was relaxed and chatty.

"No doubt you are wondering why I am here," she said, stating the obvious.

I nodded. "The question had crossed my mind."

"There are two reasons," she said. "The first is that the board of our university instructed me to visit you to ask for a donation to a worthy cause. Many of our students arrive on campus unprepared for college because our public education system is so weak. In particular, their math skills and writing ability are lacking. Rather than watch them struggle and drop out, we propose to fix that with a year of college prep before they begin their freshman year. Unfortunately, most of them can't afford this. We want to provide

100 students with this opportunity for free. But we need a sizable donation to do this."

"How much?"

"A minimum of $10 million to start with," she said.

"Make it $20 million and more if needed," I said.

"Cecelia predicted you would say that."

"My sister knows all things."

"I noted that when I talked to her," Dr. Matthews smiled. "Would you like the program to be named after you? We will have to build another dormitory. We could name that after you."

I laughed. "Not a chance," I said. "A man who wins a lottery didn't do anything to be worthy of something named after him. In fact, it would be embarrassing."

"Anyone else then?"

I thought for a moment. "Actually, yes," I said. "I would like to name the program after someone who never graduated from college but taught me a lesson about the power of forgiveness. Her name is Lizzy Miller, and she lives in a remote area of Idaho with her daughter and disabled son. Of course, we would have to get her permission."

Dr. Matthews looked at me with a concerned expression. I realized what she was thinking. "Don't worry," I said. "She's African American."

"I'm sorry," she said. "I was just thinking about how my board would react."

"That's all right," I said. "I get it."

No one spoke for a few moments. Dr. Matthews glanced around at the lavish interior of the Tiffin, but I could tell she wasn't thinking about the cherry wood cabinets or Sub-Zero refrigerator. She was contemplating what she would say next.

"You said there was a second reason you came," I noted to break the silence.

She nodded. "Mr. Mathers," she said. "I want to apologize. When we met in Alabama, I judged you. And I judged Mr. Weinstein. It didn't matter that you were making an unheard-of donation to Tuskegee; I put you both in the same box. And it wasn't a good box. It was not a box anyone can buy their way out of, even with $30 million. That is because the box was my box, and I spent my entire life making sure it was a well-tended, polished box where I could put other people. I could shrink people down so that they were small enough to fit because you can't fit a real person into it. In a perverse way, it made me feel good to put people in that box. What's worse is that I was doing exactly what I have spent my life criticizing other people for doing. I had all kinds of justifications why it was OK for me to do it and not others, of course."

"I think we all have a box like that," I said. "What changed?"

Dr. Matthews took a deep breath. "Your sister," she said. "I talked to your sister when I was trying to find you."

"Ah, the truth teller," I replied.

Dr. Matthews looked puzzled. "That's what I call Cecelia," I explained. "Some people have the gift of telling other people the truth in ways they can hear it. They are truth tellers."

"I suppose she is," she answered. "She wanted to meet me before she told me where you were. She flew all the way down to Alabama to visit me. I spent an afternoon drinking tea and talking to her."

"That sounds like Cecelia."

"The first thing she did was tell me about Mr. Weinstein. She knew a lot about him – about his parents dying in the death camps and the trauma of being transported to a new home with adoptive parents in Brooklyn. When she was done, I didn't see a rich Jewish banker. I saw a remarkable man who managed to overcome great odds – not to mention a lot of antisemitism – to get where he ended up. I saw a man who swam in the shark tank of Wall Street without becoming a shark. In fact, a man who never got married himself but worked tirelessly to help disadvantaged children in Brooklyn, whether they were Jewish or not."

"You saw a whole person," I interjected.

"Exactly," she said. "And then she told me about you."

"About me?" I tried to imagine what my sister would say about me.

"Your sister has a high regard for you," she said. "She told me about your care for your late wife while she had cancer. Then she told me about the football players you mentored – young men blessed with enormous athletic talent but not much else in life. You didn't view them as athletes but as confused teenagers in a world where 60,000 people cheered them on Saturday and then set them adrift with little education and few life skills on Monday."

"Janice and I couldn't have children because of her cancer," I said. "They became my children."

"She also told me about what you have done since you won the lottery, traveling the country."

"Buying the RV was Cecelia's idea."

"I don't know many people who wouldn't spend the money on themselves," she said. "According to Cecelia, you are giving the money away. She told me about the young couple in Alabama you bought a house for, and the Decker Medical Relief Foundation. And, of course, I know about what you are doing for Tuskegee."

I felt uncomfortable hearing about my sister singing my praises. "It isn't my money. I didn't do anything to earn it. I didn't even buy a lottery ticket. It's God's money."

"I respect that," she said. "But it's not what she said about the money that got my attention. Lots of rich people give away money."

"I don't understand."

"It's something else Cecelia said about you," she paused to reflect for a moment. "It's that you don't have a box. You don't shrink people down. She thinks that is the reason God gave you the money. You meet people where they are."

"Cecelia said that about me?"

"She was the one who came up with the analogy about the box," she replied. "I didn't think of that analogy. She used it talking about you. But the moment she did, I felt convicted."

"Convicted?"

"I not only have a box, I don't let people out of it. I didn't want to let you or Mr. Weinstein out of it. I wanted to keep you there. I had never let anyone out of my box."

I pondered what she said for a moment before I replied. "Dr. Matthews," I said. "I think you are being hard on yourself. We really don't know other people, and yet we have to interact with them. We don't even know ourselves. We are flying on instruments throughout life, trying to make sense of everything. I don't blame you for putting me in your box. I showed up out of the blue in your office and didn't tell you right away that I was the donor."

"Why didn't you?"

"I didn't want credit for it."

"A man who doesn't want credit for giving away $30 million to help poor students in Alabama doesn't fit in my box, Mr. Mathers," she said. "I had to shrink you."

"I don't know what to say."

"That's not all," she continued. "I said something to you just before you left that was wrong."

"What was that?"

"I said, 'There are some sins that can't be forgiven.'"

"I remember."

"What I should have said was 'There are some sins I don't want forgiven.' That was the reality. I didn't want the sins of Oswald Higgins to be forgiven."

"Why not?"

Dr. Matthews frowned. "Because then I would have had to let him out of my box," she said. "I didn't care if God forgave him or Simon Jackson forgave him or that he became a changed man and was beaten for marching with Dr. King. There was no way I was going to let the former Grand Cyclops of the KKK out of my box."

—--

As surprising as it was for a woman who described herself as a "city girl," Dr. Matthews came up with the idea for a hike. She didn't even bring hiking gear with her – she didn't own any, even in Alabama – and we had to stop by an outfitter to buy her some. She simply said she was interested in experiencing my life on the road and doing what I did.

"A kind of cross-cultural experience?" I suggested. I noticed how uncomfortable she appeared in brand-new hiking boots.

"You could call it that," she replied with a smile. "We should all try to broaden our horizons."

The hike itself on the east side of Flathead Lake was relatively easy and uneventful, a roughly two-mile jaunt that ended up at a stunning mountain pond. Dr. Matthews was in better shape than I expected and didn't tire out or complain. She did, however, keep her hand on her canister of bear spray the entire trip, scanning the woods for any sign of a grizzly. The trail was popular, and we passed a number of other hikers, but one never knew when a bear might show up. That clearly terrified her.

Along the way, we compared Virginia Tech and Tuskegee, and especially how minority athletes who aren't good enough to become pros fare after their four years of eligibility expire. We compared the lives of the poor whites trapped in the hollers of Appalachia with the poor blacks trapped in the low-income areas of Birmingham and other big cities. The same issues plagued both groups: drug addiction, domestic violence, out-of-wedlock births, low-paying jobs, unhealthy diets, struggling schools, and a culture of hopelessness.

"I have students who have miraculously come out of that environment to attend Tuskegee – it is almost always because someone, usually a father or other man, took an interest in them and mentored them when they were adolescents," she said. "They tell me that many of their friends don't expect to live long or, if they do, they assume they will be in prison."

"I think it's much the same is true in Appalachia," I said. "People have low expectations for their lives. Someone at a party offers them OxyContin, and they feel happy for a few minutes. Then, in a few months, they are dead from an overdose. All manufactured and distributed by the pharmaceutical industry."

"I will be honest," she said. " For all the bluster in the news media, it's not easy to think of a realistic way forward. There is no magic wand."

"Well, if you think of something, I have a billion dollars and no interest in buying a private island or a yacht," I replied.

—--

The lesson Gabe Remiel promised me was rooted in simple geography and human stupidity. That I terrified Dr. Matthews half to death made it even worse. Yet I, too, was deeply shaken, exposed by my fear.

As the crow flies, the distance between the RV park in Polson and the trailhead was relatively short. But automobiles are not crows, and the Mission Mountains blocked the direct route. We had to drive north along the shore of Flathead Lake past Bear Dance and Wood Bay to Big Fork. There we turned east and then south on Route 83 on the other side of the mountain ridges past Swan Lake to the trailhead in the Flathead National Forest. The trip took 90 minutes.

Unfortunately, as it turned out, I had bought a map of the

national forest at the outfitters. As I scanned it, I realized that if we traveled south on Route 83, we could cut our return trip in half by taking a road westward through the forest and out the other side near Polson. If someone made a movie of our trip, this would have been the point where the narrator flippantly asks, "What could possibly go wrong?"

What went wrong was the map. One of the purposes of Flathead National Forest is timber harvest, and timber harvest requires roads – lots of dirt roads that don't end up on official maps. When we took the westward turn into the forest, we were fine for the first mile. The road headed in a straight line towards Polson. As we drove, I noted the density of the forest and how a single match might lead to an inferno. I had seen photos from the late 19th century of western forests when naturally occurring fires caused by lightning strikes had kept them from becoming overgrown. After a century of fire suppression, they were bonfires waiting to happen.

After a mile, we came to a fork in the road that didn't appear on the map. I made my best guess and turned to the left. Soon, we came to another fork. I guessed left. Then another. I guessed left again.

"Are you sure you know where you are going?" Dr. Matthews asked. She tapped away on her phone, hoping for GPS, but in the middle of the forest there was no signal.

"I'm sure we will be OK," I answered. The captain never lets anyone know about his doubts. His passengers need to believe he knows what he is doing, even if he doesn't. Just a little turbulence, folks. Nothing to worry about.

It didn't take 10 minutes before we were hopelessly lost. I took a right at another fork, and the Jeep climbed up a steep slope to a ridge. The road narrowed and was just wide enough for the Jeep to navigate. Dr. Mathews gasped. A foot from our tires, the terrain fell 100 feet to a raging stream. The captain assured his passenger that everything was under control. She didn't believe him.

"I didn't come all the way from Alabama to die in a forest," she said.

"No one is dying today," I said.

"If we fall off this cliff, I'm going to kill you before you die," she said. I didn't think she was joking.

There was no way I was going to back the Jeep up on such a narrow road, so I had no choice but to forge ahead deeper into the forest. On and on we drove, going one way or the other with each fork in the road. I wondered about the last time a vehicle traveled on some of the roads. There were no ruts or tire tracks. The forest could swallow us, and no one would know what happened to us for days, maybe weeks. I could imagine the strange headline: "Skeletons of University President, Billionaire Found in Flathead National Forest." It would have been an amusing thought if it weren't a real possibility.

Dr. Mathews suddenly shrieked, a primal scream from the dawn of time. The sound caught the attention of the grizzly bear ambling across the road 50 feet ahead of us with her two cubs. She stopped and stared at us, seemingly puzzled. Dr. Mathews grabbed her bear spray but then realized she couldn't use it inside a vehicle.

"Get us out of here!" She demanded.

I slowly drove forward. The bear apparently didn't see us as a threat and continued across the road into the trees, the cubs scurrying behind her.

"Now you can tell your friends you have seen a grizzly in the wild," the captain said to lighten the mood of his passenger.

"Shut up, Joe!" she snapped. "Get us out of here!"

I drove on for another 20 minutes. The afternoon sun peeking through the trees dipped lower, and the forest darkened. I checked my watch. We had about an hour before sunset. The needle on the fuel gauge hovered just above empty. The panic light began to blink on my internal dashboard. I decided to own up to the situation.

"I don't know where we are," I said. "It's going to get dark, and I don't have much gas. We may have to spend the night in the Jeep."

"I thought you were an experienced hiker," she said with a combination of anger and fear. "We could die here."

"We will be OK in the Jeep," I said, once again struggling to be the reassuring captain.

"Nonsense, Joe. There is nothing 'all right' about this situation. If we spend the night here, we will still be lost and out of gas in the morning. No one knows we are even out here to come looking for us."

I stopped the Jeep. We stared into the forest, lost in our own fear. Once again, I thought of my sister. What would Cecelia do in a hopeless situation? What did she always do? What had she done when Janice was taking a turn for the worse and there was no hope? I thought of Gabe Remiel. He said the next lesson was for me. What lesson was lost in a forest?

I began to pray. Then I invited Dr. Matthews to pray with me. She looked at me with a bewildered expression, then gave me her hand. Together we pleaded with God to direct our path, to, in the words of Dr. Mathews, "make a way where there is no way."

The solution was obvious, so simple that it was embarrassing not to have thought of it. The Holy Spirit didn't give it to me. He gave it to Dr. Mathews. She stopped praying abruptly and looked at me.

"Joe, where does the sun set?"

"The west," I said. "Everyone knows that."

"Then start the Jeep and head towards the sun before it gets dark," she said. "Every fork, take the one that goes in the direction of the sun. We will eventually come out the other side of this forest."

——-

The large, muscular man tending a horse in a small corral next to a ranch house glanced at us, then went back to his business. The mailbox said McDermitt, but his hairstyle, with a long braid that fell down his back nearly to his waist, was Native American, not Irish. That a Jeep with an African American woman and a white man would run out of gas in front of his house, a quarter mile from the edge of the national forest, didn't seem to interest him.

"We almost made it," I said to Dr. Matthews. "I hoped we could run on fumes until we got to a gas station. I don't even know where we are. At least we are out of the forest."

"We are on the Flathead Reservation," she replied.

I spied a tractor in a barn behind the corral. "Do you think that guy will give us some gas?

"I don't think so," she said. "I've seen that look before."

"What look?"

Dr. Matthews grimaced. "Hatred," she said. "The look of hatred."

I shrugged my shoulders. "I saw the way he looked at us," I said. "But I didn't notice the hatred."

"Trust me, if you are black in America, you know that look," she replied. "But he wasn't looking at me. He was looking at you."

"I still don't understand."

"That's because you are white and from West Virginia and not from here," she said. "Before I flew out here, I did some research on this area. Remember, I enjoy books and libraries more than getting lost in forests."

"And?"

"This area is the home to three tribes –the Salish, the Kootenai, and the Pend Oreille. As with many Native American tribes in the 19th century, the U.S. government forced them onto a reservation in 1855. It signed a treaty with them, guaranteeing that the land and its resources were theirs forever. But when whites wanted to settle here in the coming decades, the government reneged on its agreement and allowed them to homestead on the reservation. Today, whites outnumber the Indians by two to one on the reservation. Your RV is actually parked on tribal land. Needless to say, there has been a lot of animosity, especially when it comes to water management, hunting and fishing rights, and law enforcement. That look you got was 175 years in the making."

"Why would he hate me? I never even heard of this place before this week. My ancestors were Irish. Based on the name on the mailbox, we may have common ancestors. They had their whole island stolen from them by the English. When the potato famine hit, the English tossed them out of their homes to starve on the roads because they couldn't pay the rent on the land that used to be theirs. You can still find the remains of the famine houses in fields around Ireland."

"There is no logic to that kind of hatred," she replied. "It infects everyone. I'm sure he's been looked at like that countless times."

"So people put him in their box," I said. "And he put me in his box."

"Yes, based on the way he looked at you."

"The look that Jesus got from the people who crucified Him?" I suggested.

Dr. Matthews raised her eyebrows. "That's probably true," she said. "I never thought about that."

"Lizzy Miller certainly thought about it," I said. I opened the door to the car. "If Jesus can deal with it, I can certainly deal with it."

——-

Maybe I couldn't deal with it.

I noticed the way the man moved awkwardly around his horse and figured it was a case of sciatica, not uncommon among riders. He silently glared at me when I introduced myself as a physical therapist and offered to take a look. I doubt he cared much about football or even had heard of Virginia Tech. I tried a different approach.

"I'm not from around here," I said. "We got lost in the forest and ran out of gas right in front of your place."

He ignored me and turned his attention back to grooming his

horse, a black and brown stallion that seemed to have an attitude on par with its owner. I pitied the greenhorn who attempted to ride it. I sensed that man and horse shared a deep connection that I understood Native Americans have had with wildlife since ancestral times, before Europeans set foot on the continent. By contrast, Janice and I hadn't even owned a dog, and I am sure the big stallion sensed that I was frightened of it.

Not quite sure what to say next, I watched as the man carefully brushed the animal. After a while, I glanced back at Dr. Mathews. I expected her to be concerned, but instead she was smiling, clearly amused. She pointed at the cell phone in her right hand. She had a signal, and the AAA was on the way, so I didn't need to bother the man anymore.

No one likes to be ignored, so maybe it was my ego, which had already taken a beating in the forest, or maybe it was something else, but I wasn't done. "I believe God brought me to this place at this moment," I said. "There is something he wants me to do to help you."

This time, the man stepped away from the horse and looked straight at me, anger in his eyes. "How are you going to help me, white man?" he asked. "Will it be the help your people gave us when they told us about their god as they stole our land?"

"I don't know," I replied calmly. "But there is something I could help you with. Maybe your sciatica or maybe something else. What do you need?"

"Since when does any white person care about my needs?

I shrugged my shoulders. "Right now," I said. "I care about your needs. And I think I can help you."

"You talk with a forked tongue," he responded. "You say you want to help me, but you really want gas for your car."

"I think the car has been taken care of," I said. "My friend has called for help. When it comes, we can leave, but then you would still need help."

"How can you help me?" he scoffed, taking a step towards me. "Are you the bank?"

"No, I am not a banker," I said. "I am a physical therapist."

"Then you can't help me," he said. "So you and your black friend over there can leave."

At that moment, a tow truck with an AAA logo came down the road. Dr. Mathews got out of the car to wave it down. The driver made a wide U-turn and came to a stop behind the Jeep.

"You never know where help might come from," I said, ignoring the implication that he felt the same way about Dr. Mathews as he did about me. "What is your problem with the bank?"

"What business is it of yours?" he snapped.

"You are the one who brought it up."

He took another couple of steps toward me. I wasn't sure about his intention, whether he intended to intimidate me with his size and strength. Fortunately, there was still a stockade fence between us.

"My family has owned this land for more than a hundred years – ever since the whites made us divide up the reservation they forced us onto and took more than half our land," he said. "Now the bank is going to force us to sell it."

"So you are in debt?"

"That's not your business."

"You are right, of course," I said. "But I can help."

The man paused and examined me closely. "I didn't ask for your help," he said.

"You didn't," I said. "But God often gives us grace before we ask for it. Maybe I'm His grace in your current difficulty."

The man folded his arms in front of him. "You can tell your god that I don't need help from someone like you. Or from your friend."

Dr. Matthews came up from behind and tapped me on the shoulder. The AAA man had given us a couple of gallons of gas, enough to get to a station in Polson. I don't know how much of the conversation she had overheard, but she was clearly eager to move on. I sensed she was uncomfortable on reservation land.

"I will tell you what," I said to the man, who had taken yet another step towards me. "I will be staying at the RV park in Polson. My site number is 14, and I have a Tiffin Allegro bus. If you decide you would like my help, come knock on the door."

"I won't."

"Think about it," I said. "It will make all the difference."

I turned away. Dr. Mathews and I climbed into the Jeep and drove off. As we reached Route 93 and turned right towards Polson, she looked at me quizzically.

"Why didn't you tell him you were a billionaire?" she asked.

I thought for a moment. "He didn't ask," I finally said.

—--

"So what do you think was the lesson?" Lara asked me when I called her two days later. The man with the horse had not come by or made any effort to contact me. Meanwhile, I spent a day driving Dr. Mathews on the Going to the Sun road in Glacier National Park. She flew back to Tuskegee from Missoula with a newfound appreciation of the beauty of God's creation.

"I've been pondering that," I answered. "I think there were actually two lessons that could be compressed into one lesson."

"What are those?"

"The national forest was a metaphor for life," I said. "We enter into it with a certain destination in mind. We lean on our own understanding to get there. But soon enough, we find that there are unexpected forks in the road and dangers we have not anticipated, such as the 100-foot cliff or grizzly bears. We do the best we can, but life is too complicated. Eventually, we find ourselves lost. There are too many turns. We might be going in circles for all we know. In the end, our bodies run out of gas just as my Jeep did. We die as the darkness falls on us."

"And?"

"There is only one answer to the hopelessness of our situation: look to the Son. Not the celestial body called the sun, but the Son who is Jesus. At every fork in the road, we take the one that leads towards Him, even if it doesn't make sense to our natural minds. At times, it may seem as though we are still lost in the forest, but we are actually safe in our journey, and our destination is as sure as the sun setting in the west."

"Wow, that is absolutely true," Lara said. "So what was the second lesson?"

"Pretty much the same. God offers a way, but we have to be willing to accept it. The Native American man is in more debt than he can pay back, and the bank is about to force the sale of his property. That land is what connects him to his ancestors, and he will soon be a landless Indian on his tribe's reservation. He has every reason to be bitter about how history has played out and how he has been treated. There has been terrible injustice. But God sent him a solution to his problem. A billionaire ran out of gas in front of his house and told him God sent him to help. But the man is so enslaved by his hatred, which is really his pride on steroids, that he will not accept help. So he will lose his land. And that will only enflame his hatred more."

"The story of salvation," Lara said, connecting the dots.

"Exactly," I said. "And the answer is the same. God has guaranteed us safe passage through the trials of this life and the next, but we must turn towards the Son."

"It is a good lesson," Lara said.

Neither of us said anything for a few moments. I thought about how I desired to be with her. I pondered all the experiences God had given me: the sacrifice of Bayou Thunder, the power of Liz Miller's forgiveness, the hike with Dr. Decker and the miraculous healing of Travis Maynard, the transformation of Dr. Williams, my descent into spiritual depression, and the resurrection life of Melissa Shoemaker's funeral. Each step of the journey, loneliness was the background music – my desire to be intimately connected to Lara. To be one with her.

"Will you come be with me?" I asked. "It is beautiful here."

Once again, she hesitated, and I sensed her heart screaming, "Yes, I will come." But her voice said differently.

"I will come when that fork in the road turns toward the Son," she whispered into the phone. "Only then."

Chapter 22

The Cloud

The Blackfeet call the Rocky Mountains the "backbone of the world." I understood why as I traveled east from Polson through the southern region of Glacier National Park. In the distance on the left was the towering peak of Chief Mountain, and to the right was the rugged Badger-Two Medicine landscape that is sacred to the tribe. For centuries, the Rockies were the western edge of the tribe's world, which stretched across the plains to the Great Lakes until the white man slaughtered the buffalo and drove the people onto a reservation, where many starved or died from smallpox.

I met Tom Hears Thunder in Browning, the largest town on the reservation with just over 1,000 people. A full-blooded Blackfoot with a rugged countenance bracketed by two braids, Tom didn't look at me the way the man with the horse outside Polson had. In fact, it was the opposite. When I entered his small convenience store to buy snacks for my journey, he greeted me warmly. As strangers usually do, we talked about the weather, and he told me that Browning held the world record for the single greatest temperature variation in a single day. In January 1916, the temperature fell from 100 degrees to minus-56 degrees in a 24-hour period.

I was about to leave with a bag full of chips and Snickers bars when his countenance suddenly became contemplative as though something significant had dawned on him. "I lead a small church here and we are having a worship service tonight," he said. "Would you like to come?"

I hadn't been to a church service since I attended Revival Christian Church and chastised Dr. Brantley Clay, D. Div., for running a business rather than a house of God. Going to church hadn't been my habit in Blacksburg, and I didn't like the awkward feeling of being an intruder in other people's services. I began each day with my own private worship before God, praying and reading the Word. I could easily have said "No," using my planned trip to Canada as an excuse, but I didn't. I told him I would be honored to attend.

He held the door open for me as I left. As I stepped through, he spoke to me. "Joe," he said. "I sense the Spirit within you, so you are my brother, but I have a question I ask everyone in my church."

"What is that?" I replied.

He put his hand on my shoulder and smiled warmly. "Do you know who you are?" he asked. "Do you know the power of the cross?"

———

I stepped out of the Jeep in a parking lot full of potholes in a rundown strip mall to drumbeats from Tom Hears Thunder's church, a storefront bracketed by a pizzeria and a barber and adorned with a simple sign, "Buffalo Christian Fellowship" above a wooden cross. Were it not for the drum beats, one could easily have passed it by without noticing it. Only later did it dawn on me that when God became a human being, He chose to be born in a manger, not in a palace. He certainly could abide in a storefront.

The inside of the church was one large room with 50 chairs and a podium. On a small stage behind the podium, six men sat around a giant drum made of an animal hide stretched over a wooden frame. Above their heads hung a large rough wooden cross. As they beat the drum in rhythm, they began to chant in a language I assumed was the ancient Blackfoot dialect. About 30 people attentively watched the men, seemingly absorbing their passion and energy. As I sat down in the back row, I realized I was one of only three white people. The rest were Native American.

A woman dressed in native garb stepped forward with a guitar and the congregation sang a hymn in the Blackfoot language, followed by a traditional English hymn, "How Great Thou Art." Tom Hears Thunder then gave a sermon about the parable of the sower from Matthew's Gospel, alternating between Blackfoot and English. He was a gifted preacher, and every ear was fully attuned to his message. At the end, he spoke a prayer in the Blackfoot language. I said "Amen" even though I didn't understand the words. I sensed in my spirit that it was a powerful prayer.

Tom then sat down in the front row. The entire congregation fell into deep silence that gradually quieted my restless mind. I realized everyone was praying, each one individually yet somehow united, and in my mind's eye I saw a cloud of incense rising out of them on its way to the ears of their Creator. I longed to add my silent prayers to the cloud, but my words seemed so inadequate, so unworthy of the presence of God.

"Prayer is a mystery," Tom whispered in my ear. I had been so entranced with what was going on that I hadn't noticed him coming over to me. "There are many types of prayer, like many streams that flow from a mountain into a great river. The Great Spirit is the mountain where all prayer begins, and the river is where it flows."

"The Great Spirit?"

"The Holy Spirit of God," he said. "The ancients called Him the Great Spirit. We now know that He is the Spirit of Jesus. They did not know who He was, but they saw Him in the buffalo, in the trees, and in everything He created. They worshiped Him in their ceremonies, their songs, and their dance. Now, we worship Him as not only our Creator but also our Savior."

I pondered for a moment what he was telling me: God Himself is the source as well as the recipient of true prayer, the Alpha and Omega, so to speak. He is both the beginning and the end of our relationship with Him. The ancient Blackfeet recognized Him in nature and worshiped Him in their own way, but now the people in the church had come to know who he is: a Jewish carpenter in a land half a globe away who paid for their sins and gave them eternal life.

"So the very people who took your land, slaughtered the buffalo – the people who broke the treaties you made with them — brought you the Good News of Jesus?"

"What man intends for evil, God uses for good," he said.

At that moment, the six men on stage began drumming and chanting again in the Blackfoot language. The congregation let the beats wash over them. Tom returned to his seat in the front. I made an attempt to pray, but I couldn't muster any thoughts or words. So I just watched, mesmerized by the sound of the drum.

After five minutes, an old woman in the middle of the congregation stood up. I immediately recognized her. She was the woman I had seen by the fire in the clearing in Yellowstone when I battled Bayou Thunder. She wore the same knee-length sheepskin dress with a deer-skin cloak. The moment she stood, the drummers stopped, and the congregation fell silent.

I had only seen her from a distance in Yellowstone. Up close, I realized that she was truly ancient in appearance, thin in the way old people are as they lose muscle mass and tone, but with a sense of strength, not fragility. She held her hands out in worship and gazed upward as though looking to heaven. Then she began to sing in Hebrew, exactly like a cantor at the synagogue where I had attended a childhood friend's Bar Mitzvah. This lasted only half a minute, and then she sat down.

Tom Hears Thunder stood up and scanned the people. "Who has the interpretation?" he asked.

A young boy rose from his chair. "I do."

"Give it to us," Tom Hears Thunder said.

"The Great Spirit says that a man who is not from here has sacrificed the great bull, but he does not know who he is or the power the Lord has put in him," the boy said. "He must go to the mountain."

"Who will take him?"

The boy didn't hesitate. "You will," he said.

———

The service continued for three hours with periods of silence and times of ecstatic prayer accompanied by the six men beating the drum. Near the end, the old woman who had spoken the prophetic word moved from person to person, laying hands on their heads and praying in the Blackfoot language. Finally, at midnight, the drumming stopped, and without a word from Tom, the congregation rose as if on cue and silently left.

"Her name is Mary Three Bears," Tom explained when we were the only two left in the church. "She is the granddaughter of a famous medicine man. She hears the voice of the Great Spirit and speaks to the people. His power flows through her to heal them."

"I would like to talk to her," I said.

"She doesn't speak English. Only our language."

"And Hebrew."

"She doesn't know Hebrew. Or Greek. Or Arabic. Or African dialects. She has spoken them all and many others I do not recognize."

"And the boy?"

"He is the one the Great Spirit touched to interpret her words to the people this time," he said. "But he could have chosen any of us. Mary Three Bears only speaks when there is someone who can interpret because she doesn't know what she is saying."

"I saw her in a vision," I said. "When I was at Yellowstone."

Tom raised his eyebrows. I told him about the fire I had to pass through and the sacrifice of Bayou Thunder.

"That is why He sent you here," he said. "You have slain the beast, but you don't truly know who you are. She will be your guide."

"On the mountain?"

"On the mountain."

"And there I will find out who I am and the power that has been put in me?" I asked.

Tom didn't respond to my question. "I will pick you up at the break of dawn. It will be a long day," he said.

The Blackfoot named their sacred mountain Ninastako, but it is commonly called Chief Mountain, a towering edifice of sedimentary rock near the border of Glacier National Park. Tom Hears Thunder picked me up at dawn in a heavy-duty truck, and we bumped along on the rough dirt roads leading to a trailhead at the base of the mountain. From there, we alternately hiked and scrambled over loose rocks and boulders for several hours, winding our way up steep slopes to the summit. Tom moved like a gazelle over the terrain while I struggled behind him despite my long experience as a hiker and backpacker. As we climbed, I asked him how he came to lead a church in Browning.

"I was raised in the Blackfoot tradition along with my twin brother, George," he said. "When I was 13, I fasted for three days and then spent two nights on this mountain alone as part of my vision quest. The first night, I was cold and frightened. I huddled behind boulders and hoped a grizzly bear would not find me. I prayed for dawn, but it seemed it would never come. The second night, I was hungry and fighting back tears when suddenly, a great cloud of light surrounded me. I was lifted up in the air a thousand feet, and I could see the mountain glistening in the moonlight and the land stretching out across the plains. A man came out of the cloud and touched me on the forehead so that it seemed as though lightning was running through me. And I heard a voice like the sound of many waters coming from his mouth. He simply said, 'Follow me.' At once, I was back on the ground. The vision was over.

"That is how I came to know that the Great Spirit's name is Jesus and He was calling me. He also called my brother in the same way during his vision quest. We decided we would follow Him together, but that has not happened. We both attended a Bible College and started our ministry. But he met some people who preached a prosperity Gospel and followed them to Los Angeles."

"Prosperity Gospel?"

"It's a belief that if you pray the right way and believe enough, God will bless you with material riches here on earth, or if you have an illness, He will heal you," he answered. "And if you give money to the pastor and his ministry, you will certainly be healed or get rich."

"Sounds like a scam," I said.

"Unfortunately, my brother fell for it, and then he got rich off of it. He changed his name to George Fuller and started a church. The last time I checked, he had 2,000 members and was living in a million-dollar house and driving a Jaguar. His services are chaotic with people falling over, barking like dogs, acting as though they are drunk – all supposedly under the influence of the Holy Spirit. He doesn't preach the cross. He preaches nothing but the Prosperity Gospel. But when the collection plate is passed around, it is full."

"And you?"

"I follow Jesus, who revealed Himself to me on this mountain," he said. "He told me to stay here and help the downtrodden and broken people on the reservation."

We reached the top, and I stopped to admire the beauty of the land stretching out before us. I imagined the legendary herds of buffalo that once covered the plains and provided sustenance, clothing, shelter, and tools for the Blackfoot. Scattered about a large flat rock on the mountain were feathers, leather bundles, pipes, and bones of animals.

"Many of our people still follow the ancient ways," he said. "In our tradition, this mountain is the home of Thunder, a fearsome and powerful spirit. Our people worship him to bring rain or stop storms."

"And your name, Hears Thunder?"

"My great-grandfather was a great chief," he said. "He could hear the voice of Thunder."

"But you don't hear his voice?"

"That voice tries to speak to me, but I do not listen," he said. "I listen to the voice of the Great Spirit, the Spirit of Jesus."

As he spoke, I noticed a small cloud in the distance, the only one in an otherwise clear sky. Tom Hears Thunder, and I watched as it drifted across the prairie towards us, growing larger. A light breeze picked up and wafted across the summit. A raven landed on a rock nearby, then took off again. I sensed a strange aura about us and understood why the Blackfeet considered the mountain to be a portal to the spiritual realm.

I scanned the summit behind me, half-expecting John Demas or Gabe Remiel to appear suddenly. They were not there, but another person was: Mary Three Bears. Perhaps I should not have been surprised: Tom said she would be my guide. Yet it seemed impossible that such an old woman could have climbed the steep slopes to the summit. She stood as she had in the church with her hands extended, looking upward to the sky.

"You knew she would be here?" I asked.

"I did," he answered. "You will see soon enough."

"See what?"

At that moment, the cloud drifted directly over our heads, blocking the sun. Another gust of wind, stronger than the first, rushed by us, and the cloud rapidly descended until it enveloped us. Power coursed through me, infinitely strong yet gentle, the arms of a father around a small child. It came from the cloud, but it also came from within me. I was not the source; rather, I was at an intersection. I was within the power, yet the power was within me.

I fell on my knees. I could not see Tom in the cloud, even though he was only a few feet away. A pair of hands rested on my head from behind. At once, a vision invaded my mind. I saw myself in a dark tomb, a body caked in a mixture of myrrh and aloes and wrapped tightly from head to foot in linen strips. Suddenly, a light like a thousand suns burst into the tomb. and I passed through the linen strips and stood up. The huge boulder sealing the tomb rolled away, and I stepped into a dew-soaked dawn. The vision ended. I heard the voice of Mary Three Bears speaking in the Blackfoot language."

"What is she saying?" I asked.

"'The Great Spirit says you must know who you are.'"

"I keep hearing that," I said. "But who am I then?"

"An earthen vessel that contains a priceless treasure," he answered.

I pondered this for a moment. "But what does that mean?"

"The Spirit who raised Jesus from the dead abides in you. You must humble yourself as He did to be a light to others. You must become broken bread and poured out wine."

"I have slain Bayou Thunder," I protested.

"That is only the beginning," he replied.

Another gust of wind rushed by. Mary Three Bears spoke again, holding her hands to the sky. I waited for the translation.

"You must be holy," Tom Hears Thunder said. "If you need

to forgive, you must forgive. If you need to be forgiven, you must seek forgiveness. If you have been ungrateful, you must be thankful. You must not judge but take the lowest place. Then the power within you will flow to others."

I immediately knew what the old woman said was true. Hidden within me was a viper's nest of unforgiveness, self-justification, ingratitude, and judgment. Others might speak well of me, and they did, but they could not see beyond the surface to the hidden places within. Bayou Thunder was dead. I no longer clung to my own identity, but the mind of Christ still needed to be formed in me.

"But how?" I asked.

Tom Hears Thunder put his hand on my shoulder. "Mary Three Bears will guide you."

Another gust of wind, this one even stronger than the others, swept across the summit. The cloud disappeared, once again revealing the vista of the prairie in bright sunshine. When I looked behind me, Mary Three Bears was gone.

———

Any mountaineer will tell you that the descent from a mountaintop is often riskier than the ascent. Far more accidents happen on the way down than up. You can't see your handholds and footholds as well, and you have to control your momentum with every step, risking a slip. As a result, it took us longer to get back to the trailhead than to reach the summit. By the time we drove back to Browning, the sun was dipping below the mountains. Along the way, I had tried in vain to get Tom to tell me what happened to Mary Three Bears, but he either couldn't or wouldn't.

"Mary appears when she is needed and only stays until she is no longer needed," he said.

"She is not an angel, is she?" I asked, thinking of how Gabe Remiel and John Demas had appeared out of nowhere.

"No, not an angel. I have known her since I was a child. She used to babysit us when George and I were little. She is as human as you and me." Beyond that, he would say no more.

When he dropped me off at the RV park, he told me that he would pick me up early the next morning again – that is, if I were willing. There was one more place he needed to take me.

"Of course," I said. "I don't think I've really had a choice since I left West Virginia."

"You are from West Virginia?" he asked.

"Blacksburg," I said. "I thought you knew everything about me already."

"Only what I need to know," he said, as he shifted the truck's transmission into drive. He drove off without another word of explanation.

――-

We traveled deep into the reservation as the sun rose the next morning, traversing miles of sparsely populated Rocky Mountain front, rarely seeing another vehicle and only an occasional ranch house. Once in a while, we came across a small town with a gas station, a tiny grocery, a liquor and beer store, and the ubiquitous casino with gambling machines ranging from keno to video poker. Eventually, we turned onto a dirt road that led to an old Airstream, a cylindrical silver RV, that has a cult-like following among its enthusiasts. This one, however, was at least 30 years old and badly stained and rusted.

"Someone lives in that?" I asked Tom Hears Thunder, trying to imagine how anyone could survive a Montana winter in an RV not designed for severe weather.

Tom nodded. "It's not unusual," he answered as he parked his truck next to the Airstream.

There were no other vehicles, so I assumed no one was home. But when we knocked, a small Native American woman opened the door a crack and peered out at us. I immediately noticed the bruises on her arms. Behind her, a small child, perhaps five years old, clung to her skirt. Tom spoke to her in the Blackfoot language. She hesitated, looking beyond us at the road, then let us in.

I was shocked to see Mary Three Bears sitting on a ramshackle couch in the main area of the RV, sipping a cup of tea. There was no ready explanation for how she could have gotten to such a remote place. Perhaps someone gave her a ride and then left. Or maybe the Holy Spirit had transported her the way He had swept up Philip and taken him to Azotus after the baptism of the Ethiopian eunuch.

Tom eyed the perplexed look on my face. "When you began to follow Jesus, you entered the supernatural," he said. "Mary shows up where she is needed."

Mary clearly was needed by the woman whose name was Hurit Hungry Crow. I later found out that "Hurit" means beautiful in the Blackfoot language, and indeed, she was a beautiful woman. The bruises that marred her body and the distant look in her eyes told the story of terrible abuse. Her child, a delicate girl, cowered behind her mother, fearful of the strange men in her home.

Mary Three Bears abruptly put down her cup and whispered in the woman's ear. Then she put one hand on the woman's forehead and another on her heart. She began to pray in the Blackfoot

417

language, a low, soothing prayer so different from the loud groans and prayers in the worship service two nights before. The woman began to cry and then fell into her arms. Mary continued to pray. I sensed the same power that had been in the cloud – that had been in me – flowing through the room. The power compelled me to cross to where they embraced and place my hand on the young woman's head. Words began to flow from my mouth: words I didn't recognize. Words of a foreign language. With each word, power flowed from me through my hand into the young woman. I looked down at her arms and legs. The bruises were fading away.

I don't know how long we prayed. Once again, time seemed to be suspended as though we were transported to a world where there is no past and no future – only an eternal now. Then the sound of screeching tires on the road outside brought our prayer to a stop. A car door opened and slammed shut. A moment later, the door to the Airstream flew open. A large man stormed through, pointing a handgun first at Mary Three Bears and then at Tom Hears Thunder.

"What the hell are you doing here, pastor?" he shouted, waving the barrel of the handgun. "No one invited you. Did she call you?"

"She doesn't have a phone, Matwau," Tom replied softly.

Matwau's eyes bulged with anger. He fired a shot into the floor of the RV. The sound reverberated around the Airstream, badly hurting my ears. All the while, Mary Three Bears continued to pray, ignoring him. I kept my hand on the young woman's head, the power still flowing through me to her.

"Shut up!" Matwau shouted at her. He reached out to grab her, but his hand seemed to be stopped in mid-air as though by an invisible barrier. This made him angrier. He pointed the gun at her. "I will shoot you if you say another word!"

Mary Three Bears finally looked up at him. She slowly withdrew her hands from Hurit's forehead and heart and spread them wide the way she had in the church and on the mountain.

"In the name of the Great Spirit Jesus, I command you to depart," she whispered. It was in English.

Matwau convulsed, his whole body shaking. He dropped the firearm. "You can't do that!" he shouted in a deep voice that was not his own. "He is mine!"

Mary Three Bears shook her head. "He is yours no longer," she spoke more loudly still in English. "In the name of Jesus, depart!"

Matwau convulsed again, then collapsed, knocking over a side table and sending a framed photograph of the child skittering across the floor of the Airstream. He lay motionless, as though in a coma or dead. Mary Three Bears bent over and laid her hands on his head and his heart. She began to pray again.

After a couple of minutes, she stood up again and looked at me. "When he arises," she said in English. "You will tell him the Good News, and he will believe it. You will pray for him. Then you will pray with him. Then he will pray. Then you will help his family."

With that, Mary Three Bears stepped over the fallen man, opened the door of the Airstream, and left. It took me a moment to recover from what I had seen and experienced. By the time I looked out the door, she was gone.

I turned to Tom, who was embracing the young woman and her child. I shrugged my shoulders.

"She leaves when she is no longer needed," he said.

———

Matwau sat up with a confused look on his face a couple of minutes after Mary Three Bears left, like a child waking up in a strange place. He saw his wife and child seated on the couch next to Tom. Then he looked at me, a white man he did not know, kneeling beside him, holding his hand. Up close to him, I recognized he had the bloodshot eyes and reddish nose of alcoholism, one of the curses Europeans brought with them to native people who had no physiological tolerance for "fire water."

"I am Joe," I said. "The Great Spirit Jesus brought me here to pray for you."

"I feel different," he said.

"The Great Spirit has freed you from your enemy," I said. "But now you must pray. You must give yourself to Him. I will lead you."

Matwau nodded. "I want to be free."

Over the next half hour, I shared the Gospel with him: the hopelessness and misery of being a slave to sin, followed by the glorious news that God Himself had taken our form and sacrificed Himself in our place that we might have life and life abundant in a new kingdom – a supernatural kingdom where pure, unconditional love reigns. Each word I spoke was infused with a radiance that penetrated the darkness of Matwau's prison. Indeed, the massive stone blocking the entrance of his tomb rolled away inch by inch, revealing the sunshine of a new dawn.

We prayed together, and the power once again flowed from within me to him. Then I stopped and he began to pray, surrendering himself to the Great Spirit Jesus with tears in his eyes while his wife and child watched with amazement from across the Airstream. Soon all four of us huddled around him, singing a song of praise in the Blackfoot language. Somehow, in a remote place more than 1,000 miles from my home, I knew the words of a song sung in an ancient language.

Mary Three Bears was right. I would take care of a man named Matwau and his family. The Great Spirit Jesus had ordained it.

Chapter 23

The Valley

The valley follows the mountaintop. The cross follows the transfiguration. The thorn in the flesh follows the third heaven. I learned this at Lake Eufaula. I experienced it in the dark tunnel of the Hiawatha Trail. It nearly crushed me in Browning.

I fell asleep in Tom Hears Thunder's truck on the return trip. We barely said a word to each other the entire journey back to the RV park. As soon as he left, I climbed into bed. I didn't leave the Tiffin for days. I couldn't even muster the mental energy to say a prayer, much less contemplate all that had happened. I had been part of something extraordinary, even miraculous, but my emotions were dormant – neither lifted up nor cast down but stuck in neutral.

It only got darker. I awoke the third morning racked with joint pain, followed by a high fever and nausea. I spent the morning on my knees leaning over the toilet, even after there was nothing left in my stomach. I longed to go to bed and sleep, but I couldn't. I prayed, but I did not get better. Hour after hour, I grew only worse. Finally, I pleaded with God: "I did what you led me to do, Lord. Your power flowed through me to a broken man and healed him. Why won't you heal me?" The still small voice did not answer. My body shivered with fever, and I spent the night begging for sleep that my stomach would not allow.

Lying in bed on the fourth morning, I heard the door of the Tiffin open. I questioned whether I really heard it or simply imagined it. But then I heard footsteps, and the refrigerator door swung open with a clunk as it hit a bulkhead. The intruder rumbled around inside it.

"Who is there?" I called out in a weak voice as another wave of nausea swept through my body.

No one answered, but a moment later John Demas walked through the bedroom door. He held an Italian roll stuffed with ham and dripping with mustard. The sight of food triggered another bout of dry heaves.

"It's just me," he said with a smirk, waving the sandwich. "Would you like a sandwich? Ham and mustard."

"I don't remember inviting you," I said.

John laughed. "You've been busy," he said. "I needed to pay you a visit."

"The last thing I need is a visit from you."

"That's where you are mistaken," he said. "I can take away your sickness. I can make it so you actually want to eat this sandwich."

I dry heaved again. "I am not interested," I said.

"You don't understand, do you?" John said. "The one I serve has authority over your body."

"Just like he had authority over Travis Maynard's body?"

"He allowed that," John replied. "He cares about Travis."

"So why would he make me sick?"

"For your own good. To get you to see the error of your ways."

Another wave of nausea doubled me over. "What error?" I asked when it passed.

"The error of surrender," he said. "You yourself admit that you haven't been in control of your destiny. You left West Virginia and haven't really had a choice about where you went. Do you think it was an accident that your GPS malfunctioned twice or that you had global transient amnesia that landed you in a hospital? You have been nothing but a puppet. And now you are sick, and the one who controls you isn't helping you. But I am."

"You want me to surrender to the one you serve," I said. "I would still be controlled."

"No," he said. "You don't need to surrender. You simply need to declare your independence. Set yourself free."

"And if I don't?"

"Then you will spend the rest of your life being miserable, just as you are now."

As if on cue, my body started shaking again with fever. I felt a pain in my chest and began to cough. I noticed a rash developing on my hands. I buried my head in my pillow and didn't respond.

"Go ahead, ask your God to heal you," John said. "He's not listening. You've been praying to im. He's ignored you. He is not the God of love. He is the God of control. You asked him to heal Janice, and he wouldn't. Or he couldn't."

Immediately, an image flashed into my mind of Janice lying near death in the family room in Blacksburg, crying out in pain while I watched her, unable to help. I knelt by her bed and begged the God of the Bible to heal her or at least to take away her pain. He did not. I saw myself holding her corpse for two hours after she died, certain I would never find peace again, much less happiness.

"You go ahead and think about it," John continued. "I will come back tomorrow."

He abruptly turned and left, leaving the ham sandwich on the end of the bed.

———

The cough worsened overnight, and the rash spread up my arm, bright red splotches that caused me to flinch when I touched them. This made sleeping on my side almost impossible, if indeed I could get any sleep between bouts of nausea. I just lay on my back and stared at the ceiling of the Tiffin above my bed. I am not sure what was worse: the nausea or desperately wanting to sleep but not being able to. It was as though my body had been invaded by a hostile enemy that was setting fire to each cell as it advanced.

Even worse, I was alone. I recalled a bad case of the flu when Janice and I were first married. She couldn't do anything to lessen the symptoms, but her presence was solace and comfort to me. Now there was no one.

I continued to beg God for healing, of course, but my pleas felt like dead prayers. I had no sense of His presence or His power within me. It truly seemed He had abandoned me. And the question rose in my mind: "Why did He guide me to all the places I had been and all the encounters I had had only to leave me dying in an RV in the middle of Montana?" For indeed, my body felt like it was in the throes of a death spiral.

For the first time, I began to be angry at Him. I accused Him of not caring – of forgetting his promise to be my great physician. The power that raised Jesus from the dead might abide in me and flow through me to a man like Matwau. But where was it when I needed it? Could such power not raise me from my sickbed?

When I called Lara, she reacted exactly the same way Janice would have: she was alarmed and tried to get me to see a doctor. It was Saturday night, however, and the last thing I wanted to do was sit in an emergency room for hours waiting to see a weary doctor who would tell me I had the flu and send me home. When we hung up, I wondered if she already viewed herself as my wife, even though she still hadn't agreed to come visit me.

I didn't tell her about John Demas. His words were like arrows that had penetrated me, perhaps because they reflected my deepest doubts. It was easy to praise God and give Him thanks when the Holy Spirit embraced my spirit in a divine dance, and His power flowed through me as it did with Matwau. But in the darkness of the valley, amid waves of pain and nausea, the assurance of the mountaintop evaporated, and the questions rose from their hiding places deep in my soul.

"Was it real?" I asked myself, thinking back on all that had happened to me. Could it have been a matter of blind luck, coincidence, and human psychology? I thought of the miraculous healing of Travis Maynard that turned a headstrong Dr. Williams into a follower of Jesus. John Demas said that God had nothing to do with it, but, in fact, the one he serves deserved the credit. It was preposterous, of course. The enemy of Travis' soul would never heal his body, even if he had the power. Yet Demas' claim nagged at me.

I did tell Cecelia about John Demas when I called her.

"God allowed you to get sick, Joe," she said. "It's a messenger from Satan."

"Why would He do that?"

"Paul said he was given a messenger from Satan to keep him from being puffed up with spiritual pride," she said. "But I don't think that's the case with you. I don't think you are at risk of spiritual pride."

"Then what is it?"

"Well, what was the message?"

"He said I didn't need to surrender to anyone," I replied. "He said I just needed to declare my independence."

Cecelia laughed. "Joe, there is no such thing as independence," she said. "You will be a servant of either iniquity or of righteousness: a child of hell or a child of heaven."

"Yet where I am right now, it seems so reasonable," I said. "Just let go, and I will be set free from the sickness and the loneliness I feel."

"And that is exactly why God gave you the thorn in the flesh."

"I don't understand."

"It is a battle of the will, Joe," she said. "John Demas doesn't care about your physical suffering, although I suspect he enjoys it. He has his sights set on your will. His arrows are aimed at your will."

"But I have given my life to Jesus," I protested.

"You have," she responded. "But what happened to Matwau echoed in the halls of hell. John Demas doesn't want it to happen again. He may not be able to reclaim you or Matwau, but he can stop you from what you might do next."

"But why would God let him?"

I sensed Cecelia smiling on the other end of the line. "Because he has something even bigger than Matwau for you to do. And you need to be ready for it."

—--

A battle of the will.

When Cecelia hung up, I thought about the battleground not being in my body but in my soul. John Demas wanted me to focus on my physical pain and God's apparent indifference to my suffering. I thought of Job's wife, who, in the middle of his suffering, encouraged him to curse God and die. Job refused and in the end, when God blessed him, he prayed for his friends who had doubted him.

Then I remembered Jesus on the cross in agony, surrendering His Spirit not to despair but to His Father, who had turned His back on Him because of sin. Surely, he was tempted to use His power to come down from the cross. He refused, and the veil of the temple was torn in two so that we could enter the presence of God, not as sinners facing judgment but as beloved children receiving abundant life more than we can ask or imagine.

"I have been crucified with Christ," I remembered Paul wrote. Was Paul tormented by illness and faced the same battle? Did God want battle-hardened warriors who had learned that no matter what happened to their bodies or how deep the valley, they were more than conquerors? To learn that they could not be separated from His love even if their emotions proclaimed otherwise?

Even as I pondered these things, the pain grew worse. A fresh wave of nausea, this one a tsunami, had me retching so hard that I fell off the side of the bed and lay on the floor. My body shook with fever. The rash had spread to my thighs. I heard the voice of John Demas. He stood at the door again.

"Have you had enough?" he asked. "Are you ready to give up your hope in the one who allowed Janice to die. You know she is with us now. I will let you see her again."

With all the energy I could muster, I hoisted myself back up on the bed. John Demas was eating a meatball sub, its sides dripping with cheese. The sight of it caused my stomach to turn violently.

"When I first met you, you tried to convince me God didn't exist," I said, my voice barely a whisper. "Now you are saying the God whom you argued doesn't exist has abandoned me."

"It was all for your benefit, Joe. To keep you from being swept up in the delusion."

"And the raging bull who spoke with your voice?"

"That was all imaginary. A hallucination. It only happened in your mind. Your pain right now is real. Your depression is real. You need to focus on what is real and set yourself free."

A thick fog descended on my brain. My thoughts seemed stuck in thick syrup. Across from my bed, I saw my reflection in the television mounted on the wall. I looked like the survivor of a plane crash. My hair was tangled, my eyes blurry, and my skin pale except for the bright red rash. Everything was in slow motion except the jabbing doubts that emerged like snarling wolverines from dens deep in my soul. The miracle of Travis Maynard's healing and the power that redeemed Matwau seemed a distant memory – an unreal memory. Did these things actually happen?

"My sister says this is a battle of the will," I said.

John Demas nodded. "It is," he said. "And you need to claim your own will, not surrender it to the One who is tormenting you."

I tried to formulate a response but couldn't. I just wanted it all to go away. I wanted to sleep.

"You are so close, Joe," John Demas continued. "Just set yourself free."

I would have. I would have said anything at that moment to be free of the pain. But once again, a scripture I was forced to memorize in my childhood rose out of the morass of my confusion.

"Though he slay me, yet will I trust in Him," I whispered the words of Job.

This clearly annoyed John Demas. He took a step forward and spoke angrily, firing a volley of arrows. "You are a fool, Joe," he said. "What has He done to earn your trust? He took Janice away from you and gave you money you didn't want that upended your life. He has left you all by yourself in the middle of nowhere. Where is that idiot Tom Hears Thunder, who ignores us? And that whore Mary Three Bears? Have they come here to see if you are all right? No, they don't care. They just want your money. He won't let you have Lara. She wants to be with you, but he won't let her come."

Another thought rose out of the mire. A clear thought. A question. "What about Mindy?" I asked.

John Demas was taken aback. "What are you talking about?"

"What happened to Mindy when she went home to her husband?" I had no idea where this was coming from. I had barely thought about Mindy since I left Memphis. I would never see her again, and I just as soon would have forgotten the margaritas and the midnight temptation to have her.

"That's irrelevant," he snapped back. "It has nothing to do with the reality of where you are."

His reaction gave me a strange jolt of energy. I sat up in bed. "Something happened to her, didn't it? Something you didn't like?"

"We are dealing with that whore," he shouted furiously. Then he quickly caught himself and spoke calmly again, "She is ours and we will reclaim her."

"So you lost her, didn't you?" I asked. "She turned away from debauchery and adultery and turned to God?"

"Shut up! This is about you! Your reality! Your sickness!"

As if on cue, another tsunami of nausea caused me to buckle over. When I recovered, I looked him in the eye. "Cecelia is right," I said. "This isn't about me. You've lost me. This is about Mindy and Matwau and others you are afraid of losing."

"That's a lie!" John Demas said, his face bright red. "This is about your reality. It's about you discovering that you have been deceived. It's about you being set free from your prison."

I ignored what he said and continued my point. "If you are so worried about what I might do, why haven't you killed me?" I asked.

"We are trying to set you free, not kill you."

"Because you can't," I said. "Because he won't let you kill me."

"He has no power over us! We have killed many people like you."

"Then kill me right now," I dared him. "If you can."

John Demas pointed at me, his eyes full of venom. "You are a fool, Joe," he said. "You don't know who you are dealing with. You need to deal with reality."

It seemed every cell in my body exploded in pain. I couldn't help but cry out and fall back on my pillow. The ceiling of the Tiffin began to spin. It should have been enough to crush my will, but somehow it wasn't. There was something inside me that refused to surrender. Something that would rather have my body die than give in to John Demas.

Then the words came to me, falling into my mind as they had in the past. "There is a greater reality than my reality, isn't there? That is what you are afraid of – that I will truly embrace that truth and then help others to see it."

"That is a lie," he said. "The only reality you have now is that you are sick and abandoned. This world is your reality. You live in it."

I shook my head. "Though He slay me, I will put my trust in Him," I said.

John Demas raised a fist and shook it. "We will make you regret that," he snapped. Then he abruptly turned and left, slamming the door of the Tiffin behind him.

I lay in bed, still in pain, still exhausted, still desiring a sleep that could not come. But somewhere deep in my soul, I heard a trumpet sound a triumphant note.

—---

John Demas had been gone only 10 minutes when I heard a knock on the door. I struggled out of bed to open it. Tom Hears Thunder stood outside, bathed in the first sunshine I had seen in days. He took one look at me and shook his head.

"You look like a corpse," he said.

"I feel worse than a corpse," I replied.

"I thought you had left town, but when I drove by, I saw your coach," he said. "I wanted to invite you to church again tonight."

"Thanks, but I can barely get out of bed."

"That's the other reason I came by," he said, then paused. I heard the door to Tom's truck open and shut. A few seconds later, Mary Three Bears appeared. "She asked me to bring her by. She's been fasting."

Mary uttered what I assumed was a greeting in the Blackfoot language. Then she climbed the stairs and waved at me to sit in the captain's chair. I quickly obeyed. She may have been just five feet tall and less than 100 pounds, but she had an air of authority. I was sure that people in her church did what she said, even Tom.

The prayer was shorter than I expected. She laid her hands on my head and prayed in the Blackfoot language. Then she put her hand on my chest and said another prayer. Finally, she put her hand on my thigh and again prayed. When she was done, she quickly left. I didn't hear the door of the truck open or close. I wondered where she had gone.

I looked at Tom, hoping for a translation or an explanation. He shrugged his shoulders. "She prayed for your healing," he said. "She shows up when she is needed and leaves when she is no longer needed."

The healing didn't happen instantly. Rather, it came over several hours, like a high tide gradually receding from the shore. First, the nausea faded. Then the fever broke, leaving me in a sweat. Finally, the rashes turned from bright red to pink, then disappeared. I found the Italian roll stuffed with ham in the refrigerator and ate it.

Then I went to church.

Chapter 24

Dinosaurs

My mother would not have been surprised where I ended up next. Like many little boys, I was obsessed with dinosaurs as a child. I had plastic models of triceratops, velociraptors, tyrannosauruses, and other raptors and herbivores in my room. She borrowed every book on dinosaurs in the public library over and over again. By the time I was seven, I could identify scores of them from the smallest, the hummingbird-sized Oculudentavis to the largest, the 122-foot-long, 70-ton Patagotitan.

When I left Browning two days later, I drove the Tiffin north four hours to the badlands in Alberta – to a place where more dinosaur fossils have been unearthed than anywhere else in North America. Dinosaur Provincial Park appears with breath-taking suddenness like a smaller version of the Grand Canyon on the vast Canadian prairie, 130 miles east of Calgary. Paleontologists have found specimens of 35 dinosaur species from the sedimentary layers in the Red Deer River valley.

In the park's visitors center, I met one of them, Dr. Paul Phillips, a don at Oxford recognized as one of the world's foremost experts on the mass extinction that occurred 66 million years ago in the Cretaceous Period. That is, if it actually happened 66 million years ago and not in 2,350 BC when the Bible records that a worldwide flood wiped out the world's land animals. It was a date calculated by Irish Archbishop James Ussher in 1650, a century and a half before anyone even thought of the field of paleontology.

When I met him, Dr. Phillips was engaged in a friendly debate with another visitor, the Rev. Perry Mitchell of Sioux Falls, South Dakota, about the actual age of the earth and the dinosaurs who met their fate in the valley. He was dressed in a blazer and tie, an odd choice for hiking through a park. After introductions, they allowed me to participate in their discussion, although I didn't have much to say at first.

"I respect your religious beliefs, especially when they motivate charity," Dr. Phillips said in a crisp British accent. "But you do realize that science has completely undermined your Bible?"

"You will have to explain that to me," the Reverend replied, more calmly than might be expected in response to a comment that completely negated his life's work. He was an average-sized man in his late 50s who had the look of a former athlete who had kept himself in shape. He projected an air of confidence.

"It's simple," the don answered. "If the first 11 chapters of Genesis can be proven to be mythology rather than history, then the entire foundation of the Bible crumbles. And I can prove to you that they are mythology."

"Why does the foundation of the Bible crumble?" Rev. Mitchell asked.

"If there were no Garden of Eden and no Adam and Eve who disobeyed God and became subject to death, then there would be no need for a Redeemer – a second Adam, Jesus," he said. "And Jesus Himself cited Noah as a historical figure, so if Noah and the great flood were just a myth, then Jesus was either deceived or lying, certainly not the Son of God."

"I see you have studied theology," replied Rev. Mitchell in a calm voice. He clearly was not one of those people who are offended when people question their faith.

"Quite a bit. One can't be truly educated about Western civilization if one doesn't study the Bible."

"But you don't believe it?"

"My vocation as a scientist will not allow it," Phillips said. "How can I believe the universe is 6,000 years old when we have fossils and rocks that are millions of years old, not to mention relics of human civilization dated much earlier. There are cave paintings in Spain from 64,000 years ago."

"That's assuming you are dating them correctly," Reverend Mitchell said, again with no sense that he had taken offense.

The don smiled thinly as though correcting one of his students. "Radiocarbon dating is not perfect and has its limits, but it has been proven accurate for objects less than 20,000 years old. It can be used to categorically dismiss the notion that the world is 6,000 years old or even 10,000 years old," he said. "Not only that, consider that our advanced space telescopes can see stars that are in distant parts of the universe. We are observing light that was emitted 13 billion years ago, not 6,000 years ago."

"You are assuming that when God said 'Let there be light,' He didn't fill the universe with light at that moment. Perhaps the light you are seeing was created 6,000 years ago and its source is God, not a distant star," Rev. Mitchell replied. "Not to mention that those telescopes are revealing fully formed stars and organized galaxies, which shouldn't be the case since you are looking back in time to when your Big Bang occurred."

"I see you have studied some science," the don said.

"Just as you have studied the Bible. I am no expert or even a scientist. I am a theologian."

"If you were a mathematician, you would realize that there is no way the eight people who survived in the Ark could populate an entire world of seven billion people in 4,500 years," he said. "Not to mention that inbreeding and lack of genetic diversity would doom the population."

"That is assuming a Creator didn't invent DNA and, therefore, can alter it as necessary."

Dr. Phillips shrugged his shoulders. "So you categorically reject the idea that Genesis could be mythology or poetry?"

"Hebrew scholars will tell you there is no question that Genesis was written as a narrative, not as poetry or mythology. It is an account of real events and real people."

"Certainly the author believed they were real, whoever that author might have been," Dr. Phillips said with a hint of British condescension.

The conversation lagged as the three of us agreed to hike a trail to some fossil exhibits. We left the visitor center and passed through a copse of cottonwoods. When we had gone a short distance, Rev. Mitchell took the opportunity to go on the counterattack.

"The problem you have, Dr. Phillips," he said. "Is that while you claim science disproves Genesis, you have no reasonable alternative explanation of the origin of life on this planet. The so-called theory of evolution is so full of holes from a scientific standpoint that it is truthfully a religion, requiring even more faith than believing Genesis is history.

"You mentioned mathematics. Even if you could explain their origin, which you can't, the mathematical possibility of a massive cloud of hydrogen atoms in a lifeless void leading to a human being through a process of trillions upon trillions of sequential accidents is so infinitely minute as to be unbelievable except to those pre-determined to believe it.

"The answer evolutionists offer to any questions about their theory ultimately comes down to time. Time overcomes the odds. But that is merely a form of denial because if we could label anything impossible, it would be inorganic chemicals in a tidewater pool spontaneously combining to form amino acids, then proteins, then a living being with the ability to immediately reproduce itself."

Dr. Phillips smiled, a university professor being challenged by a bright student. Both men clearly enjoyed the repartee.

"There is ample evidence of the evolutionary process in nature," he said. "We can clearly show you where species evolved through DNA analysis."

"By accident?"

"Of course. Given enough time."

"If I showed you a Model T Ford, would you believe it evolved into a Corvette by accident? After all, they both have wheels, engines, axles, and many other similarities. Of course not. You would say that there was a designer. Yet you are willing to look at an amoeba or an ape and say that it evolved into a human being by a series of accidental mutations. And human beings are far more complicated than automobiles."

The two men fell silent for a moment, thinking about what they would say next. I took the opportunity to speak.

"It seems to me, gentlemen," I said, "that neither of your positions can withstand a single concession. They must be completely true or, as Dr. Phillips said about the Bible, they collapse. An evolutionist cannot concede anything that implies intelligent design, and a believer in Genesis cannot concede anything that says Earth is more than a few thousand years old.

"To use an analogy, both of you have your own magic wands to answer problems with your position. Reverend Mitchell's magic wand is an all-powerful Creator, and Dr. Phillips' magic wand is time, which effectively takes the role of Creator. Neither of you believes the other's magic wand is a reasonable answer, and compromise is impossible."

The two men thought about what I had said, and then Reverend Mitchell asked, "What do you believe, Mr. Mathers?"

"I could say I believe part of each is true, but I won't. Many people do take this position. They concede a Creator exists because the complexity of the universe and especially living beings is too intricate to have happened by accident, but they say that God could have used evolutionary processes to create life. As a Creator who stands above time, He could shoehorn billions of years of geologic time into six 24-hour days so that Genesis is true. After all, the Apostle Peter noted that a thousand years to God is but a day. So in this view, He could engineer a step-by-step evolution of species until finally He created human beings, all in a 24-hour period.

"As attractive as that position seems, it doesn't pass Biblical muster. Why? Because the Bible says that corruption, violence, and death only entered the world when Adam and Eve disobeyed God and sought to live independently of Him. Before the creation of man, you could not have had hundreds of millions of years of creatures devouring each other in a fallen world as they gradually evolved through natural selection.

"Therefore, if there is no compromise possible, I am forced to take a position. I believe the Bible is the Word of God and is the one book that I can absolutely say is truthful. I know this because I have a personal relationship with its Author, and His Spirit has testified to my Spirit that the Bible is His living word.

"Dr. Phillips is right that the Bible cannot stand if Genesis is mythology rather than history. As much as questions about rocks and fossils perplex me, I believe Genesis indeed must be history. In short, if one knows something is true and it is dependent on something else to be true, then that something else must be true."

"So you are saying that if the New Testament is true, then Genesis must be true?" Dr. Phillips asked.

"Precisely," I said. "The New Testament is filled with events that modern scientists would deem impossible. Take, for example, Jesus walking on water. It's impossible according to physics. Yet no one sits around debating whether Jesus walked on water. You either believe it or you don't.

"Genesis is different because we are surrounded by evidence of God's creation that can be examined according to the scientific method. This allows people such as yourself to say to those who believe the universe was created 6,000 years ago that their faith is unscientific – in fact, absurd. You have rocks you say are too old and light that left distant galaxies billions of years ago. People who would never bother to argue that Jesus didn't walk on water will snicker at the idea that the world was created in six days."

"Well said," Reverend Mitchell exclaimed.

Dr. Phillips nodded, conceding I had made some good points, but then pressed his case.

"Your belief that the New Testament is true, of course, is a matter of faith, and you cite as evidence a personal relationship with a

Creator," he said. "That is subjective, of course. People all over the world say that God, or their version of God, spoke to them. Sometimes people commit horrible crimes, saying they heard God commanded them. They have used the Bible to justify everything from war crimes to slavery. How can you possibly test whether you are actually hearing the voice of a Creator rather than your own imagination?"

I hesitated. "That's going to take a few minutes."

"I have nowhere else to be," Dr. Phillips said. "This is a fascinating discussion. We don't have many at Oxford or even in our local churches who would defend belief in a six-day creation. Or at least any that would admit to it. Their careers could be ruined."

I took a deep breath as we crested a hill in the trail. "Let's start with the fact that I am a billionaire," I said.

"A billionaire?" Dr. Phillips looked dubious.

"Yes," I said. "I have more than a billion dollars invested in various securities and bonds on Wall Street. But the interesting part is that I didn't earn it, nor did I inherit it. Six months ago, I was living a middle-class life as a physical therapist in West Virginia. I won the largest Powerball lottery in history."

Dr. Phillips nodded. He looked at me differently, the same way people looked at me in Blacksburg when they started to laugh at my jokes. A billion dollars will do that. "Someone has to win it," he said.

"Sure, someone does," I said. "But I had never bought a lottery ticket in my life, and I still haven't. A hospice volunteer who was sitting with my late wife as she died from cancer left the winning ticket on a nightstand. I couldn't find her despite a lot of looking. The hospice organization had no record of her. In the end, I became a billionaire. What do you think the odds of that happening are?"

"Highly unlikely," he said. "But it is possible. I suppose you would say that your faith in God made that happen."

I laughed. "I didn't have any faith in God," I said. "Not the God who allowed my wife to die a slow and painful death despite my desperate prayers. I was done with God. He didn't exist, or He was powerless, or He didn't care about my wife or me. Besides, I had no interest in the money. It turned my life upside down, and I had to quit my job. I've done nothing but travel the country since."

Dr. Phillips thought for a moment, perhaps contemplating how anyone could say that winning a billion dollars was a bad thing. "That's all very interesting," he said. "But what does that have to do with a relationship with a Creator?"

"I've met a lot of people in my travels," I said. "I've seen things a rational scientist would have difficulty believing."

"Give it a try," he said.

"I met a traumatized Vietnam veteran who was hopelessly addicted to drugs instantly set free from his addiction through faith in Jesus. I also saw a Native American man instantly freed from alcoholism and become a completely changed man, from a brutal drunk to a man who loves and cares for his family."

"Unlikely, but explainable," Dr. Phillips said. "People can sometimes demonstrate great courage and determination in the face of addiction, and the human brain has a remarkable capability to heal itself."

"I suppose that is true, but, as you say, 'highly unlikely,'" I replied. "But consider this. In Washington state, I saw Jesus

Himself enter a hospital room and heal a man who was dying of brain cancer."

"Jesus Himself?"

"In bodily form," I said. "The surgeon who had operated on the man was utterly perplexed. There was no evidence of a tumor that had shown up on a previous MRI, nor was there a scar or other evidence that he had ever operated on the man. The surgeon reluctantly conceded it had to be a miracle and then became a Christian."

"Lots of people claim faith healing," Dr. Phillips said. "They are either unprovable or complete hoaxes."

"The doctor graduated from Johns Hopkins Medical School and did his residency at Mass General. He was the head of neurosurgery at a prominent Seattle hospital and an atheist at the time."

"I am sure there was a rational explanation and, in any event, it doesn't prove it was Jesus – did he give you a business card?" he asked with a chuckle. "Nor does it explain your claim to have a relationship with a Creator."

We came to a fork in the trail. After discussing it, we decided to turn right into a valley where there was an exhibit of fossil remains still embedded in the mudstone. I realized that Reverend Mitchell hadn't said a word for quite a while. He was letting me take the lead in the debate.

"That's the interesting part, Dr. Phillips," I said. "One can hear about a miracle or even see a miracle and still not enter into a relationship with the miracle giver. It is not a matter of miracles but of revelation. And then a willingness to accept that revelation."

"And you had that revelation?"

"I did," I said. "In a small church in the backwoods of Arkansas, pastored by a retired U.S. Senator."

Dr. Phillips raised his eyebrows. "There must be a story in that."

"Not much of one," I said. "As I mentioned, it was a matter of revelation. God directed my path to that church by means of a faulty GPS. Jesus touched my soul in a way that was unmistakable. It was pure joy. I surrendered my life to Him. I could have refused to surrender. Many people do. But I made a choice."

"Praise God," Reverend Mitchell exclaimed.

Dr. Phillips was unimpressed. He shook his head. "I am a scientist, Mr. Mathers," he said. "I deal with hard evidence, not emotion. Measurable evidence like those fossils." He pointed at some fossils in an exhibit by the trail. "A man may believe with all his heart that he is a rabbit, but that doesn't make him a rabbit. Or a man may believe Noah could fit two of all the animals in the world into a wooden ship only slightly longer than a football pitch, not to mention the world's one million insect species, but that doesn't make it true."

Reverend Mitchell started to answer, but then thought better of it. I'm sure he would have noted that Genesis doesn't say Noah brought every species of animal into the Ark, but merely "every animal after its kind." The total number could have been as low as 600. But that would have led to a discussion about how horses became zebras and donkeys in 4,000 years, and Dr. Phillips would immediately point out that it would require a condensed evolutionary process that is unscientific. Besides, Reverend Mitchell and I had already rejected evolution.

"So you are a materialist and don't believe we are spiritual beings?" Reverend Mitchell asked, taking another tack.

"What we perceive to be our spirits are simply an evolutionary development in our brains to deal with things we cannot explain. That is why religion is universal. The more we learn about the world, the less we need religion. A caveman might have thought that lightning was the wrath of an angry god. Now we know it is a meteorological phenomenon caused by static electricity in clouds."

"Doesn't that make the unscientific assumption that simply because we can't detect something, it doesn't exist?" the Reverend asked. "Like dark matter?"

"The burden of proof is on you," Dr. Phillips replied.

"True," the Reverend said. "And the existence of God cannot be proved or disproved by the scientific method. Nor can we explain with certainty how Noah managed to get all those animals into the Ark any more than we could explain how Jesus walked on water."

"But we can prove the universe is billions of years old using the scientific method. And I can prove that the fossils we are looking at right now are millions of years old," the don replied.

"So either the Bible is true or the current consensus among secular paleontologists is," I said. "And never the twain shall meet."

"I will stand by what I can see and measure," the don said.

"And I will stand by the Word of God," Reverend Mitchell said.

The conversation ended. We shook hands, and the other two men went in a different direction at a fork in the trail.

I was soon a child again, marveling over Hadrosaurs, Ceratopsians, Theropods, Ornithomimids, and Paravians. I stood in awe of the God who imagined such creatures and then crafted them like a potter skillfully fashioning an ornate urn from the mud of the earth.

A verse from my childhood came to mind. "The whole earth is full of HIs glory." I silently gave thanks for Noah's Ark.

Chapter 25

The Shepherd

More than 200 miles west of Dinosaur Provincial Park and 20 miles from the town of Banff, a pair of gondolas carry their passengers to the top of the Canadian Rockies. During the winter, the peaks are a skier's playground and during the summer a hiker's paradise, with trails weaving through the mountain landscape under bright, crystal blue skies. It was there that I saved a life, although I don't believe I saved anyone.

I was not the same person I was when I left Blacksburg. In the spiritual calculus of God's creation, I had died and been resurrected with Jesus when I fell on my knees in the Senator's church in Arkansas. I was a new creation. I had been born again into the kingdom of God. It was an idea that Dr. Phillips would call foolishness. Indeed, to the natural mind, it is foolishness. Yet it is true. In one of those mysterious phrases written by Paul, only those with the mind of Christ can know it is true. Others simply shake their heads.

A new creation, however, is not a finished creation. A sapling and a towering 350-foot-high tree may both be redwoods with the same DNA, but they are different in just about every other way. The towering tree lived through hundreds, if not thousands, of years of freezing winters, scorching summers, wildfires, earthquakes, volcanic eruptions, droughts, and floods – each leaving its mark as its roots descended deeper into the earth, allowing it to reach for the sky. The sapling knows none of that – yet.

Leaving the Tiffin in an RV park in Banff, I rented a chalet near the base of the gondolas with a view of the mountains. The following morning, I rode them to the ceiling of the Rockies, then hiked three miles on a weather-beaten trail through Alpine meadows dotted with wildflowers. Eventually, I came to a powdery blue lake fed by melting glaciers where I sat down to rest. I was alone.

The quiet was the first thing I noticed. It was one of the rare places in my life where I could hear no sound. Nothing moved, not even the wind. Everything was completely still. But it wasn't just the absence of sound. The quiet was animated like an encroaching flood tide. The longer I gazed at the still waters of the lake and the snow-capped peaks, the deeper it penetrated.

Grief came first. Grief deeper than any I had experienced before. Janice was not with me. She would have delighted in the rugged beauty of the mountains, the pure chill air, and the milky lake. It had taken 2,000 miles on the road and the quiet of the mountains to open the door to the place where my deepest emotions were hidden and release the fullness of my sorrow. The tears I could only shed in droplets before, even when I buried her, poured out of my eyes in a torrent.

"I miss her," I cried to God. The words echoed across the lake with no one to hear them.

I also missed Lara. She was the one who could assuage my grief and take away the loneliness. Yet she would not come, even when I pleaded with God to change her mind. I was certain that if she were with me, my soul would be comforted and I would find joy in the wonder of His creation, rather than gnawing despair. But those prayers, like those I had sent heavenward on my knees at Janice's bedside, were not answered. The God whose existence I had questioned when Janice died gave me a billion dollars I did not ask for and didn't want. But He would not take away the pain of my loss and my loneliness.

"Why, Lord, am I here?" I asked out loud. "What is the purpose of my sorrow?" The quiet swallowed my words. There was no answer.

I sat by the lake for a few minutes before I spotted a tiny dot far up the trail descending towards me. Gradually, the outline of a fellow hiker came into view. When he grew near, I saw that it was a slim young man in his early 20s with an orangish beard dressed from head to toe in black clothing – a black ball cap, black shorts, a black tee-shirt, and even black sneakers. He wasn't carrying anything: no backpack, no water bottle, and no hiking stick. When he drew nearer, I recognized the matching logos on his cap and tee-shirt of a heavy metal band called Raven under the words "Nevermore Tour" in Gothic font.

"Hello there," I greeted him when he came to the place where I was seated.

"Hi," he replied with a bass voice that contrasted with his thin build and pale, somewhat pasty complexion. He had the appearance of someone who didn't spend much time outdoors. His beard, hair and black attire suggested Halloween, an effect magnified by the skulls tattooed on either bicep.

"Nevermore, quoth the Raven," I said. He gave me a puzzled look, and I realized he might not know the origin of the band's name or the verse from Edger Allen Poe. "From the poem 'The Raven.' I see you are a fan of the band."

He shrugged his shoulders. "I like the music," he said. "I don't know anything about a poem."

I considered explaining it to him, but then thought better of it. "What brings you all the way out here…?" I stopped myself before I finished the sentence with "dressed like that?"

"I don't know," he replied. "Just seemed like the place to go."

"Just woke up this morning and decided to take a gondola up here and then hike out into the mountains?"

"Something like that," he said.

"So you are from around here?"

He shook his head. "Los Angeles."

Neither of us spoke for a few seconds. I thought about urging him to turn around. It was foolish to hike into the mountains so lightly clothed and unprepared for a sudden change in the weather. A cold front could sweep in at any moment and drop the temperature to near freezing, even in the summer. I decided against it: he seemed like someone who had been told what to do all his life and had rebelled against it.

"So are you here with your family?" I asked.

"I don't have a family," he said quickly. "At least really."

I nodded. We fell silent again. He could have continued past me down the trail, but he didn't. Instead, he gazed at me in a strange way, as though he were trying to figure something out.

A thought entered my mind. "You've been here before, haven't you?" I asked.

He was surprised, then nodded.

"But you weren't alone then?"

He shook his head. I waited, letting the pause elicit more information. "I was with my dad," he finally said.

"So why are you here without him this time?"

"He's dead."

"I'm sorry," I said. "That must be hard."

"He died when I was 13. Killed by a drunk driver."

"I'm sorry," I repeated. Then another thought fell into my mind. "You looked at me strangely. Do I remind you of him?"

He looked away, biting his lip. "I don't know," he said. "When I saw you from up there, I thought you were him. That he had come back to stop me."

I pondered this for a moment. "Stop you from what?" I asked.

He looked back at me, a tear appearing at the edge of his right eye. "I can't talk about it," he said.

"Your father loved you very much, didn't he? That's why he would come back, right?"

He wiped the tear from his eye and nodded.

"Maybe someone sent me here instead of him," I said. "What were you going to do?"

The young man hesitated. I sensed he badly wanted to tell me but was struggling. Finally he spoke softly, almost in a whisper. "I came here to end it all," he said.

"To kill yourself?"

He looked at me sheepishly. "What else can I do?" he blurted. "I'm all alone. No one cares about me. After my father died, my mother got remarried to some guy who resents me. He wanted her, but not a step-son. I was an inconvenience. I turned to drugs and alcohol. I was so stoned all the time that I flunked out of college. Then I tried to be gay. It was a big fad among the stoners I hung out with. But after two one-night stands with men I didn't even know, I felt dirty – and I still wanted women even if they didn't want me. To make money, I sold drugs, but I got robbed by other dealers. I lent my customers money, and they wouldn't pay me back. They laughed at me. I was lucky I didn't end up in prison. Now I work at McDonalds and live in my mom's basement. My step-dad puts up with me only because of my mother, and he is always giving me lectures about how I need to straighten up and get a life. My real father would be ashamed of me."

I was startled at how his pain gushed out of him like a dam bursting. I considered telling him I, too, had suffered a terrible loss and was in pain, but I didn't. It wasn't what he needed.

"Why here?" I asked instead.

The young man pointed at a nearby peak. "My father brought me here just before he died."

"So it's a special place for you?"

"It's a place where I experienced real peace, hiking to the top of that peak with him," he said. "Everything after that was miserable."

"So you came all the way from Los Angeles to kill yourself in the one place where you had peace?"

"I sold all my possessions, even my guitar, to pay for the ticket. I won't need them anymore," he replied.

"You are going to jump off the mountain?"

"There is a cliff there," he said. "No one will miss me."

I took a deep breath. "Come sit with me," I said, gesturing for him to join me on the log.

"You can't talk me out of it," he said. "I've made up my mind."

"I won't try," I said. "It's your choice. But there's no hurry, is there? Maybe you and I could talk a bit."

He hesitated, then slowly stepped over to where I was seated and sat down. I didn't say anything. We watched a light breeze ripple across the water towards us.

"Tell me about this peace," I said. "The one you experienced when your father brought you here."

"What's there to say?" he replied. "It was a perfect moment. I was with my father, and I just sensed that everything was good. I was where I was supposed to be. I was cared for. I was all right."

"You were loved?"

"Yes, I was loved," he said. "I knew who I was. I was loved for who I am."

"Like touching the face of God?"

He turned to look at me with a perplexed expression. "Do you believe in God?"

"Yes," I said. "But I haven't always believed. Now I do."

He leaned over and picked up a flat rock and tried to skip it across the surface of the lake. It took one skip, then plunged into the water with a splash.

"I believe in Him, too, I think," he said. "But no one else I know does. So I haven't told anyone. But if He exists, I don't know why He allowed my life to stink."

"Your life is not over yet."

"It will be soon. You are not going to talk me out of it."

We again fell silent. My thoughts drifted back to the locker room at Virginia Tech, where I massaged and stretched football players who were just as lost as this young man, clinging to the one thing that gave them meaning in life and a sense of belonging. A sense of being approved. And yet as soon as their eligibility was over, they were cast aside, treated as young men with little education and no marketable skills. They had been someone in the world's eyes. Then they were nothing.

"You didn't come here looking to kill yourself, did you?" I asked.

"Of course, I did."

"No," I said. "You came here seeking what you experienced that day with your father. Except it wasn't a "what." It was a Who. God touched you and showed you the truth – that you are priceless in His eyes because He made you and He loves you."

"He abandoned me!" he snapped loudly. The words echoed across the lake as mine had earlier.

"Do you really think so?"

"Why would he let my father die?" he shouted. "Where was he? Couldn't he have stopped that drunk? Couldn't the guy have lost his car keys or turned down another road?"

I thought of Janice, shriveled and semi-conscious, crying out in pain. "He doesn't need to explain Himself," I said. "But He never left you. You were never alone."

It dawned on me that I was talking not just to the young man but to myself. Just a few minutes before, I had accused God of abandoning me in my hour of pain.

"Then where is he?" the young man challenged me.

I stood up. "Let's go find out," I said. "Together."

His name was Seth. He didn't agree to go with me, but when I started up the trail towards the peak, he followed. Along the way, he became chatty. He told me that as a child, he was enamored with roller coasters and wanted to be an engineer who designed them. All that changed when his father died. No one had taken him to an amusement park since. His mother was too busy dealing with her own grief and then getting remarried that she didn't have much time for him.

"I didn't really like getting high," he said. "But the stoners were the only kids at school who would accept me. So I did what they did. Sometimes I pretended to get high just so I could fit in. Eventually, it just became a habit. I was never addicted. But drugs were what I did. They became my identity. I was a stoner."

I pointed at the summit of the small peak ahead of us on the trail. It didn't have snow on it like the taller peaks. "But you remembered this place?" I asked.

"I just remembered being with my dad and feeling so much peace."

"Maybe we will find that again."

"You aren't going to change my mind," he said.

We hiked for half an hour, climbing the steep slope to the peak. With each step, the panoramic view of the high Rockies grew more and more spectacular until we finally reached the summit. Seth was right. There was a sheer cliff face on the far side. We sat on a flat rock overlooking the valley below.

"Have you ever heard of Virginia Tech?" I asked.

Seth shook his head. "I've never been to the East Coast," he said.

"It's a university in western Virginia," I said. "You could study engineering. Maybe you could design roller coasters."

That got a brief smile out of him, which he quickly suppressed. "My mother would never pay for that, not after I flunked out of UCLA."

"I think I could afford that," I said. "I would like to help you out."

Seth frowned. "It's too late for that," he said.

"Think about it," I said.

"You don't see it," he said. "I'm all alone. No one cares about me. I got bullied in high school and brushed off in college by anyone who wasn't high. I'm an inconvenience."

"Maybe you are the one who can't see," I said. "Maybe there is more going on than you have eyes to see."

"I don't know what you mean," he said.

Our conversation lagged for a minute. I doubted he would actually jump off the cliff. I figured that people who would actually kill themselves don't pour out their feelings to another person before doing it. Rather, they decide to set themselves free from their misery and perhaps exact a measure of revenge and guilt on those who had hurt them. That's what John Demas would whisper in a person's ear: "Take control and set yourself free!"

Gabe Remiel would say that no one can set themselves free. Only God can do that. I wondered if Seth had his own John Demas tempting him moment by moment to make himself his own god, even to the point of choosing the time and manner of his death.

I didn't know what to say to him, so I thought about what Cecelia would do. The answer came quickly. I put my hand on his shoulder. He flinched but allowed it to stay there. "Would you allow me to pray for you?" I asked.

"You do what you want, but you are not going to talk me out of it," he said.

"I agree. I don't think I am," I said. "But it would be good for someone to pray for you before you end it all."

He considered this for a moment. "If you want to," he said. "No one has ever prayed for me before. But it won't change anything."

I bowed my head and prayed while he stared off in the distance. "Father in heaven, you made Seth. You knit him together in his mother's womb and counted his days before he ever was. Show him the reality of who you are and let him know your love for him. I pray this in the name of your Son...."

I never finished the prayer. Over Seth's shoulder, a man appeared – an olive-skinned man wearing the garb of an ancient shepherd. He carried a shepherd's crook with which he guided a half dozen sheep trailing behind him. I had seen so much on my journey, I wasn't completely surprised. It occurred to me later that perhaps that is one sign of growing into a towering oak: the supernatural becomes natural. You expect prayers to be answered and mountains to be thrown into the sea.

Seth looked up at me, puzzled why I had stopped abruptly. Then he turned and saw the shepherd.

"You!' He gasped. He shot to his feet and ran to the man. "You are here!"

"I am why you came back here," the shepherd said.

His voice was the sound of dawn over a tranquil lake. At his words, I sensed something change in my heart: his voice silenced a kind of background chatter of anxiety that I had become so used to over the years, something that I barely noticed until it was no longer there.

"Where have you been?" Seth asked. "You said you would never leave me."

"I have been with you the entire time," the shepherd replied. "Every moment. Every second."

"I talked to you," Seth said. "Did you hear?"

"I heard."

"I thought I imagined you. That it never happened. That I never met you here with my father. And then he died."

"I know," the shepherd said, stepping forward and embracing him, holding him close to his heart. "I know."

Seth looked up at Him, tears again falling down his cheeks. "Can you show me again?"

The shepherd nodded. He let Seth go and then waved his hand in the direction of the cliff. Instantly, everything changed. The mountains, valleys, and lakes were still there, but the light was different. It was the same radiance I saw in the woman who sang at Melissa's funeral, except it filled the entire landscape. In the valley below, I saw hundreds of people looking up at us. They began to sing a melody I had never heard before – in fact, it seemed to be beyond the octaves of any music on Earth, as though there was an entirely different musical scale.

"Worthy is the Lamb," they sang. "All praise to our Creator! Worthy is the Lamb who was slain! All praise to our Creator!"

The song enveloped us, and I found myself singing along, my voice somehow able to match the pitch. I sensed a new tide flowing into the uplands of my soul, bringing with it not grief or loneliness but comfort as mysterious as the music itself.

"Look!" Seth suddenly exclaimed, pointing. "Look!"

I followed the line of his finger to the front row of singers. A tall man stood in the center who, unlike the others in white robes, was dressed as a well-equipped hiker holding a walking stick.

"That's my father!" Seth shouted. "My father!"

"It is," the Shepherd said.

"Can I see him? Can I talk to him?" Seth asked.

The shepherd shook his head. "You will someday," he said. "But it is not possible today."

Immediately, I scanned the throng of singers looking for Janice, but she was not there. The shepherd knew my thoughts. "You have seen her, Joe," he said. "And you will see her again."

I understood that he had let me see her in my dream when I had a picnic lunch with her, and she told me to marry Lara. That was my moment. This moment belonged to Seth.

At once, the singers disappeared and the landscape returned to normal. The shepherd put his hand on Seth's forehead and seemed to be praying. Another verse from my childhood came into my mind.

"He is also able to save forever those who come to God through Him, since He always lives to make intercession for them."

Then he raised his hand in benediction and said one word: "Shalom."

Peace. Peace as deep and mysterious as the music from the singers. Peace that passes understanding. Peace that overshadows the soul. Peace that knows no end.

Seth and I fell on our knees, overcome. I don't know how long we were there. Once again, the past and future ceased to exist. We were in His time: an eternal Now. When we finally arose, the sun was descending towards the ridges across the valley. The still small voice I had come to recognize over the course of 2,000 miles spoke to me.

"Seth is your son now," he said. "Take care of him."

Chapter 26

Reunion

Seth had not been to an amusement park since his father died, so two days later, we left the Rockies and drove 100 miles east to the annual Calgary Stampede, a major rodeo and fair celebrating western Canada's cowboy heritage. In the meantime, he called his mother to let her know he was all right and staying in a chalet in the Rockies. She had a hundred questions and obvious concerns about his boarding with a stranger, but he was 22 years old and an adult. He could make his own decisions.

If his mother had been paying full attention – and I am not sure she was – she would have noticed a new attitude in her son. He had gone to the Rockies to end his life. Instead, Jesus had given him new life – abundant life. Eternal life. The Good Shepherd had embraced him and held him close to his heart. Rather than take his own life, Seth had surrendered his life. There might be a day in the future when he would tell his mother, but at that moment, she wouldn't have understood.

As for me, I found it ironic that after all I had been through, God had chosen to give me a son – at least in a figurative sense. Janice and I had badly wanted children, but then she got sick. Now, like Abraham in his old age, I was a father. I told Seth what the Holy

Spirit had said to me. His eyes lit up. I couldn't replace his late father, nor could he heal the wound of childlessness caused by cancer, but we could give each other what the other lacked.

Seth delighted in the rides and roller coasters at the Stampede like the 13-year-old he had been when his father died. I had talked him into wearing blue jeans and a red polo shirt. The Gothic stoner clothes went in the trash. I rode a few of the rides but then retreated to a bench to eat poutine, the traditional Canadian comfort food consisting of French fries, cheese curds, and gravy, while he continued to rekindle a lost adolescence. Poutine is heart attack food and somewhat odd for those not used to cheese and gravy on fries, but I figured when in Canada, eat as the Canadians do.

As I watched Seth enjoy himself, I pondered whether he really might end up designing roller coasters someday. I had no problem getting him admitted to the engineering program for the fall semester at Virginia Tech. The university president was overjoyed to hear from me, especially as I agreed to fund the new weight room for the football team he had mentioned when he came by my office before I left Blacksburg.

Despite his drug use, Seth had a decent high school transcript and SAT scores. The president immediately accepted him into the freshman class without even calling the admissions office. A billion dollars will do that. He also arranged for a paid internship with the training staff of the football team. The Hokies would start training camp the next week, preparing for the fall season.

As I watched the crowds thronging the fair, I thought about loneliness. It struck me that it is possible to be as lonely – maybe even more lonely – among thousands of people as it is by a remote mountain lake without another soul in sight. I had visited New York City a few times and sensed the loneliness: thousands upon thousands of people riding subways and packing sidewalks, avoiding any eye contact. How many hearts weighed heavy among the bustling masses, craving human touch and someone to be interested in them – to care for them?

I no longer felt lonely. The beauty and solitude of the Canadian Rockies proved to be the final classroom in my solo journey across the continent. I came to understand I had not been alone when I held Janice's body in my family room. I had not been alone on the long stretches of highway. I was not alone turning the lights off in the Tiffin and lying in bed, wondering where I was going or what I was doing. The Shepherd was with me: watching me, guiding me, blessing me – drawing me closer to His heart.

I still desired Lara, but I did not need her. Nor was she the one who could assuage my grief and fill the hole in my heart left by Janice's death. No human being could do that. Only the Shepherd could: the One who laid down His life for the sheep. The One who rose again to overcome all that is tragic and painful – to conquer death itself, even the death of the one I loved so much.

After a few minutes, a man on the loudspeaker announced the day's rodeo had begun. I left Seth to his rides and found my way to the large arena in the middle of the fairgrounds. It was similar to the one in Cody and crowded with spectators. By the time I found a seat in the top row of the stands, squeezed in next to a large man, cowgirls were racing fast horses on the arena floor, making sharp turns around barrels in a skillful display of horsemanship.

As I watched them, I thought about Gabe Remiel and John Demas, two supernatural beings – angels – on opposite sides of a titanic struggle waged in an invisible spiritual realm that so many people either ignore or deny exists. I was the prize they were after. The Shepherd would allow me to suffer, even let John Demas inflict sickness on me, to win the prize. For it could never be won apart from my will. Only through my surrender would it be won.

When the cowgirls finished their barrel racing and a winner was announced, the rodeo moved to the main event, the bull riding. I watched intently, still incredulous that any sane human being would attempt to ride a 2,000-pound animal. A few cowboys managed to stay on for eight seconds. Several limped out of the arena, injured by either the fall from a bull's back or from being stepped on or gored when they hit the ground.

"Now, ladies and gentlemen," the announcer said. "Pete Michaels, the top money earner on the Professional Bull Riders tour, will attempt to ride the world's number one bull, Bayou Thunder!"

The crowd let out a roar. I looked down at the chute where the cowboy was wrapping his bull rope around his right hand, and indeed there was Bayou Thunder, the massive animal Gabe Remiel had tamed with a single wave of his hand: the beast who had tormented me in the darkness in Yellowstone, and I had sacrificed on the altar of light.

The gate swung open. Bayou Thunder bolted out, jumping high in the air while rotating to the left. Pete Michaels' head snapped back, but he gripped the bull rope tightly and managed to stay centered on the animal's back as it landed. Enraged, the bull pivoted to the right and then bucked again, his rear hooves at least six feet off the ground. The cowboy skillfully adjusted his weight to stay centered even as the force of the bull's bucking whiplashed his body.

Around and around they went, brute force against sheer athleticism. The crowd buzzed as the clock counted higher: six seconds, then seven. Finally, the buzzer sounded when the clock hit eight. Pete Michaels managed to jump off the bull, which immediately attempted to gore him, but the bullfighters intervened and distracted the animal. The cowboy threw his hat in the air while the crowd roared. The great Bayou Thunder had been ridden!

"That's incredible!" I shouted, swept up in the cowboy's moment of triumph.

"It certainly is," a voice to my left replied.

It took me a moment to recognize the voice. I turned to see Lara sitting in the seat that just a moment ago had been occupied by the large man. She was smiling as she leaned over and kissed me lightly on the lips.

"I am here," she said. "Will you marry me?"

I was stunned. "With all my heart," I managed to reply.

I kissed her. It wasn't a quick buss but a long, passionate kiss, months in the making, that drew stares from the people around us.

I didn't have a ring to put on her finger. I expected to be the one who would make a marriage proposal if Lara ever showed up. I figured she would let me know she was coming, and I would meet her at the airport. I would have time to visit a jeweler and spend a small fortune on a big diamond. As it turned out, she had the ring. When our kiss was over, she handed it to me. It wasn't much, but she didn't want much: just a one-carat diamond solitaire on a white gold band she had bought from a jeweler in Foley.

I could never adequately describe the joy that filled my heart. On the mountain peak, I had surrendered the painful longing for her and the worry that she might never come. That was the key that opened the door I had been vainly pounding on in my heart and mind.

Lara may have asked me to marry her first, but I wasn't going to be deprived of my moment. I got out of my seat and knelt on the concrete of the grandstand and asked her if she would marry me.

She laughed. "A thousand times yes," she said. "I would have married you in Foley if He had let me."

I slid the ring on her finger and rose to embrace her. It was pure joy feeling her arms around me and her body pressed up against mine. The spectators nearby realized what had happened and began to cheer. Cowboy Pete Michaels had had his moment of glory. Now we had ours.

———-

It was a conspiracy, of course. Lara and Cecelia had planned it all. It is a mystery how they were able to do it – something that would have been impossible except that a billion dollars sometimes makes the impossible possible.

"We are going to be married tomorrow," Lara told me with a chuckle as we drove back from Calgary to Banff with Seth, still transformed into his 13-year-old self, eating cotton candy and crackerjacks in the back seat. "This is the last night this poor widow will sleep alone. Tomorrow, I get my man."

"Can you get married at a courthouse in Canada?" I asked. I didn't care where we got married. Even waiting one more day seemed like torture. If we were in Las Vegas, I would have gone to a drive-thru wedding chapel to have Elvis marry us.

Lara laughed. "No courthouse for us," she said. "Your sister is in town."

"Cecelia is here?" I exclaimed.

"Are you surprised?"

I took my eye off the road to look at her incredulously before it dawned on me that there was a conspiracy.

"And who else is here?"

Lara smiled. "A pastor named Brian and a few other folks," she smiled, enjoying having me on the hook and reeling me in. "He is the one who is going to marry us."

"But how? Where?"

"The Banff Springs Hotel," she said. "That's where you are taking me. I'm staying there tonight. Tomorrow you're staying there – with me. Don't plan on much sleep."

By the time we arrived at the ornate hotel, built in the 19th century by the Canadian Pacific Railroad in the style of a French chateau, Lara had told me that Cecelia had arranged a ceremony on the hotel terrace. She asked me to drop her off at the front entrance and not to contact Cecelia.

"I am not going to insist on anything," she said, taking my hand. "That's not how our marriage should start. But with Cecelia's help, I planned this to be a surprise."

"And a surprise it will be," I said. I didn't care how she and Cecelia had arranged the wedding as long as she said "I do" at the right time.

"Good," she said. "You and Seth go into town and buy nice suits. I am not marrying a slouch. Come back here at 4 o'clock tomorrow, ready to go."

"But I do want to spend time with you today," I said. "Can you meet us for dinner?"

She shook her head. "You can't see the bride the night before a wedding. After tomorrow, I am all yours," she said, shutting the Jeep door behind her. "You will never get rid of me."

I watched as a bellhop opened the door and she sauntered into the hotel like a princess returning to her castle. Seth moved from the back seat to the front. "She seems like a pretty take-charge lady," he said.

"You haven't met my sister," I said. "Peas in a pod."

"Is that OK with you?"

I smiled. "Trust me," I said. "None of us is in charge."

———

I don't know that I really heard a single word Brian said as he married us under an arch of roses and carnations on the hotel terrace with a spectacular view of the Bow River Valley and, in the distance, the towering peak of Rundle Mountain. My eyes stayed fixed on Lara the entire time, amazed that the God I had said probably didn't exist had gifted me such a beautiful woman to be my wife. When the moment came, I said "I do" so enthusiastically the guests broke out in laughter and then applause.

The "few other folks" Lara had mentioned included just about everyone I had met during my journey. Cecelia flew them in on private jets. Lionel Jackson was there. He brought his saxophone and jammed with the band at the reception, bringing the house down. Dr. Arlene Matthews took time away from Tuskegee University to attend, bringing with her architectural drawings of the new Simon Jackson Hall.

Peter and Sally Flynn showed up, awestruck by the majestic mountains and bearing the good news that she was pregnant. They brought with them Mountain, who had gone back to using his real name, Jerome Mancini. He proved to have an aptitude for repairing diesel engines and, along with Peter, was enabling Jake to expand the business in Red Bay. Cecelia had also tracked down

Meadow, whose real name was Jane Allen. I was surprised and gratified to see her embrace Jerome at the reception and forgive him – they both had been deceived and then separately came to know the truth.

Will Slye, of course, came, along with Dr. Brantley Clay and Kiff Bellingham, who was now overseeing an active recovery program for addicted gamblers at Revival Christian Church. Meanwhile, a limousine ferried Senator Randall Farris, Dwight Moore, and Dr. Ethan Williams from the airport. I learned that Dr. Williams regularly traveled to Arkansas on weekends to attend the senator's church and hunt with Dwight.

Travis and Clara Maynard also showed up, still exuding gratitude for Travis' healing and for the help the Decker Medical Relief Foundation was providing their neighbors in Idaho. Tom Hears Thunder drove up from the Blackfoot Reservation. He told me that with the help of the Hears Thunder-Three Bears Foundation, Cecelia and I established, Matwau and his family had moved to a house in Browning. He found a calling as an evangelist – a living testimony to the power of God's love and mercy – and spent his weekends driving around the reservation, sharing his story with anyone who would listen.

Gaylord and Sarah came with Cornelius, whose law firm had prospered, attracting new donors who allowed him to hire two more lawyers to help the poor in Oklahoma. Their new farmhouse was half completed, and they expected to move in by the end of the year.

Perhaps the most surprising guest was Buster Blanchard, who insisted on driving from Idaho to Banff with his wife and Lizzy Miller. They had become fast friends and started a Bible study in Lizzy's home. So great was his transformation that I hardly recognized him: his countenance that had been so filled with bitterness and hate seemed to shine with an inner light – or more accurately a radiance like the one I had seen on the mountain peak when the Shepherd gave us a glimpse of heaven.

The reception, held in one of the hotel's ornate halls, was a whirlwind of reunions and joyful celebrations as the guests swapped stories of how they had come to be there. What were the odds that an Alabama saxophone player, a Nebraska farmer, and a Blackfoot pastor who had never met each other would end up together at a billionaire's wedding in the Canadian Rockies?

I was eager to catch up with Cecelia and Brian, but that would have to wait until another time. Too many people wanted to congratulate us and thank me, although I deserved no gratitude. When dinner was served, I stood up to offer a toast. I welcomed the guests and thanked them for coming, then I remembered the one person who was not there – at least in bodily form.

"Janice is here in spirit," I said. "Most people wouldn't believe me if I told them that she told me in a dream to marry Lara. But I know everyone here does. You have been touched by God and seen what He can do. He used me – a crushed and angry man who had lost the love of his life to a horrible disease – to cut a swath of grace and mercy across the continent. Each step of the way, He showed me who He was. He taught me. He molded me. He led me to trust in Him – to not be surprised by miracles or answered prayers: in fact, to expect His hand to be supernaturally upon everything in my life, even if I don't understand His ways or the winters that sometimes come before the rebirth of spring.

"Along the way, He blessed each of you, for God's blessings are never limited. He allowed Janice to die and gave me a fortune I never wanted so that He could give you new life. Abundant life. His life. Some of you for the first time. Others, so you could grow closer to Him. And most of all, He gave me Lara, not to replace Janice because Janice could never be replaced, but to walk with me on the journey He has in store for us. He even gave me – in a figurative sense – the son that Janice and I could never have. Who knows what He will do with Seth – what an explosion of grace may come through his life as he follows the Good Shepherd.

"Lara and I begin our life together with a mission: what to do with a billion dollars. It is an unfathomable amount of money, and we will spend the rest of our lives giving it away. My RV is parked just a few miles from here. We could go west. We could go east. We could go north or south. We don't know yet. That is the joy of being God's child. It's always an adventure. At the end of the day, even the hardest day, there is always a blessing. There is always a blessing."

It was 10 o'clock when the reception finally wound down, although Lionel Jackson kept playing for another half hour. To the lullaby of his saxophone, I finally got Cecelia alone to ask her a question.

"How much did you know in advance about all that happened to me?" I asked.

"I didn't," she said. "Except in the most general way. I knew you would meet God on your journey, but I didn't know whether you would surrender to Him. He always gives us the choice. I knew He intended Lara to be your wife, but I didn't know whether you would reach the place where He would let her marry you."

"Why wouldn't He?" I asked.

"Because of the way He designed marriage," she said. "You and Lara are equal partners in every way, but you have the role of leader. He wasn't going to allow you to marry her until you were ready to lead, and she wasn't going to come to you until He gave her permission."

I looked puzzled. "Ready to lead? She doesn't seem like a woman who needs to be led. Neither do you, for that matter."

"Every wife needs to be led: in fact, deeply desires to be

led," Cecelia replied. "But it's Biblical leadership, not secular leadership. It's servant leadership. Jesus loved His bride, the church, by laying down His life for her, and husbands are called to lay down their lives for their wives. You lead to serve and you serve to lead."

"I don't know who could meet that standard," I said.

"You can't by yourself," she said. "But God showed you what He can do through you. You just need to be obedient, and He will enable you."

I pondered this for a moment as the last of the guests left for their hotel rooms. Lara waited patiently for me by the doorway.

"If every woman desires to be led, then why haven't you gotten married?" I asked.

"God hasn't sent the right man," she said. "Yet."

"Do you think He will?"

She laughed. "The odds are about the same as winning the Powerball," she said. "And we know that never happens."

Chapter 27

Presence and Power

Lara and I met Fulton Sanders in the hotel's Vermillion Room four days after our wedding, when all the guests had departed and Seth had flown east for his internship in Blacksburg. I was surprised we were still at the hotel to meet him. I would have taken Lara anywhere in the world for a honeymoon, but she wanted to stay in the Canadian Rockies.

After a day of rest, we drove to Lake Louise for an afternoon. The next day, we rode the gondolas and hiked to the lake where I had met Seth. In the morning, we met Fulton. We were planning to hook the Jeep up to the Tiffin and head north along the Columbia Icefields Parkway up the spine of the Rockies to Jasper National Park. God had other plans for us.

A balding man in his 60s with the stocky build of a former offensive lineman, Fulton was alone, sipping coffee and staring out the window at the mountains with a pained expression on his face. After the waiter brought our breakfast and I offered thanks to God, Lara nodded towards him.

"We need to invite that man to have breakfast with us," she said in a tone that conveyed certainty. I learned later that when Lara spoke that way – and she didn't do it very often – she had heard something in prayer. She was rarely wrong. When I asked Fulton if he would like some company, he immediately accepted my invitation. In fact, he seemed relieved for the distraction from whatever he was pondering as he gazed out the window.

Lara was not shy when she believed the still small voice of the Holy Spirit had spoken to her. After Fulton sat down at our table and we introduced ourselves, she immediately cut to the chase. "You seem to be troubled," she said to him. "What is troubling you?"

Fulton was briefly taken aback by her forthrightness, but the way she spoke to him was disarming. I was impressed at how she could be both blunt and gentle at the same time. It dawned on me that Jesus was that way: He spoke the truth boldly yet in a way that comforted people and drew them to Him. Indeed, when the religious leaders sent guards to arrest Him, they came back empty-handed, saying, "No one ever spoke like this man!"

"Is it that obvious?" Fulton replied.

Lara nodded but didn't say anything. Fulton took a sip of coffee and looked out the window. "My wife – her name is Sophie – is upstairs in our suite. She is semi-conscious and dying of breast cancer. I left a nurse with her. I've been up all night with the nurse giving her morphine. I am almost certain this is her last day. I needed a few moments away from it."

"You brought your sick wife here?" I asked. Lara shot me a disapproving look. I hadn't meant to judge the man. I was just surprised. Apparently, I needed to keep my mouth shut and let Lara handle the conversation.

Fulton seemed unfazed by my question. "It's where she wanted to be," he said. "She is a Canadian from Banff, and she wanted to come home to die, not that she has any relatives here anymore.

Everyone moved away. But she loved the mountains, and this is where she wanted to take her last breath, not in a hospital room in New York."

"I am sorry to hear about your wife," Lara said.

"I am sorry too," Fulton said. "I'm sorry that it took her getting cancer to finally get me to pay attention and love her the way she deserved to be loved."

"I'm sure that's not true," Lara said. "I'm sure you have loved her."

Fulton shook his head. "No, I have not," he said. "I spent my whole life being in love with myself — or at least my image of myself and left her to struggle through life being married to a man who wouldn't, and couldn't, love her. Now it's too late. I had my chance and I fumbled it away."

"Are you sure you aren't being too hard on yourself?" Lara asked.

Fulton took another sip of coffee and looked straight at Lara. "I married Sophie the week after I graduated from Harvard," he said. "I met her when I was skiing up here. She worked at the resort. We were very much in love and had a wonderful honeymoon in Greece. But when we got back, I took a job in an investment banking firm on Wall Street. Sophie lost me for the next 40 years while I worked 100-hour weeks and became fabulously wealthy. In fact, I was making $50 million a year. I have a net worth of a quarter billion dollars. Most people can't imagine such wealth."

"That is hard to imagine," I said. Lara gave me another disapproving look.

"What is all that money worth?" Fulton asked. "I gave Sophie every material thing I could think of. We had a house in Malibu and another house in the Hamptons. She had maids and cooks and all kinds of servants. I hired a chauffeur to drive her around Manhattan in a Bentley. We went to lavish parties hosted by Wall Street titans and politicians. Yet she saw so little of me. And the little she did see was still back at the office. Even making love to her, I would be thinking of some deal I was working on and not her.

"But she was different from the wives of my colleagues. She didn't divorce me and take half my assets. She didn't even divorce me when we found out I was physically unable to father a child. I don't know why she didn't. She always wanted children of her own. Maybe that was a blessing because our children would have grown up with a father who was never around. All through my self-centered life, she stuck with me, year after year.

"Only when she got sick did I wake up and realize what a wasted life I had lived. I quit my firm. People were shocked. I was only in my 60s and one of the titans of Wall Street. I was making the kind of money people dream about. But I left to take care of Sophie. To try to be a husband to her. I had money to get her the best possible care in the world. I flew with her everywhere to see specialists – anyone who might be able to cure breast cancer. But no one could. She has an aggressive form of the disease, and she just got sicker and sicker. And now she is going to die, and I will be alone.

"I discovered that once I left Wall Street, no one thought much about me anymore, except the politicians and charities that wanted donations. People I thought were my friends lost interest in me once I was out of the game. I had ignored all my relatives for years, and they didn't know me at all. I missed weddings and funerals if there was a deal I was working on – and I was always working on a deal."

"Did you ever pray?" Lara asked.

He shook his head. "I'm not a religious person," he said. "Sophie is. Maybe that's why she stuck with me. She got me to go to church on Christmas and Easter – that is, if there wasn't a deal pending – but it was not my thing. She was always involved in church stuff and charities. When she dies, we will have a big funeral in New York. Hundreds of people I don't know will show up. I doubt the people I worked with will be there. I am not a player anymore. Maybe they will if they think they can get me to invest in something they are working on. The politicians will show up, of course, thinking it will help get me to give them some money."

"Having a lot of money can be a bit of a curse," I said. "You don't know if people like you for yourself or for your money."

"You can't imagine," he said. Lara gave me a look, and I didn't say anything.

"Fulton," Lara said. "I know we just met you. But I was wondering if Joe and I could go with you up to your suite and pray for Sophie."

He didn't answer for a moment. "Sophie would like that," he said, then a couple of seconds later added. "I would like it."

————

As it turned out, Fulton's suite was just two doors from ours with the same breathtaking view of the Bow River Valley and Rundle Mountain that was the backdrop for our wedding. Sophie lay in a hospital bed next to a window where she would have been able to see the view if she had been conscious. The nurse stood over her, adjusting her blankets and making herself look busy when we came in.

I immediately had a flashback of our family room in Blacksburg, of Janice in the same state as Sophie: the gaunt face and frail body, the shallow breathing, and the smell of impending death, awaiting the moment when the cancer encroached upon the part of her brain that controlled breathing or other vital bodily functions. The room was full of floral arrangements intended to brighten the mood with aromas and beauty. They could not. Despite the view and the flowers, the room was a sepulcher waiting for a corpse.

I don't know why the scene didn't overwhelm me and drive me to tears. It should have, but I had been transformed. I still empathized with Fulton. I had been where he was, and I shared his sorrow. However, death itself had lost its sting.

Sophie belonged to Jesus, and I sensed His presence in the room. I thought of Dr. Decker —-Melchizedek — and wondered if He were standing next to her, invisible to the eyes, holding her hand. I was certain he had been with Janice when she died, although I hadn't had eyes to see Him at the time. When Janice breathed her last, he took her to the place he had prepared for her, the place where I had met her in my dream. She had told me the beautiful forest where we had our picnic together was just one atom in the fabric of heaven. No one could ever explore it completely because it went on forever, from one glory to the next.

When we entered the hotel suite, Lara immediately walked to the side of the bed and took Sophie's hand, a woman on a mission. I thought she would begin to pray. She didn't. Instead, she turned to me.

"Joe, will you pray for her?" she asked.

I crossed the room to her bed and got on my knees, exactly the same way I had just months before with Janice. I laid my hand over Sophie's hand and then waved Fulton over to join us. He didn't quite know what to do, but after a moment's hesitation, obediently came over and put his hand on top of mine.

"Father in heaven," I prayed. "We lift up Sophie to you in prayer, asking you to do a miracle of healing in her body. Send your Holy Spirit to drive out all cancer cells from her body and everything else that is evil and leads to death. Bathe her in the blood of your Son, Jesus, by whose stripes we are healed. Lift her body from this sick bed into new life. Let not death have its way in her body. Have mercy on her and on all who love her. We pray in the name of Jesus. Amen."

It was a simple prayer, the prayer of a child, which is often the best prayer. While I spoke, I sensed power coursing through my hand. Lara and Fulton felt it as well. Out of the corner of my eye, I saw his surprised look. Lara had her eyes closed and her head bowed.

At once, light bathed us. Again, more than light: radiance. It engulfed us with peace. In fact, more than peace – shalom: the perfect peace of heaven I had experienced when I was with Janice in my dream and on the mountain with Seth. Unspeakable power overshadowed us: the power that could create the universe with just a spoken word and could resurrect a tortured and murdered man from the dead. Both Fulton and Lara fell on their knees next to me. No one could possibly stand in the presence of such radiance and power.

Time ceased. Once again, I found myself in a state with no past and no future, just the eternal Now. We watched as the radiance transformed the dying woman in front of us. Her body began to glow. Her muscles gained mass and tone. Her sallow eyes brightened. It was a miracle in slow motion.

The radiance faded away as quickly as it had appeared. Sophie sat up in bed, fully awake. She looked at her husband and the two strangers holding her hand.

"Where did He go?" she asked. "He was right here beside me."

—--

I suppose I would not have been human if I didn't wonder why God let Janice die yet healed Sophie. I knew the answer, of course, but knowing it didn't erase my grief or the pain of missing her. Jesus wept even when He knew He was going to bring his friend Lazarus back to life. The last enemy, death, has been conquered but not yet vanquished.

What John Demas did not understand, nor was capable of understanding, was the power of redemption. The God who used the most heinous murder in history as the way to set us free from the prison of self and the fiery judgment of Flathead Lake had used Janice's death to rescue me – and not just me but the people I had met in my journey. The last one was Fulton Sanders on his knees in a Canadian hotel with his healthy wife holding his hand, asking God to forgive him for a wasted life and receiving His grace and salvation – indeed for the Spirit of the God of the Universe to dwell within him.

As for Lara and me, we decided to continue traveling in the Tiffin. After praying, we turned east along the Trans Canada Highway through the places with strange names like Moose Jaw and Medicine Hat. Lara placed a sign on the front dashboard of the Tiffin with a quote from Oswald Chambers:

"Faith never knows where it is being led,
but it loves and knows the One Who is leading."

Just in case we were ever tempted to forget.

Reviews

"Drawing from his own experience of grief, Hugh Vickery weaves a tale of redemption and hope. Reminiscent of John Bunyan's classic, The Pilgrim's Progress, Vickery takes us on a rollicking good adventure replete with colorful characters and problems along the way. It is a tale of America, a cross section of her people, their struggles, and one man's question for answers to an age-old question."

Stanley Reahard, Author, "The Island Then and Now"

"What a wonderful life-affirming read. The protagonist is a likable, flawed man, like all of us who make the journey from darkness into the light of redemption."

Celia Marzsal Iannelli, Columnist, Riverhead Local and News Review

"After heartbreaking personal loss, Joe Mathers sets off on a journey to seek help and hope. Along the way, he finds himself to be the one sought by the very Source of all help and hope. Readers will be encouraged and challenged to expect the Seeker who seeks, and the joy of responding to Him in faith and devotion."

Glen Davis, Orange Moon Ministries

About the Author

Hugh Vickery is a former journalist and speechwriter for the Secretary of the Interior. He has taught the Bible for 30 years, served on church boards, and participated in a wide variety of ministries including mentoring homeless youth, providing food to needy families, and leading marriage and step-family support groups. His first novel, *"The Autobiography of Judas Iscariot"* was published in 2024 and is available on Amazon and other sites. He and his wife, Kathryn, live in Palm City, Florida with their Havanese dog, Zena.

Veritas Resurgance Publishing

The Autobiography Of Judas Iscariot
Hugh Vickery

The Other Side Of Reality
A Trilogy
G.L. Durham

You Can Find More From Veritas Resurgence Online
https://www.veritasresurgence.com